Amelia Henley

'The most gripping and moving novel I have ever read
. . . I couldn't put this book down and yet I didn't want
it to end at the same time. This novel really put my
heart through the wringer, it was brilliant and life-
affirming . . . This whole novel was just on another level
and I thoroughly enjoyed it and would highly recommend'

'It is rare that a novel touches me in this way so it is
definitely one that will stay with me for a long time'

'A stunningly written story of love and loss that made
me smile and brought me to tears in equal measure'

'This book is special. Something about this book has
ruined all other books for me . . . All I will say is thank
you, Ms Henley, thank you for writing this story'

'I laughed, I cried, I was humbled. Beautiful modern love
story to beat all others. You won't regret buying this'

★ ★ ★ ★ ★

'It was an absolute honour to have been given the chance to
fall in love with this beautiful story . . . The best book I have
read so far this year, and I have no doubt whatsoever that
Amelia Henley will be touching hearts all over the world with
such a detailed, emotional and . . . . . of true love'

Amelia Henley is a hopeless romantic who has a penchant for exploring the intricacies of relationships through writing heartbreaking, high-concept love stories. Her debut novel was *The Life We Almost Had*.

Amelia also writes psychological thrillers under her real name, Louise Jensen. As Louise Jensen she has sold over a million copies of her global number one bestsellers. Her stories have been translated into twenty-five languages and optioned for TV as well as featuring on the *USA Today* and *Wall Street Journal* bestsellers list. Louise's books have been nominated for multiple awards.

The Art of Loving You is her second book.

Also by Amelia Henley

The Life We Almost Had

Writing as Louise Jensen

The Stolen Sisters
The Family
The Gift
The Sister
The Surrogate
The Date

The Art of Loving You

Amelia Henley

ONE PLACE. MANY STORIES

HQ
An imprint of HarperCollins*Publishers* Ltd
1 London Bridge Street
London SE1 9GF

www.harpercollins.co.uk

HarperCollins*Publishers*
1st Floor, Watermarque Building, Ringsend Road
Dublin 4, Ireland

This edition 2021

1

First published in Great Britain by
HQ, an imprint of HarperCollins*Publishers* Ltd 2021

ISBN: 978-0-00-837577-5

MIX
Paper from
responsible sources
FSC™ C007454

This book is produced from independently certified FSC™ paper
to ensure responsible forest management.

For more information visit: www.harpercollins.co.uk/green

This book is set in 11/15.5 pt. Caslon

Printed and Bound in the UK using
100% Renewable Electricity at CPI Group (UK) Ltd

For Callum and Rebecca.
May every chapter in your love story be filled with joy ♥

Prologue

Four phone calls.

It took four phone calls to tip my world off its axis. I remember them all with sharp clarity; the things I wanted to know, the things I wished I'd never been told. The disbelief, the fear, the hope. The impossible, impossible choice I am faced with. I want everything to slow down.

Stop.

'I can't …' What I can't do is look my sister, Alice, in the eye. It's too much. All of it.

'Say yes, Libby.' She's crouching before me, reaching for my hand. I snatch mine away. As vivid as the memories of the calls are, it's the time in between each one I am struggling to recall. Alice says shock has the power to whisk memories behind a hazy curtain, sometimes replacing them with a better, shinier version – the way we wished things were. The way we wished they could have happened – and she's probably right. Right about that at least, but the rest? I *have* to remember if I'm to make the right decision. Again, I try to summon a slide show in my mind but the images are as fuzzy as an out-of-focus photo, nothing quite making sense. 'I think …' I tail off, unsure what I think. What I know. Alice has been telling me a new life, a better life is what I need. What I deserve.

That word plucks a hollow laugh deep from my belly. *Deserve.*
Do I deserve … *this?*

'You *know* what you have to do, Libby.' Her voice is thick with tears. 'For your sake. For Jack's.' She adds softly, 'For mine.'

Sometimes I hate her.

Should I do what she is asking? If I agree, it's an admission that my life has been built on a lie and the childish part of me taunts; why should I give her what she wants when I can't have what I want?

'Please, Libby, please,' she pleads. 'I know it's a big ask. I know you weren't expecting this – none of us saw it coming but …' One whispered word. 'Please.'

Neither of us speak. The clock ticks. In the distance the thrum of a tractor. Alice's perfume fills my throat, something light and floral.

'Jack—'

'Don't speak his name,' I bite.

She flinches but still she doesn't leave. She's waiting for an answer as she tucks her long blonde hair behind her ears. My eyes flicker towards the nicotine-yellow ceiling we never did get round to painting bright white, as though I might find the right response written there.

Yes or no?

Yes or no?

Yes or no?

The words are loud. I raise my hands to my head, fingertips digging hard into my scalp. I can't decide. I won't.

Jack.

I have to.

Think.

'You know if I could change things, I would,' Alice says softly. She places her palm against my cheek; it's cool and I lean against it, allowing her to take the weight of my head which is heavy with thought. With doubt. For the first time I look at her properly. Her eyes, the same green as mine, are rimmed red. The whites streaked with tiny blood vessels from where she's been crying. She is no more together than I am. This is as torturous for her as it is for me. 'If I could go back …' She falls silent before she can blame herself again. I can't bear her guilt. Her shame. I have enough of my own.

I shift my gaze around the room which was once warmed with love but now feels as chilly as my cold, cold heart. If we *could* go back, I would return to the exact moment everything changed. It was the day Jack and I moved in here. I allow my mind to travel, tumbling down the rabbit hole to that ordinary Thursday when it all began.

The point which had led to *this*.

The memories bring me pleasure.

Pain.

Think.

I have to make my choice.

Yes or no?

I have to give Alice my answer.

Yes or no?

I have to tell her now.

Before it's too late for her, for me.

For Jack.

Think.

Choose.

Time is running out.

Yes or no?

PART ONE

Chapter One

The day it all began was almost seven months ago now. My hand had rested on Jack's knee, both of his gripping the steering wheel as we bumped down the potholed lane, exchanging a look of pure pleasure as we curved into the driveway.

Before the van had fully stopped I was opening the door. Despite suffering from the tail end of flu I could smell the difference in the air; honeysuckle and happiness.

'Do you want to unload—'

'Nope.' I couldn't wait to get inside. Our scant possessions crammed into the back of the hired transit could wait. Our rental flat had been fully furnished and we didn't own much. There was nothing I needed in that moment except to step over the threshold of our new home with the man I loved.

Jack took my hand. We crunched over the gravel, our fingers linking together the way they had a million times before, as we gazed in wonder at the decrepit three-storey detached with its smattering of outbuildings that had somehow become ours. Despite the hard work that lay ahead it felt like the right decision. The warm breeze on my cheek, the birds singing from the trees, the lazy buzzing of bumblebees – everything seemed to welcome us.

'This is it, Libby.'

Despite my thumping headache, streaming nose and sore throat I tingled with excitement as I drank it all in. The pops of yellow in the jumble of the overgrown garden as daffodils poked their cheerful heads through the tangle of stinging nettles. The peeling paint on the front door; I was itching to restore it to a glossy British racing green, to shine the brass lion's head knocker back to its original glory. Tall and proud against a back-drop of a clear blue sky, the towering chimney. In the winter smoke would curl from the fire while Jack and I lazed in front of it, dipping toasted marshmallows into melted chocolate. It was easy to romanticise. We'd never owned our own home before but the four years spent in our cramped modern flat already seemed part of our distant past.

'I don't know whether to run away or run inside.' Jack turned to me. 'We're sure about this, aren't we?'

'Yes.' We'd had endless conversations. A volley of reasons why we shouldn't do this, taking it in turns to be the one with doubts and fears that the other would bat away with logic and reassur-ance. 'Let's get a selfie. I want to capture every second of today.'

I used my phone, rather than the camera looped around my neck.

Our heads touched, goofy smiles on both of our faces. A paint-plastered beanie on Jack's head. He dangled the key at the lens, the sun glinting off the metal. Behind us a single bird glided through the sky.

'Perfect.' I stuffed my phone back into my pocket.

Jack offered me the key. I shook my head. 'This is your moment, Jack. Your dream.'

Uncertainty passed across his face.

'*Our* dream,' I corrected and that was partly true. A long and happy life with Jack was my dream and the rest? I was happy to support Jack in his new venture the way he always supported me in mine.

'Always the photographer.' He grinned. 'Never off duty.'

'Always the artist.' I reached up to wipe at a smudge of paint from his cheek.

'This is it!' He slipped the key into the lock. His joy was palpable. For a second I forgot my raging temperature, the ache in my bones, how dreadfully this spring bout of flu had hit me, instead feeling nothing but an immense pride for this man who was going to make a difference to so many lives the way that he had to mine.

'Jack?' I raised my camera.

He turned to look at me over his shoulder. His unruly dark hair flopping slightly over his left eye, the grey of his irises darkening to slate the way they did when he was joyful. His mouth stretched into a smile displaying his white teeth, the front ones slightly crooked. It was the picture-perfect moment I would pore over again and again in the following months, my fingertips lightly brushing the glossy photo paper, almost feeling everything we had felt that day.

Now …

My feet left the ground as he scooped me into his arms.

'What are you doing?' I laughed.

'Shouldn't I carry you over the threshold?' He grinned down at me.

'We're already inside, idiot. Besides, we're not married.'

Our eyes locked, an unspoken *yet* hung in the air trailing anticipation down my spine.

'Remember the first time I took you to bed?' he murmured.

'Always.' He had carried me effortlessly into his bedroom but then he had worked out at the gym regularly.

There was a spark in his eyes as he asked, 'Are you up to christening the place?'

'Are you?' We both peered doubtfully at the staircase. He stepped onto the bottom step and a cloud of dust rose. I dissolved into a coughing fit.

He set me down.

'Sorry.' I pulled a tissue out of my pocket to wipe my streaming eyes before shrugging off my jacket and slinging it over the bannisters. As I headed towards the kitchen, my eyes lingered on the dark rectangular marks on the faded burgundy walls where family photos once hung. One day we would display our own pictures, adding to the already rich history of this house. How sad would we feel if we had to pack up our belongings and leave? I couldn't imagine.

Jack wrapped his arms around my waist. I leaned back against him. I knew he was thinking about the same thing I was.

Sid.

'We'll fill the house with new memories,' Jack whispered, kissing my neck.

The mood broke as another sneeze drove me into the kitchen. It was unkempt – cobwebs stretching across the dark wooden beams that striped the ceiling – but not unloved. This had been a happy home. A place filled with laughter. I promised that it would be again, not knowing I was making a promise that would be impossible to keep. I had a strange sense of déjà vu as I looked around. A sense I had lived here before almost, it felt so meant to be.

There was a black range cooker which I had no idea how to use, and country pine cupboards; cabinet doors hanging skewwhiff and shelves coated with grime, stacked with mismatched plates and bowls. I was exploring every nook and cranny, running my finger across the tiles where faded images of ducks and chickens marched across the cracks. Before I could open the pantry door, Jack brought in a box from the car.

'If my amazing organisational skills are right, there should be a kettle in here.'

'Thank goodness. Couldn't have you going for more than an hour without a cup of tea.' Jack was obsessed with the stuff, strong and sweet.

'I'll make you a Lemsip.'

'I don't know where I put them but I've got some paracetamol in my bag.' I popped two out of their foil cocoon.

The water from the tap gurgled and spluttered as Jack filled two mugs, handing one to me, raising his.

'To Sid.'

'I think it's bad luck to toast with water.' I wasn't superstitious but I didn't want to tempt fate either.

'Rubbish.' He clinked his mug against mine. 'We have *all* the luck today.'

Now, I can't help wondering how things might be different if we hadn't toasted. Would life be better? Easier? Smoother?

Different.

'I'm going to fetch another load and then we can unpack a few bits.'

'We could do that tomorrow.' I wrapped my arms around his neck, my chin resting on his shoulder.

'Tomorrow, I have plans. Tomorrow,' his voice sultry, 'I'm going to strip,' his voice warm, 'the paint from the front door.'

'You're so hot.' Laughing I pushed him away as his phone buzzed. He pulled it out of his pocket. 'It's the care home,' he said.

He jabbed the accept button and Sid's weatherworn face appeared.

'Hello!' Sid shouted. 'Helen's helping me do Face-to-Face Time with you.' He turned his head to the side and we could hear him ask his favourite care assistant, 'Am I doing this right?' Helen's soft reply reassured him that he was and he didn't have to shout.

He turned back to us. 'Are you in yet?'

Jack panned the phone around the kitchen. 'We just got here.'

'Have you found it? My surprise?' The excitement in Sid's voice made it easy to visualise him as the eight-year-old boy he once was and not the eighty-one-year-old man he was now.

'No. Where is it?' I asked.

'You have to find it yourselves. Like a treasure hunt,' Sid said.

We began to head towards the hallway.

'Don't go away from the larder!' Sid said.

'Is it in the larder?' I tried to keep a straight face.

'I couldn't possibly tell you, duck. You have to find it yourself.'

The box was sitting on the shelf. I lifted it out.

'That's where Norma used to store all our homemade jams and chutneys,' Sid said. 'She'd use fruit and veg from the garden. See that little room off to the back?' Jack walked towards it with his phone and stepped inside. It was only a few square feet, empty, too small to have a purpose, but the view from the window was stunning. 'We would sit there in the evenings, catch the last of the sun, and eat cheese and crackers heaped with chutney, scones piled with strawberry jam. There was just room for our two burgundy leather armchairs and a small table. I got rid of the chairs when Norma passed. Couldn't bear to go in there. Look at it now. A shell. Take me back to the kitchen.' He flapped his hand as though he could propel Jack. I gently closed the door on Sid's memories, wishing we could have met Norma, the love of his life.

'Right,' Sid said. 'That's enough of the maudlin stuff. I'll leave you to open the box now.'

'Don't you want to—'

'No.' Sid cut me off. 'It's a special day and you two should celebrate together.'

'Jack will come and visit on Saturday,' I promised. 'I'm not sure about me, I'm still getting over the flu and even though I feel so much better than I did, I don't want to pass on any germs.'

'That's thoughtful of you, Elizabeth, but we're a tough old bunch. Think it's 'cos we ain't like your generation – all vegan and pesky whatever where you only eat fish. We all like a good steak here. Well those of us that still have teeth.' His laugh morphed into a hacking cough and we waited until it passed before we said our goodbyes and turned our attention to the box. 'Shall we open it together?'

We each slid our fingers under a cardboard flap, pulling them open simultaneously.

From inside Jack lifted out a wooden skittle, while I retrieved a warm bottle of ale with a faded label.

'I don't get it?' Jack shook his head.

'There's an envelope.' I pulled out a letter written in Sid's shaky handwriting.

Dear Jack and Elizabeth,

If you can be a tenth as happy in this house as Norma and I were then you'll be living a life full of joy. There's a bit to do, I know it needs a good clean and a lick of paint, but on the days it gets a bit much I've left a reminder to you that life ain't all beer and skittles but as I've said to you before – everything will be okay. It usually is.

Lots of love, Sid.

P.S. The nearest pub is The Crown and if you pop in for a pint, best not mention this. Their nine pin table hasn't been quite the same with only eight skittles.

We both laughed. 'Should we make another toast with the ale, now? You know, in case toasting with water before cursed us.'

'I don't believe in curses. Anyway, thanks to Sid we can rest assured everything will be okay.' Jack placed the skittle on the windowsill, the beer bottle next to it.

I conceded he was right, that the old wives' tale was rubbish, because my mobile beeped with an email alert from Greta, my partner in the photography business we ran.

Joyfully, I read the email once, twice, three times but still I couldn't quite absorb it. 'I've got it! Jack, I've got it!' My eyes flickered across the email again to make sure.

Jack picked me up and swung me around. I was dizzy with it all, the house, him, the good news I'd just received. The news I didn't have to explain because we were so in tune with each other. Or so I thought.

Then.

'Finally a yes.' He planted a kiss on my lips.

Today was the day our stars had aligned. Everything was falling into place. The Hawley Foundation Prize for photography was a huge deal. It wasn't only the large cash sum if you won, but the exposure. It lent a sense of credibility to the winner. Photography was such an overcrowded market; it was difficult to make a mark. You had to be selected to enter the themed competition and I'd pitched unsuccessfully for a place for the past four years.

But now not only an acceptance but a 'Your submission photograph "trust" evoked a strong emotional response from the panel.' The picture I had sent was of Sid, crouching in the alley behind Jack's studio, holding out a piece of ham in his gnarled fingers towards Whisky the stray ginger tom with the torn ear and skinny body, who stalked the area like he owned it. He never usually let anyone touch him.

Until Sid.

I scanned my screen again, hardly daring to believe it was true.

'The theme is "hope". Possibilities already whirred around my head. I could feature this house. Jack's project. What could be more hopeful than our future plans? It felt so apt.

But then came the first phone call.

The first star shifting out of alignment. My universe already veering off its perfect path.

But I didn't know it then.

Chapter Two

The first of those four fated phone calls was from my sister, Alice. 'I have something to tell you,' she blurted out before I'd even said hello. 'Can I pop over?'

I pressed my mobile to my chest, mouthing, 'It's Alice,' to Jack. 'She wants to drop in.' I had told her we wanted some alone time to settle, so I arched my eyebrows in a 'you-know-my-sister' way and he raised his own in a 'you're-going-to-say-yes-anyway' response but he wasn't annoyed; he loved her almost as much as I did.

Moments after I'd told her she could stop by the doorbell rang.

'That can't be her already!' But it was. She must have made the call from outside.

She had the grace to look sheepish. 'Sorry for turning up today but I have something to tell you.' She lowered her voice as she stepped inside. 'Where's Jack?'

'I'm here.' Jack appeared behind me. 'This is a nice surprise.'

'I hope so.' She forced a smile. 'Do you want to show me around?'

'Love to.' Jack's face glowed at the prospect. 'We haven't made it upstairs yet today, let's start there.'

The stairs creaked in the way that old houses do. My fingers curved around the wooden handrails that sat atop the spindles and I wondered about the hands that had come before me – Sid and his family – and the hands that would come after.

'It smells of damp.' Alice wrinkled her nose.

'It needs some work but we'll get there.'

Jack's confidence had always brought me comfort but that day I had to fight to cling on to my optimism which wriggled further from my grasp with each room we peered into. Peeling wallpaper and flaking paint. Yellow ceilings. Curtains billowing in the draughts snaking in from the gaps around the sash windows. It was far worse than I had remembered. When we'd visited previously our enthusiasm had tinted everything with a rose-coloured hue.

The main bedroom was habitable at least. A cast-iron bedstead. Pink floral paper covered the walls. Edging the room, dark mahogany furniture: a wardrobe, set of drawers. A large oval mirror balanced on top of a dressing table. This was the home Sid was born in, raised in and the place he'd brought his young bride, Norma. They hadn't been able to have babies, 'not through lack of trying' he had told us.

'I'm sorry.' I had placed my hand on Sid's knee covering a faded patch of rough corduroy.

'Don't be sorry. One thing I've learned, young Elizabeth, is that even if things don't seem like it, everything will be okay. It usually is. This has been a real home, one filled with laughter.'

It would be full of joy again.

'You're not going to sleep in that bed are you?' Alice broke through my thoughts.

'We've brought our own mattress, but the frame is staying.'

'Didn't Sid want any of his furniture?' Alice ran her finger through the dust on the bedside table.

'No. His room at the home is furnished. It's ours. All of it.' Jack pulled me close to him. We grinned at each other.

Ours.

'It's overwhelming really,' Jack said. 'Imagine if I hadn't met Sid. If he'd taken up a different hobby. If—'

'If. If. Ifs. You can't think like that. It's unhealthy.' Unselfconscious in front of my sister, I pressed my lips against his.

'Get a room,' Alice said.

'You're in it!' Jack and I chorused, perfectly in sync.

'I guess I am.' There was something melancholy in her response and I glanced at her, but she was gazing out of the window across the sprawling fields at the back of the house, dark green and peppered with grazing sheep. We could hear the bleating of the lambs as they trotted after their mothers.

Before I could ask her what was wrong she said, 'We should raise a glass, to your new home and to Sid.'

I nodded. After all, if it wasn't for the kindly old man we wouldn't be here today.

Jack said it was luck but I believed it was fate that had led Sid Butler to Jack's art studio. He had told me later that Sid had reminded him of his late grandfather, who he'd adored, with his thatch of white hair and pale blue eyes full of kindness.

I had felt that instant bond with him too when I met him. Sid was unobtrusive, unassuming.

Undemanding.

There was just something about him and I loved spending time with him and hearing his stories. We both did. I had taken to popping in after Sid's lesson, checking out the progress on his painting. He'd shown a natural talent, despite the shake in his hands, his difficulty in holding the brush for prolonged periods. He'd managed to capture Whisky the cat over the following few weeks once he'd enticed him inside with pieces of meat from his sandwich.

One day it had finally been finished. Sid had untied the apron he wore over his once white shirt and moss-green tank top.

'It's fabulous!'

I had studied the finished piece. The pink nose. The long whiskers. I could almost feel the softness of Whisky's fur beneath my fingers.

'Thanks. Me and Norma had a cat just like him once. Our one and only pet. Seventeen he made it to. People say black cats are lucky but the ginger ones have more personality, don't they?' He studied his canvas before turning to me. 'I want you to have it, duck.'

'Don't you want to hang it at home?' I asked.

'There ain't nobody to see it.'

Jack's eyes met mine, full of pain. I understood. The thought of Sid being lonely, alone, was unbearable.

'Don't you go feeling sorry for me.' Sid nudged me. 'You're a good girl, Libby. Always bringing me sausage rolls and making me tea and whatnot. You've always time for a chat with an old man.'

'Thank you. I'll treasure it.' I could see that giving me the painting meant as much to him as it did to me.

Jack was quiet, eyes downcast. 'You won't stop coming now you've finished, will you Sid?'

'Depends if you're still here.'

Confusion crossed Jack's face. 'Why wouldn't—'

'Sit down, laddo.' Sid patted the stool next to him. Jack sat down, swallowed hard, emotional. His grandad had always called him 'laddo', not that Sid knew that of course.

'I see the work you do here, with the kids.'

After the local youth centre had closed down because of cutbacks, Jack had noticed an increase in crime – petty vandalism, fights breaking out. Gangs of hooded youths had hung around the car park, frightening his students. Leaving late one night he had exited the building to the pungent tang of aerosol. A boy had been spraying the wall with an intricate pattern.

I had flinched when Jack had told me he'd clapped him on the shoulder; I'd felt Jack was putting himself at risk. 'You're really talented,' Jack had told the boy before he could react.

'Yeah, gotta talent for trouble, me mum says.'

'No. Really. The lines. The colours. Why don't you come back tomorrow and show me what you can do on a canvas?'

'Nah.' The boy had shrugged. 'Ain't got no money.'

'I'm not asking for any. See you at four.' Jack had headed back to his car without waiting for an answer. He told me the less talking it through, the more chance the boy had of coming back the next day.

And he did. Liam he was called. He was fifteen then. Soon he brought a friend, two, three.

Jack had taken on an assistant, Faith – an ex-secondary school art teacher who had despaired about the creative cuts to the curriculum. With the extra help, Jack was in a position to apply for grants and offer free classes for the kids in the area, and over time they had built in popularity. Jack had told me that Aarav, the police community support officer, had called in to the studio and told Jack that crime on the estate had reduced; it hadn't stopped completely, but still it was a smidgen of hope that despite the bleak picture the tabloids painted of broken Britain – the stabbings, the swell of hopelessness – that things could be improved with kindness, love.

With time.

'So.' Sid had coughed the cough of a lifelong smoker and we waited while he composed himself and carried on. 'I've got this house that I can't manage. It's a performance to climb the stairs to the first floor, let alone the second. There's outbuildings too. You could run retreats. Art holidays. Take kids from further afield. Those that ain't never seen the countryside. The cows and the sheep.'

'But …' Jack glanced at me. I knew he was trying to find the right words to let Sid down gently.

'I'm going into a home. Can't manage any more. You could take the house, and …' His vicious cough chopped his sentence in two. He popped a Polo mint out of his jacket pocket and began to suck.

My mind hopped from thought to thought while we waited for him to carry on. He couldn't be giving us a house, surely? That sort of thing only happened in movies or books, a legacy from a long-lost relative or a gift from an anonymous benefactor, and it had me rolling my eyes each time.

If only that ever happened in real life.

But no. Sid explained, 'I can't just give you the house which is daft because I ain't got no family since Norma passed and the bloody thing is mine. I've seen a solicitor and 'cos I'm moving into a home there's rules and stuff. I've got to pay for me own care, but there's a way for you to buy it on the cheap, all legal like. It needs a bit of tarting up, mind.'

Jack looked elated and crestfallen all at once. 'Sid, the funding we've got, it wouldn't stretch to renovations. Besides, there's strict rules about what I can spend it on. I have to account for every penny.'

'Don't fret. I can put some money into a trust to help you out.

Me and Norma were never blessed with kids to spoil so I ain't short of a bob or two. Earned a decent wage as an engineer – got a generous pension too.' Sid's nicotine-stained fingers had strayed to his chin, scratching his nails against his grey bristles. 'You're a good lad, Jack. If I'd had a son, a grandson, I'd hope he'd be like you.'

Jack covered his heart with his hand. Our eyes met. I knew we were both thinking the same thing, wanting the same thing. Wishing that Sid was our family, that the house could be ours.

And now it was.

'We *should* toast,' Jack replied to Alice. 'But not today. We don't have any champagne. Libby hasn't felt well and hasn't been drinking and—'

'I haven't been drinking either.' Alice sank down onto the bed, the mattress sagging under her weight, springs sighing. 'I'm pregnant.'

For a moment there was silence before I spluttered, 'But … how? Who? When?'

'The how you should know. The who doesn't matter. I'm due around 6 November according to Google. I … I think I'm pleased. I think …' Her voice trembled. 'Be happy for me, Libs. I can't do this without you.'

It was hard to believe my little sister, my single sister, was going to have a baby. I felt many things in that moment. Sadness that she was doing it alone, worry she was only twenty-four, excitement I was going to be an auntie and, if I'm brutally honest, a twang of envy that she was doing it before me.

'Does Mum know?' I asked Alice.

'Christ no.'

I wasn't surprised Alice had told me before Mum, she was a flapper. Not in a stylish 1920s type of way but a worrier. No matter what the situation, she always seemed to know someone who had experienced the same, with disastrous results.

Nobody spoke, the atmosphere sombre until Jack clapped his hands together lifting the mood. 'Right. This is cause for a celebration. A baby! I'm going to be an uncle. Bags I buy him his first paint set.' Unlike Mum, Jack could always find the sunshine through the clouds. 'I'm going to nip out and get us something fizzy. I can't promise champagne but prosecco? You can both have a small glass can't you?'

'Absolutely.' My throat was raw and the last thing I felt like was alcohol but Alice looked so young, so unsure. I wanted to prove to her that I was on her side. That if she was happy, then so was I. 'Can you pick up a box of Lemsip too while you're out?'

'Of course. I'll light the fire in the snug before I go. Keep yourself warm, Libs. See you soon.' He kissed me goodbye and then he was gone and instantly I was looking forward to his return. I was looking forward to everything the future had to offer.

Then.

The butterfly effect. The delicate flutter of wings. The tiniest change leading to chaos, catastrophe, an ordered life falling apart.

If Alice hadn't called, Jack wouldn't have gone out for prosecco.

If. If. If.

Chapter Three

In the snug, the fire crackled. Jack had stripped off the dust sheets that had draped the sofas and although they weren't to my taste – a mustard-colour velour – the cushions moulded to my body as I sank down onto them. The fabric smelled faintly of smoke and I imagined Sid sitting here, cigarette in his hand, ashtray on the side table.

The care home Sid had moved to had given him nicotine patches and the last time we'd visited he'd sat in their garden, patch on arm, smoking.

'You're not supposed to do both, Sid,' Jack had said.

'Roll-ups.' Sid tapped his tobacco tin with his arthritic finger. 'They don't really count. Anyway, you're not supposed to do anything any more according to the news.' He flicked his ash onto the grass. 'Don't drink alcohol, don't smoke, don't eat fat. Sounds bloody miserable if you ask me. Want to know the secret of a long and happy life?'

Jack and I had exchanged a smile. 'Do tell.'

'Doing whatever brings you pleasure. For me that's ten fags a day, a bottle of beer before bed and a pork pie on a Saturday.'

Alice now found evidence of his love of pie as she brushed the arm of the chair. It's covered in crumbs.'

'It's probably pastry.'

Craving a sugar fix, I reached for the packet of Jammie Dodgers that Jack had left on the table, hoping the strawberry zing would perk me up. It wasn't only the lingering effects of flu leaching my energy but the thought of everything we had do.

'So.' I tossed the pack to Alice and waited while she pulled out a biscuit.

'So.' She met my gaze, knowing what I was thinking. 'Is it terrible if the baby doesn't have a dad? We didn't.'

'Yeah and look how screwed up we are.'

'It wasn't the perfect childhood but it was better than having two parents fighting all the time.'

'Maybe.' But it still stung that our dad had left and hadn't kept in touch. 'Have you told him? The father?' I asked.

'No. He's … he's in a relationship. I really don't want to talk about it.'

'Is it Kris?' I couldn't help pushing.

'No, thank God. Do you know he never once took his socks off during sex?'

'Alice!'

'Well he didn't. Hardly husband material is he?'

'Bare feet in bed isn't a requisite to getting married.'

'Well it should be. Still he wasn't as bad as Leyton. I remember bleaching his filthy bathroom and finding a pile of toenail clippings behind the loo.'

'Gross.'

'We can't all find the perfect boyfriend straight off,' she said.

'I didn't.' It was convenient for Alice to rewrite history sometimes. To forget that before Jack there had been Owen. My first … not love although it felt like it at the time.

My phone lit up. The screensaver a photo of me and Jack. In the picture our faces were pressed together, yellow and blue paint splattering our cheeks, foreheads, noses, my dark ponytail swinging into the frame from the tilt of my head. That day I had come home to find him poised in front of a canvas, his brush sweeping fluffy clouds over a tranquil sea.

'You were supposed to start dinner?' I had been tired. Hungry. Instead of apologising Jack turned back to his painting, adding a crab to the scene before pointing to it.

'That's me.'

'A crab?' I was puzzled.

'Shellfish.'

I couldn't help laughing. 'Yep.' I dipped my finger in the paint and smeared it over his nose. 'You are selfish.'

He flicked paint back at me and the result was messy faces, dirty clothes, that photo and the memory of what came after we'd showered together. While we were showering together.

I was smiling to myself as I opened the text. An image of a box of Lemsip, a bottle of prosecco with the message, **Wild times ahead! Home soon xxx**

The word 'home' was more warming to me than the fire.

'What did Jack say?' Alice asked.

'That he's on his way back.' I put my phone down. 'How did you know it was him?'

'Because you get that look whenever you think about him. That's what I want. That look. A Jack.'

My stomach briefly seized with guilt that I was so happy when Alice obviously wasn't, but that wasn't fair. I'd kissed my frog before I found my prince.

'You always want what I have.'

'I do not,' Alice retorted.

'My Barbie doll camper van, my Girl's World, my crimpers.' I smiled, counting them off on my fingers.

'It's just that you always had cooler stuff than me. I wished I was the older sister.'

'Babysitting, helping you with your homework, reading you a bedtime story.' This time my tone didn't feel quite so light. Although only three years older than Alice I'd stepped into the role of mother when our own mum was working long hours.

'I am grateful you know. For everything.' Alice took my hand and squeezed it.

'I know. Sorry if I sound off. I just don't feel great and, Alice, honestly, life hasn't always been a bed of roses for me. I know I'm incredibly lucky to have Jack but ...'

'Owen.'

'Owen,' I confirmed.

I had given that boy my seventeen-year-old heart and he'd squeezed it painfully for three long, wasted years before throwing it onto the floor and stamping on it for good measure. Looking back it was unthinkable that I hadn't known he was deliberately, consistently, lying to me about virtually everything; where he was, who he was with. How he felt about me. It left me wearing a protective cape of mistrust – don't trust and you can't be hurt – but Jack had gently untied the fastenings and shrugged it from my shoulders which had borne so much unhappiness.

'It gives me hope you know,' Alice said, 'that after Owen you found somebody who treats you like a princess. It makes me certain that I can do the same. I don't want somebody who never takes his socks off or leaves his toenail clippings lying around.'

'Everybody does something that somebody else finds irritating.

It's whether you can put up with it. Whether the good outweighs the bad.'

'Was there any good with Owen?'

I cast my mind back. My first kiss. First Valentine's. First meal cooked for me – garlicky spaghetti. But the memories of those firsts were all replaced by the firsts I'd rather forget. First time I was cheated on. Stolen from. Dumped.

'There must have been once but all I remember is that being lied to over and over made me feel as though I wasn't worth being honest with.' There's a question on my tongue and I taste the bitterness of it. 'Alice, who is the baby's father?'

'Libby. Please don't ask me that.'

'But you and me.' I didn't understand. 'We've always being truthful with each other, haven't we? Had each others backs?'

'We still do. Libby, don't compare me to Owen.'

'I just want you to be okay.'

Looked after.

Loved.

'I am. One day … one day the baby might have a father but until I can find the right one …'

'Life isn't all about perfection, Alice. Relationships are about compromise. Nothing is perfect. Jack isn't perfect.' I was trying to make her feel better.

'How so?' she asked.

I stalled for time, wiping my nose, clearing my sore throat. I could tell her a million things that were right with him, but I looked at the expression on Alice's face and I knew it was important that she realise we are all flawed.

'He's too optimistic.'

'That's a fault?'

'It can be. Like this place. Look at it. He sees what it can be. We've a real challenge here but he's all "it'll be fine".'

'It will,' said Alice. 'Because he's a hard worker and passionate.'

'So hard-working that he often forgets to eat, which is okay when it's just him but when it's his turn to fix dinner it's annoying.' I don't tell her that he always puts this right as I'm pulled back towards that photo on my phone, thinking of the after, curled up in towelling robes in bed, hair shower damp, spicy pepperoni pizza with stringy mozzarella stretching between our slices – a *Lady and the Tramp* moment in time but with cheese rather than spaghetti.

'And!' I added triumphantly. 'He's too focused on helping other people sometimes, sacrificing what he should be doing to help someone else out. What he's done for the kids he teaches is amazing but sometimes …' I faltered, feeling terrible for even thinking it.

'Sometimes?'

'It can encroach on the little time we have together. They look up to Jack—'

'He's a great role model.'

'He is but … Liam, in particular, seems so reliant on him, even more so since he left school and started his art and design course at college.'

'How's that going for him?'

'He's not crazy about it. Level 1 covers such a broad spectrum of areas from 3D crafts to textiles and graphic design. Liam really wants to focus on the painting but it was this or an apprenticeship in God knows what. His GCSE grades weren't high enough for the school to accept him into sixth form and he had to do something. He was always dropping round to the flat to show Jack his assignments, unannounced, uninvited.'

'Unwelcome?'

'Not exactly. I always asked him in and usually fed him. I feel sorry for him. He's permanently hungry. It's nice to see the way he's changed. He was so … angry when I met him. Defensive, but now he's softened. Particularly around Sid.' The teenagers had bonded with Sid in a way neither Jack or I had envisaged. He told them stories of the past and they gazed at him with such respect. The fact he also shared his tobacco with them probably helped forge their unlikely friendships. But then you couldn't help loving Sid. 'I just wish Jack would set some boundaries sometimes.' It was unfair to say this. Jack would always put me first, I just hadn't asked him.

'Riiight,' Alice drew out the word. 'So in proving Jack's not perfect all you've come up with is that he's too happy and kind. Poor you.' She covered her heart with her hand. 'I don't know how you cope.'

I picked up a cushion and threw it at her. As it flew through the air dust motes danced in its wake triggering a bout of sneezing which, in turn, exacerbated my pounding head.

'You sound so rough,' Alice said.

'I've felt better,' I admitted. 'Those things I just said—'

'Were because you were trying to cheer me up, Libs. I know you love him to bits. He is taking ages though.'

I text him. **Where are you?! I'm dying here!**

Minutes later my phone began to ring.

The first phone call, the earlier one from Alice, had changed so much. I was to be an auntie. Already I had begun to feel the weight of responsibility towards the new life along with the worry of a big sister that she was doing this alone. But that phone call had brought, ultimately, happy news. The second phone call though ... God, that second phone call.

'Are you going to get that?' Alice had asked.

'It's an unknown number, probably marketing.'

'If it's someone flogging a cut-price man who would make a great dad, sign me up,' she had said.

I remember now I had been laughing when I answered.

Couples should have this sixth sense when something is wrong shouldn't they? Especially when something is wrong with the other? Today, I still burn with shame that I had no idea.

I was laughing.

Chapter Four

Four words.

Four words and everything changed.

'There's been an accident.'

For a second I froze; the smile on my face, my whole body motionless, lungs ceased to function.

I couldn't breathe.

The person on the other end of the line continued talking.

My hearing sharpened, my voice muted. Vision tunnelled.

I shook my head as though I could make it stop. She must be mistaken.

Must be.

'Accident? Jack?' I was repeating random words. 'I don't …'

My eyes met Alice's; hers were full of confusion. It didn't make sense. Jack had only nipped out for a box of Lemsip and some booze.

'You can't have the right person. Jack … Jack's on his way home. He texted me, he …' My voice cracked.

Gently, Alice took the phone from me. She spoke for a few moments before hanging up.

'Libby.' She cupped my face with her hands. She felt cold. I felt cold. 'We need to go to the hospital.'

'But I don't understand—'

'Now.' She pulled me to my feet.

Like I had done for her so many times growing up, she coaxed me into my shoes and jacket. We stepped outside. Bewildered, I gazed around the front garden we had skipped happily through just hours before. Now the daffodils seemed to hang their heads with sorrow.

Jack.

Was he … Was he …? I tried to recall what I'd been told but it was all a blur. Surely if … if the worst had happened, we wouldn't be speeding to the hospital?

'Alice …' I wanted reassurance but I was too scared she wouldn't be able to give it to me. Instead I placed the thought that Jack must be alive on the palm of my hand and clenched my trembling fingers around it, holding on tightly, the sharpness of my nails cutting into my soft flesh.

We ran into the hospital when all I wanted to do was to run away, to travel back through time to a place where Jack was okay. Where we were happy.

The smell of disinfectant stuck in my throat. The tropical heat, combined with my raging temperature made my head spin. We pelted through endless corridors. All around me streamed the sick and the dying, anxious relatives and worried friends. My scant experience of hospitals so far had been solely positive. Visiting a couple of friends who had given birth. Marching onto the maternity ward trailing pink or blue helium balloons embellished with congratulatory storks. Now … now I saw this place for what it was.

Frightening.

Life-changing.

'This is us.' Alice smiled at me encouragingly, although her face was drained of colour. Her lips almost blue. Her fingers trembled as we rubbed antibacterial gel into our hands from the dispenser under the 'Accident & Emergency' sign. She pushed open the double doors and I stepped through them, flinching as they slammed behind me.

Once more it was Alice who took charge, speaking to the receptionist. Leading me to an orange plastic chair as hard and uncomfortable as the ball of dread that lay heavy on my chest. I'd have thought that night-time would be when this department was busiest – drunken fights, drunken falls – but the waiting area was rammed. A small boy, swinging his legs, wailing that his tummy hurt. A man pressing a bloodied rag against his forehead. A woman doubled over in pain, her toddler pulling at her skirt, whining for chocolate from the vending machine.

Jack wasn't here. He was obviously being seen. Was that good or bad? I just didn't know.

'Libby Gilbert?'

I raised my face to a man with a bushy beard and a white coat. 'Emerson. I'm Emerson. Jack and I aren't married.'

Yet. I wanted to add yet but I was so scared that it was too late for us. I glanced at my bare ring finger. The other day Jack had made a throwaway comment about 'happy wife, happy life' and I swear my heart momentarily stopped beating. Marriage was something we'd discussed in the past. Jack wasn't keen because his parents were no longer together, but it was because my parents weren't together that I longed for the stability. It hadn't been mentioned for a long time; it meant a lot to me but I hadn't wanted to pressure him. I'd rather be with him and happy than force him into something he didn't believe in. But then, unbeknown to Jack, a couple of months ago I'd seen him rummaging around in my jewellery box, trying one of my rings on. It was hard to keep a neutral expression on my face when, over the next few days, he had casually asked what my favourite gemstones were, whether I preferred yellow gold or platinum.

'Is he …?' I searched the man's face for an answer to the unspoken question that fear had shackled to my tongue. His expression was inscrutable.

'I'm Dr Corcoran. Follow me please.' He led us into a room. Even if he hadn't gestured for us to sit I would have collapsed onto the faux-leather sofa. My legs just couldn't support me when the ground felt like it kept shifting beneath me. My future slipping away.

The relatives' room. Again I had the strange sense of déjà vu. I'd watched enough TV dramas to know there was no good news when you were led to the relatives' room. I was quietly crying before he even spoke.

'Jack's been stabbed.'

The words sliced into me.

I covered my mouth with the horror of it. Of all the things I had steeled myself for when I'd heard the word 'accident' – tripping over a paving stone, a car ploughing into his van – a stabbing had never entered the equation.

'Where?' Alice asked. She took my hand and I gripped her fingers tightly.

'He's been lucky. We've X-rayed him and the blade missed all of his vital organs. A few millimetres lower and it would have pierced his bowel. We've stitched and dressed the wound and—'

'So he'll be okay? He is okay?' I nodded in the vain hope that my affirmation would make it so.

'Is he conscious?' Alice spoke at the same time.

'Yes. We're going to keep him in overnight for observation but all being well you'll be able to take him home tomorrow.'

'But … who? How …?' *Stabbed*. I had so many questions and I couldn't form any of them.

'The police are with him now. I'll get somebody to take you to him.'

Even as I stood it still felt like the floor was moving beneath me, my future not as solid and as certain as it once was.

Jack's face was as white as the pillowcase he rested his head upon. His hospital gown was a washed-out grey.

'Jack!' I rushed to his side, barely registering the uniformed officer that hovered in the corner. I couldn't contain my tears as I scattered kisses onto his mouth, his nose, his forehead. What would I have done if I'd never seen his face again? It was incomprehensible that somebody young and healthy could walk out of the door never to return. I sat on the bed and leaned into him until he was looking at me, but instead of love and life in his eyes there was nothing, and that emptiness caused my stomach to plummet.

'You're okay. You're okay.' I tried to convince him, myself. But we both knew he wasn't, not really.

'I dropped your Lemsip,' he monotoned.

'Shh.' I took his hand, pressing the tips of his fingers against my lips. 'Don't worry.'

'Elizabeth?' The officer stepped forward. 'I'm PC Nowak.'

'It's Libby, please. What happened?'

'Jack was mugged—'

'I hope you catch the bastard,' Alice said from the doorway.

'He's dead,' Jack said dully. 'He ran out of the alley by the side of the chemist, straight into the road. A car … A car …'

'Oh my God.' It was all too horrific for words.

'He was known to us. He had a record as long as your arm,' PC Nowak said and then his face softened. 'Victim support will be in touch the next few days. We retrieved Jack's things, they're on the cabinet over there. I'll be off now.'

'Thank you,' I said, but I wasn't watching him leave, instead staring with revulsion at Jack's phone and wallet. The mugger's hand had touched them, his fingers now cold and stiff.

Dead.

I'm dying here I had texted Jack, trying to hurry him home, when unbeknown to me he was fighting for his life.

Somebody *had* died today, it could easily have been Jack.

I leaned into him, burying my face in the hollow between his shoulder and his neck and inhaled, but instead of his usual comforting Jack smell my nostrils were filled with disinfectant, a washing powder I didn't recognise.

Hospitals.

I raised my head, meeting his gaze, but it was the eyes of a stranger staring back at me.

He was in shock, that was all. A man had died in front of him. Once he was home and showered and felt safe again he'd get back to normal. *We'd* get back to normal, wouldn't we?

We'd fall back into the life we had so meticulously planned and have many happy years together.

Wouldn't we?

For a long, long moment we didn't speak. Our fingers remained linked together, tight, but not as inextricable as I'd once thought.

As though on some level I knew what was to come.

Chapter Five

Jack was dozing, the tea I'd bought him from the vending machine growing cold and unappealing.

'A decent cuppa makes everything better,' he was fond of saying, but it would take more than tea to fix this.

To fix him.

The medication and the shock had collaborated to whisk him somewhere else entirely.

Frequently I reached out to touch his shoulder, reassuring myself that he was here, safe, but my hand was shaking and my mind screamed the what-ifs.

Alice had gone to grab a sandwich.

'Sorry, morning sickness seems to last all day,' she had said. 'Food is the only thing that keeps the nausea at bay.'

I didn't mind her nipping off. The canteen was right over the other side of the hospital and I relished the time alone to gather my galloping thoughts.

My mobile beeped – a text from Greta. **Has the news sunk in yet?!!** For a few moments I couldn't process what she meant, how she knew. But then I remembered she'd emailed me earlier to let me know about The Hawley Foundation Prize. How was it possible that we had been so happy a few hours ago, that this was even the same day?

I texted her back, **Jack's had an accident. He's in hospital, but he'll be fine.**

He'll be fine.

There was something reassuring about typing those words, seeing them in black solid letters, a declaration, a promise.

I wrote them again, this time to Jack's assistant and our friend, Faith, but then after I had sent it I was overcome with guilt that I'd told friends before family and so I dropped my phone back into my bag. Once I didn't have anything else to occupy me the sick dread built again in my stomach.

I placed my hand lightly on Jack's chest feeling the reassuring rise and fall of his ribcage.

He'll be fine.

He *is* fine.

'Hello. It's Libby isn't it?' I'd no idea how long had passed before a nurse bustled through the thin blue curtains hanging around the bed. 'I'm Angela. How's everything here?'

'Jack's … he's okay?'

'Yes. But what about you?' Her kind eyes studied me.

'I'm … I'm …' Tears rose in my throat. I tried to swallow them back down.

'Let it out.' She rubbed my back. 'You've had an awful shock.'

'He could have … He could have …'

'But he didn't. He's fine. The stitches will be out in a few days and he'll be as good as new.'

Physically he might but mentally? Emotionally? Not all scars are visible.

'Libby?' Breathless, Alice pushed through the curtains, her

cheeks pink, two plastic packs of sandwiches in her hands. 'Sorry, the canteen was miles away.'

'It's okay. I'm okay.' I wiped my eyes.

'I'll leave you to it.' Angela squeezed my arm before she slipped back onto the ward.

'Cheese and tomato or tuna mayo?' Alice asked.

'Neither.'

'You need the calories or you won't have the energy to—'

'Cheese.' I held out my hand. Our relationship had suddenly turned on its head, her making sure I ate, repeating the words I used to say to her when she was teenager, heading out for the pub. It was never her energy levels I was worried about though, it was lining her stomach because when the shots she'd downed came back up it would be me holding back her hair, cleaning the toilet bowl.

I bit a small piece of the sandwich. The tomato was slimy on my tongue, the bread stiff, cheddar tasteless. I chewed and chewed before I could swallow it down.

The curtain swished back again.

'I believe these two belong to you?' Angela gestured to Faith and her husband, Michael.

'What are you doing here?' I stood up and hugged them both.

'We were having lunch in town when we got your text.' Faith was peering over my shoulder towards the bed.

'Well technically *I'm working from home*,' Michael made inverted commas with his fingers. 'I can catch up in the evenings though so it isn't really skiving.'

'I said they could have a quick peek to reassure themselves that Jack's okay but they can't stay.' Angela kept hold of the curtain, ready to draw it closed.

Faith stepped closer to Jack and in her usual tactile way, rested her fingertips lightly on his arm. 'Oh, Jack.' Her voice was barely audible. Michael placed his hands on her shoulders and kissed the top of her head protectively, and inexplicably the gesture made me want to weep. They were as close as Jack and I were and the thought I might have lost that …

'What happened?' Faith asked. 'A car accident?'

'No.' I lowered my voice. 'He was stabbed.'

'What?' Faith spun around to face me. 'When you said accident I assumed—'

'He was mugged. The doctor said he was lucky, it could have been … The man that stabbed him missed his vital organs.' My voice now a whisper.

'He's going to be fine.' Alice gave my shoulders a reassuring squeeze.

'Christ,' Faith said softly. 'Have they caught the mugger?'

'I hope they string the bastard up!' There was no speaking in hushed tones for Michael but I was touched by his outrage.

'He … he died at the scene,' I told them, pausing for breath.

'You don't have to go through it all again,' Alice said.

But Faith's eyes were wide with expectation.

'It's fine.' It still didn't feel real. 'He ran into the path of a car after …' The police said he had a record but …' While Jack had been sleeping I'd been turning it over and over. It was incredibly sad. The mugger was someone's son. Possibly a husband, a father, a brother. Almost certainly a friend. What drove someone to crime? I'd been trying to figure it out. Was it something inherently damaged in them since birth or was it their upbringing? Neglect? Lack of love? I kept circling back to Jack's students who'd been restless and bored before they'd discovered art. 'I've been sitting here thinking that without Jack's guidance, Liam could have turned to crime, ended up in prison or … or worse. Any one of his group of friends could.'

'I always knew that Jack's vision for a centre could be life-changing,' Faith said. 'I never actually thought of it being life-saving.'

There was a beat before Michael asked, 'Is there anything we can do?'

'Actually, yes. You could find the van we hired. It must be around the chemist's somewhere.'

'Michael doesn't need to do that,' Alice said. 'I can get a cab there and drive the van myself. Do you have the keys?'

'Yes. But, Alice, the van needs emptying and returning, our cars collecting, and it would be good for you to have help … you know … lifting.' My eyes flickered to Alice's stomach and she placed a hand across it, her cheeks burning red. I turned to Faith and Michael. 'There isn't much, no furniture except a mattress, mainly clothes, records, books and some kitchen stuff.'

'We'll figure it all out and we can work off that sticky toffee pudding and custard,' Michael said. 'We'll pick your cars up when we drop the van off too.' Faith brushed her lips against Jack's cheek and whispered goodbye before we all swapped hugs.

'Alice?' I called her back as she started to leave. 'You've been amazing today. Really.' Usually I was the one in charge. The way Alice had kept calm, taken control, had shown a real strength of character. I lowered my voice to a whisper. 'You'll be a great mum. A great mum *and* dad.'

She nodded and with one last, lingering look at Jack she hurried to catch up with Faith and Michael.

I curled up on the visitor chair, staring out of the window. Night had drawn in. The sky dark but clear. Popping with stars. A sliver of a moon cast a silvery glow across Jack's face.

His eyelids fluttered. I leaned forward, wanting me to be the first thing that he saw.

'Hey, you.' I smiled as he focused on my face. His eyes now more familiar, still sad but definitely Jack.

'How are you feeling?' I climbed onto the bed next to him. His hands covered his abdomen as the mattress shifted beneath him. 'Does it hurt?'

'Not much.' His voice was hoarse.

I picked up a glass of water and angled the straw between his lips. 'Small sips.'

He drank, wiping his mouth with the back of his hand as I set the glass back down.

'What happened?' I didn't want to bring it up but I couldn't help it.

'It was all so quick. One minute I was heading back to the van with the prosecco and Lemsip. The next I was handing over my wallet and phone. I saw the silver of the blade and … oh, Libby …' It spilled from his lips in a garbled rush. 'All I could think of was getting back to you. Our life. I love you so much. I was waiting until our anniversary but …' He took my hand along with a deep breath. 'Libby, will you—'

'You're awake.' It was a different nurse, unsmiling. 'Can you get off the bed please.' She glared at me. 'Patients only.' She folded her arms while I slid back onto the chair. Jack pulled a mock angry face behind her back. I was heartened to see he hadn't lost his sense of humour.

'You were saying?' I prompted once she'd gone.

'Get back on the bed.' He patted the space next to him.

I glanced down the ward.

'I dare you,' he said.

'I can't.'

'Scaredy cat.'

'Would you risk her wrath, if it were the other way round?'

'God no. She's terrifying.' He flashed a brief smile.

'So …' I took his hand. 'You said, "will you".'

'It'll wait. We have a lifetime together, Libs. Five years on Sunday.' He looked at me so tenderly.

'Five years.' I couldn't wait for the rest of our lives.

'It's eight o'clock.' The hostile nurse had returned and was looking pointedly at her watch. 'Time for you to leave.'

'But … Can't I sleep here? In the chair?'

'I'm afraid not.'

'Go home and get some rest, Libby,' Jack said. 'I'll see you in the morning.'

Grudgingly, I kissed him goodbye, feeling the nurse's eyes burn into my back. I was still wondering what he wanted to ask me as my reluctant feet trudged out of the ward.

Before I jumped in a taxi I rang the care home.

'It's ten past eight,' I was told indignantly. 'Most of our residents are beginning to wind down before bed.'

'Please. It's important.'

It took Sid an age to reach the phone and when he did I told him what had happened. 'I'm sorry but Jack won't make it in on Saturday now.' Every weekend we took Sid a pork pie from the butchers he liked. 'But I wanted to let you know he's okay.'

'Libby, you'll *both* be okay.' For once Sid didn't crack a joke.

'I hope so. Thanks, Sid.' My voice was barely audible, the words stuck behind the lump in my throat.

We both knew that I'd called not to reassure him, but because talking to him reassured me. Jack and I both loved our surrogate grandfather who thought we looked after him when really it was he who took care of us. 'Everything will be all right.'

There was a pause. Sid's rasping breath. My own troubled thoughts loud inside my mind. 'What if … What if this changes him somehow, Sid?' I couldn't have voiced this to anyone else. It felt wrong. Selfish. 'What if Jack realises how close to death he was and he wants … more?'

'Develops an urge to travel, chucks his things into a rucksack and disappears halfway around the world?'

'Something like that.'

'Then you'll be by his side, Elizabeth, sharing the adventure, taking glorious photos, and—'

'You'll be—' I began

'Look forward to your postcards. I can't see it though, duck, really. Can you? He'd never get a decent cup of tea.'

The mood lighter, Sid told me to go home and get some rest.

I took one last lingering look at the hospital.

Jack.

I whispered his name. Feeling the shape of it on my tongue. Wondering if he was asleep again. If he was dreaming of me.

Home.

Where the heart is. Though my heart was here, with him.

Today, despite everything that has happened between then and now, my heart is still with Jack.

Always.

Chapter Six

Although I had rung the hospital the second I had woken after a fitful sleep, I hadn't quite believed the assurances that Jack was okay. Forgoing breakfast and a shower I raced across town. My heart was in my mouth as I pushed open the door to the ward with my elbow, still rubbing the squirt of antibacterial gel into my hands, the small cuts around my nervously bitten fingers stinging.

Angela was in the small office scribbling on some paper. When she noticed my arrival she hurried over to me.

'Oh lovey.' She scanned my face. 'It doesn't look like you got much rest. Jack's going to be fine. He *is* fine. He should be discharged later,' she told me as we walked towards Jack's bed.

'Already? You don't just want him gone because it's almost the weekend?'

'Honestly. We do try to free up beds for the weekend but we wouldn't be sending him home unless he was ready.'

'Hey you.' I kissed Jack hello. 'How are you feeling?'

'Good.' He caught my expression. 'Okay, perhaps not good, but a lot better. Really. The shock's worn off and the pain is under control. Honest, Libs. Relax. You're not getting rid of me any time soon.'

Relieved, I clutched his hand tightly.

'Very true,' Angela said. 'I was just telling Libby that you should be able to leave today. You can take care of each other. Libby, it looks like you slept in those clothes.' Angela nodded towards the creased shirt of Jack's that I had, indeed, slept in.

'At least she's wearing clothes today,' Jack said. 'The first time I met her she was naked.'

Although I was mortified I couldn't help laughing.

'Tell me more.' Angela crossed her arms.

'It isn't how it sounds,' I said.

'So you weren't naked?' Angela asked.

'Well, technically ...'

'As bare as the day she was born.' Jack had a wicked glint in his eye. He still looked pale, awful, but he was trying to cheer me up, remind me of a time I could never forget.

'I definitely need to hear this,' Angela said.

Jack gently squeezed my fingers in a can-I-tell-her? way and I stroked his thumb – yes, you can.

I had been modelling for life classes for about a month, saving up for a new camera. I'm not the bravest person but I knew from my own experience with photography that the amateur artists would be viewing me as a subject, nothing more. At least I had hoped that they would.

Jack had run in ten minutes late, white shirt blotchy with paint, brush in his hand.

'Sorry I'm ... Oh.' He had skidded to a Tom and Jerry halt. Our eyes had met. Heat crept into my cheeks as the air between us fizzed. I had never experienced such an instant attraction before.

'You're ... new?' he asked. 'Sorry, don't let me distract you.'

He attempted a jog around the outskirts of the room but his

foot caught on an easel causing a pot of water to crash to the floor. 'Sorry,' he said as he mopped it up.

Laughter bubbled in my stomach and I fought to hold it in but when Jack took his place behind his own easel and our eyes met I was suddenly serious, hot. I diverted my gaze, staring at the floor, trying to think of everything but him as his brush swept paint across his canvas with a light touch, but it was impossible not to imagine his careful hands on me.

My body felt heavy, arms aching from holding the pose, the weight of Jack's stare. I couldn't stop checking whether he was looking at me, which was ridiculous because it's what I was there for. Every time our eyes met he quickly looked away, acting like he hadn't been looking at me – which was just as absurd.

About halfway through the class he packed up his things and with one final 'sorry' in my direction, he left.

I couldn't get him out of my mind as I held my position, immune to the pins and needles which pricked at me to move. Had I imagined the connection between us? Had I repulsed him?

Afterwards, I had wrapped myself in a fluffy white towelling robe and headed to the loos to get dressed. He was waiting in the corridor, leaning against the wall.

'Hello, you,' he said.

I tightened the belt on my robe, feeling exposed. Vulnerable.

'I'm sorry I rushed out. It's just … It didn't seem appropriate to see you like … that … when … when I knew I wanted to ask you out.' This time it was his cheeks that coloured. Coming from somebody else this might have sounded like a cheesy line, but there was a sincerity about him I was drawn to.

'I …' I fiddled with the fraying towelling of my belt. Where were my words?

'God. Sorry. Go and get changed. Have a think. I'll be waiting, in a non-creepy way of course.' It was his turn to be unsure. Nervous.

'What did you have in mind?'

'Food? Do you eat? Of course I can tell you eat. I don't mean … I'm not implying you overeat. You're not fat. You're lovely. You're … shut up, Jack.'

'Jack?'

He slapped his palm to his forehead. 'Christ I haven't even introduced myself. I'm such an arse. I'm Jack.' He stuck out his hand.

'Libby,' I called over my shoulder as I pushed my way into the toilets to get changed. I wasn't trying to be seductive by not shaking his hand but I was holding my robe together. I was trying to hold myself together.

I had known that it was the beginning of something.

'That's a lovely story!' Angela said. 'Certainly something to tell the grandkids, although I hope you kept your clothes on for your first date.' She peered at me over the top of her glasses reminding me of my old English teacher.

'Yes, let's talk about *our first date*, Jack.'

'Do we have to?' he asked, knowing what was coming.

Payback.

'Jack offered to cook me a romantic meal. Now what was it again?' I tilted my head to one side, pretending to think. 'Peanut butter and mashed banana on cream crackers.'

'You're having a laugh?' Angela put her hands on her hips in mock anger.

'Don't knock it til you've tried it,' Jack said.

'Lucky you're a handsome boy then isn't it, if that's the limit of your culinary skills?' Angela shook her head sadly.

I had arrived that first night and tentatively knocked on the door, unsure what I was doing. There had been an undeniable spark between us but still, this was a stranger's flat. A stranger who had seen me naked. I was about to turn around, flee for home, when Jack had answered the door wearing a black-and-white-striped butcher's apron, splattered with something that looked like blood. I took a step back.

'It's tomato, I promise!' He held his hands up. Even then, he could read me. 'I'm making lasagne. Come in.' He seemed delighted I'd turned up. His eyes fixed on mine, not travelling to other places on my body which he'd already seen.

I stepped over the threshold, towards the smell of garlic and basil.

We settled on the sofa with a glass of Rioja. From the stereo, sounds of 'California Dreamin'.

'A fan of The Mamas & the Papas then?'

'It reminds me of being a kid,' Jack said. 'Sometimes I wonder whether I should listen to something cooler. More modern. But when I paint I like to listen to music that makes me *feel* …'

Suddenly the room was plunged into darkness.

'Sorry,' Jack said. 'That's the third time today. I'm not sure what's going on. Wait here a sec.'

I listened to his footfall as he crossed the room, a bang. 'Shit.' Followed by a 'Sorry. Walked into the bookcase.'

The opening and closing of a door. A spark of light. A glowing candle.

'Everything is as it should be in the fuse box. I don't know what the problem is. Dinner is off unless we fancy raw pasta. Unless … unless you want to go out? There's a nice Chinese at the bottom of the road.'

But right there, in Jack's flat, just he and I, was exactly where I wanted to be.

'We could have a sandwich?' I suggested.

'My kind of woman.' I could feel myself glowing under the light of his smile. 'I'll be right back.'

It took several trips, more candles, a new bottle of wine, and then Jack placed a plate before me laden with ...

'Sorry. I was out of bread.'

'Is this ... banana?'

'Yep. And peanut butter on cream crackers. Don't knock it til you've tried it.'

Hesitantly I had nibbled the edge, the sweet and the savoury exploding on my tongue. Another bite, bigger this time.

'Told you,' Jack said fiddling with his phone. The Beatles began to play.

After we'd eaten Jack offered me his hand. 'Dance?'

John Lennon crooned 'In My Life' and we spun slowly around the furniture; in the flickering candlelight our long shadows mirrored against the the walls. Jack's lips softly butterflied across mine.

That was the exact moment I opened myself up to the possibility that I might, one day, love again.

Angela's eyes flickered between me and Jack. 'That sounds like a pretty awful first date.'

'I've just been stabbed!' Jack wore a wounded expression. 'Leave me alone!'

'A right pair you two are. Anyway, I've got other patients to check on. I'll see you both later.'

We barely noticed her leave, our eyes locked together, our fingers linked. The affection I had felt for him that night in his flat, a million times stronger now.

There was nothing left to do but wait. Sometimes Jack and I discussed our plans for the future but mostly we were silent. Drained. The minutes stretched, time feeling like a vast lake we had to wade through before Jack could go home. The doctor had discharged him but the wait for Angela to bring the paperwork was interminable. I'd drawn the curtain, was lying on the edge of the bed, my head on Jack's chest, his arm around me. His breath slow and steady, his soft fingers lazily running around the skin between my jeans and shirt. My eyelids were heavy. I was just relaxing into sleep when the curtains swished open. Guilty, I sat up, straightened my top, swung my legs off the bed but it wasn't a nurse.

'Faith.' Her dark hair was piled on top of her head, face pale.

'She couldn't relax until she'd seen Jack,' Michael said from behind her.

'Sorry. I called the ward but they wouldn't tell me anything and I rang your mobile but …' She shrugged.

'It's on silent.' I stood and after hello hugs I linked my fingers together, stretched my arms above my head to loosen my stress-tightened muscles.

'So how are you?' Faith sat on the edge of the bed and sandwiched Jack's hand between hers. 'You scared us all there for a moment.'

'I'm okay. I'll be going home soon.'

'That's a relief,' Michael said.

'Yes. I want a shower, a decent cup of tea and then some pineapple,' Jack said.

'Pineapple?' asked Faith.

'The hospital food has left me craving something fresh.'

'You've only been here for … what? Less than twenty-four hours,' Michael said.

'I was *stabbed*.'

'You're never going to hear the last of it, Libby.' Michael laughed. We chatted for several minutes until Angela brought the paperwork.

'Here you go, lovely.' She pressed a sheet of paper into Jack's hand. 'Here's what to do. What not to do. Keep yourself dosed up with painkillers. Don't suffer. The district nurse, Maggie, will drop in every day and check your dressing. I've given her your mobile number as a contact, Libby. Any concerns in the meantime, the phone number of the ward is here.' She pointed. 'Give us a ring any time. And look after each other. I would say keep your clothes on but—'

'It's our anniversary this weekend,' I blurted out as though that would constitute us getting naked.

'I hope you'll have a more romantic meal than … What was it? Peanut butter and banana on crackers.'

'Hey!' Jack said. 'Don't—'

'Knock it til you've tried it.' Angela shook her head. 'Go on. Get away with you both.'

Michael drove us home.

'Do you want to come in and see our new place?' I asked Faith and Michael as they dropped us off, secretly hoping they would say no.

'It's okay,' Michael said. 'We saw it when we unloaded the van. We'll give you two some alone time.'

Faith twisted around in her seat. For a split second it seemed like she wanted to say something else. She glanced at me before her eyes shifted back to Jack. There was an expression on her face I couldn't read, a silent question, but Jack was already climbing out of the car.

By the time we went to bed it was raining, the rhythm comforting against our windowpanes. Yesterday, without Jack, the bed had been Papa-bear-big but now it was Mama-bear-just-right.

Jack winced as he turned onto his side. 'I'm not sure I'm up to taking Sid his pork pie tomorrow.'

'He's not expecting you. You can always call him. That reminds me, I still have your phone in my bag. Do you want me to get it?'

'No. I ... it's awful isn't it? The thought of ... him ... the mugger touching ...' Jack began to cry. It was unexpected. Distressing. Something I rarely saw. I wrapped my arms around him, wishing I could absorb his pain. It was heartbreaking but, I hoped, ultimately healing, the dark of the room allowing him to feel all of the things he'd tried to suppress.

'I was so scared, Libs.' His voice was muffled. His mouth pressed against my hair.

'Shh. It's okay. You're okay. Try not to think about it.' But now he'd mentioned it I couldn't think of anything else.

I slipped my hand inside Jack's T-shirt, feeling his heart thudding underneath my palm.

The warmth.

Those fingers of the mugger, icy and still. Fingers that had touched Jack's things.

I decided that I'd buy Jack a new wallet and mobile as soon as possible but until then I'd leave his where they were.

But keeping his phone turned out to be a big mistake.

Huge.

Chapter Seven

The overhead lights were harsh and bright, the corridor endless. Rockets of pain fired up my shins as my feet pounded against the hard floor.

Jack.

I pushed my way through another double door. On the wall, in big bold letters, A & E and an arrow pointing forwards. I increased my speed.

Jack.

There was no one else here but me. No one to ask for help.

Again, a door. I shouldered my way through it. Another sign for A & E but this time the arrow pointed back to the direction I had come from.

Jack.

Here was here. Hurt. I couldn't find him. Couldn't reach him. I was stuck in a never-ending loop.

Jack!

'Libby.' His voice soft in my ear. His fingers touching my cheek.

'Jack.' My eyes snapped open. For a second I was disorientated. The walls unfamiliar. Grey morning light filtered through the bare window which was framing the country view like one of

Jack's oil paintings. I burst into noisy tears, curling into a ball on my side.

'It's okay. I'm here.' He rhythmically stroked my back while I cried it out. I didn't need to share the details of my nightmare with him. He just knew. I reached for a tissue and while I blew my nose Jack shifted back against his pillows, covering his abdomen with both hands.

'Does it hurt a lot?'

'It … burns. It's like I can still feel it there. The knife.'

I shuffled closer to him. 'Do you want to talk about it?'

'No.' He shook his head. 'No, I don't. What I would like to do is take some painkillers and go to the studio.'

'Jack, no. You're supposed to be resting.'

'There's something I need to finish.'

A message beeped its arrival and I checked my mobile, sighed. 'Mum's coming round.' I spoke just three words, laced with disappointment and edged with irritation. The last thing I needed today was Mum's doom and gloom. Not while a blizzard of fearful what-ifs was still whirling fiercely around my mind. I could still feel it, that insistent quiver of fear in my stomach that had been ever present since the hospital had called, and perhaps now it would always be there.

'Then I'll stay here, with you.' Jack held me against him and my heart beat out *thank you, thank you, thank you*, against his chest.

The house was the best I could make it in the forty-five minutes between Mum's message and her arrival. I shouldn't have felt so apprehensive that she was coming but I was agitated as I plumped the cushions in the snug for the fifth time, scanning the room, momentarily removing the hopeful lenses our eyes saw it through and noticing it for what it was. Tired. Run-down. In need of more than a sprinkling of fairy dust and a vague idea of what it could be.

'Relax,' Jack said but I couldn't. Partly, I think, because I wanted Mum's approval and I'd never felt like I'd had it. I wanted to feel like the centre of her world, like me and Alice were the centre of her world, but she loved to talk about other people more than she did about us as though everyone else was more interesting than her own children. She worked in a bakery and spent so much time – too much time – telling us the ins and outs of the customers' lives. She knew them in a way she didn't know us – her own daughters – and I found that sad. Our father had been absent while we were growing up and sometimes it felt that Mum was missing too. Rationally, I knew that was unfair. It wasn't her fault that she had had to work full-time when other mothers picked their kids up from school, but even when she had been at home she didn't talk to us properly and I had never felt as close to her as I'd have liked.

There was a knock at the door but it wasn't Mum. It was Faith and Michael.

'Ta-da!' From behind their backs they both produced a pineapple.

I laughed. 'Mr "I've-been-stabbed" will be pleased.'

'How many times have you heard that then?'

'Oh, only when he wanted another cup of tea, to choose what he wanted to watch, to pick the first room to be decorated … Do you want to come in?'

'If that's okay? I'd like to see Jack,' Faith said.

'She's done nothing but worry about him,' Michael said. 'It'll put her mind at rest.' His concern for her was touching. They'd been together since they met at uni, twenty years ago. I'd never heard them argue.

But before they could step inside, Mum's car pulled up.

'Libby.' She pulled me into a quick hug before turning to Faith. 'Lovely to see you again, and is this your husband?'

'Michael,' Faith said, introducing them, 'this is Caroline, Libby's mum.'

'We should go.' Michael gently tugged Faith's hand. 'We don't want to overwhelm Jack.'

'You're right,' Faith said. 'Can you give Jack my … my best?'

By the time I'd waved them goodbye, Mum had gone inside to find Jack. When I joined them in the snug he had the imprint of her orange lipstick on his cheek and she was holding his hand. I hovered in the doorway, holding both pineapples, feeling like Baby did as she'd carried a watermelon in *Dirty Dancing*. Out of place.

'Are your mum and dad coming, Jack? They must have been frantic when they heard?' Mum asked.

'It's a long way for them to travel.'

Jack dodged the question. His parents had divorced a few years ago and they had both moved to opposite ends of the country, as far away from each other as possible, leaving Jack in the middle, bouncing between them. They didn't understand Jack, nor did they try to. An artist wasn't a credible career in their disapproving eyes; they had wanted him to be a lawyer, a doctor, anything but a creative. Jack hadn't told them about his mugging – I don't know if he was afraid they wouldn't come, or afraid they would.

'It's not like the house is habitable for them to stay in yet. I want them to see it when it's finished,' Jack told Mum.

In truth, his parents would be horrified at the enormity of the project we had taken on. 'Pipe dreams' was a phrase bandied around whenever Jack had tried to share his plans with them. He genuinely wanted to help the local kids with this centre but deep down he also longed to make his parents proud too.

'But still … you could have *died*.' Mum's eyes widened dramatically.

'I'll make some drinks.'

It was a relief to escape into the kitchen for a few minutes leaving Jack to deal with my mother. He didn't mind her. He was our bridge, the structure holding us together.

Balancing a tray laden with mugs of tea and a plate of biscuits I walked as slowly as possible down the hall.

'I would have come to see you in hospital, of course, if Libby had told me,' Mum was saying. 'Not that they make it easy for visitors. Did I tell you that Alan Watkins – he's the one that likes an apple Danish – visited his neighbour after he'd had his gall bladder removed and his car was clamped in the car park. Alan couldn't afford to get it released and now …'

I gritted my teeth.

Jack stood as I entered the room. He winced, his hand seeking out his wound.

'It's okay.' I set the tray down on the coffee table and gestured to him to sit. 'Mum.' I passed her a mug. As I sat down I sneezed.

'Still not feeling well?' Mum asked. 'Mary Phillips, you know Mary – six chocolate eclairs at a time that she swears aren't all for her, but we know she lives alone – anyway, she caught a cold and sneezed so hard the blood vessels in her eye burst—'

'How's Mabel?' Jack changed the subject.

Mabel Mackay was Mum's neighbour. She was nearing eighty-three and lived independently, partly because she had no family telling her she shouldn't. Since she'd had her hip replaced she hadn't been quite the same and Mum took her some dinner every day. There was a kindness in Mum, I could see that, it was just that sometimes, selfishly, I longed for that kindness to be centred around me.

'She's okay. Knitting bootees; Shona Wilkens across the road is going to become a grandma. Can you imagine?' She looked hopefully between me and Jack. Perhaps she'll be pleased with Alice's news. 'Shona said—'

'So, Caroline.' Jack put a calming hand on my knee. 'What do you think of the house?'

My shoulders rose with tension. This was the part where she would tell us that one of the customers had a friend who had bought an old house and there was an unexploded bomb or something in the garden. But she surprised me.

'What you're planning is really remarkable. I know what it's like to be a single mother raising children and worrying what they're up to when you're out working. If there had been a place like this they could come to, somewhere they could have had a little holiday when I couldn't afford to take them away, it would have made so much difference.'

'Mum, that's lovely.'

'You're both very brave for trying to make a difference.' I basked under the warmth of her unexpected praise. 'And if you fail, you mustn't be too hard on yourselves. Most new businesses do. Jenny Ward – her that brought the bread back because the slices weren't the same width – her son had a start-up and lost all his money and now he lives in a caravan.' And there it was. Give with one hand and take away with the other, but for once I let it pass over me, exchanging a look of amusement with Jack.

'But it's not just you two is it?' Mum asked. 'There's Faith.'

'Yes,' Jack said. 'But she's not putting any money into the

project. Some of that will come from Sid and we've secured three-year funding from the Lottery as well as some other, smaller, bursaries for both art projects and young people. But Faith's experience is really valuable. She'll be great at running workshops and after-school classes as well as helping out with the retreat side of things. That's the part we've secured most of the funding for. Giving underprivileged kids the chance to experience something new.'

'And you'll be teaching photography, Libby?' Mum turned her attention to me.

'Not straight away. I'll be involved of course, but we'll need my income at first. Wedding season starts soon and I'm booked up until the autumn.'

'That's not all.' Jack grinned at me. 'Tell her your news.'

I looked at my lap. I hadn't wanted to tell Mum about the exhibition next year. Sometimes she brushed things off and left me feeling hurt – a child flourishing an A* report card, waiting for praise, being ignored or compared to the children of people I had never met.

'There's this thing called The Hawley Foundation Prize.' I hadn't expected Mum to remember, but she did.

'The one that keeps turning you down?'

'Umm. Yes. I've been invited to take part next year.'

'That's wonderful, Libby.'

'Thanks.' I smiled at her; this version of my mum, when she was positive and paid attention, was my favourite. 'The theme is hope.'

'Michelle Walker, who always buys a four pack of sausage rolls and gives one to her dog, had a daughter called Hope and she ran off and became one of those pole dancers and Michelle—'

'Libby won't be photographing her,' Jack cut in. 'You've a very talented daughter. You must be proud of her.'

'She knows I am,' Mum said. 'She doesn't need me to tell her.'

Oh but I did.

Mum stayed for another drink and a tour of the house. By the time she left Jack was visibly flagging. I was about to suggest we go and lie down when my phone rang.

The third call.

It seemed so innocuous.

'Libby? It's Maggie, the district nurse. I'm really sorry I haven't reached you yet. We've never enough cover at weekends – department cuts – and I've had an emergency and ended up twenty miles in the other direction … Now I could get to you but I've had a dickie tummy and—'

'It's a shame you're not feeling well but Jack has been *stabbed*.' My tone was curt and I was instantly ashamed. It wasn't her I was cross with. 'Sorry, I didn't mean to sound rude.'

'No. No, luvvie. You're quite right. How is he?'

'I'll let him answer that.' I passed the phone to Jack and rinsed the mugs, gazing out into the inky dark. The stars that blistered the sky.

Jack's arms slipped around my waist. 'Maggie's not coming.'

'What? Why?'

'I'm okay. She seemed satisfied that my dressing was clean and dry. I don't want to sit around waiting for her. I'd rather have an early night. She's going to come in the morning, hopefully early, before … Well, we don't want her arriving later and interrupting … anything. It's a special day tomorrow, isn't it?'

Tomorrow. Tomorrow we'll have been together five years.

'I was waiting until our anniversary but … will you—' Jack had begun yesterday before the sour-faced nurse had interrupted him.

Will you ... be my wife? I filled in the blanks with my heart's desire.

Was he going to propose? My heart swelled with happiness. The answer already siting on my tongue waiting to be released.

Yes.

Yes, of course I would marry him. He was my happily ever after. Had always been my happily ever after.

Later, in bed, I couldn't sleep. The hands crept slowly around the clock.

1 a.m.

2 a.m.

3 a.m.

I was still wide-awake, dreaming of what the day would bring.

It wasn't what I'd imagined.

Chapter Eight

It was early on Sunday when I woke. We hadn't drawn the claret velvet curtains, not wanting to spoil the view, the shades of green patchwork fields under a crayon blue sky. It was early spring but lambs on shaky legs nudged their mothers with their heads, wanting milk. I was glad we didn't have double glazing so I could hear the soft bleat of sheep, the low rumble of farm machinery, birdsong. The cacophony of living in the countryside. Life had transformed, rich with new colour, sounds.

This.

This is what we had both wanted for so long. Somewhere rural but not too far out of town. A place we could call our own, make our own. I reached for the glass of water on the nightstand and took a sip. For the first time in what felt like forever my throat didn't feel as though it was full of razor blades when I swallowed. I was over the worst of my illness and now I was feeling better I began to see the potential as I scanned the room. The original ceiling rose we could paint a bright white. The ornate fireplace. We had floorboards to sand, cracks to fill on the walls, but today things didn't seem quite as dire as they had. But then today was cause for celebration.

Our anniversary.

Jack was still sleeping. He'd had a restless night, flinging the covers off before dragging them back up to his chin. I'd tried to cuddle him but his body was a furnace, skin damp with sweat. Had I pass-the-parcelled my sickness on to him?

I wondered what the day would bring. Last week I had offered to book a table at the Italian we liked, the one with the extra buttery garlic bread with melted cheese on top, but Jack had said no.

'Let's not make arrangements to go out. It will be our first weekend in our new home and we'll be far too busy having sex in every room to—'

'Oh will we now?' I had placed my hands on my hips. 'You're very sure of yourself.'

'Sure that you can't keep your hands off me.' He had caught me around the waist and pulled me close. 'Seriously, Libs. I want to cook. I want it to be perfect.'

'You're perfect.'

'Am I now?' He smiled.

'No. No.' Immediately I had taken it back. 'You'll be unbearable now. You have lots of faults. You can't keep track of time, you can't—'

To cut me off he had kissed me, gently at first before his mouth moved more urgently against mine, our movements frenetic as we tugged at our clothes, until there was nothing but that moment, the words I had been going to say lost in an all-consuming passion.

Jack's eyelids twitched before he prised them open. He'd been in bed for ten hours but he still looked worn-out.

'Happy anniversary,' he croaked. 'I think I've caught your flu.'

'Sorry.' I darted across the bedroom, floor cold against my bare feet, and pulled a present from the wardrobe. 'Here.' I placed it on his bedside table before I climbed back into bed. 'This might make up for it a bit.'

'I haven't picked your present up from the studio yet. I must …'
He raised himself onto his elbows. 'I really don't feel good, Libs.'

Under different circumstances I might have made a joke about man-flu but I knew how unwell I had felt over the past couple of weeks. It would be much worse for Jack with the pain from the wound to his abdomen as well. I placed my palm against his forehead.

'You're burning up.' I shook the foil-clad paracetamol from the box. 'There's not many left. I could pop out for more and pick up some—'

'Please don't go out for Lemsip. That never ends well.' He tried on a thin smile which slipped away in a flash.

'You can't have Lemsip with the paracetamol anyway. It's ridiculous the hospital didn't give you anything stronger.' I felt so helpless, hopeless, watching the pain furrow his brow as he propped himself up against his pillows. 'Bloody district nurse. Do you reckon Maggie will come this morning?'

Jack shrugged. 'She said so but perhaps being Sunday we're more likely to see her tomorrow.'

'Shall I call the ward?' Angela had been so kind.

'And say what? Jack's caught my flu? No, it's just lousy timing. I had something memorable planned as well. You could drive me to the studio—'

'Absolutely not. You need to get your strength back, mister. We can celebrate when you're feeling better and next year …'

'The stress of doing up this place will have—'

'Hey.' Jack was always my silver-linings optimist. 'Don't get all blue because you're sick. We have builders quoting next week and it'll be fine. Let's not dwell on it today. Open your present.'

He carefully peeled back the Sellotape. Unfolded the ends of the paper that sparkled silver like the starry night sky.

'Libs. It's beautiful.' He opened the lid of the mahogany wooden box. Inside nestled paintbrushes, handles made of maple.

'I know you have a ton of brushes already but ...'

'These are special.'

I smiled. Pleased he loved them. I didn't share that I had bought them because wood is the traditional five-year wedding anniversary present. It seemed so lame because we weren't actually married.

Yet.

Will you ...

We lay together under a patch of sunlight beaming through the glass, my leg slung over his, trailing an unhurried finger across his chest. He kissed me tenderly and I could feel the heat of his hands in my hair.

'Sorry,' he said after a few minutes, a wistful edge to his voice. 'I haven't got the energy.'

'That's okay.' I gave him a careful hug before we settled back down, gazing outside as a red kite swooped across the wisps of clouds.

'What do you think about getting a pet?' he asked unexpectedly.

'What brought that on?' It was a discussion we'd had before. There had been a strict no-animals policy in our flat but we had agreed to wait until the renovations were finished.

'It's just ... after Thursday. Life's too short to wait.'

Inside I felt a slackening of tension. I had confided in Sid that I was worried a near-death experience might make Jack want to do something extreme, backpack around the world. Of all the ways I'd thought our lives might change, this was the very best outcome.

'I'd love that.'

'What do you fancy? Apart from me of course.'

'You're not doing it for me right now with your raging temperature. I'd rather have a puppy.'

'Charming. How about a goat?'

'Now you're delirious.'

'Seriously, I don't know how we're going to tackle the back garden. The goat could eat his way through the undergrowth.'

'And probably our underwear.' I had visions of the laundry being tugged off the washing line. 'What about a dog? Imagine a springer spaniel with floppy ears sleeping in a basket in front of the fire in the kitchen.'

'It's a nice idea but it's not the right time, Libs. You're always out on shoots. We've so much to sort out with this house before I can let go of the studio and be here every day. When would we walk it?'

He was right. 'A cat?' I could picture a kitten curled up on the windowsill above the radiator, or watching Jack paint, me edit my pictures.

'What sort of cat would you like?'

'Black with white feet. We could call him Socks.'

'And then you'd want a second called Shoes.'

'No. One is enough. What do you say?'

'I say if you can find a black cat with white socks then it's meant to be.'

Jack was sleeping once more. I dressed quickly in jeans and T-shirt and padded downstairs, hungry for the first time in days. In the fridge were the basics, courtesy of Alice. After three slices of thick granary toast and honey I called her to say thanks.

'How's Jack?' she asked immediately.

'Sore and now he has flu on top of everything else.'

'Poor him. And you? How are you holding up?'

'I feel so much better physically but …' I'd wandered into the dining room, scanned the stack of boxes. 'There's such a lot to do.'

'Do you want me to come over?'

'It's okay. Jack's asleep so I want to keep the house quiet. I just wanted to touch base. How are you?'

'Nauseous pretty much all of the time. I don't know why it's called morning sickness. It never goes away. God, I want to chuck just talking about it. Speak later?'

She hung up.

I spent the next few hours cleaning. Unpacking. Taking it slowly, my energy still low. Focusing on one room at a time. Firstly the snug. We already knew this would be one of the last rooms we fixed up, our private quarters secondary to getting the art centre up and running. The house creaked its delight as I rested ornaments on the mantelpiece, hung a mixture of my black-and-white photos and Jack's oil paintings on the hooks that remained, Sid's painting of Whisky, the ginger cat, in the centre of the wall. I draped my faux-fur throw over the sofa and heaped on pink and turquoise cushions. Unrolled my patchwork rug.

Intermittently, I checked on Jack. It was almost teatime before he woke.

'Are you hungry?' I asked.

'Not really,' he muttered.

'You need to keep your strength up and it isn't good to take painkillers on an empty stomach. I'll bring you some soup.'

'I'll come down. I've been here all day. Sorry, Libby, some anniversary dinner.' He needn't have looked so dejected, I had a plan.

The dining room flickered with the flames of every tealight I had been able to find. Candles lined the mantelpiece, the fire surround, the top of the bookcase which I had filled with Jack's beloved art books. The rich mahogany table shone with polish and pride. The room looked the way it was always supposed to, warm and inviting. Ready for an intimate dinner for two. I wondered how many meals Sid and Norma had shared here. Had they made plans for their future? Believed that they would fill the four spare chairs with children? For a moment I let my mind travel to the future. Pouring too-thick gravy into the dip of a Yorkshire pudding. Our kids who would have Jack's unruly brown hair and my green eyes, chomping on roast potatoes. Jack and I making chicken wishbone wishes that we'd always be this happy. Socks, the cat, curled up in a patch of sunlight beaming through the French doors. A chocolate spaniel under the table, nudging knees with her forehead, desperate for scraps.

Jack's footfall on the stairs startled me from my daydreams. Quickly I slipped his favourite album, *Rubber Soul*, from its inner sleeve, the faces of John, Paul, George and Ringo encouraging me from the cover.

'Wow!' Jack spun around the room taking everything in. 'I wish I'd dressed up.' He was wearing a white T-shirt and navy joggers. 'You're a proper miracle worker, Elizabeth Emerson.'

'The mood lighting is making things appear cleaner than they actually are but I've made a good start today.'

'You're feeling better then? I can't believe I haven't asked you how you are.'

'Crab.' I smiled.

'Shellfish.' he nodded.

'Sir.' I pulled out a chair and gestured with flourish for him to sit. In front of him was a silver cloche I'd found in the pantry. 'Ta-da!' I lifted it, revealing his dinner.

'Libby it's … perfect.' Jack's face lit up.

His plate was piled with cream crackers topped with peanut butter and banana. I sat down opposite him. Revealed my own plate bearing the same.

'I will make this up to you—' he began.

'Shh. This is exactly what I wanted for an anniversary meal. It's my favourite,' I said.

'It is not.'

'Hey. Don't knock it til you've tried it. Let's make a toast.'

Our wine glasses were full of Ribena.

'May all of our dreams come true,' said Jack. I took a sip of my drink, not saying that all of my dreams had already come true. This. Jack. The house. His expanding business, my entry into The Hawley Foundation Prize. All of it made my heart sing.

'I love you, Elizabeth Emerson. I'm sorry tonight isn't … it isn't what I'd imagined but—'

'No need to apologise.' Understanding the meaning behind his words I lowered my eyes so he couldn't see the tears I knew coated my lashes. He wasn't going to propose tonight, *of course* he wasn't going to propose here, now. It was all wrong, he was in pain, this wasn't what he'd planned and yet … my optimistic heart had clung on to a smidgen of belief that, perhaps, he would.

'Are you okay?' Jack's voice gently asked and I smiled at him.

'Yes. I am.' And that was the truth. As disappointed as I was, I knew that there was no rush; we had the rest of our lives.

From the record player John Lennon sung about people he

had known before. 'In My Life' had been our song since that very first date.

I could see the monumental effort it took Jack to stand and walk to me but I could also see how much it meant to him. I took his hand. We stood, feet barely moving, his arms wrapped around my waist, mine around his neck.

If anyone had peered through the window what would they have seen? A man leaning heavily on his girlfriend for support? A room full of hope and plans for the future? A couple at the start of a new adventure? I'm not sure how anyone would have interpreted the scene, but love. I think they'd have seen love.

If I could have frozen one moment in time, it would have been that one.

It was the last time I would know what it was to be truly happy.

Chapter Nine

Monday morning and Jack was still asleep. Downstairs, I gazed out of the kitchen window while I waited for the kettle to boil. The view was obscured by a milky mist, the sun quivering behind a cluster of cloud. March felt like February once more.

Grey. Everything was grey.

The landscape.

My mood.

We'd arranged some time off work to get the house as straight as we could before the tradesmen arrived to give us quotes but Jack was sick and I was still weak.

I was contemplating whether I should cancel the appointments when my phone began to ring.

Sid.

I tucked the handset between my shoulder and cheek and spoke to him as I poured boiling water onto teabags.

'Are you okay, Libby? You sound tired.'

I hesitated, not wanting to sound ungrateful. 'Now we're in, I'm a little concerned about all the things we have to do before we can get the centre up and running.' It had all sounded so romantic; moving into a rickety house, renovating it so we could follow our dreams, but it was daunting, the sheer volume of faults the house had, and they were only the ones that were visible.

'It just needs—'

'Tarting up and a lick of paint, I know, Sid.'

'I was going to say it just needs vision and you both have that. It looks a state but we did that structural survey thingy so you know the bones are sound. You just need to add the meat. We went over the budgets and the trust fund before you took out the mortgage, and young Jack sorted the grants so don't worry, duck. It might seem like a mountain now but you can only reach the peak step by step.'

'Thanks, Sid.'

Reassured, I carried Jack's tea upstairs. He was still sleeping, cheeks pink, hairline damp with sweat. The patch of skin underneath his nostrils was dry and red where he'd frequently blown his nose on toilet paper because we'd run out of Kleenex. He stirred as I placed his mug on the bedside table.

'Hey.' The bed frame creaked as I sat on the edge of the bed. 'How are you feeling?'

He licked his lips. 'Rough.' He didn't try to sit up.

'I've made you a drink. Do you want it now?' I asked but his eyes had already closed and within seconds he was dozing again. I was worried, already dialling Maggie, the district nurse, but she didn't pick up. I was pondering what to do when seconds later I received a text from her. **With a patient. Will be with you around eleven**.

It was a relief.

Back downstairs Jack's phone trilled from inside my handbag. I pulled it out. The battery was almost flat but there were several missed calls from Faith – she must have called while I was upstairs and couldn't hear – and a text from her. I would never normally have gone through Jack's phone but I opened it so I could reply. When I saw what she'd written my stomach somersaulted. I had to read it a second and then a third time. **Have you spoken to Libby yet? It's so awkward when I see her. XX**

My brain stuttered for a moment while my thoughts caught up with each other. Why did Faith know something I didn't? It must be about the business, but still, awkward seemed an odd word to use.

Were we in trouble financially?

I drummed my fingernails on the worktop. My uneasy feet itched to march upstairs and demand that Jack explain it, but he felt so under the weather it didn't seem fair. Besides, I'd know if it was something serious.

Wouldn't I?

We knew each other inside out but then I thought I knew Alice better than anyone and she was keeping the identity of the baby's father from me. Do we ever properly know anyone?

I scanned the text again, trying to figure it out. Faith had been quiet when Michael had driven us home from the hospital but we all were, Jack and I both spent. But was there another reason they hadn't made conversation? Not wanting to let a secret slip? What could Jack possibly have told her that he hadn't told me? Suddenly a memory came to mind, pushing my doubts aside.

The month after we had begun dating, Jack and I were strolling across the park, his arm slung over my shoulders when we'd passed Owen. I'd felt myself begin to shake.

'Who was that?' Jack asked, throwing a glance behind him.

'That was my ex.' My voice was small.

Jack stopped walking. 'Did he ... did he hurt you, Libby?'

He tilted my chin with his fingers so I was looking into his eyes. I could see the concern in his own.

'Not physically but … he wasn't a good man. He lied to me. A lot.'

'Do you want to tell me about it?' Jack led me to a bench and we sat, the sun warming our backs. I raised my face to the cloudless sky and closed my eyes, feeling the heat in the day, the slight whisper of a breeze against my cheeks. Plump ducks quacked as they waddled around the edge of the pond.

Jack didn't rush me and when I was ready to speak again my words were quiet; shame had shrunk my voice.

'Owen was my first boyfriend. I was seventeen and … I'd never been outgoing like Alice. I was grateful when he took an interest in me and at first … it was … I was happy.' I turned to Jack, feeling the tears welling in my eyes. 'I don't know when it stopped being okay.'

I took a moment to compose myself, watching the bees hover around the bright yellow flowers in front of us.

'He began to break dates, lie about where he'd been. He was seen in the pub kissing another girl. I confronted him and he told me he was comforting her because her mum was ill and he put such a spin on it I believed him.' I couldn't look at Jack. I could feel my skin burning with humiliation and yet there was something about him that made me feel safe as he listened, holding my hand, not judging me. 'He began stealing from my purse and … I don't know. Not growing up with two parents, I didn't know what was normal in a relationship. I knew it wasn't right though. Each time I tried to talk to him about his behaviour he had an excuse and most of the time I ended up feeling it was my fault. For three years I let him walk all over me.' I swiped the tears from my cheeks.

'When he finally ended it he looked me in the eye and told me he was really sorry for the way he'd behaved. He said … he said he knew he'd treated me terribly but that he realised he'd never loved me. He'd fallen for somebody and had learned from his mistakes and wanted things to be different with her. The worst thing was, he sounded so sincere, it's probably one of the only times he was honest with me.' That honesty had sliced through me, the cold, hard truth that I wasn't good enough to be treated with respect.

I had to take a deep breath before I could meet Jack's gaze, wondering what I'd see in his eyes – sympathy, disgust, a realisation I was unlovable? – but instead there was a tenderness that made the tears form once more.

Jack tucked my hair behind my ear. 'I promise you, Libby, I will never lie to you.'

And he hadn't.

I was reading too much into Faith's message; I'd find out eventually what she meant but Jack had never let me down.

It was almost ten o'clock. I had time to nip into town, stock up on Lemsip and Soothers and extra soft tissues before Maggie arrived.

It felt odd to be driving through country roads to reach the shops, rather than walking everywhere as we would have done from the flat. The car climbed a hill and it seemed as though I was driving into the swirling mist.

It only took fifteen minutes to reach civilisation. The houses dark and drab, too close together. Pavements glistening with damp.

I'd slotted my car into a sixty-minute parking bay and was striding in the direction of the chemist when I realised I'd be passing it.

The alley.

The thought stopped me in my tracks. I didn't want to see the place Jack could have died. My toes scrunched inside my shoes as I willed my feet to move. I couldn't avoid this street forever. I reassured myself that Jack was at home safe and sound, tucked up in bed. There was nothing here that could hurt me.

It was just a place.

But still, that's what Jack would have thought on Thursday. My heart beat faster. The world didn't seem quite so safe any more. I knew bad things happened, of course I did. I read the news, watched the TV. Part of our plans were to give restless teenagers a purpose other than roaming the streets looking for trouble, but knowing the statistics of crime and having somebody that you love experience something so brutal were two different things entirely.

Dizziness engulfed me. I steadied myself against a wall, my hands pressing against the rough bricks.

It took several deep breaths before I could set off again at a slow walk. I rounded the corner and the sight in front of me was wounding.

Flowers.

Flowers taped to the lamp-post at the end of the alley.

This was where the mugger died. This was where he ran into the path of an oncoming car. I was almost in a trance as I moved towards the already wilting carnations. Underneath them, a picture of a laughing boy, freckles dotting his cheeks, a gap in his front teeth. 'RIP Kenny' was written on the photo in black marker. Although I knew that Kenny wasn't the innocent child depicted in the photograph, it was hard to equate him with the adult Kenny who had almost torn my life apart. Had his mother left the photo and flowers? His father? It was incredibly sad his life had been cut short. It was all such a waste. I fought back tears, not quite sure who I was crying for; Jack? Me? Kenny? His family? All of us? I just couldn't unpick my twisted feelings – all I knew was I had to leave, get away. The buildings were shifting towards me, the sky pressing down. The smell of bacon drifting from the burger van up the road turning my stomach.

I shouldn't have come here. I'd thought that once Jack was discharged from hospital the worst was over but the hidden scars, the emotional scars, would be harder to heal – for both of us. When the police had mentioned victim support I had dismissed the idea. I hadn't felt like a victim, and that wasn't how I saw Jack but now … now I felt small and scared and overwhelmed.

Unsafe.

I couldn't feel the solidity of the pavement under my feet. I was detached, not fully present in my body.

Don't faint.

It was a few minutes more before I was composed enough to go into the chemist. Again, I had the light-headed feeling. I was in the same shop Jack had stood in on Thursday. His shoes had trodden where my shoes were treading. What had he been thinking about? Me? The house? Alice's news? He wouldn't have been thinking he might be stabbed as he headed home.

I threw things onto the counter, extra soft tissues, lip balm, vapour rub, and asked for paracetamol and Lemsip, impatiently telling the pharmacist that yes, I was aware you couldn't take them together. I knew it could be dangerous.

Everything could be dangerous.

Thoughts of the flowers taped to the lamp-post caused me to shake again.

Kenny.

Once in my car, I locked the doors. All the way home I repeated '*I am okay, I am okay*' as a mantra.

At home I burst through the front door, pounded up the stairs, desperate to hug Jack.

I am okay.

'Jack?' I pelted into the bedroom. Not caring if I woke him. He needed to be up soon anyway for Maggie.

He didn't move. Didn't answer.

'Jack?' I was cautious now as I approached him. Some sixth sense whispering that something was wrong. Tentatively I touched his shoulder. 'Wake up.' He didn't move. I pressed my hand against his cheek, whereas earlier it had been burning, now it was cool.

'Jack?' There was an hysterical twinge to my voice. My brain was telling me he had to be all right. He was young, he was fit, but my eyes were telling me a different story. He wasn't moving but he had moved over the opposite side of the bed – my side – nearest the door.

'Jack!' I screamed, shaking him hard. Had he tried to get up? Call for help? I still had his mobile and wallet in my bag. 'Wake up. Please wake up.'

But he didn't.

I had left him this morning without access to a phone and now …

And now … this.

I would never, ever forgive myself.

It could have been seconds, minutes, an hour later when Maggie arrived.

I was still shaking Jack.

Still screaming.

Chapter Ten

I wish I could say the days that followed passed in a blur but they didn't. Every second was sharp and painful.

Jack was gone.

I wandered around the house like a ghost, touching the things that he had touched. We hadn't been here long enough to make memories but still I saw him everywhere. Not the life we had but the life we could have had. Sprawled on the mustard velour sofa in the snug, sketchbook on his knee. Standing at the window in the dining room, head bobbing to the beat while The Beatles crackled and hissed from the turntable. In the kitchen, cream crackers snapping under the weight of his peanut butter laden knife, mashing banana with a fork to heap on the top. In bed – the bed we hadn't yet made love in – patting the space beside him, his eyes an invitation.

He was everywhere and nowhere.

Gone.

Sometimes I just sat. Still and silent.

Alice floated around, giving me space, urging me to eat. Drink. Leanne, the owner of the café where Alice was a supervisor, had been understanding about letting her take some unpaid leave. Sometimes I was grateful for her company, sometimes I just wanted her to go away.

'Tell me what you need, Libby,' she'd ask, her eyes mirroring mine, filling with tears that she wouldn't allow herself to release either, knowing that she couldn't give me what I needed. The *only* thing I needed.

Jack.

It was inconceivable that someone could be here and then suddenly not. I couldn't make sense of my thoughts, let alone voice them.

Sid had taken to calling every morning. 'I … I don't know what to say,' was all I could manage the first time he had rung.

'You don't have to speak. Just know I'm here. With you,' he had said and oddly it was comforting. Sid was the only person I knew who had lost a partner, the only person who came close to even understanding the sharp and sudden loneliness that was ever-present, deep in the pit of my stomach.

I would hold the handset to my ear, no pressure to spill out my feelings, hearing the rattle of Sid's breath, his occasional cough, the crunch of a Polo mint. It was easier than being face to face with Mum and Alice, seeing the sympathy in their eyes. Sometimes I spoke. Sometimes I didn't.

'It isn't fair,' I had said this morning.

'It isn't, Elizabeth. It really isn't,' Sid agreed.

'Was this … was this how you felt when you lost Norma? This …' My hand covered my heart, feeling it as I voiced it. 'This searing pain that never eases.'

'Grief is a unique experience. My feelings won't be your feelings, Libby, but … it will diminish, that pain. I promise you.'

'When?' I had asked the impossible question.

'One day, it will hurt a little less, and then a little less after that and—'

'I don't want—'

'It won't mean you're forgetting him.' He read my fears and we'd fallen into our usual silence once more.

I couldn't settle.

'You need to get some proper rest, Libby,' Mum said. 'I wish you'd change bedrooms. I don't know how you can sleep in that room, on that mattress.' She shuddered dramatically.

I couldn't explain it myself. It sounded horrific to lie on the bed I found Jack in but it was our bed. It still smelled of Jack. The last memory of him alive, of us together, was on that mattress so as much as Alice and Mum offered to burn it, move my belongings to another room, another floor, I just couldn't.

'You know you can come and stay with me, or with Alice?' Mum asked again but if I left here it would feel like I was leaving Jack, leaving us. In this house I remained wrapped in Jack's things, in Jack's dreams.

'I want to stay here, Mum.'

'At least, let me take you to the doctor, get you something to see you through. The funeral won't be easy.'

'I don't want anything.' Nothing was easy but Mum insisted. It wasn't like her to take charge but shock had forced us all into unexpected roles. I wasn't capable, somebody had to be.

Hours later we were sitting in front of the impossibly young-looking GP, Mum squeezing my hand as he said, 'I can give you some antidepressants,' after Mum had explained why we were there. Unshed tears had trapped the words in my throat.

'Libby needs a good night's sleep, not to mask her feelings. Grief isn't an illness, young man, and Jack's only been gone a week,' she had said.

'I appreciate—'

'Do you?' she asked him. 'Have you ever been in love? Have you had your heart broken? Mary Phillips' grandfather passed and her grandmother followed him days later and she hadn't a jot wrong with her. It wasn't like she ate six chocolate éclairs at a time like Mary. Lack of sleep can make you ill. I heard about—'

'I'll prescribe two weeks' worth of sleeping tablets. It isn't something I encourage. They can be addictive.' The doctor tapped onto his keyboard before the printer whirred and spat out a prescription which he handed to Mum. We left and I hadn't even spoken. I touched my face to see if I was still there. To see if I was invisible. It was disappointing to feel the solidity of my cheekbones beneath my fingertips. I wished I could disappear.

Mum drove to the nearest chemist – *the* chemist – and pulled into a lay-by. I closed my eyes against the sight of the alley, wilting flowers still bound to the lamp-post, the photo of Kenny drooping in the drizzle. I could feel myself shaking, teeth chattering together. The engine thrummed once more and we began to move.

'I'm so sorry,' Mum said. 'I didn't think. We'll go to the pharmacy in the big Tesco near the roundabout.'

I didn't tell her it was okay because it wasn't.

I didn't tell her I was fine because I wasn't.

At the supermarket I waited in the car watching shoppers stream in and out of the automatic doors; a couple pushing a little girl in a trolley, a deflating pink '3 today' helium balloon tied around her wrist; a harassed-looking man shepherding four kids with the same red hair as his, like sheep – this way, this way; a heavily pregnant woman and … Jack. My spine stiffened, heart jolted.

Jack.

I wrenched open the car door and half fell from the car before finding my footing and pelting across the car park. The screech of brakes, the blast of a horn didn't slow me. I ran around the car that had almost hit me and barged past a couple holding hands, separating them.

'Jack!' I called loudly, my hand reaching to touch the man in front of me, his dark hair curling around his collar. He turned round and my disappointment was crushing. He was a she and not only the wrong gender but the wrong age, race.

'Sorry ... I ...' I turned and ran away from her, hurtling into a man pushing a long row of trolleys, backing away, hitting something hard, the A-board I'd knocked over clattering. I was a frantic pinball, ricocheting, lost, directionless.

'Libby?' A man's voice, a warm hand on my arm.

'Jack!' I turned but it was Michael, Faith next to him, a worried expression on her face.

'I thought I saw ...' I shook my head, trying to dislodge my confusion.

'It's okay,' Faith soothed me. 'When I lost my dad I was convinced I was seeing him everywhere. Are you on your own?'

'Mum's inside,' I muttered, my eyes searching, not for my mother, but for the impossible.

'Do you want me to go and find her?' Michael asked.

'No. I'll go and wait in the car.'

Faith and Michael walked either side of me as we made our slow way across the car park. I sat in the passenger seat while Faith slid into the driver's side.

'Libby ...' She lightly touched my arm. 'If you ever want to talk, I'm here for you. I know it's difficult. You might feel awkward ...'

Awkward.

With a jolt I remembered her text to Jack from that day.

Have you spoken to Libby yet? It's so awkward when I see her.

The words formed in my mouth to ask her what she meant but I was aware of Michael sitting in the back seat, scrolling through his phone. It wasn't the right time.

Instead of speaking I stared into my lap, picking at a stray piece of cotton hanging from the hem of my top, casting my mind back to the last time I'd seen Faith before she had come to the hospital. It was Valentine's night. She'd turned up as we were getting ready to go out. After hearing the doorbell, I'd wandered into the lounge, fastening a silver chain around my neck to find her and Jack deep in conversation. They broke apart the moment they noticed me.

'You look lovely, Libby,' she'd said. 'Sorry for turning up unannounced. I was passing and I needed to tell Jack something. I'll leave you to enjoy your Valentine's.'

'Don't worry. Glass of wine before you go?'

Jack had uncorked a Sauvignon. One glass led to two and after she'd received a text from Michael saying he was working late, we'd ended up cancelling our table and ordering in, the three of us sharing crispy chilli beef and egg fried rice. Dipping battered chicken balls into sweet and sour sauce.

It's so awkward when I see her.

But we'd had a nice night and later she'd shrugged on her coat and, after hugging and kissing us both, she had stepped out into the freezing night. In bed Jack had given me my gifts, a pair of panda slippers that were far from sexy and some chocolate body paint, that was. I hadn't given her a second thought.

Have you spoken to Libby yet?

Is it connected to why she came around that night?

The car door opened, bringing me back to now. Faith stood outside with Mum muttering things I could not hear.

I turned away from her whispered words.

What *had* I been thinking?

Stupid-stupid-stupid.

Over and over I berated myself that for one single, joy-soaring moment I had believed that I had seen Jack. Had believed his death had all been nothing but a mistake.

At home, I put the medication in the bathroom cabinet alongside Jack's razor which was clogged with shaving foam. On the shelf above lay his comb, strands of brown hair still entwined around the teeth. His toothbrush was dry and I dampened it under the tap before placing it back in the glass next to mine. I closed the cabinet, the mirror tarnished, the reflection of my pale face patchy through the dark spots. It was such a contrast to the light, bright bathroom in our old flat. The way Jack would slip his arms around my waist and nuzzle into my neck as I tried to do my make-up.

'You don't need all that stuff, Elizabeth Emerson. You're beautiful just as you are.'

Days passed without me resorting to the tablets I had been prescribed. I would fall into brief snatches of sleep only to wake again, drenched in sweat, ribcage heaving, convinced hours had passed but at the most it was twenty minutes. Always twenty minutes. Not long enough to forget. There weren't those few moments of oblivion I'd heard about from others. The 'I'd forgotten they were gone when I first woke'. I knew. For every single excruciating second, I knew and it was agonising. And I welcomed the agony, felt that I deserved it. I didn't take the tablets because I didn't want to be medicated, placated. I wanted to feel.

I wanted to feel it all.

The 'if-onlys' were tangled threads I couldn't help pulling at, despite knowing that they would be my unravelling.

If I hadn't let Alice come round and share her news, Jack wouldn't have gone out for prosecco.

If I hadn't had the flu, Jack wouldn't have been near the chemist buying Lemsip.

If I hadn't let Jack tell Maggie he didn't need her to come, she might have spotted early signs and been able to save him.

If I hadn't kept Jack's phone, he might have been able to call for help.

If. If. If.

The road of guilt stretched out before me and I studied each alternative fork I could have taken, despairing that I could have made a difference. *If* we hadn't have moved to this house.

If we'd never met.

The last one was my undoing. The realisation that if Jack hadn't asked me out that day after the life class, if I hadn't agreed to have dinner with him, he might still be alive. Happy. In someone else's arms, in someone else's bed. His pulse beating strong and steady.

That was what I fixated on. How different it could all have been. The butterfly effect. The delicate flutter of wings. The tiniest change leading to chaos, catastrophe, an ordered life falling apart.

My crying bout left me weak but I had to pull myself together.

Today, I had to fight for Jack.

Chapter Eleven

Jack's body had been released after nine harrowing days of waiting for the post-mortem and today I was meeting the vicar – *we* were meeting the vicar – Rhonda and Bryan, Jack's parents were coming too. A churchyard wasn't where Jack would have wanted to be laid to rest and I was nervous as I dressed, hoping they'd let me have some say in the service at least. They hadn't listened to me on the phone when I'd said that Jack wanted to be cremated, scattered.

'It must be a burial,' his mum had said. 'We have a family plot. It's near you so you can still visit him.'

'But Jack wasn't religious.' I had gripped my mobile tightly. 'He didn't want—'

'He's our son.' Rhonda's voice had been steel. 'And this is what Bryan and I want.'

'That's not fair.'

'Life isn't fair.' She had softened her voice. 'Look, Libby, I appreciate you loved him—'

'Love him.' I couldn't think of him in the past tense.

'We're happy … not happy, bad choice of words. We're …' She had gathered her composure. 'You can come and meet the vicar with us but the arrangements are our choice. Bryan and I are next of kin. It's not as though you were married is it?'

The phone had dropped heavily from my hand. Alice had picked it up and finished the conversation but I couldn't make out what she was saying. The poisonous truth of Rhonda's words still filled my ears.

It's not as though you were married.

My future had been yanked from under me and I wanted to tell her that we *would* have been married.

'I was waiting until our anniversary but ... will you—' Jack had begun at the hospital.

Will you ...

I could almost hear his soft voice saying, *I love you, Elizabeth Emerson* but now I wouldn't hear him whisper *I love you, Elizabeth Gilbert*, would I?

It's not as though you were married.

And now we never would be. I thought it was impossible for my heart to hurt even more, but somehow it did.

Alice and I arrived before Rhonda and Bryan.

The vicar opened the door and told us to call her Elaine as she ushered us into a cosy living room with white walls and oak furniture, logs piled next to a fireplace. Bronze bowls brimming with potpourri were scattered over side tables, the smell of lavender lingering in the air. I sat on the pale pink sofa, Elaine one side of me, Alice the other.

On the wall was a large framed photo of two young girls flying a kite on a beach.

'Your children?' Alice asked.

'My sister and me,' Elaine said. 'I'm not married.'

I wasn't sure whether being single was through choice or a stipulation of her job.

'We don't know much about the Church.' I fidgeted in my seat. 'I don't believe in the Bible.'

'Libby!' Alice gasped.

'That's okay.' Elaine placed her hand on my knee, heavy and warm. I wished she wasn't being so nice. An angry debate about religion I could cope with, I'd already rehearsed my questions in my head. My scathing responses to her justification of a God who was so cruel. Her kindness, her lack of judgement was unsettling.

'When somebody as young as Jack is taken—'

I cut her off. '*Taken?* Don't make it sound like he was purposefully chosen for something. He was *stabbed* because the world is awful and people make terrible choices. The sutures broke open on his wound and there was blood seepage under his dressing – something the district nurse might have picked up on if she'd come but she didn't because *people make terrible choices.* Jack died because of acute sepsis secondary to his infected stab wound.' I trotted out the words from the coroner. 'Jack might have seen his dressing was stained. He might have known something was wrong, but not wanting to worry me on our anniversary, brushed it aside thinking Maggie would sort it out when she came. If he'd told me … if he'd just said …' I clenched my hands into fists. 'But he didn't say anything because … People. Make. Terrible. Choices. People … not … Not God.' I was shaking. My nails carving crescents into my palms. If she told me I was wrong, if she ran through the different stages of grief the way that Mum had, reassuring me it was natural and normal to feel angry, sad, lost, everything, I would scream.

'You're right,' she said. 'They do.' A beat. 'I'm going to make some tea.'

'I don't want tea. I want—'

'Jack,' she said simply.

His name took my breath away. I nodded.

Jack.

I just wanted Jack.

While Elaine clattered around the kitchen the doorbell rang. I crossed to the living-room window and scooped back the net curtains. There was a shiny BMW outside.

'Sorry we're late.' Rhonda's shrill voice reached me in the lounge. 'Bryan was supposed to meet me at the services an hour ago but he was late and—'

'It's not my fault there was bloody traffic.'

'Don't swear in front of the vicar, Bryan.'

Even now they couldn't be united.

I sat back down and didn't get up as they entered the lounge.

Alice shot me a look as she crossed the room and introduced herself, shaking their hands.

Elaine clattered a silver tray back into the room. 'Apologies for the lack of tea cups. I've broken the last saucer – I'm so clumsy.' On the tray was a selection of mugs, one with 'Need an ark? I Noah guy' and another with 'How does Jesus make his tea? Hebrews it.' Instead of a bowl, the sugar was still in its bag. Ginger nut biscuits cocooned in their wrapper. It made her more human somehow, this stranger I had directed my rage at.

Suddenly my stomach clenched into a fist of shame.

'I'm sorry,' I whispered as Rhonda and Bryan took an armchair each, as far away from each other as possible.

Elaine patted my knee in response. 'I've heard worse.'

There were a few minutes of uncomfortable silence, everyone intently stirring their tea. Bryan reached across and took three biscuits, placing them on the arm of the chair. Rhonda glared at him.

'Tell me about Jack.' Elaine looked to Rhonda.

'We've chosen the passages we'd like read from the Bible. There's a particular prayer—'

'Don't worry about that just yet. Tell me about your son.'

'Well …' Rhonda hesitated. 'He was always a dreamer. Head in the clouds. He … he wasn't naughty but he drew on the walls once, a picture of a cat sitting on a wall, facing the moon. I don't think he'd realised he'd done anything wrong.'

'We wallpapered over it,' Bryan added.

'Do you think it's still there, Bryan? Underneath the paper?' Rhonda's voice cracked and she dabbed her eyes with a tissue. 'He liked nature. Flowers. We've arranged for "SON" in white carnations to go on top of his coffin in the hearse.'

'That will look beautiful,' Alice said but heat rushed over me. I couldn't bear it.

Those three letters shouting to the world that they had more claim on him than I did.

It's not as though you were married.

'We'd like three hymns.'

'Can't we have *normal* music?' I asked. 'Sorry,' I added to Elaine. I was being rude I knew, but everything had spun out of my control. From the moment Maggie had arrived at that house on that fateful morning I hadn't had a say in anything. Jack's body had been removed while Alice had held me back, held me up as I screamed his name over and over. Jack's parents making choices he'd have loathed.

'Hymns *are* normal to us,' Bryan said.

'When was the last time you went to church?' My gaze was

93

challenging, flitting between Jack's mum and dad. 'I didn't think so.'

'I went at—'

'And Christmas or Easter doesn't count either.' I cut Rhonda off.

'I'm sorry,' Alice apologised for me and I resented her for it. 'Obviously Libby is upset, we're *all* upset, but Jack loved music. It was a big part of his adult life.'

'We know our own son.' Bryan snapped a biscuit in two.

How could he eat? Didn't he care? Rhonda, at least, was showing some emotion.

Elaine soothed, 'Of course you do, but Libby knew another side of him. I'd like to hear from all of you today. The memory you shared of Jack drawing the cat was lovely. Now, Libby, do you want to tell me about your Jack?'

She smiled as she handed me my tea. I wrapped my hands around the warmth of the mug and thought carefully about how to reply. I could tell her Jack was kind, loving, generous. Words she could use in her eulogy but it wouldn't tell her who he was to me. Who he was to the world.

'He wasn't materialistic but his prized possession was a vintage Gibson guitar,' I began falteringly not sure where I was going.

'He was a musician?'

'No. He had it hanging on the wall of his flat when we met.' My hands began to shake and I set my mug back on the table. I closed my eyes, remembering our first date, after we'd eaten crackers by candlelight.

'Play me a song,' I had said.

'I …' He had run his fingers through his hair. Later I would learn that he'd do that when he was unsure. Embarrassed. 'I can't actually play.'

'You have a guitar on display and you can't play?'

'I'll try and explain. Songs mean so much to me.' He gestured to his record player. The vinyl LPs stacked everywhere. 'My granddad passed away when I was eleven and it was around the time I discovered music. Grandad left me some money and I wanted to be Bob Dylan so I spent it on a turntable, his *Slow Train Coming* album and the Gibson. But ...' He pushed up the sleeves of his black jumper and sat cross-legged in the armchair opposite me. 'A funny thing happened. Each time I picked it up to play along I ... felt the lyrics, the melodies. I saw them all in my mind and started trying to imitate what I was hearing but ... I felt ...' He shook his head. 'Don't think I'm mad, but I felt ... compelled, I guess is the best word, to get all the emotions music made me feel out of my head in a visual and not an auditory way and so I began to draw them. Paint them. That probably doesn't make sense.'

'It does. I'm not the same with music but when I hear a news story, see the way a couple look at each other in the street, I interpret the feeling and put it into a photograph.'

He nodded, relief on his face that I got it. That I got him.

'It would be kind of hot if you could play though,' I had said, grinning.

It was two weeks later and we were back at Jack's flat. This time the electricity hadn't cut out but the lights were low, candles lit. Wax dripping onto the windowsill. Flames casting dancing shadows against the walls. Jack handed me a glass of Malbec and said, 'I've a surprise for you.' I curled my feet under myself on the sofa, watching as he lifted his guitar from the wall. He began to play 'Lay, Lady, Lay', slowly at first, his voice thin, but growing stronger as his fingers strummed the strings. The song ended and his eyes found mine. There was a shyness about him.

'You told me you couldn't play!' Had he been purposefully modest?

'Some things are worth making the effort for. *You're* worth making the effort for.' He removed the strap from his neck and leaned the guitar against the wall. He crouched down before me.

'I was right.' I trailed my fingers down his neck.

'About what?'

'You playing the guitar. It was hot. Very hot.' I pressed my lips against his, our kisses gentle and then frenzied. He carried me to his bed. His hands mapped out my body as I trembled under his touch, until he was moving inside me and nothing existed but him. I was lost and found and his completely. That was the first time we had made love.

'Libby?' Elaine asked me now. I realised I still had my eyes closed. Was still lost in the memory. Alice's fingers entwined with mine, her gentle squeeze reassuring.

'Sorry, I—'

'Know a million things about Jack and don't know how to share them with me,' she said.

'It all sounds nondescript. The guitar—'

'The Gibson?' Bryan said gruffly. 'He bought that with the inheritance money from my father.'

'He still has it,' I said.

'I guess it's mine now,' Bryan said. 'Ours.' His eyes met Rhonda's and just like that I was reminded of my place again, my insignificance.

My hold on Alice tightened. I could feel the tension in her grip too.

'Perhaps we could have two hymns,' Elaine said. 'And Libby could choose one of Jack's favourite songs to play.'

'Does it have to be religious?' I asked.

'As long as it's not worshiping Satan it should be fine. What do you think?' She swept a glance around the room.

'I suppose that would be okay,' Rhonda conceded.

'Would any of you like to say something at the service?'

'I couldn't. Every time I think of my boy …' Rhonda dissolved into tears.

'I couldn't either. Libby, you can if you want to?' Bryan said.

Could I stand up in front of a church of mourners and share my memories? Even now, here, sadness had closed my throat.

'Or is there anyone who might? Someone who knew Jack well?' Elaine asked.

Bryan and Rhonda didn't answer. They knew little of Jack's adult life, his friends.

'I … I'll think about it.'

'Okay. Now, let me run through what will happen on the day. The hearse will park outside the church and the pallbearers – have you chosen them?'

'Some of Jack's artists friends would like to be involved. They'd—'

'We're using the ones we met at the funeral director's. We don't want a bunch of strangers carrying our son.'

But they weren't strangers to Jack, I wanted to say. I knew the funeral wasn't about me but it seemed it wasn't about Jack either.

'We've decided on the wording for the headstone,' Rhonda said. I let out a low moan, I couldn't help myself.

Elaine squeezed my hand. 'We advise on waiting for a least six months before erecting any sort of memorial; the ground needs time to settle.'

The thought of Jack's name on cold marble, the date of his death was too much.

It was time to go.

I said a stiff goodbye to Bryan and Rhonda.

'You'll send Jack's things? His guitar?'

I nodded. I didn't have a choice. At least, legally, Jack's half of the house belonged to me, even if nothing else seemed to.

It's not as if we were married.

'You can choose two songs for the service,' Rhonda relented before she turned away.

By the front door Elaine swept me into her arms.

'Can you let me know if there is someone who wants to speak so I can factor it into the order of service?'

There was one person I could ask. There was something else I needed to ask them too.

Something I'd been avoiding.

Too scared of the answer.

Chapter Twelve

Outside the vicarage Alice looped her arm through mine. 'Are you all right?'

'Rhonda and Bryan didn't know Jack.' I was despairing. 'He'd have hated hymns and prayers and … all of it.'

'I'm so sorry. It's so unfair. And asking for his guitar is awful.'

'I guess it got me an extra song though.'

'Home?'

'No.' I told her where I wanted to go. As she drove, I watched a bird, its wings flapping through the cornflower sky. It landed on the spire of the church perching against a backdrop of fluffy white clouds. It looked so small, so insignificant and yet something about it stood tall and proud. 'I am here,' it seemed to say as it puffed its chest out. 'I can make a difference.'

That was what Jack wanted. 'Be the change you want to see', he was fond of quoting. What did I want said about him at his funeral? I thought I knew him so well, all of his hopes and dreams tightly parcelled up with mine, but now he wasn't here the string was lax and some of the little pieces that had made up Jack were slipping away.

Have you spoken to Libby yet? Faith had texted.

Regretfully I realised there were so many things I didn't know about him. So many things now I wished I'd asked. Things I had thought inconsequential were now of the utmost importance to me. What was his favourite flavour of rock?

Not long after we'd started dating we had taken a trip to Norfolk – it was somewhere Mum had often taken me and Alice when I was a child. There was a particular place I had wanted to revisit but I hadn't known exactly where it was. Jack had driven along the coast while I had peered out of the windows, eyes searching for something familiar. Regularly we'd climbed out of the car to explore. Sipping sweet cider in pub gardens, eating chips doused in vinegar, ears full of the screech of the gulls as they circled for scraps. Trudging over dunes in the midday heat. Every now and then I'd turn to the sea to glance at the lighthouse for direction, leading Jack more to the right, to the left until finally we stumbled across it.

I crouched down and parted the long grass.

'There's a bunker under here.' It was covered now, by a man-hole, but it used to be open to explore.

Jack tried to lift the heavy metal cover but it had been fixed down somehow.

'This was my favourite childhood place. Me and Alice had been running up and down the dunes to get warm after being drenched by freezing waves as we paddled and we found it.'

'And why did it mean so much to you?' Jack had brushed dry sand from his hands as he stood.

'I thought …' I considered how to put it into words. 'I thought that this was it …' I swept my arm across the coastline. 'The ocean, the beach, the long grass. But then suddenly there was this hidden world. There never used to be anything covering it up so me and Alice would run through the tunnels exploring. The first time we found it I had a disposable camera with me and I remember getting the film developed and seeing the pictures of us just feet away from the bunker before we knew it was there and then the excitement on our faces after we'd discovered it. I realised that' – again I gestured to our surroundings – 'what we see is rarely all that there is. There's so much under the surface that we can't even imagine. Sometimes we're lucky enough to uncover it but sometimes we have no idea it even exists.' The breeze blew my hair across my face and I tucked it behind my ears. 'There's an entire world waiting to be discovered. Imagine? That's when I first became interested in photography. Wanting to capture the hidden things, a look, an emotion.' I tugged the metal ring of the manhole fruitlessly but it didn't budge. 'An entire universe.'

'How old were you?' Jack asked.

'About ten.'

'Blimey, that's deep. Whenever I went to the seaside around that age I was obsessed with rock.'

'Geology?'

'Sticks of.' He grinned.

'Then we must get you some.'

'And that's why I love you.'

He'd never said it before and my expression must have demonstrated my surprise because he had cupped my cheeks with his hands, fingers holding my hair back away from the wind that whipped around us.

'I. Love. You,' he said again.

He kissed me, his lips sea salt and hope and something else, home.

'I love you too.' And right there, right then, it was everything I ever wanted.

Later, we found a small shop, yellow, green and blue buckets and spades stacked outside, a stand crammed full of wish-you-were-here postcards. Jack picked out three sticks of rock for £1.00. A pink minty one, a striped fruit one, a black aniseed one. I hadn't asked him what his favourite flavour was.

Now I would never know.

Before I came to the nursing home I'd never understood the expression 'the air seemed thicker' but here it was heavier. Stagnant. A smell that was both familiar and not, lingering in the myriad corridors that I travelled down, my feet swallowed by the dark brown pile carpet. However did residents with dementia navigate this place? There were many rooms, straight-backed chairs pushed against sensibly painted walls. A splash of cheap art breaking up the endless magnolia. A TV blaring in the corner of the main lounge. Almost everyone here asleep, thick blankets covering knees, and those who were awake were staring into space, somewhere else, somewhere happier I hoped.

The conservatory at the back of the building was lighter. Brighter. It was here all the action took place, Sid had told us when we'd moved him in. It was here we always found him when we visited, playing dominoes, cards, betting matchsticks and sometimes money. Crunching Rich Tea biscuits and slurping tea.

Not today though. Frowning I asked one of the carers, 'Where's Sid?'

She shrugged. 'In his room?'

Upstairs I tentatively tapped on his door. 'Sid?' I stepped inside. Guiltily he dropped the cigarette in his hand, closing the window and wafting his hand to dispel the lingering smell of tobacco.

'Sid! There's smoke alarms everywhere. They'll chuck you out.'

Normally he'd have a retort – 'they'd have to catch me first' or something similar – but today there was nothing.

'Sid?' I dropped to my haunches and took his liver-spotted hand, rubbing his fingers with my thumb. I could feel his bones underneath his loose skin. He'd lost weight.

Our eyes met for a few seconds, long enough for us to recognise the terrible loss we had both experienced before he lowered his gaze to his lap.

'I'm sorry I haven't been in to see you.' My throat swelled – his pain was swallowing him whole.

'That's okay, Libby duck. I've been grateful for our phone calls.'

'Even though we didn't speak half the time.' I tried to smile, to lift his sprits.

'Sometimes, there just isn't anything to say. That's doesn't stop your mum from nattering away though.' This time, it was him trying to cheer me up.

'Mum's called you?'

'She came to visit a couple of days ago. We shared our memories of young Jack. She bought me wine gums.' He picked up the open packet on his table and offered me one. I shook my head trying to process the fact that Mum had come to check on Sid; it was such a kind thing to do. She *was* kind.

Sid plucked out a black sweet before dropping it back into the bag. 'I ain't got much of an appetite neither, duck. It ain't right a young 'un like that. I should have gone before Jack. If I could swap—'

'Don't say that,' I said urgently. Sid may have had a bad hip, bad knees. His body might have creaked with protest when he rose slowly from sitting to standing, but he still had a zest for life. He'd made friends here, enjoyed the games they played.

We all have a right to life, don't we? I think no matter how old we get, how frail we are, perhaps none of us ever feel ready to leave this earth and, truth was, I needed Sid. He'd become such an integral part of my life. Just sitting, hearing his breath drift down the phone line, had been more comfort to me than he could ever imagine.

'I've set a date for the funeral. Sid, I don't mind if you don't feel up to it but Elaine, the vicar, wondered whether someone might like to say something about Jack to make it more personal. I'm not sure that I could but—'

'Libby.' His expression a complicated mix of pride and sadness and gratitude. 'I'd be honoured to. Jack had so much good inside of him, so many plans—'

'That's the other thing we need to talk about. Jack's plans.' Sweat prickled under my armpits; I could be making myself homeless but it was the right thing to do. 'I want to offer you the house back. If you can give me what we paid—'

'I don't—'

'Listen. You let us buy it for less than it was worth because you wanted it used for good—'

'It still can—'

'I can't, Sid.' I lowered my face. 'I just can't. You could sell it for a better price. You know you could.' I stood and circled the room. Five paces to the door. Three to the en-suite. Back to the window. I couldn't look at Sid but I could feel him watching me. 'It wouldn't be the same.' My voice was low. 'Without him. Even if I knew where to start with it all, which I don't.'

'You're forgetting, Libby, that first and foremost I wanted that place to be a home for you and Jack, the way it was for me and Norma. We'd planned to fill it with kids but that wasn't to be. Jack wanted it become an art centre and I dunno, maybe that's not to be either, but it's yours, Libby. Yours to do with it what you will.

Live in it. Sell it. I ain't gonna say be happy, 'cos I know that right now you'll feel you'll never be happy again. Felt the same meself after I lost Norma. She was ill and I was expecting it but it didn't make it any easier when she died in her sleep, God rest her soul, but … it will be okay, young Elizabeth. It always is and there ain't no pressure from me but I believe you can do anything you set your mind to, although you don't have to do anything don't want to do.'

'I don't want to bury Jack, Sid.' I sank onto the edge of the bed and covered my face with my hands while I wept. The mattress dipped as Sid sat beside me. His fingers threaded through mine, my head dropped onto his shoulder. We sat side by side, my heartbreak dampening the shoulder of his white shirt. Eventually I stopped crying. Sid pulled a handkerchief from the pocket of his cords and I dried my eyes, blew my nose. He offered me a Polo and I took one, cracking the mint between my teeth.

'I was thinking earlier of a place in Norfolk that Jack and I went to.'

'What about it?'

'It was the first time Jack told me he loved me.'

'It's a special place, Norfolk. Norma's family were from a little village south of Cromer.'

'But you're from here?'

'I am.'

'Where did you meet her?' I couldn't believe I hadn't asked him before.

'My dad was in the Navy, based in Norfolk. He didn't make it through the war.'

'I'm sorry.'

'Don't apologise, duck. Lots didn't. Life ain't all beer and skittles is it?'

A memory landed in my heart; moving-in day, unpacking Sid's surprise gift. A reminder that life wasn't always smooth. Who'd have thought that ... I exhaled, forced myself to focus on what Sid was saying. 'Anyway there was a memorial service one year, I must have been about seventeen, and I went to pay me respects. I was on the beach, clambering over rocks when I heard this loud rip and I could feel the wind on me arse cheeks. I heard this laughter and I looked up and I couldn't properly see her in the glare of the sun, only her shadow, but her voice was kind when she said, "I'm a seamstress, I could try repairing them if you'd like?"'

'That was lucky.'

'It was. It wasn't like today where you'd chuck 'em away and go and buy a new pair. They were me only decent slacks. I climbed back up to her and when I saw her face ...' He tilted his head back, closed his eyes and smiled, still seeing her. 'She was beautiful, like an angel. If I'd have known that, I'd never have been brave enough to speak to her. We went back to her house, well her parents' house but they weren't in. I had me hands covering me bum the whole of the way there, and when we got there it were her turn to be shy. "I'll ... umm ... need you to ..." She lowered her eyes. "Blimey, I've known you five minutes and you're trying to get me trousers off," I said. Her cheeks turned red as rhubarb and ... well, that was it, really. When you know, you know, don't you?'

'You do.' That life drawing class, Jack's eyes meeting mine over his easel, both of us looking away before stealing another glance at one another. Feeling the spark of connection even then. 'And now I'll never feel it again ... Sid, how do you bear it?'

He didn't answer, instead simply saying, 'It'll be okay.'

But when I got home later there was a grubby white van parked on the driveway and it wasn't okay at all.

Chapter Thirteen

'Whose is that van?' Alice asked as she manoeuvred her Mini onto my driveway.

My heart sank. 'I forgot we'd arranged appointments for tradesmen to have a look around and give us quotes.'

'Well he looks classy,' Alice said of the man who was kicking gravel with the toe of his DM. He wore faded ripped jeans and a too-small black T-shirt which showed the podge of his hairy belly. She raised her eyebrows as she read the side of the van. Someone had written 'I wish my wife was this dirty' into the grime.

'I can't deal with this.' It was too much. Too soon.

'I'll speak to him,' Alice said as we climbed out of the car. 'So sorry,' she called over. 'We don't need any quotes right now after all.'

'What the fuck?' He glowered.

'Please don't swear at me—'

'I've driven nearly an hour to find this place. I've plenty of other customers I could be with—'

'If you'd listen—'

'I'm going to bill you for my time.'

'Don't you dare try billing my sister.' Alice placed her hands on her hips. 'She's had some terrible news and—'

'I'll give you some more shall I? If you don't fix that roof, next time it rains it'll be pissing down indoors.'

I scanned the tiles. Was he right? They did look patchy but they could have been like that before. I hadn't paid that much attention.

'I can start today. Now,' he said.

'I thought you had plenty of other customers?' Alice said. 'What part of "no" don't you understand? We're not in a position right now—'

'The only position you'll be in is with your arm above your head while you hold an umbrella as you watch the telly.' He strode back to his vehicle. 'If you don't get it fixed pretty pronto you'll have bigger problems further down the line.'

'Dick!' Alice muttered as he screeched down the driveway.

'Is he right?' I asked. 'Could the storm last night have dislodged some tiles?'

'I don't know. Don't worry,' she said, but it was impossible not to. If I took that worry and stacked it with all my others I'd have enough to build a wall, a house, a city.

A new roof at the very least.

Another smaller van pulled up, this time with 'Electrician' plastered across the side.

'Go inside.' Alice patted my arm. 'I'll deal with them all.'

And she did.

Funeral day dawned dank and dismal. Thunderous clouds squatted over the house lashing rain against the windows, obscuring my view to the world which still turned, turned, turned for some people. Not for me. This next chapter in mine and Jack's life was incomplete. My life was on pause; I'd been so focused on today, I hadn't really thought about the after.

I wasn't ready.

I just wasn't.

For a few seconds I toyed with the idea of running away and there was one rash moment when my legs were ready to carry me far from here. Instead, my trembling hands pulled my black shift dress from the hanger. It used to fit snuggly but now it zipped up easily, hanging loose at the waist. My stomach was a clenched fist of regret that our story would remain half told as I stared at myself in the bathroom mirror, trying to find myself in my own reflection. My heart skipped a beat as I caught a glimpse of Jack behind me. It was so real I turned around.

I was alone.

Turning back to the mirror I ran a light fingertip across the glass, willing his face to appear.

It didn't, of course.

I needed to hold it together today.

From downstairs came the sound of the front door knocker. Mum and Alice were due soon but I knew they'd let themselves in with the spare key they had taken.

The knocking came again. I had no intention of answering it – I didn't want to speak to anyone today until I absolutely had to. Besides, it was likely the postman with another batch of sympathy cards to add to the unopened pile on the telephone table. I couldn't bring myself to look at them or throw them away. It was as though once I read them I'd be accepting that Jack was never coming back and I still wished for the impossible.

The tap-tap-tapping came once more, sharp and insistent.

I flung open the door with more force than necessary. 'What do you want?'

In front of me was a man of around my age, bleached blond hair, red plaid shirt tucked into black jeans.

'I'm sorry to disturb you but—'

'We've put a hold on getting quotes right now so—'

'I'm sorry but—'

'My … Jack … he …' I was going to have to say the words out loud some time but they were stuck to the roof of my mouth. 'He's not here.' I slumped against the door frame, my fingers clutching at the wood. If I let go I feared I'd fall.

The man took a step forward, hands outstretched, flustered. 'Can I … Are you okay?'

'No. No I'm not.' I didn't know what made me answer so honestly, but I couldn't allow the British 'I'm fine' to leave my mouth, it was so far from the truth.

I stared at him, this stranger who looked uncomfortable but didn't leave. There was a kindness in his hazel eyes. 'I don't know how to deal with everything,' I whispered.

'Can I help?' There was compassion in his face; he knew I was talking about more than the house.

'There's a funeral, today.' I almost buckled under the weight of that one sentence, the magnitude of my loss sweeping over me.

His gaze dipped to his shoes before meeting mine once more. 'I'm so sorry,' he said sincerely.

I nodded once, before gently, and wordlessly, closing the door on him and sinking down onto the bottom stair.

Please. I silently pleaded. *Send Jack back to me and I'll do anything. Give anything. Please.* I linked my fingers together in a prayer. *If I get through today please send him back.*

When Mum and Alice arrived I was still sitting on the stairs. Lips still moving in silent prayer.

Please.

Please.

Please.

'Come on, Libby, it's time to go.' Mum gently touched my shoulder.

But I didn't move.

I couldn't.

Chapter Fourteen

There was a straggle of mourners from the previous funeral heading back into the car park, tissues dabbing eyes. The downpour was now a drizzle. The hearse already here. I hadn't wanted to follow Jack's parents in the funeral car, like an afterthought. I kept my eyes fixed on the horizon as we trudged towards the church, me in the middle, Mum and Alice flanking me, arms linked through mine.

'Look, Libby,' Alice said softly.

At first I couldn't make sense of what I was seeing. A throng of people wearing hoodies. Was the church being robbed? My stomach spasmed; the memory of that alley, Kenny's photo taped to the lamp-post, the wilting flowers from his family.

RIP.

But no. Taking a closer look, I could see it was the kids that took Jack's classes. The ones he had been setting up the centre for. I watched as Liam ushered them all into place. In military formation they lined the entrance in two rows but instead of raising sabres to form an arch they each held a paintbrush aloft.

My lip trembled.

As I walked slowly, reluctantly, into the church my eyes met Liam's and I saw my own anguish reflected. I nodded once, slowly, *thank you*, and he nodded back, *you're welcome*. Jack had touched so many lives in so many ways. Did he know how loved he was? Not just by me but by the crowd that had wedged themselves inside the church. Each pew crammed, people squeezed together at the back.

By the time we were halfway to the front row I was drawing in breath in short, sharp bursts. Lungs full of the smell of roses and polish. I had dreamed of walking down the aisle towards Jack, the organist playing 'Here Comes The Bride' but instead I walked unsteadily towards his coffin, The Beatles singing 'In My Life'.

I love you more.

I took my seat.

Elaine took her place and began to speak, a sombre expression on her face as she said, 'We are here today to celebrate the life of Jack Gilbert which was tragically …'

Celebrate.

That word again. It was too cheerful for the occasion. Too cheerful for the darkened church. It was as though all of my grief had been poured into the angry black cloud outside which blocked out the sun that would normally stream through the stained glass windows.

I realised she had stopped speaking. Sid was making his way to the lectern, one hand gripping his walking stick which thwacked against the stone flooring.

He turned to face us. Took a moment to gather his breath, likely to gather his thoughts too.

'People often believe that we are here to make an impact, leave a mark on the world, the bigger the better. I don't believe this is always the case. Those bigger acts are often at some-one else's expense, another person's, the planet's. The smaller things – the caring for others in your community, a kindness towards a stranger – are the things that leave an indelible trace. Make a difference without causing damage. Those things that are done out of a genuine concern for others, not to feed an ego or for something to boast about. Jack …' Sid began to cough, bowed his head, fumbled in his pocket. I held my breath wondering if he could go on but he stuffed a Polo into his mouth and swept his gaze around the mourners. 'Jack,' he said simply, 'is someone we all knew in different ways. For Libby, a life partner. For his parents here today, a son. For the young 'uns at the back with their paintbrushes, a mentor. To me, a friend. To all of us, an inspiration.' He wobbled on his feet, his weathered hands tightly clutching the wood in front of him.

'The first time I met Jack was when I went to ask about his art classes. He was just locking up the studio to go home when I got there. "Is it too late for a dinosaur like me to learn?" I asked him. "It's never too late to learn," he said. "What sort of life would we be living if we stopped being curious, stopped trying new things? Come in and have a go."'

Sid nodded. 'He was leaving but he stayed to help an old man. We didn't have creative classes and all that whatnot at school when I was a lad and me mum couldn't afford canvases and brushes and the like, so that day I painted me first picture. "It's good," Jack said. "It ain't," I told him, "but I'm eighty today and this has been one of the best birthdays I've had in years. I ain't ever going to be Picasso but that's okay. I haven't achieved much in my life—"

'"Have you loved?" Jack interrupted. "Been loved?" The question took me by surprise. "Yes," I told him. "Then what greater achievement could there be?"'

Sid put another mint in his mouth, took his time before he spoke again. 'Jack … Jack was loved. You only have to look at the amount of people here to see that. Bet you ain't had it so packed in years?' Sid looked at Elaine. 'But he also loved. He loved his art. His community – he had great plans. First and foremost, he loved Libby.' Sid nodded as he looked directly at me. 'He never stopped talking about you, girl. So although you wouldn't find Jack in a church I think he very much lived by "do unto others as you would have them do unto you", so let's all be kinder to each other. Let's all be more Jack.'

Sid climbed down and Mum took his elbow, bringing him back to sit with us. The church filled with the sound of The Mamas & the Papas singing 'Dream a Little Dream of Me' and although I'd vowed to hold it together I couldn't.

My heart shattered. I could almost feel fragments of it leave my body in a bid to reach Jack. Noisy tears escaped me. An arm slipped around my shaking shoulders; I didn't know whose it was and it brought me no comfort. Sid pressed a handkerchief into my hand and I balled it against my mouth, trying to be quiet as Elaine stood and talked of love and forgiveness and hope. The rest of the service passed in a haze until the pallbearers lifted the coffin as though it contained nothing but air, and for a single, ridiculous moment my heart soared as I allowed the transient notion that perhaps Jack wasn't in it to form. I scanned the church hoping I might find him standing there, watching me in that way of his, smiling that smile.

You didn't really think I'd leave you, did you?

Alice gave me a gentle push. 'Come on. It's nearly over.' But it wasn't nearly over. The searing pain born from the overwhelming thought of living a life without Jack was only just beginning.

Later, at the wake, Sid offered me a pint glass of something dark and frothy. 'Get it down you, girl,' he said. It was warm and bitter. I drained my glass, ran the back of my hand across my upper lip. 'Remember' – he patted my shoulder – 'you can do anything you set your mind to, Libby.'

I shook my head, catching sight of Liam and the other kids huddled by the buffet tables, cramming Scotch eggs into pockets, shovelling quiche into their mouths. I didn't want to be responsible for them. I barely felt responsible for myself. It was claustrophobic. I couldn't breathe. Telling Sid I'd be back in a minute I headed towards the beer garden, sinking heavily onto a bench, staring longingly at the overflowing ashtrays – for the first time I wished I smoked.

'Fag?' A packet was waved in front of my face. I hadn't heard Liam join me. The table creaked as he sat on it, pulling his hood over his head.

'No thanks.'

We sat in silence. I breathed in the smoke that curled from the butt in Liam's fingers. After a few minutes he pushed the dog-end into an empty bottle of Budweiser. It sizzled as it went out.

Liam jumped down, his trainers sending up a puff of dust where he landed heavily on the ground. He waited until I looked at him, the desolation on his face. I couldn't offer him any comfort, I was just as broken.

'Libby?' There was a beat. He pushed his hood down, and without shadows his face looked so young, freckles dotting his nose. 'I'm gonna do what Sid said. I'm gonna be more Jack. Kinder.' He stopped speaking. I didn't know what to say but when he made no move to go back inside I offered a 'great'.

'Do you think … Will you still do it? The centre?'

'Liam … I don't know. It was Jack's dream.'

'Not just Jack's dream,' he said firmly. 'All them times at yours when you cooked me dinner. You were both excited about it. You were.' His mouth turned down at the corners, a toddler about to cry.

'I know we both were but … there's only me now.'

'There doesn't have to be. I can help. The lads. Without Jack … without something … half of us are going to end up inside.'

'That's not true. You've all left school this year, there's college and—'

'Courses we don't care about and apprenticeships in things we don't want to do because the government say we have to do something til we're eighteen and the school don't want us back.'

'But you all have … something.'

'Something to keep us out the way. Make the statistics look good. Keep the unemployment figures down. It's all bullshit. The centre would be … We *need* it. Jack was the only person who ever saw the good in us. No. That ain't right. You saw the good in us, Libby. You could do it for him. For Jack.'

'I'll think about it but—'

'If you don't do this, what are you gonna do?'

'I don't know, Liam.' It was the heartbreaking truth. What was I going to do? How could I live Jack's life when I didn't know how to live my own? 'I'll think about it' was as much as I could promise him.

Alone again, through the window I saw Faith crying against Michael's shoulder, inconsolable.

If I were to go ahead with the centre I'd need her help.

Have you spoken to Libby yet? she had texted.

If we were ever to work together I'd have to know what she

meant. My memory of Jack was fragile as it was. If he was keeping a secret from me, would I really want to know what it was?

Could I trust her to tell me the truth?

There was only one way to find out.

I had to ask her but not when she was with Michael. I pulled out my phone and texted her. **We need to talk. Alone.**

I watched through the window as she read the message, saw her face fall.

As if she sensed me watching her, Faith's puffy swollen eyes met mine before she quickly looked away.

Chapter Fifteen

Faith had replied to my text after the funeral, promising to set up a date, but it was a week before she messaged again. **Can we talk today? I'll come alone.**

She'll be here after lunch.

'What does she want to talk to you about?' Alice asked. 'Is Michael coming too?'

'No.'

'I'll stay.'

'You need to go to work. If you take any more time off Leanne might sack you. I'll be fine. We have things to discuss.'

'Like what?' Alice bit the edge of her thumbnail.

I hadn't told her about Faith's message to Jack, not wanting to hear her theories. I wanted cold, hard facts.

'The studio. The centre.'

And something else, something darker. *Have you spoken to Libby yet?*

'What are you going to tell her? Have you made a decision yet?'

I shook my head. I had promised Liam I'd really consider it and I wanted to. Jack would want me to. Memories of Liam teaching Jack to rap in our kitchen while chicken roasted in the oven were still prevalent in my mind. Jack got just as much out of mentoring as the kids did. Sid's words rode the merry-go-round in my mind: *you can do anything you set your mind to.* But could I?

Faith stood on the doorstep and at first I didn't know how to greet her, opening my arms but then closing them seconds later when I remembered her text.

It's so awkward when I see her.

We stared at each other for a moment before falling into an uncomfortable hug, rearranging our arms until we fitted together.

'How are you?' She stepped back and studied me.

I shrugged in response.

She offered to make the tea and I let her. It had always been so mindless, pouring boiling water onto teabags, adding milk and sugar, but now it was overwhelming. Everything was overwhelming. There was no way I could imagine opening the centre without her help.

We sat at the small pine table where I imagined Sid and Norma would once have eaten their breakfast. His toast dripping honey, the way he liked it.

'I wanted to ask—'

'I've something I have to tell you,' Faith spoke in unison.

Have you spoken to Libby yet?

I fell silent.

'It's difficult …' She pulled out a tissue and screwed it up in her fist, just in case. 'I … I'm sorry.'

'For what?'

'I'm leaving,' she said quietly.

'Leaving? Leaving what?'

'Town.'

'But when? How far are you going? What about the centre?'

I was flustered, asking too many questions, too fast, but she couldn't just *leave*. Could she?

She didn't meet my eye.

'Faith … Liam … the other kids … they're all relying on me. On *us*. I can't do it without you.'

'I know the timing is lousy.'

'Why now? Is this something to do with Jack?'

'No. Of course not. Michael has been relocated again and … Why would it be to do with Jack?'

'You wanted to talk to me alone. You texted Jack "Have you spoken to Libby yet?" and said you felt awkward around me.' A new thought occurred to me as I remembered how tactile she was with him. 'Were you only helping with the centre because you were in love with him? Is that why you crashed our Valentine's meal?'

Faith placed her palms on the table and stood as if to storm out, but instead she said, 'I came alone because I have something for you and you don't need an audience when you see it. I'll be back in a minute.'

I didn't follow her, instead wondering whether I was being irrational. Nothing was making sense.

She came back into the kitchen carrying a painting. I couldn't see what it was of.

'This is what Jack was working on,' she said. 'The last thing he'd been working on. He'd been trying to source an image to copy but he couldn't find one online and Google Earth was no help at all. I was going away for a few days in that direction anyway so I offered to try and find the place for him; he couldn't lie to you and make the trip himself.'

'I don't understand.'

'I found it and I was so excited. I took some pictures and as soon as I was home I wanted to show Jack the images right away and see if it was the right place. I didn't mean to sabotage your Valentine's, I should have just texted the photos.'

'Stop.' I placed a hand over my forehead. 'You're not making things any clearer.'

'Sorry.' Faith turned around the picture and when she did I covered my mouth with shock. 'I wanted to know if he'd told you that he'd tracked down the place and that he wanted to take you back there? Told you why?'

Lightly, I touched the painting, running fingertips over the oils. It was the spot in Norfolk where Jack had first told me he loved me. He had captured the landscape perfectly, the brilliant sun bouncing off glistening waves. The lighthouse stood to the right. In the foreground the wind was whipping the long grasses we had made love in and, underneath the greenery, if you knew what you were looking for, you could just make out the silver glint of the manhole cover that led to the bunker, a hidden world that nobody knew about. I could smell the salt. Hear the gulls. Feel Jack's hand in mine.

On the top of the painting, trailing in a plane's frothy trail, written in beautiful swirling dark blue letters across a bright blue sky was 'Please will you'.

'Please will you?' Puzzled I looked at Faith.

'He hadn't quite finished it.'

'What was the end of that sentence going to be?'

'Libby …' Faith shook her head sadly.

'Please what?' I demanded. 'Tell me, Faith.'

And when she did, my heart broke all over again.

Chapter Sixteen

Jack had been going to propose. I knew it, hoped for it at least, but to have it confirmed cut me deeply. He had planned to give me the painting on our anniversary. That was why he'd been so eager to go to the studio that weekend, both to finish it off and to bring it home. Not only was he going to propose, he'd spoken to a celebrant about conducting a ceremony at our special place in Norfolk, made enquiries at the registry office about signing the paperwork before we went so it was all legal. Faith had been on hand to help finalise the details once he had spoken to me about it all.

She held me while I cried and even when she'd gone I couldn't pull myself together. After staring at the picture most of the night, in the early hours of the morning I carried it to one of the spare rooms on the third floor, as far away as possible, and shrouded it with a sheet. I just couldn't deal with looking at it knowing what it signified.

Forever.

It's not as though you were married, Jack's mum had said, but we would have been. We could have had the wedding and children and the happily ever after. I tossed and turned in my lonely bed, teetering on the precipice of sleep before being wrenched away from slumber.

I could smell Jack's aftershave.

Sense his presence.

'Jack?' I fumbled for the lamp. Honey light cast shadows on the wall. A flicker. A movement in the corner catching my eye. It was the curtain moving in the breeze that pushed through the gaps around the sash window.

The room was empty.

I was alone.

Of course I was alone. I breathed in deeply, desperately, trying to recapture the smell of aftershave but it had been a figment of my imagination, a hopeless desire.

Eventually I snatched a few scant hours of fitful sleep and now Alice was here to pick me up. Our journey to the hospital for her scan was silent. Alice had one hand on the wheel, the other at her mouth as she nervously chewed her fingernails. I didn't reassure her that everything would be fine because Jack had taken all my promises with him.

It wasn't until we'd parked and were walking towards the hospital that Alice asked, 'What did Faith want yesterday then?'

'She …' I glanced at her. Her attention wasn't on me but on the appointment letter in her hand. I didn't want to tell her that Jack was going to propose, it wasn't the right time or place. Instead I shared, 'Faith and Michael are moving away.'

'What? Running away?' she said bitterly, glancing at me. 'I mean what are you supposed to do with the house and the studio and everything now without Faith's help?'

'I don't know. I want to try for Jack … For Liam—'

'No, Libby,' Alice said. 'It has to be for you. What do *you* want?'

'I don't know. I'd have to get all the contractors back and—'

'I could help. If you wanted to go ahead. I can organise and make calls and … I don't know. We can figure it out together. We don't need Faith and Michael. We have each other. You and me, we're a team. And the baby. We'll muddle through it all, won't we?'

She scratched furiously at her wrist.

'Hey. We'll be fine.' I gently stopped her and examined her skin. It was red and inflamed.

'Is this stress?'

'It's pregnancy-induced eczema. It's not uncommon apparently. I've been given some cream for it.'

'It looks so uncomfortable, why didn't you tell me?'

She avoided my eyes. 'It didn't seem important.'

And there it was. The cold, stark fact that in the game of trumps, Jack's death would always score the most points. Everyone was tiptoeing around me like their problems were insignificant in comparison to mine. I needed to take more interest, in Alice at least. She needed looking after if the elusive father of her unborn child either wouldn't or couldn't.

Our arms linked, we carried on towards the entrance. Sitting on the wall outside was a figure in a hoodie, hunched over a mobile phone. When he looked up I gasped.

'Liam?' I hurried over to him. 'What happened?' His face was bloodied and bruised, SteriStrips covered his forehead. There was a throbbing in my chest borne from a desire to comfort him. Desperate to give him a hug but certain he'd push me away. 'Have you been in a fight?'

'Yeah but …' He shrugged. 'You should see the other guy.'

'Are you all right?' I asked helplessly, unsure what to say.

'Are you?' His gaze was unwavering but when I didn't answer he jumped off the wall and stalked away, hands in his pockets.

'Wait.' I wanted to know if he was going into college.

'Come on.' Alice gently tugged my arm as Liam disappeared around the corner. 'We're going to be late.'

Alice gave her name and then we sat on plastic chairs. I didn't know whether it was nerves or a desperate need for the toilet that caused her knees to jiggle up and down but she couldn't keep still. I checked out the other women waiting. Some had still-flat stomachs like Alice. Some had bumps they stroked. Could the baby feel their touch? I knew nothing about pregnancy. Jack and I had both wanted children; we'd had that conversation before we moved in together but we had wanted to wait until our careers were established.

'Although I could still paint if the baby was in one of those sling things,' Jack had said.

'You'd get paint over her.'

'Her?'

'We'll have two girls.' They could play together like me and Alice had.

'What if I want a boy to play football with?'

'Girls play football too. Anyway, when was the last time you played?'

'Umm. Year 10 probably. Fair point. Boys just seem easier. I don't know how to work girls.'

'You know how to work me.' I had slid onto his lap, my arms wrapping around his neck.

'Is that so?' His fingers played with the buttons on my blouse. 'I think I need some more practice.'

'Practise away.' Our lips met. Jack had …

'Alice Emerson?' a voice called over the tinny speaker. 'Please make your way to room three.'

Taking one last lingering look at the couple I followed Alice into the room.

'This is my sister, Libby,' Alice said.

'Fiona,' the sonographer said, smiling.

Soon, Alice was lying on the bed, her shirt unbuttoned, her stomach shiny with some sort of gel-like substance.

The screen was turned towards us. Fiona ran the probe across Alice's belly.

'Say hello to baby.'

I leaned forward, squinting, not able to make out a little person at all, more of a dark moving mass with lighter parts.

'That' – Fiona pointed – 'is the head. There's the heartbeat, and that' – her fingers curved across the screen – 'is the spine.'

Alice's hand squeezed mine. We were both too overcome to speak.

A life. A new life. Suddenly it all felt so miraculous. I was ashamed I'd ever, however momentarily, resented this baby, felt they were to blame for what had happened to Jack.

Alice squeezed my hand back. And that squeeze told me she understood and more than that, that it was okay.

'So … are you ready to know when you'll meet your little one?' Fiona asked.

'My midwife said around 6 November?'

'Yes, I'd say around 7 November which makes him—'

'Him?' Alice squeezed my hand.

'Or her. It's too early to tell the sex but their star sign is a Scorpio.'

'I'm not big on astrology,' Alice said.

'I'm no expert but I think Scorpio's are brave, passionate and artistic.'

'Artistic!' Alice beamed at me. 'He'll take after Jack. Not take after,' Alice hurriedly added, 'but he'll love to paint. Imagine that, Libby, another artist in the family.'

'Do you want an image?' Fiona asked.

'Yes please.'

'And one for dad?'

'I … I'm on my own.'

'That's okay. Nothing wrong with being a single parent as long as baby is loved.'

'I love him – or her – already.' Alice smiled at the screen. 'To think I never planned on having a baby so young. When I first started throwing up and suspected I was—'

'Was it just because you were sick that you suspected you might be pregnant?' It hit me hard and fast. Taking the nausea I had felt lately and teaming it with other facts. When had *I* last had a period? I'd unpacked a new box of tampons when we'd moved in weeks ago; they were still unopened. I'd thought stress had messed up my cycle but what if it wasn't? What other symptoms were there? 'Everyone feels sick sometimes don't they?' My gaze flickered desperately between Alice and the sonographer, my own stomach spinning wildly. 'There are lots of different reasons for nausea aren't there?'

'Well, yes but—'

'Why are you asking, Libby?' Alice asked.

Because …

'What else? Feeling tired. You feel tired don't you, Alice?' Exhaustion was a heavy weight I carried every day.

'Shattered. And my hormones! A cereal advert reduced me to tears yesterday.'

My heart skittered around my ribcage; I couldn't unpick whether I was anxious or hopeful.

'We're done here.' The sonographer handed Alice a wad of blue paper towel to wipe her stomach.

'The giveaway was the lack of periods though.' Alice was still chatting away but her voice grew fainter.

Missing periods.

Feeling sick.

Tired.

Mood swings.

Was I pregnant?

Was I having Jack's baby?

Alice carefully carried the brown envelope containing an image of her baby as though it was the most precious thing in the world, and to her, it was.

We were leaving the department as another couple were approaching it.

'Alice,' I hissed. 'It's Owen.' There was my ex, his hand on the small of the back of a woman I assumed to be his wife or girlfriend, her hands cradling her bump.

With force, Alice pushed me in the opposite direction, linked her arm through mine and dragged me quickly around the corner.

'Thank goodness he didn't see us.' I was shaken. 'Who in their right mind would want to have a baby with that—'

'People do change ...'

'Not him.'

'Let's just get home.' Alice sounded weary. Anger increased the speed in my step. How could Owen still be here, be happy, when Jack wasn't?

On the way back to the exit, we passed the hospital pharmacy.

'I'll meet you in the car park,' I told Alice. 'I just need some migraine tablets.'

'You've a headache again—'

I didn't stop to answer her. I was already through the door, searching out the pregnancy testing kits.

I was scared. Confused.

Desperate to know.

At home I told Alice to go to Mum's and tell her now she knew everything was okay with the baby, that she was pregnant. I wanted to be alone with my thoughts and my fears and my hopes and my dreams.

I dashed into the house. Tore open the packet which could contain my future, scanned the instructions. After I'd peed on the stick I replaced the cap and forced myself to walk away from it. I paced the landing, counting the seconds in my head.

One, two, three.

Please let it be positive.

Four, five six.

I'd give anything for Jack's baby.

Seven, eight, nine.

Universe, let me have this one thing.

Ten.

Please, Please. Please.

Finally two minutes.

I walked slowly back into the bathroom. For a brief moment I imagined Jack was sitting on the edge of the bath, holding the test towards me, smiling the biggest smile but there was only me checking the test window on the stick.

Crying when I read the result.

Chapter Seventeen

The pregnancy text screamed negative at me. I hurled it at the wall to shut it up. That plastic stick had ripped away my future in less than three minutes. The tiny smidgen of hope that I'd have something left of Jack. Not solely my memories or a heart full of love for him but something new. Something solid and tangible that would grow. On the shelf above the radiator stood my make-up and my angry arm swept everything onto the floor. It was after kicking the side of the bath in frustration, forgetting it was cast iron, that my rage turned to hurt.

Physical.

Emotional.

I sank to the floor. One hand clutching my throbbing toes, the other hand resting on my belly as though there was a life inside of me that I needed to protect.

There's nothing there. There's nothing there. There's nothing there.

Time leapfrogged into May. Victim Support had been in touch; apparently although Jack was the one who was stabbed, I was a victim too and just hearing that word made me feel weaker. Powerless. I'd been assigned a support worker but I had told her I'd be in touch whenever I was ready to talk about it, just as I'd told Greta I'd return to work when I felt ready, but it wouldn't be until wedding season was over. I couldn't take photos of someone else's happily ever after, knowing that I wouldn't get my own.

On my phone I opened up the web page for the online support group I frequented, but today reading other people's pain to reassure myself I wasn't alone didn't bring me any solace. I scrolled through a post from a woman called Ivy whose husband died three years ago and she was still deep in grief, had cut off her family and friends and, except for shopping, never left the house.

'Bill would be heartbroken if he could see me now,' she acknowledged.

I hadn't yet left the house without Alice or Mum.

What would Jack feel if he could see me now? It was time to try and be more positive. I didn't want to be like Ivy.

I wanted to feel like me.

There was an ambulance outside the care home.

Sid.

The sight of it caused my heart to swell in my chest, like it might explode if I experienced one more loss.

Sid.

I sprinted through the building, the doors shushing against the thick carpet as I hurled my shoulder against the doors.

Sid.

By the time I'd checked the conservatory, his bedroom and reached the residents' lounge with its floral sofas and curtains – its decor tragically trapped in the Eighties – I was breathless, shaking with relief at the sight of Sid swiping biscuits from a plate.

'Hello, Libby duck. This is a nice surprise.'

I couldn't speak while I gathered my breath and my composure and when I finally found my words again all I could say was, 'You're okay, you're okay.'

'Libby …' There was understanding in his kind eyes. 'Ethel pulled her groin doing yoga. She wanted me to have a look but I wasn't putting me hands up her skirt. The ambulance was called as a precaution. She's fine.'

'Yoga?' I cast my eyes doubtfully around at the residents.

'It's in an armchair. None of that wrapping your legs around your neck malarkey. But Ethel insisted on trying it on the floor. Honestly that woman's about as flexible as the chef here who serves fish every Friday, pie and mash on a Saturday like the world would stop turning if we had a bloody sausage at the weekend.'

'Do you join in?'

'Do I heck. That young instructor tried to teach me to breathe. I said, "You don't get to be eighty-one without knowing how to breathe." I do hang around for the refreshments afterwards though. There'll be more later. It's crafting this afternoon. Our Norma would have loved that.'

'Did she like to make things?'

'She did. There's probably still a box or two in the house crammed with scraps of material and knick-knacks she'd collected to make stuff out of. Come on, duck. There's something I'd like to show you.'

In Sid's room he ignored the chairs and lowered himself onto his bed then patted the space next to him. He reached for a folded quilt and flapped it open; it was a patchwork blend of different types of material, rainbow colours and monochrome, all cut in various shapes and sizes.

'Norma made this,' he told me, stroking it tenderly. 'She used to have the room next to the bedroom as a hobby space. She had a rocking chair by the window overlooking the fields.'

'It's beautiful.'

'It's our memories. Our life. Remember I told you when we met I'd torn me kecks?'

'Yes.'

'This ...' He showed me a charcoal square of heavy fabric. 'This is a piece of them. You see this one?' It was ivory, delicate. 'That's part of Norma's wedding dress.'

'It's wonderful.' I ran my fingers over it, marvelling at the small, neat stitches. 'There's a story behind every square?'

'Yep. This floral one here is the pillowcase from the first time we shared a bed.'

'It must have brought her much joy.'

'Not always and that's the point of it, duck. Sometimes it served as a distraction, keeping her going when things were hard, when we couldn't have a baby, when she became ill. There was also a book she wrote in ... It was extraordinary, just like her. She called it her ...' He bowed his head, trying to recall the details. 'No matter. It's been lost over time.' He looked so wistful. 'But ...' He draped the quilt over both of our knees. 'The point is Norma found things that lifted her, that kept her going. What's keeping you going?'

'I ... I don't know. I'd love to make something like this.' I fingered the soft material. 'But I really can't sew.'

'It doesn't have to be a quilt, young Libby. Or a journal. But there should be something, because while you're using this' – Sid tapped my head – 'and these' – he touched my hands – 'you ain't wallowing and I don't mean that to sound ... you ain't a hippo or nothing but ... you need a focus. A project.' He let his words hang until I caught them.

'The house?'

He shrugged. 'Maybe. Maybe not. That's a big task but it would be like this quilt you see. A square at a time. A room at a time. There ain't no rush to complete it. Norma never finished this. Right up until the end she was adding to it. You see this one here …' Sid pointed out a red chequered piece of material. 'That was the napkin from an Italian restaurant we went to. She was pretty sick by then, she knew somehow that it would be the last meal out we ever had, and it was. If she was here, she'd still be sewing patches onto this' – he smoothed out the quilt – 'because this, life, it's a work in progress, not a race and Jack knew that. He was always making plans, moving forward. He'd want you to do the same. A square at a time.'

At home I couldn't stop replaying Sid's words.

You need a project.

I wandered through the house. There was so much to do it was an enormous undertaking. Every room needed something; plastering, flooring, decorating. But I didn't need to do it all at once, did I?

A square at a time.

But just one room would take an immense amount of planning and the thought was daunting, frightening, knowing that the success or failure was wholly dependent on me.

The sun shimmered through the grimy windows encouraging me outside. I gazed across the countryside; it was so beautiful here. In the distance, the joyful swoop of a swallow, fearless and free.

Still I felt that low-level anxiety in my stomach, a trapped bird that cawed that everything was transient, breaking me apart with each ferocious beat of its wings.

To clear my mind of its tumultuous thoughts, I decided to go for a walk.

The lambs, bigger now, skipping in buttercup-yellow fields as I meandered along the lane. I walked until my calf muscles were tight and a stitch burned in my side. I walked until a film of sweat coated my skin. I walked until I saw the church spire. And then I knew, subconsciously, that I had had a destination all along.

Despite it being so close by, I hadn't visited Jack's grave although Alice had tried to persuade me. She'd been several times, but I was adamant I wouldn't, couldn't – and yet my feet had different ideas. I wanted to tell Jack about Norma's quilt, share that although I wasn't sure I could manage the renovation, that perhaps I might try.

One square at a time.

He'd have loved that analogy. Although happy still seemed impossibly out of reach I was willing to try positive on for size.

My stomach churned with nerves as I slipped through the black wrought-iron gate. My breath was rapid, sweat prickled my armpits. This first time would be the worst, I knew. Slowly, I headed over to the far side of the church, to the new extension, to Jack, careful not to step on anyone else's plot, painfully aware that underfoot were people who had once lived, loved, had left behind grieving families and friends.

At last I was under the willow tree overlooking the fields. Shock brought me to an abrupt halt.

There must be some mistake.

I stared in horror at Jack's grave.

There must be some mistake.

But there wasn't.

Chapter Eighteen

No.

I dropped to my knees.

No.

Bile stung my throat. I was going to be sick. I swallowed down the saliva that flooded my mouth. Covered my face with my hands desperately hoping that when I lowered them my tired eyes would have deceived me.

They hadn't.

No.

My tears didn't come as I glowered at the white marble head-stone with a cherub on the top. It was garish and tasteless and Jack would have hated it. And … and … It shouldn't be there.

'It's advisable to let the ground settle for six months after a burial,' Elaine had said that day at the vicarage when I had brought it up. 'If not longer. The stone carries a risk of tipping forward otherwise.'

How had this happened? When had this happened? Alice would have mentioned it if it had been here a couple of days ago when she last came.

But I knew from the pretentious swirling lettering *exactly* how this had happened.

Jack Gilbert.

Beloved son of Rhonda and Bryan Gilbert.

There was no mention of me.

None at all.

'We're next of kin,' Rhonda had said. 'It's not as though you were married is it?'

But we would have been.

There must be something I could do to get the headstone changed. Removed. It shouldn't even have been erected. What if it collapsed? What if the plot sank and Jack was left …

No! This time I screamed out loud. If I rang Elaine she'd only tell me I had no legal right to interfere. If I rang Rhonda she wouldn't care; she'd demonstrated that by this … monstrosity. I bet she and Bryan had bulldozed Elaine into agreeing to have one now so that they could go back to their opposite ends of the country. Back to hating each other. Forgetting they had a son the way they had when he was alive. But that was callous. They had lost a child and they must be heartbroken, but … what about me? My grief? My right to mourn him. Reading the headstone it didn't feel I had any right at all.

Beloved son.

Jack was so much more than that.

I curled up on the patch of turf that was darker than the rest, the blades of grass not yet integrated with their neighbours, and I wept.

'So.' It was some time later before I stopped crying. My earlier positivity had vanished. I was, as Sid would say, wallowing. The sun at its highest in the sky was pumping out the promised heat. I sat cross-legged on my denim jacket, my back leaning against the headstone so I did not have to read it. 'I'm a mess.' I tugged a daisy from the ground, plucked its petals off one by one.

He loves me. He loves me not.

'Faith doesn't want to keep the studio running,' I sighed. 'That's unfair. It's not that she doesn't want to but she's moving away, her and Michael.' I paused, waiting to see if Jack might answer, if only in my head. Muttering how cross he was that they were relocating again for the sake of Michael's career when Faith had forged a good life for herself here.

He didn't.

'The house is … as it was, I guess, although there was a storm and some of the tiles have blown off the roof. One of the builders said if we don't patch it up it'll get worse. It'll leak. I need to do that much at least but … everything is just so *hard* without you.' It was the understatement of the century. 'Alice sent all the tradesmen away because I wasn't ready to deal with it all. I'm still not ready to deal with it all but the roof needs looking at.' I leaned towards the ground, my mouth close to the grass. 'Come back, Jack,' I whispered conspiratorially. 'Come back and I wouldn't tell anyone. I can't do this without you. Any of it.'

Silence.

I straightened up, feeling dizzy as I did so. I wiped my brow with my arm, wishing I had thought to bring some water with me, some money at least so I could find a shop. I hadn't even brought my phone so I couldn't call Mum or Alice to pick me up. I felt so peculiar and it was such a long walk home.

'I'm an idiot,' I said.

'Are you okay?' a male voice answered. There was a nanosecond when I unfeasibly thought it was Jack but then a shadow fell over me. I looked up, shielding my eyes. Nerves jumping around my belly. Once strangers were just people I hadn't met but after Jack being mugged they were something to be wary of.

Feared.

'I'm fine.' My tone was clipped.

'You didn't sound it.'

He made no move to leave. 'I was just wishing I'd brought a drink,' I offered him as an explanation. 'The sun's given me a blinding headache.'

'There's a Co-op not far from here.'

'I know. I didn't bring my purse.'

'I could—'

'No. I … I don't know you.'

'I'm Noah,' he said reminding me of the joke about the ark on the vicar's mug. Perhaps this man had been sent to save me.

'I'm Libby. I don't suppose you have a phone I could use please? It's a local call.'

He handed me his mobile but I didn't know who to call. I was loath to ring Alice, she'd already taken so much time off work: Mum too. I couldn't remember anyone else's number. I would have to walk home but it must have taken me at least an hour and a half to get here. I needed to hydrate.

'Actually, if you've a pound I could borrow instead please?' I stood, swaying as the world began to spin. He caught my elbow.

'Let's get you sitting down. Can you make it to that bench over there?' He pointed to a seat in the shade. We walked, me unsteadily, until I sank down onto the hard slats adorned with the brass plaque proclaiming 'Frank loved this place'.

'I'll be back as soon as I can.'

While he was gone I gazed out across the emerald fields, placing one hand on my scalp, feeling the heat still in my hair.

'You should always wear a sun hat. Gail Everest's grand-daughter – the one who likes those creamy meringues – went out without one and her brain got so hot she couldn't remember the alphabet,' Mum would have said, had she been here. Perhaps, sometimes, she was right.

The man returned and sat next to me, handing me a bottle of orange Lucozade. 'Here. It's what Mum always gave me and my sister Bethany when we weren't feeling quite right.' He also offered me a box of paracetamol. I pushed out two tablets and popped them into my mouth, washed them down with the syrupy sweet liquid. On his arm, a tattoo, the name Beth inside a heart. They must be as close as me and Alice.

'Thanks.' I wiped my mouth with the back of my hand. 'I haven't drunk this in years.'

'Me neither. Beth said it gave her super powers. She'd run up the stairs and slide down the bannisters, pretending she could fly.'

'That would be the sugar then.'

'Yeah.' He put the top back on his bottle. 'I believed her though. Thought my big sister could do anything. She really was my hero.'

'But not any more?'

'She … she's not here now. She's … gone.'

There was sadness in his voice. Of course, he was visiting a grave. Nobody came here for fun.

'I'm sorry.'

'It's okay. It was a good few years ago,' he said.

'That doesn't make it okay,' I said.

'No. It doesn't.'

We fell into silence. Both thinking of what we'd lost. Who we'd lost.

'Does it … does it get any easier?' I asked, my eyes fixed on the distance.

'It gets …' There's the longest pause. 'I don't want to say normal because my life without Beth in it … it doesn't feel normal at all, but … I guess you get used to it. Get on with it. It's early days for you though.'

'How do you know that?'

'From the date on the headstone.'

'Ah. The headstone.'

'Not your choice?'

'No it wasn't my choice but I don't get to decide anything. It wasn't as though we were married.' My sour words left a coating on my mouth and I took another swig of Lucozade to wash it down.

'Tell me about him. Jack.'

'You don't want to—'

'I do. Really.'

'Jack was twenty-nine and I loved him more than I ever thought possible.' I still didn't look at him. My eyes firmly on the thin distant line where the sky merged with the fields. I didn't want to see the sympathy that I knew would be on his face. 'He was mugged. Stabbed.'

'I … I'm so sorry. He was so young. Was it … quick?' Noah's voice was thick with sympathy.

'Yes and no. He was fine afterwards, well, not fine but discharged from hospital. He was home when … when his wound became infected and …' I sniffed hard. 'Whatever age Jack was taken it would have been too soon. There's so much I wish I'd have told him.'

'So tell him. Talking about those … we've lost … talking *to* them … it keeps their memory alive.'

'Is that why you come here?'

For a moment there's no answer, and then, 'I pretend we're having a conversation sometimes, me and Beth. I tell her things and I imagine what she might say. If I've a decision to make I ask myself "what would Beth do?" She was a better person than me in every single way.'

'I'm sure—'

'I want … If she were here. Now. I'd want her to be proud of me and I don't think she would be.'

'Why not?' I turned to face him. There was something familiar about him. His bleached blond hair. His hazel eyes. And then I remembered seeing his kindness-filled gaze before, 'You're the builder who came to the house to quote?'

He didn't answer straight away. Had I misplaced him?

'It was the day of the funeral,' he said quietly. I had got the right person then.

'I'm sorry I was so rude to you.'

'You weren't really.' His cheeks were already red but now a creep of pink crept up his neck.

'I shut the door in your face.'

'It's only natural,' Noah said. 'Under the circumstances.'

'I just don't feel like myself any more. I don't know who I am without Jack, or who I want to be.'

'I get that.'

'Is that why you think Beth wouldn't be proud? Because you don't know who you are?'

Noah's lip trembled. 'I know who I want to be, Libby,' he said.

Again we fell silent. We'd used all the words. It was exhausting, his grief, my grief. It might have been selfish but I couldn't help him deal with his loss when I hadn't even begun to process my own.

'I need to go.' I didn't want to be here any more.

'Can I give you a lift?'

'No. Thanks for the drink and these.' I tried to push the paracetamol back into his hand but he shook his head.

'Keep them.'

I could feel his eyes on me as I walked away, or perhaps it was just the burning sun.

Halfway home the sky darkened, lightning cracked and thunder rumbled. Rain pelted down, bouncing out of the potholes, turning the countryside a deep moss green. It took an age before I was trudging up our lane. I was soaked, my limbs heavy, my head light. I had thought going out was hard but coming home was harder. Putting my key into the lock, knowing there wasn't anybody waiting the other side of the door. Perhaps I should have let Noah drive me. I would be dry now and I could have invited him into this cold empty space where Jack should be but wasn't.

But I didn't want Noah here. He might have understood that grief is a thief. It steals your rational thoughts, your words, your feelings. Your peace of mind. It robs your contentment, leaving in its place a constant unease. What will happen next? Who will leave me next? It's exhausting. But Noah was still a stranger and it was cutting hearing him refer to loss as something you get used to. I didn't want to get used to it and the thought that I one day might was devastating. I climbed upstairs to fetch a towel and change my clothes. On the first-floor landing droplets of water were splashing onto the stairs, coming from the floor above. I checked it out. There was a pool of water on the floorboards. The builder had been right. The roof was leaking.

It was all too much.

I didn't know how to do this without Jack: the house; be happy; live – any of it. It was inconceivable that it had even crossed my mind that I perhaps could.

Without conscious thinking I found myself heading back to the bathroom, opening the cabinet and staring at the box of sleeping tablets.

I could make it all stop.

Everything.

It was wrong, I knew it was wrong but still my trembling fingers curled around the packet, the prick of a thousand needles jabbing against my skull.

It was wrong, but still I lifted the box from the shelf, closed the cabinet door. My wide scared eyes stared back at me from the mirror.

I dropped my gaze to the box in my hand.

It was wrong.

Drip-drip-drip, the rain pattered in.

It was overwhelming.

I could make it all stop.

Sleep.

Restful.

Eternal.

Life without Jack was too hard. Too colourless. Too painful.

You get used to it.

I hadn't.

I wouldn't.

I couldn't.

One square at a time, Sid had said but even that seemed too much. Every time I tried to pick myself up I was knocked back down. The headstone was the tipping point.

I couldn't get up again. I just … couldn't.

Downstairs I opened and closed the cupboards until I found a bottle of vodka. I'd heard somewhere that alcohol helps accelerate the process.

Process.

My hands shook as I filled a pint glass with water to sip. If I drank too much vodka too quickly I'd be sick and then I'd have to start again.

I counted out the tablets onto the table. How many would I need? Half of them? All of them? I wouldn't know until I tried.

Filled with a strong sense of calm and feeling more certain than I had in weeks, I pressed out the first tablet, placed it on my tongue.

Chapter Nineteen

I didn't want to be here any more, I wanted to be with Jack.

The tablet felt dry in my mouth.

Bitter.

My hand shook as I unscrewed the bottle of vodka. I was crying as I pushed thoughts of Alice and Mum away. I told myself they'd understand that I had to be with Jack. I told myself that although they'd be sad, in a strange way they might also be happy for me.

I told myself lies.

The bottle was cold against my lips.

For a moment the only sound that filled my ears was the frantic pounding of my own heart, but then I heard it.

A noise I couldn't identify and then one I could.

I plucked the tablet off my tongue and rested it on the table.

As I crossed the room I could see the old cat flap in the bottom of the door lifting before dropping once more. I opened the back door and there it was.

A black cat, mewing pitifully.

He bumped his head against my legs, tail high, purring happily before he padded confidently into the kitchen like he belonged there.

With one leap, he settled himself on the table, studying me as I studied him. Licking his white paws.

'What sort of cat would you like?' Jack had asked me on our anniversary.

'Black with white feet. We could call him Socks,' I had replied.

'And then you'd want a second called Shoes.'

'No. One is enough. What do you say?'

'I say if you can find a black cat with white socks then it's meant to be.'

Meant to be.

I didn't believe in meant to be. I didn't think that what happened to Jack was fate, part of some great universal grand plan.

I didn't believe in miracles and yet … I tentatively stroked Socks' fur, warm and silky under my fingers. He batted my hand with his head, tilting his chin up so I could scratch underneath it. He was real and solid and part of me wondered whether my imagination had conjured him up.

I hurriedly scraped some tuna into a bowl before Socks could run away and while he ate, unashamedly, the sound of his chewing loud and unselfconscious, I fetched my camera. It felt heavy in my hands, strange, belonging to my before life, not to now, but I took several shots of Socks before I viewed them on the screen. It was reassuring to see he was real.

I pushed the pills back into the box, screwed the lid back on to the vodka bottle.

Not today.

A week later the June sunshine threw out a surprising amount of heat as we sat in the pretty courtyard at Sid's care home. Pink clematis and white rambling roses entwined around wooden trellises pinned to the wall. Bees buzzed lazily around a hydrangea bush. Alice leaned back on her chair, raising her face to the sky. I slipped on my sunglasses to dull the brightness. I had a headache forming. Alice's cheeks were flushed. As the summer and her pregnancy progressed, she would find it more uncomfortable but in the second trimester now she was blooming. Pretty in her floral maternity dress. Mum kept smiling at her bump. She'd been thrilled with the news although, predictably, Alice had been subjected to multiple pregnancy-related horror stories Mum had heard from her customers.

'Happy birthday!' We all stood as Sid joined us then kissed his dry, crepy cheek.

'Shall we do presents while we wait for our drinks?' Mum was already pushing a brightly wrapped parcel in front of Sid. 'This is from all of us.'

I raised my camera; since Socks had entered my life, all swishing tail and soft purring, I'd begun to take the odd picture again.

Sid grinned at me, his teeth yellowing and uneven.

We leaned forward as he painstakingly peeled off the Sellotape. Slid the box from the paper.

'A smartphone?' His voice was neutral. 'It's too much. Take it back.'

Alice and I weren't sure about the gift. Sid had always said he was too old for new technology, wouldn't use a mobile even if he had one, but Mum had insisted.

'We know most of your friends, your social life is here, but it'll make it a little easier for us to get in touch with you rather than calling and waiting for somebody to try and find you. You can text us any time. I've already put our numbers into your contact list.

Look.' Mum showed Sid how the phone worked. 'It's a camera too: you can take photos of the birds.'

'Ain't that classed as stalking?' Sid winked at me.

'I meant the kind with wings.'

'Well, thanks.' Sid placed the phone back down onto the table; I wasn't convinced he'd ever use it. He opened up his cards.

Tea was brought to us on a tray, cups and saucers clattering against each other.

'Shall I pour?' Mum asked.

'No. You're my guest.' Sid picked up the pot. The lid rattled as his hand shook. Tea splashed on the table. He set the pot back down again.

'Let me,' Alice said. 'I need to practise being mum.' She let Sid think he was doing her a favour.

'You've got a few months left before you need to worry about that,' Sid said, but still he relinquished his hold on the handle.

Once we all had a drink in front of us, Mum nodded to the carers who were gathered behind Sid. They advanced, carrying a huge cake Mum had brought from the bakery, the sponge covered in smooth white icing, 'Sid' piped in blue buttercream. Pushed into the cake were two candles, an eight and a two.

We all sang happy birthday. Tears sprung to Sid's eyes and he wiped them away muttering 'bloody pollen' as Alice and I exchanged a smile.

'Good job you didn't buy eighty-two candles,' Sid said after he'd blown both flames out to applause. 'Or they'd have cost more than the bloody cake.'

I laughed.

My hands automatically covered my mouth wishing I could

stuff the sound back in. Jack had been dead for less than three months and here I was having a good time.

Laughing.

'Excuse me.' I grabbed my bag and hurried to the toilet where I splashed my face with cold water to wash away my shame, my confusion. Laughing was something I'd never given a second thought to. Now it felt like a betrayal.

I was trying to compose myself when my mobile beeped. I took it out of my bag.

It will be all right. It always is. Enjoy the beer and skittles days. Jack would want you to laugh.

This was followed by a second text.

This is Sid.

A third.

Am I doing this right?

Through my tears I laughed again, and this time it didn't hurt quite so much.

It was an odd afternoon. Lovely, but odd. The thought that Socks was waiting for me at home made being out seem almost bearable. Sometimes I fixed my smile in place the way I had learned to do, my cheek muscles aching with the effort of curling my lips into a position that was forced and unnatural. On occasions Sid would make one of his jokes, and then my smile was genuine, spreading across my face before I realised it was there. Unsure how to feel about these brief periods when I was momentarily relaxed and unguarded.

I yawned.

'It's time you left.' Sid began to gather his presents, his cards.

'We don't have to rush off,' I said. Although I was worn out with trying to focus on the conversation, of pretending I was okay, I didn't want Sid to be alone on his birthday.

'I've got a game of bridge to play. You never know, I might make a few quid.'

'Sid. You shouldn't be gambling,' Mum gently chided.

'It ain't my fault. Ethel wanted to play strip bridge. Offering her money was the only way I could persuade her to keep her clothes on,' he whispered loudly.

My last smile of the day was for Sid, and Sid alone.

'I'm counting my blessings today,' he said. 'And you should too, duck. It'll all be okay, Libby. It usually is. I have a present for you before you go.'

He handed me a squashy silver parcel, wrapped with a big red bow. Intrigued I slipped off the ribbon. Inside the paper was Norma's quilt.

'Sid!' I was overcome. 'I can't take this.'

'You ain't taking it, I'm giving it to you.' He hugged me tightly. 'You're stronger than you think, Libby. If you want to do up the house, then you can.'

'One square at a time,' I whispered against his white shirt that smelled of tobacco and mint and comfort.

'And you can send me photos as you go on that fancy phone. It does receive photos too?'

'Yes. It does everything. You can even watch the horse racing on it and place a bet.'

'Well there's a thing. You see, Libby, life gets better when we least expect it, always.'

'Can we stop at the Co-op, Mum?' I asked on the way home. I needed cat food for Socks.

Mum parked. A figure I recognised strolled out of the shop. Noah.

I groped for my bag while fumbling with the door handle to get out and call his name. I still owed him the money for the Lucozade and the paracetamol he had bought me at the churchyard that day, but before I could get out of the car he had ambled down the path leading to the house next to the shops, and let himself in with a key. I would repay my debt another time. I couldn't face the inescapable questions from Mum and Alice if I were to knock on his door.

The carrier bag was heavy, laden with tins of Whiskas, a bag of litter, a feather on a stick and a stuffed mouse laced with catnip sticking out of the top.

'I've got a cat now,' I said by way of explanation when I climbed back into the car.

'A cat? From where?' Mum asked.

Distracted by thoughts of Noah, I answered, 'Jack sent him.'

Mum and Alice exchanged a look before my sister said, 'Jack … *sent* him?'

'He … I …' The judgement in the car stiffened my spine. 'Socks is the cat me and Jack said we'd get.' I didn't care how it sounded.

I knew Jack had somehow sent him.

I just *knew*.

Back at my house, Mum and Alice insisted on coming in 'to meet the cat', their voices sceptical, not quite believing he existed.

But there he was; I opened the front door, stepped into the snug. Socks, curled up on the chair, but he wasn't alone.

He was on Jack's lap.

The carrier bag thudded onto the floor, tins of cat food rolling under the sofa. Spooked by the noise Socks ran away.

I couldn't take my eyes off the armchair.

'Jack?'

In the time it took me to blink he had vanished. The moment had fallen away from me and although I'd only seen him for one painful second, I felt his absence keenly.

'Come on then,' Mum said from behind me. 'Where's this cat then?'

But I couldn't speak. Couldn't move. I'd forgotten the most fundamental of skills as I stood rooted to the spot, pulse accelerated, palms damp, chest aching with both longing and loss. The endless chasm of grief opening up its demanding jaws once more while I fed it another shaft of my intense sorrow.

'Libby?'

Utterly bewildered, my eyes searched the room.

Socks had gone.

Jack had gone.

Had either of them really been here?

What *was* happening to me?

A startled scream.

An 'oh my God, I don't believe it.' Alice shouting, 'Come quickly' from the kitchen.

Chapter Twenty

Alice's scream kick-started my feet. One thought boomeranged around my brain as I rushed down the hallway – Alice must have seen Jack too.

Panting, I reached the kitchen, feeling dizzy, afraid.

Excited.

'Jack?' The word burst from me.

Alice raised her face to me, puzzled. She was crouching on the floor, rubbing her fingers together, trying to coax a quivering Socks to come out of his hiding place under the table. 'There's a dead mouse on the doormat, Libby. This little terror must have dragged it in.' But she was smiling as Socks hesitantly butted her hand. She scratched her fingers between his ears. They twitched with pure pleasure.

'What's going on in here?' Mum asked confused. 'Why on earth did you scream, Alice?'

'Sorry, Mum. Unexpected dead rodents tend to do that to me.'

'And why did you call Jack's name, Libby? Surely you haven't named that cat—'

'The cat is called Socks, Mum.' I was sure I'd already told her that.

'But then why did you shout for Jack?'

'Because I thought I … Leave me alone.' I turned and pelted upstairs. Ignoring Mum's 'Libby!' which trailed after me, I ran into the bathroom, locked the door. My hands rested on the sink as I caught my breath. The mirror me staring back reproachfully, my skin pale, dark circles under my eyes. My image was haunting, like one of the brooding monochromes I took during an arty phase at college.

What was happening to me?

I'd sensed Jack before, smelled his aftershave before, but this time I was positive I had seen him.

How was that possible?

It wasn't.

I held up my shaking hand, never tearing my eyes away from my reflection.

Counted my five fingers.

I folded my thumb across my palm.

Four.

Quickly dropped down my index finger, observing whether my eyes could be fooled into thinking they still saw the finger when it wasn't there but no …

Three.

My middle finger.

Two.

Ring finger.

One.

Little finger.

My eyes and my brain agreed.

Nothing. There was nothing left. Nothing to give, nothing to see here. Move along.

Libby.

A whispered name.

Jack?

What was happening to me?

Libby.

I turned towards the sound. It was only the breeze drifting in through the space between the sash window and the frame. A breeze that sounded like my name.

I was hearing what I wanted to hear.

Seeing what I wanted to see.

And yet, it had all felt so real. The sense of Jack still being around growing stronger with each passing day.

I cast my mind back; snuggled up on the sofa with Jack, the opening credits to *Ghost* on the TV, him pre-empting my tears with tissues already placed on the coffee table. Sharing buttery popcorn, warm from the microwave. Me gulping chilled Chardonnay, forcing it down my throat which was already beginning to swell at the thought of what was to come.

'We've seen this movie a million times and it still gets you,' Jack said affectionately.

'But Patrick Swayze … he's right there.' I gestured at the TV. 'And Demi Moore should just know.' Jack had pulled me close to him and dropped a kiss onto the top of my head. 'I'd know if it were us,' I had muttered. 'I'd be looking for signs.'

Is that what was happening? Was my subconscious recalling the times we'd watched *Ghost*? Jack's promises he'd never let anything take him away from me? 'Nothing in this world, or the next could keep me from you, Libs,' he had murmured into my hair.

Was I remembering? Manifesting?

Hoping?

I closed my eyes.

If you're here, Jack, show yourself to me. Give me a sign.

Three slow taps to the door.

My aching heart stuttered.

And then, 'Libby?' My sister's voice, the knocks faster this time. 'Are you okay?'

'I'll be down in a second, Alice. I'm fine.'

But I wasn't. I could no longer meet my own eyes in the mirror. I was *such* a fool.

Muted voices greeted me when I reached the bottom stair. Snatches of conversation drifting from the snug.

'She's not herself …'

'Counselling …'

'Some sort of support group …'

'I'm fine,' I said with force as I entered the room. I sat heavily in the chair – *the* chair I thought I saw Jack in – drawing a cushion on my lap and hugging it close to me.

'We're worried, Libby. You haven't seemed quite right since—'

'You don't know how it feels to lose someone—'

'My parents,' Mum cut me off. 'I lost both of my parents.' There was a wobble to her voice. 'And I *do* know it's different losing a life partner. Gail Everett – pink meringue Gail—'

'Shut up.' The words slithered from my mouth; my voice was calm but cold as metal. I couldn't stand it any more. I was feeling so much pain I didn't know what to do with it. Mum's obvious distress should have been a sticking plaster over my mouth, but it wasn't. 'We're sick of hearing it. Sick of hearing all about your concern for your bloody customers. You know more about their lives than you do about ours. We know more about them than we do about you.' I swallowed hard. 'You care more about them than you do about us.' The accusation rushed from me almost before I was sure I wanted to make it.

'Libby! Of course I don't!'

'You trivialise everything me and Alice go through.' I couldn't stop myself, even though it wasn't really her that I was angry at.

'That isn't true—'

'Comparing our experiences to complete strangers—'

'Enough!' Alice's face drained of colour. She placed her hands either side of her small bump as though she could shield her baby's ears from the shouting. Shame silenced me. Whatever the first impression was that my niece or nephew formed of me, whenever that might be, I didn't want it to be this. Years of pent-up anger and frustration spewing out onto these dusty wooden floorboards that creaked with a lifetime of memories from those that had trodden them before us.

Norma.

Sid.

He'd be so sad if he heard me and Mum arguing like this.

'I'm sorry.' It was only partly true. The timing was terrible but this dark cloud had always hung over my childhood, jammed full of strangers whose names were uttered in our home far more frequently than mine or my sister's. It was inevitable that one day it would burst.

'I'm sorry that I've ever made you feel that you girls aren't enough for me when … when it's the other way around. It's me who isn't enough for you.' A tear trickled down Mum's cheek.

'What … what do you mean?' I fought against a sudden punch of emotion and stood and crossed the room. I had made my mother cry. Quickly, I took her hand. Alice scooched in closer.

'It's a bit like when apple Danish Alan Watkins said—'

'*Mum.*' If she was going to rewrite the script of our childhood, she needed to do it from her own point of view. 'Tell us what *you* feel.'

'I feel that …' She inhaled slowly, then released the air in one long exhale. 'I felt that I'd let you down, right from the start. Most of your friends had two parents, oh I know times have changed now and "blended families" are the norm but then … It was hard. On my own. I hated leaving you to the care of others after school but I had to work. I didn't want to claim benefits. I wanted you to see that women could be breadwinners. Strong. Only … only you stopped seeing me somewhere along the way. You became your own little unit of two, and clever … goodness …' She gave a high laugh. 'You were both far cleverer than me. Over dinner you'd chatter about your friends, your teachers. As you grew, your social life expanded and my world … my world was so small. I had nothing to say and so I began to talk about my customers because their lives were far more interesting than mine.'

She slowly turned her head to face me, eyes searching for understanding, a seedling unfurling to seek out sunshine when it knows it could instantly be crushed.

Everything inside me softened. 'Oh, Mum.' It was desperately sad that I'd known so little and assumed so much.

'I need you both so much. You girls. You're so inspiring. You don't need anyone.'

'I do.' My voice broke. 'Jack.'

'You *want* Jack, of course you do, my darling, but you don't *need* anyone. You're strong. Stronger than I ever was.'

'I don't feel it, Mum. Sometimes … sometimes I think he's still here.' I wanted to open up to her the way she had to me.

'That's perfectly natural, sweetheart.'

'Is it?' I sniffed hard.

'Yes. Michelle Walker told me …' There was a beat. 'When your grandad died, I could hear him for a good few days. "*Don't cry, Caroline. Turn that frown upside down.*" In my mind. As clear as a bell.'

'What happened?'

'I don't know. I suppose he gradually faded away.'

A whimper sprang from my throat.

'I don't mean I forgot him, Libby. I mean that I found a way to … be without him. To carry on. Eventually, to move on. You will too and … I'm sorry you've thought that I'm not as interested in your lives as I am in others. I know you've always needed—'

'You.' I rested my head on her shoulder. Out of my peripheral vision I could see Alice do the same on the other side. 'We've both always needed you. To know you.'

'Yes,' said Alice. 'I really don't care that Michelle Walker always gives a sausage roll to her dog when she buys a pack of four.'

'Her daughter, Hope, became a pole dancer you know,' I said, recalling the comment Mum had made when Jack told her I'd been entered into The Hawley Foundation Prize.

'Seriously?' Alice said.

'She makes a fortune apparently,' Mum said. 'She's got massive boobs like her mum. It's probably all the flaky pastry they eat.'

Her shoulders shook, my shoulders shook, but this time not through crying but laughing.

That afternoon was full of frank conversations. Unanswered questions were resolved even if Alice refused to tell us who the baby's father was. We learned a lot about Mum, viewing our childhood through her lens. Many tears were shed. Mum's. Alice's. Mine.

'I'd like you to come with my for my scan next week, Mum.' Alice glanced over at me *is that ok?* and I smiled back *that's a lovely idea.*

'Are you sure? Weren't you going, Libby? Could we all—'

'You go. Meet your grandchild. I've a lot to do. I … I've been talking to Sid and I've decided to start work on renovating this place.' Until I said it aloud I hadn't realised I'd come to a final decision. 'I'm not going to put myself under pressure, it's pretty overwhelming and I'm not committing to opening the centre right now but … one room at a time.'

'Libby. That's … you see? You're amazing,' Mum said.

'I haven't done anything yet.'

'But you will. Can we help?' Alice asked.

'Thanks, but I need to figure this out on my own.'

For Jack.

One square at a time.

The three of us had never felt so close and after they left, following a fish and chip supper at the kitchen table, I changed into my pyjamas and fed Socks the leftover cod, feeling content. While he ate I wrapped myself in Norma's quilt and opened up the notes app on my phone.

Things to do to get the centre up and running.

I studied those words until they blurred, hopping and skipping on the page, rearranging themselves into something else entirely.

I can do this.

Jack's whispered voice echoing, 'You've got this'.

It was a small start, but it was a start.

Tomorrow I'd do more.

Later, Socks sat on my lap, my fingers picking bits of mud out of his fur, loving thoughts of my family filling my mind. I could get through this, with them.

Of course then I was unaware that the following day a crack would appear in my relationship with Alice. That I'd discover something she'd been trying desperately to keep hidden.

A secret.

A lie.

Chapter Twenty-One

It was early when I woke, the sun already bright, the sky wide and clear. The world had shrugged off the last vestiges of spring and leaped into summer. June so far had been glorious. The air fresher, days lengthened. Today my thoughts didn't linger on Jack; instead I replayed the conversation of yesterday with Mum and Alice, drawing the memory to my chest. It was a warm hug, a promise of a future where we were closer as a family. Socks jumped onto the bed, sprawled across my lap and began to lick his paws.

'I said I'd renovate this house.' His black fur shed over my crisp white duvet as I rhythmically stroked him. 'Do you think that I can?'

Yes.

It was Jack's voice I heard and I believed him.

Step by step.

Square by square.

It was a day of possibility, but despite my positivity I knew my emotions were still turbulent and I didn't want to risk despondency if I stayed here, hemmed in by myriad empty rooms, each one demanding attention. Instead, I decided to take my laptop to Alice's café and contact the contractors there. I'd drink cappuccinos, eat cake, surround myself with people who had been out there living a life while mine had been paused.

I was ready to press play again.

If I'd known what was to come, perhaps I'd have stayed at home.

I drove the long way into town, avoiding the chemist, unsure whether there still might be flowers taped to the lamp-post along with the photo of Kenny but knowing that even if there weren't, I would see them anyway.

There were road works on Brampton Avenue, temporary traffic lights, a diversion sign pointed down Brown Street. If I took that route I would pass Jack's studio. Flustered, I frantically tried to map a way out of the queue of traffic but the shunting engines and blaring horns prevented me from making a U-turn, pushed me forward until …

Oh God.

Oh God.

Oh God.

And there it was, Jack's studio. Slowly I pulled over to the kerb and rested my forehead on the steering wheel both wanting to and not wanting to look.

I waited for my stomach to settle again before I raised my head. The sparks of joy that once ignited whenever I came here were now nothing but ashes of despair.

He was gone.

Everything was gone.

Ridiculously, I had expected Jack's studio to remain empty after Faith and Michael had moved out all of his stuff and sent it to his parents. It hadn't even crossed my mind that another business would take over the lease, particularly not within a matter of weeks, but in the car park was a white transit van and a black Ford Focus. Inside the studio, a couple in the empty space, his arms around her waist, her smiling up at him. She was talking animatedly, gesturing to the wall, the grin on her face breaking me apart.

'So, over here …' Jack had taken my hand the first time we had viewed the studio and led me beneath the skylight, 'imagine a row of easels.' He paced out a stretch of floor without once letting go of me. 'And …' we had headed into the smaller room, 'a couple of sofas in here. Somewhere to sit and sketch.'

Now the space would be full of someone else's hopes. Someone else's dreams. A new sign hanging on the hooks where Jack's sign had once swung, 'Alethic Art' painted in swirls of midnight blue.

'What does it even mean, alethic?' I had asked.

'It's a philosophy term meaning various modalities of truth. You can't get more honest than drawing what's in your heart.'

'That's clever. If I was naming a business I'd name it after something I loved, chocolate ice cream or custard creams.'

'Naming a business after something you love is …' Jack had stared at me intently. 'Alethic, it does mean modalities of truth, although I'm not quite using it in the right context, but I didn't choose it for its accuracy. More for what it represented. I … I took all the letters from Jack and Elizabeth and kept playing around with them until … Alethic.'

Overcome, I had stood on tiptoes and given him the most heartfelt of kisses which contained all the feelings I had felt, all the things words could not cover.

Now I turned my attention away from the couple; it was too painful to watch them.

Before I could start the engine I noticed a figure darting across the car park, keeping to the shadows. Hood up, aerosol in hand.

Quietly I got out of my car. Crept around the van to the side hidden from view. Liam had his arm raised, poised to deface the white panel.

'Liam,' I hissed. He turned to me. Emotions slid lightning fast across his face, shock, fear, anger, before vulnerability settled. 'What are you doing?'

'Writing BASTARD.' His chin tilted defiantly.

'It's not their fault … It's business.'

'It's not fair.' His voice was as deep as a man's but he looked as despairing as a child who couldn't get his own way. I didn't know what to tell him. The bruises he wore on the outside the last time I had seen him had faded but the hurt he carried on the inside was worse.

'Why aren't you at college?'

'Got a project to do. Don't have to go in often for teaching.'

'And do you go in? When you're supposed to?'

He shrugged. Didn't anybody care if he was bunking off? He wasn't my responsibility and yet responsible was how I felt towards him.

'Are you hungry?' I asked. 'My sister works at The Happy Bean, the coffee shop down the road. I'm on my way there. Fancy a bacon sarnie?'

'Ain't got no cash.'

'I'm not asking you to pay.'

He shrugged again but he began to walk and I fell into step beside him, leaving the car where it was.

*

It was lunchtime-busy. The coffee machine hissed. The comforting smell of tomato and basil hanging in the air – that was soup of the day then. Alice wasn't behind the counter. I could only see one spare table, by the door; there could be others beyond the arch where the coffee shop opened up but I didn't want to risk losing this one.

'Let's grab those seats.' I ushered Liam in front of me. He sat, eyes lowered, knee jiggling up and down.

I set my bag down on my chair to save it. 'I'm going to see where Alice is. Have a look at the menu.'

My *excuse mes* were on repeat as I squeezed through the gaps between the tables, making my way towards the arch, the space beyond.

It was then that I saw them.

Alice and *him*.

My ex.

Owen.

They were deep in conversation. A bunch of pale pink roses on the table between them. He took her hand. Ran his finger across her wrist. The gold wedding band on his finger caught the light. She smiled.

My mind travelled back to the question I had asked Alice when she had first told me that she was pregnant.

'Have you told him? The dad?'

'No. He's in a relationship. I really don't want to talk about it.' She had been cagey.

No wonder she hadn't wanted to talk about it.

Owen.

A waitress pushing between the tables dropped her order. The sound of breaking crockery lifted Alice's head, her happy expression contorted into one of horror as she caught sight of me. For a second neither of us moved. The coffee shop faded away, the world disappearing until there was only me and my deceitful sister.

She wrenched her hand away from Owen, scraped back her chair. He looked over his shoulder, his eyes burning into mine.

My skin crawled with a thousand unwelcome memories.

I turned and pushed my way back to the front of the coffee shop.

Liam had gone.

My bag was still resting on my chair but it was unzipped, my laptop and purse missing.

I was a fool in so many different ways.

'Libby, wait. I can explain.' Alice was close behind me, shielding her bump with one hand as she squeezed through the customers to reach me, stumbling against a table.

I was conflicted, desperate to get away but not wanting her to hurt herself.

Reluctantly I stopped. Turned. She ushered me outside.

'You know what Owen put me through, so—'

'He's changed.' Alice defended him before she hurriedly added, 'But it wasn't what it looked like.'

'Really? Because it looked very much like you were holding hands with my ex? Like he had bought you flowers? Are you together?'

'No! He's married.'

I recognised the treacherous slope I was teetering at the top of but I couldn't help hurling myself down it. 'So is the father of your baby, isn't he?'

The colour from Alice's face drained away.

'Is Owen the father of your baby, Alice?'

Neither of us spoke. I was hurtling down that slope, feeling it physically, the dizzying sense of being out of control, bracing myself for the impact.

There was nothing left for me to say, no words. Only me and my duplicitous sister.

Time stretched as I waited for a denial that didn't come.

Slowly, reluctantly, heartbroken, I turned and walked away.

Chapter Twenty-Two

At home I sat at the kitchen table, open bottle of wine in front of me, drinking too fast to try to blunt the edges, but the memory of Alice and Owen holding hands was still sharp and painful. Like a teenager waiting for a boy to call I checked my phone with frequency, unable to stop myself picking up my handset even though it hadn't rung, disappointment lurching when I saw she hadn't tried to call me.

The hours passed, the bottle emptied and still I waited, too angry, too stubborn to make the first move but hoping that she would. Not understanding why she wouldn't offer, if not an olive branch, an explanation.

I had accused her of sleeping with Owen.

She hadn't denied it.

I seesawed between being confident she wouldn't, to doubting her loyalty.

She hadn't denied it.

Again, I checked my mobile. I could call her, but …

She hadn't denied it.

A shiver shimmied down my spine; I wasn't sure if it was the sliding temperature or the fear that my relationship with my sister might be irrecoverably damaged. I tottered unsteadily into the snug, flopped onto the sofa and pulled Norma's quilt up to my chin. I stared up at the nicotine-yellow ceiling. Yesterday's hope had been brutally cast aside by utter despair. Everything had already seemed unachievable without Jack, but without Alice's support it was all so impossible.

'I can't do it,' I slurred as I spoke. 'I can't fix this bloody house up.'

My heavy eyelids closed.

'You can do it, Libby. Don't give up.'

Jack's soft voice was the last thing I heard as too much alcohol and too little sleep dragged me deep into an unsettled slumber.

A loud knocking roused me.

Disorientated I pushed myself up onto my elbows, Norma's quilt slithering to the floor. There was a rank taste in my mouth, a blinding headache behind my eyes.

The knocking came again.

I wobbled as I stood; outside the window the sky was goose-feather grey and I checked my watch, surprised to see it was still the same day. My body felt heavy as I stumbled into the hallway and answered the front door.

On the step, Mum and Alice. Alice's eyes were threaded with tiny blood vessels and I knew she'd been crying. Part of me wanted to tell her to go away, go back to Owen, but then I caught sight of her bump and I softened. Even if the baby was part Owen, he or she was still half Alice and stress couldn't be good for them. I led them into the kitchen. Mum made a tsking sound behind her teeth as she removed the empty wine bottle from the table, flicked on the kettle.

Alice took a seat at the table while I leaned against the worktop near the sink. The lingering smell of alcohol was turning my stomach.

'Now Alice has told me all about the misunderstanding earlier,' Mum began as she searched for clean mugs.

'Is *that* what she called it?'

'It's been a long time since you girls had a falling-out and a long time since I had to step in. Libby, I know it must have been a shock—'

'That's an understatement. And had she told you about this … this *relationship*?' I crossed my arms.

'It's not a relationship.' Alice didn't sound angry, she just sounded sad.

'He bought you flowers.' I could still picture that delicate bouquet of baby pink roses, the image of them pricking like a thorn.

'They were for his *wife*.'

'You were holding hands.' She couldn't deny that.

'He wasn't … he … it's my rash.' Alice stood and thrust her wrist towards me. 'The eczema cream isn't working. Owen is one of our suppliers, gluten- and dairy-free cakes. He thought cutting out dairy might be good for my skin.'

'You've had …' I made a show of checking the time, 'six hours and that's the best excuse you've come up with?'

'It isn't an excuse.'

Mum opened her handbag and pulled out a glossy leaflet. 'This is the health business Owen runs with his wife.'

I studied the pages. A woman – the woman I'd seen at the ultrasound department at the hospital – smiled out at me holding a bowl of fruit, Owen behind her.

A wholesome couple you'd think, if you didn't know him.

'Owen's a health freak?'

'Yes. He's been helping me with food plans. He was checking out my wrist to see if it looked any different.'

'Wait? What? Checking if it looked different? So this wasn't the first time you've seen him.'

'No. But …' she began, falteringly. 'We … we're *not* friends. Really. I was shocked when he came into The Happy Bean touting his goods a few weeks ago. I gave him a flat no, but Leanne was there that day and she called him back. She asked me why, when we'd already talked about finding a local supplier who could offer gluten- and dairy-free cakes, I had turned him down. My face gave me away because she said if I was letting my personal life influence my business decisions then perhaps she'd been hasty in promoting me to supervisor. I was so stressed I began scratching my wrists and Leanne said … she said my skin was unsightly and could put the customers off their food and Owen said he thought he could help. He *has* helped.' She hadn't broken eye contact once.

Instinctively I knew she was telling the truth. I tried to form an apology in my head but my words were inadequate, diminutive, not enough. Instead I sat down next to her and leaned in; our fingers found each other, our noses were almost touching.

There was a beat or two before I asked softly, helplessly, 'Alice. Why didn't you tell me?'

'If it had been before … Jack, I probably would have done but … I don't know. I didn't think, in the great scheme of things, it needed addressing. I am sorry you were upset though.'

'You can't … you can't treat me as if I'm made of glass forever because of Jack.' My eyes meet Mum's over Alice's shoulder. 'Both of you.'

Mum stepped forward and wrapped her arms around both of us and I felt both an adult and a child, happy and sad, and loved.

I felt loved.

Later, we drank coffee and ate beans on toast. Alice drenched her plate with tomato ketchup and Mum told her off for using too much sauce, spoiling the taste of the food.

'You've been telling her that for over twenty years,' I said. 'And it doesn't make any difference.'

'That's because ketchup enhances the flavour of *everything*,' Alice said.

We shared a smile. Some things never changed.

'I know we only talked about it yesterday but have you had any more thoughts about the renovations?' Mum asked.

'That's why I went to the café, to do some research online but ...' I trailed off. I didn't want to tell them about Liam, not only to protect him, but to protect Jack. Liam was Jack's mentee and I didn't want them to think his trust was misplaced. Besides, they'd only want me to tell the police and I hadn't yet decided what to do.

'Don't give up,' Mum said. 'You can do it.'

'That's what Jack said earlier.' I realised my mistake when I saw the horrified expression on Mum's face.

'Jack *said*?' Mum and Alice exchanged a glance.

'You know ...' Miserably I mashed beans with my fork. 'Like you said yesterday you'd felt Grandad was with you after he died, I just feel Jack's encouraging me. That's all.'

'But you know he's not here? That you're not really hearing him?' Again Mum and Alice swapped a look.

'Yes. I know that.' I gave them the answer they wanted to hear because the truth was that I did believe I'd heard Jack, but that was impossible, wasn't it?

After Mum and Alice had left I carried a mug of tea to bed, the remnants of a hangover still poking behind my eyes. On my iPad I searched for an explanation for the feelings I had felt, the things I had heard – the sense of Jack's lingering presence. I discovered a man called Dr Louis LaGrand. He'd spent over twenty-five years researching what he termed 'extraordinary experiences' and found over seventy million mourners who had experienced a similar thing to me.

I read on, feeling a sense of kinship, of hope. Apparently there were fourteen categories of extraordinary experiences ranging from feeling, hearing or seeing the loved one to having vivid dreams about them. I scrolled through multiple accounts from people who were convinced a loved one had visited them in their dreams. There were also categories for feeling you'd been touched, kissed, or embraced by the person. My face creased with pain. That was what I wanted, more than anything, to feel Jack's touch. His kiss.

I willed Jack to visit me tonight and I was certain it would happen because I wanted it so much.

I slipped into sleep, convinced he'd be waiting for me with open arms.

Chapter Twenty-Three

My sleep had been deep and uneventful. I woke at dawn, lay listlessly in bed, gazing out the window at the pink and orange streaked sky. Why hadn't I dreamed of Jack? I'd wanted it *so* much.

Jack.

I turned away from the window, away from the world with its colours and its beauty, hugging his pillow tight to my chest.

He felt further away than ever.

It was the sound of a heavy tread pressing against the gravel outside that made me reach for my dressing gown, a feeling of unease squirming in my belly. It was too early for the postman.

Who was outside?

Downstairs, I wrenched open the door as a figure disappeared out of sight.

On the step, my purse and laptop.

'Liam?'

I ran after him, the ground cold and damp beneath my bare feet.

'Liam, wait.'

He threw a panicked glance over his shoulder.

'Please,' I pleaded.

He slowed, stopped, his spine and shoulders rigid. Turned slowly to face me.

I wasn't sure what I wanted to say to him, how to convey that what I felt wasn't anger. I'd had a cold and empty place inside of me where trust used to sit before Kenny stabbed Jack and now Liam had returned my possessions he'd also handed me back a little of my faith that most people were inherently good.

It was a lot to say and so I simply said, 'Thank you.'

'You shouldn't thank me you should … I'm really sorry, Libby. I didn't take any cash from your purse. I just … I forgot to be more Jack.'

Immediately I was transported back to the funeral, to Sid's speech, to Liam's promise.

Neither of us spoke. He shoved his hands in his pockets and toed the path. The same path Jack had trod on, Jack with his hopes and his dreams and his longing to make the world a better place.

'I forgot too,' I whispered. 'I'm going to try, Liam. The centre. I can't promise but … I'm going to try and …'

'Be more Jack,' he said softly.

I nodded, my throat swollen with emotion.

After a beat I asked, 'How did you get here?'

'I walked. It took me ages.'

My heart ached for him as I imagined him trudging through country lanes in his worn trainers.

'Want a lift back to town?'

'You going to get dressed first?' He smiled.

Suddenly I became aware of the damp beneath my soles, the early morning air penetrating my thin candy-striped pyjamas. I wrapped my dressing gown tighter.

'Yes. I might even have breakfast. Fancy a bacon sandwich?'

'Yeah. I can make them while you get ready?'

'So you can cook?' I asked.

'I can fry.' He told me about his legendary sarnies as we walked back to the house – bacon, sausage, egg, mayo and ketchup.

Jack would have loved them.

Yesterday's rain had washed everything with a vibrancy, the fields a brilliant emerald, the rapeseed a dazzling yellow. Breeze from the open window ruffled my hair as I drove Liam to college, the radio playing TLC's 'Waterfalls'. I glanced across at him, wondering whether to tell him the story of when Jack and I visited a waterfall but he was lost in his own thoughts and I didn't think I could share that memory yet without crying.

Twenty minutes later I had dropped him at college and was ringing Noah's bell, hoping he'd be in.

'Hello?' A nervous-looking woman greeted me. She was probably around Mum's age, but without make-up, without hair dye covering up her grey, she appeared older.

'Is Noah here?' I asked.

'He's in the shower.' She didn't ask me in.

'Can I leave a note?'

'Yes. Of course. I'm Sandra, his mum.' She waited while I patted my pockets, knowing that I didn't have a pen or paper. 'I don't suppose you have something I can write with?'

After a brief pause she stepped back and let me inside. The hallway smelled of furniture polish.

'Come into the kitchen,' she said. It was impossible not to stare at the array of photos lining the walls, the childhood of Noah and Bethany spread out before me.

A beaming toddler with long blonde hair holding a baby.

Bethany and Noah at primary school, matching jumpers and toothy grins.

On a beach, striking a pose in front of a sparkling sea.

The last photo of Bethany was when she was around eighteen. There was the odd one of adult Noah after that, but the light from his eyes had gone. His smile had disappeared from view.

'How do you know Noah?' As she spoke his name he wandered into the room.

'Libby?' Noah filled the tiny remaining space. 'What are you doing here?' He threw a worried glance towards his mum. I smiled a reassuring I-haven't-upset-her smile.

'I wanted to ask you a favour, and pay you back for the paracetamol and Lucozade of course.'

'Oh …' Sandra's fingers found the silver locket around her neck and she began to twist it on its chain. 'Bethany and Noah used to love Lucozade,' she said.

'We did.' Noah's face was ashen as he ushered me towards the front door, calling a hurried 'See you later, Mum' to Sandra. 'Sorry. She gets upset at the thought of Bethany and she's quite unsettled by visitors. You really didn't need to pay me back. Do you fancy a coffee or something? You said you wanted a favour?' He studied me with kind eyes.

'Shall we go to the church? Is that too morbid? It's peaceful there. I can visit Jack and you can visit Bethany.'

A tortured expression briefly crossed Noah's face before he said, 'Of course. If that's what you want.'

We walked up to the church, after stopping at the Co-op for drinks on the way.

Lucozade.

On a whim I bought some pale pink roses for Jack's grave and once I'd placed them carefully in the flower holder, talking softly to Jack as I arranged them, I joined Noah on the bench, the wooden slats warmed by the sun.

'So … the favour?' he asked.

'I've decided to go ahead with the renovations on the house.'

'Wow. That's a positive thing to do.'

'I hope so. I veer between thinking it's a good thing and thinking I'm absolutely crazy.'

'It's a big place.'

'It is but one square, one room at a time.'

'You can't eat an elephant in one bite and all that.'

'Yep. I rang Faith. She was Jack's assistant; she was helping to set up the centre. She's given me some good tips and she's going to give me all the notes she'd made when she and Jack discussed it.'

'Is she coming back?'

'No. She said she'll email them. She's settling into her new home. Besides she told me that she and Michael are trying for a baby. Sorry, I'm oversharing.' I was veering off track. 'I was wondering if you'd help?'

'Me?'

'Yes. I didn't mean favour as in free. I know it's your job, I didn't even catch what trade you are when you came round to quote the day of the funeral. Please say you're a roofer.'

'I'm afraid not. I'm more of a decorator. I can paint your walls but you might need a plasterer before that, but there's no point doing that if the rain is going to leak through the tiles.'

'Right.' There was such a lot to do.

'Hey, don't looked so daunted. I didn't mean to put you

off. I'll come and have a look round. Help you make a plan. I'm between jobs right now, I had something fall through. It's exciting.'

'I don't feel excited. I feel like … like I'm trying to make amends. Do you ever feel guilty?'

'About?' he asked gingerly.

'I don't know what … how … I don't need to know what happened to Bethany but … I wasn't there when Jack died and yet I blame myself. Constantly.'

'It wasn't your fault,' Noah said.

'So people keep saying but he'd been out for me that day. To the chemist.'

'Libby.' There was such sadness in Noah's voice as he reached out and touched my arm.

'Is this too much? Talking about grief?' Sometimes I wanted to keep mine contained and hidden. Other times, like now, I wanted it to spill out.

'We can talk about whatever you want,' Noah said.

Jack.

We talked about Jack and it was comforting.

Later we wandered back to the Co-op and bought a couple of chicken pasta salads for lunch and I drove us back to the house. That was how I always referred to it now – *the* house. I couldn't say *our* house and I couldn't bear to call it *my* house. I hoped one day to call it home.

On the doorstep, I hesitated, key in hand.

'Are you okay?' Noah asked.

'Yes … It's just …' I couldn't quite put it into words.

'Just?'

I turned to face him, trying to tell him with my eyes what I couldn't with my voice.

'It feels strange, you bringing me back here?' he guessed.

I nodded.

'That's natural, Libby. This is yours and Jack's place.' He understood.

'It's not like I'm bringing you here as a man or anything, not that you're not a man of course, but I don't look at you like that and—'

'We don't have to do this today, if you're not ready,' he said gently.

No time like the present, Jack would have said.

'It's okay. I'm being—'

'Never apologise for your feelings, Libby,' Noah said. 'Christ, I don't know how you've coped. Jack going out for a Lemsip and then… it's a lot.'

'I'm not always sure if I am coping.'

'You're going to have highs and lows. Grief is a very personal experience. We don't have to tear everything down to start building it back up.'

I wasn't sure whether he was talking about the house, or about me. Either way it was reassuring.

We'd take it slowly.

Square by square.

'Socks?' I called as I clattered my keys into the china bowl. 'My cat,' I explained to Noah.

'Thank goodness for that. If you'd started talking to inanimate objects I'd be worried.'

'Are you hungry? Shall we eat first?'

'Let's pop the salads in the fridge. I can't wait to have a look around, this place is fabulous.'

'Why have you got an old skittle on your windowsill?' The question drew me away from my bleak thoughts.

'That was a housewarming gift from Sid. This was his house once.' I told Noah how we'd met Sid and the story of the beer bottle and skittle.

'He sounds a real character.'

'He is, if a tad too optimistic. He said this place just need a bit of tarting up.'

'Let's see what we can do, shall we?'

'I don't know where to begin.'

'Why don't you fetch a pen and pad and we can make a list.'

'I love a list.' It was familiar, cheering.

Armed with a notebook I led Noah upstairs and into what had once been Norma's hobby room. Sid had said that she'd sit on her rocking chair, unfinished quilt draped across her lap, gazing out across the fields as she stitched together her memories.

'If we do this room first there'll be somewhere for Alice, my sister, and the baby to come and stay. She's pregnant.'

'That's something to look forward to,' Noah said. 'I always wanted to be an uncle.' I knew he was thinking of Bethany.

He paced over to the window. 'This is a lovely big space. Nice and light. That looks like an original ceiling rose.' He crouched down. 'Do you mind if I peel off a bit of wallpaper?'

'No.'

The strip he tugged at came away easily in his hand, plaster crumbling to the floor.

'Thought so, it'll need plastering. Can I have a wander round upstairs?'

'Go ahead.' While he was gone I sat on the window seat, the lemon-checked cushion faded and flattened with age, and I wondered if Norma had made that too. I gazed down at the tangled garden below and while I waited for Noah to clatter back down the stairs I turned to a fresh page in the notebook and began to sketch some plans for the outside.

'It's a bit of a mess up there,' Noah said when he returned. 'You've got a leak, I'm sorry. So the first thing to do is to get someone to look at the roof before it causes irreparable damage. There's some mould too which we can try to treat; it might only be a recent thing because of the rain coming in, but we should get a professional to take a look. Structurally, otherwise it seems sound. You said you had a full survey so there shouldn't be anything too frightening to tackle. There's a lot of scope upstairs if you wanted to open the centre. Some of the rooms are big enough to add an en-suite or you could knock down some internal walls and—'

'Wait.' I held up my hands. It was disconcerting to hear of his plans, his constant use of 'we' tugged the control away from me and I grappled to retain my grip on it. 'Slow down.'

'Sorry. What would you like to do?'

'I'll contact a roofer and—'

'I can do that.'

It was tempting to let Noah take charge, to pass over the shell of Jack's dream and wait for him to hand it back to me when it was finished, wrapped with a shiny red bow but this was something I had to do myself.

'I'll arrange for the tradesmen to come out and once the roof is fixed and this room is plastered can you decorate please?'

'Yes. If you're getting the plasterer out though, it might be worth getting him to do a couple of rooms at once.'

'No.' I quoted Sid. 'It's a work in progress, not a race.'
Square by square.

After lunch, Noah left and I found myself drifting around the house from room to room, trying to see it through his eyes. I hadn't been up to the second floor since the day we had moved in when Jack had shown Alice around with boundless enthusiasm.

'It needs some work but we'll get there,' he had said. I lingered outside the room where I'd put some of his possessions that Rhonda and Bryan hadn't wanted and the 'Alethic' sign from the studio, the painting Faith had given me.

Biting down on the urge to cry I moved on to a small dark space at the back of the house. There were still some of Sid's things here in boxes, cardboard damp and disintegrating. Kneeling on the dusty floorboards I began to carefully lift things out to see if there was anything salvageable. I knew Sid hadn't been up to the second floor in years. A musty smell emanated from the scraps of material as I sporadically uncovered feathers, pebbles – Norma's crafting supplies. Nestled deep at the bottom of the box, wrapped in swathes of silk, a book, its soft leather cover the colour of marzipan.

Stretching out my legs, wriggling my toes to get rid of the pins and needles, I opened it. On the first page she had written a title in swirling letters.

Oh, Norma.

'There was a book. It was extraordinary. She was extraordinary,' Sid had said, and reading this I understood why. I picked up one of the pebbles, smooth and cold in my hand. If this was dropped into a pond the ripples would spread, creating a change below the surface that we couldn't always see.

That's what Norma created, a change.

I held the book to my chest as I rose to my feet. I needed to take it to Sid. 'It's been lost over time,' he had said wistfully. But now …

Finding it had given me faith. Everything lost can be found, can't it?

Everyone?

Chapter Twenty-Four

Sid was in the garden for once, alone, face upturned, catching the last of the day's sun.

Butterflies hovered around the buddleia, their pink wings fluttering around violet flowers. Apart from birdsong, it was quiet.

'Hello,' I called out as I approached, not wanting to startle him.

He waved. 'Libby, duck. This is a nice surprise.'

'Where is everyone?'

'Afternoon naps.' Sid shook his head. 'Honestly, old people. Lightweights, the lot of them.'

'I've found something.' Before I'd even sat down I was pulling the leather book out of my bag and handing it to him.

I sat onto edge of the chair, my knees bouncing up and down with excitement.

Sid took the book from me and tenderly stroked the cover before opening it up, turning the pages. I could see how overcome he was, his finger trembling as he ran it down the list. The rapid movement of his Adam's apple as he kept swallowing his emotion back down.

'This is the book you meant? The extraordinary book you told me about the day you showed me Norma's quilt? It has Book of Kindness written inside the cover.'

'Yes.' There was a crack in his voice. He cleared his throat, began to cough. He reached for his packet of Polos and took his time peeling back the wrapper, composing himself while he took a mint and placed it into his mouth.

'There was a time Norma had … the blues we called it then. Guess you'd call it depression now. It wasn't talked about much then, it was shameful, not like now, all that hashtag mental health and whatnot.'

'Sid! Where did you learn about hashtags?'

'One of the carers put that tweeting thing on me new phone so I can keep up to date with what's what, you know, what's … trendy? Trending? Not that I use it much. Bunch of people being offended by everything far as I can see. But anyway. Perhaps it's a good thing talking about things that bother you. Norma … well it was after we found out we weren't ever going to be blessed with kiddies. She took it hard.'

'I'm so sorry.'

'Life ain't all beer and skittles but knowing that … well it didn't help none. One day I bought her this book. Thought it might help her to write her feelings down, keep a diary like, but instead she wanted to use it for something else. "I can't keep thinking of myself all the time, I've got a lot to be grateful for, Sid. I've got you," she said. "I'm going to start doing nice things for other people and I'm going to write them down so when … if … I'm feeling sad I can think that perhaps, in some small way, I've made a mark in this world."' Sid lowered his head, sniffed hard, took his time before he spoke again. 'She made a mark on my world,' was all he could say.

'What a lovely thing to do. May I?' I reached for the book and Sid slid it across to me. I began to read aloud.

22 January 1966 – Mrs Wilson – cleared her drive of snow.

'Mrs Wilson had the farm down the lane,' Sid expanded. 'Her husband had died and she was all alone.'

I picked another entry, *1 March 1966 – Fred Haycock – wedding dress.*

'His daughter was getting married and he couldn't afford to buy her a decent frock so Norma cut her wedding dress up and fashioned her something new. She kept a scrap of it herself though, for her quilt.'

I read on. *11 March 1966 – Joey Watson – milk & blackberries.*

'Ah now, little Joey Watson. The milk had been going missing off our step for weeks when Norma stayed up half the night to see who was taking it. It was Joey. He were only a lad, about twelve. "Sorry." He hung his head in shame. "Me mum can't afford milk and I've three younger sisters and …" "Take it," Norma said. "I ain't no charity case." Joey was indignant. "Well you can help me pick the fruit and I'll pay you a fair wage and you can buy your own milk." And that's what happened. She saw the good, Norma, see. Much like Jack.'

'Jack certainly saw the good in everyone. Everyone had written off most of those kids he taught. Thought they were nothing but trouble.'

'Nobody is completely one thing,' Sid said. 'And boys … well I got in some scrapes when I was younger. Had the odd fight.'

'Liam's been in a punch-up.'

'Reckon he's lost his way a bit again. Poor lad. How's college going for him?'

'He's not going as much as he should; the course isn't what he thought it would be and …' I didn't want to betray Liam but I trusted Sid. 'He also stole my laptop and purse yesterday.

He returned it though. He … he wants to help with the house. The centre.'

'And you? What do you want to do?'

Be more Jack.

Be more Norma.

'I could find him *something* to do. As long as he keeps up with his coursework. I don't want to be responsible for him getting kicked out of college.'

'I'm sure he could do his assignments *and* work part-time. Some of the carers here are students. Spend more time out of college than in it. The trust could pay Liam a wage, give him a bit of self-respect. Might do wonders for him.'

'It could be the making of him. What could he do?'

'What about gardening? That's an honest day's work.'

'Perhaps. I've been mulling over some plans for outside. I'll show you.' I fished into my bag for my notebook and showed him my earlier sketch where I mapped out everything at the back of the house, marking the sprawling lavender, the apple tree. 'What do you think?'

'I think Jack definitely had the talent for drawing.' Sid pointed at the page. 'What are those sticks poking out from under the clouds?'

'They're legs! It's the sheep in the field beyond the garden …' I realised from his smile he'd been teasing me. 'Why don't you, Mr Discovered-I'd-a-talent-for-art-at-eighty, draw instead?' I turned to a clean page.

Sid picked up the pen and slowly, carefully began to draw what he could obviously still see in his mind's eye.

'Here' – he tapped to the left of the house with his finger – 'was Norma's herb garden. I'd built her a little rockery and in between the stones she grew parsley for the sauce for our Friday night haddock, sage for the stuffing for our roast, and thyme she'd sprinkle over a rack of lamb. There were others too. We kept the mint in a pot of its own, mind. It'll take over if you don't keep it contained.'

Since I lost Jack I'd been living mainly on M&S ready meals or the kindness of Mum and Alice. It might be nice to cook from scratch again. Fresh basil leaves shredded onto spaghetti. Now I was focusing on the future, I could start looking after myself properly.

'You want things that are easily maintained. The lavender under the windows has probably gone all leggy. Cut it right back and see how it fares. Norma used to make little bags out of it and put in our drawers. Here' – Sid pointed – 'was a pond. Norma always wanted one but I'd covered it when the herons kept snatching the fish, bloody things. I'd put netting over the surface too but that didn't stop them. You could uncover it?'

'But Socks might take a swipe at the fish. Besides, what if he fell in?' I loved that cat with all my heart; the thought of anything happening to him was unbearable.

'Cats ain't daft. They ain't keen on water so he'll stay away.'

'What else did Norma like?' I wanted to remain true to her vision.

For the rest of the afternoon Sid taught me about plants, the things that would grow in the soil, the things that would perish.

I was buoyant when I left, feeling that the past couple of days I'd taken my first teetering steps into the future, not away from Jack – working on the house and the garden would keep him close. I couldn't wait to get started, couldn't wait to ask Liam to help. I didn't know where he lived so on a whim I drove around the town, slowing down each time I passed a group of teenagers congregating outside a shop or kicking a ball around a car park until at last I saw a cluster of kids I knew had been at the funeral.

I wound down my window. 'Is Liam around?'

'What's it to you?' one of them said.

'Are you Mrs Jack?' another asked.

The words hit me in the heart. 'I am.' *Still. Always.* 'Do you know where Liam is?'

'Is he in trouble?'

'No, just the opposite. I have good news for him.'

I was given his address, a part of town where I'd never ventured before.

I heard the shouting before I'd knocked on the front door. Loud angry voices.

It was a woman who yanked open the door. The smell of deep-fried food came at me. She eyed me confrontationally, smoke spiralling from a cigarette in her hand. She was older than she looked under the bleached blonde hair and thick layer of make-up. 'Yeah?' As she spoke the stench of stale alcohol wafted from her breath. It wasn't that I thought Liam had a happy home life, but seeing her, the state of the flat beyond, made me want to whisk him away from all of this.

'Are you Liam's mum?'

'Are you from the college? He said he didn't have no lectures—'

'I'm not from the college.'

'Copper? What's the little bastard done now?' She scowled. 'Oi, Liam!' she hollered.

When he appeared and saw me, the colour drained from his face.

'He hasn't done anything wrong,' I said quickly, picking up on his fear. 'In fact, I want to offer him a job.'

'A job? This lazy thieving toerag can't …' She rearranged her features. 'How much you paying? He's loving his course and if you expect him to drop out—'

'I don't. This would be part-time and I'm sure Liam and I can come to some arrangement. That's if you're interested?' I smiled at him. 'Helping me with the house and the garden.'

'Umm. Whatever.' He shrugged. 'Yeah.'

'Do you have lectures tomorrow?'

'No.'

'Great. We'll sort the details out then? I can pick you up at nine?'

There was a crash from inside the flat. Liam's mum stalked away.

He stared at his shoes. 'Yeah, great. Thanks, Libby. For a minute I thought you'd come to tell Mum I'd nicked your stuff.'

'You brought it back. No harm done.'

'And you really want me to help? This isn't a wind-up is it?'

'No, Liam. I promise.' I offered my hand and he shook it.

'To being more Jack.' He smiled.

'Bring some old clothes because you'll probably get filthy,' I said.

His smile dropped and too late I took in his too-short tracksuit bottoms and tight shirt, realised he wore virtually the same things all of the time.

At home, in my bedroom, I slid open a drawer, my breath catching in my throat at the sight of Jack's things: neatly folded jumpers and T-shirts, clothes for seasons he would never see again. Rhonda and Bryan hadn't asked for them and I hadn't offered.

I unfolded a blue-and-white-striped shirt, remembering the

time I had slipped it on after a shower, hair in a loose bun, padding barefoot to find Jack, leaning against the wall as I watched him paint, noticing the contours in his muscles each time he moved his arm from palette to canvas. He'd caught sight of me and gasped, he actually gasped, and that one sound was so full of wanting I could scarcely breathe as his frenzied fingers undid my buttons, his mouth on my neck, my mouth, back to my neck. My back arching, the shirt crumpled on the floor.

Now I hugged it tightly to me. I couldn't bear to see someone else wearing this, but the rest?

That pebble in the pond, the ripple effect. A small gesture that might mean the world to Liam.

'Should I give some bits to Liam, Jack?' I closed my eyes, focusing on the extraordinary experiences I was obsessed with reading about. I felt a change in the air. A sudden drop in temperature.

I thought I heard Jack whisper 'yes' but when I opened my eyes there was nobody there.

Chapter Twenty-Five

The sky was cloudless, an optimistic blue, the sun gilding the edges of the buildings. Liam was outside his block of flats, bouncing up and down on the balls of his feet while he waited for me. He looked far younger than sixteen as he walked uncertainly towards the car, rucksack slung over his shoulder, his expression a blend of anticipation and nerves. I thought about The Hawley Foundation Prize, how a photo of Liam right here, right now, would capture the theme of hope perfectly.

'Morning,' I said brightly, while he clipped in his seatbelt.

The radio was playing Nineties hits.

'Do you want to change the station?' I asked him.

'Nah.' He scratched his chin. 'It's fine.'

'This can't be your sort of music?'

Liam shrugged. 'I really don't mind it. Faith played this old stuff at the studio.'

'Did she?'

'Yeah, she was obsessed with S Club 7.'

He lowered his gaze to his mobile, thumbs flying over the keypad and as I drove my thoughts wandered to Faith. Since she'd emailed me her notes on hers and Jack's plans we'd exchanged multiple messages, grown closer in a way than we were when she lived here. She was lonely, not having yet made new friends. Was it strange that I knew her new neighbours argued late at night, that she hadn't yet fallen pregnant and was worried she had left it too late at almost forty to have a baby, but I didn't know she loved sugar-sweet pop songs?

Do we ever properly know someone?

At the house I could feel the tremble in my voice as I said to Liam as nonchalantly as I could, 'I've put some things of Jack's in the bathroom so your stuff doesn't get ruined. Some joggers and tops.' I shrugged as though it wasn't a big deal, as though my heart was not hammering out of my chest.

'Cool. Thanks.'

By the time Liam came back downstairs, I had steeled myself for the fact that he'd be wearing Jack's Levi's T-shirt but the reality of it almost floored me, the knot of grief inside of me pulled tighter and tighter by the sight before me. Self-consciously, Liam fiddled with the drawstring around the waistband of the joggers.

A knock on the door was a welcome relief.

'Noah …' I ushered him quickly inside. 'Meet Liam. He is … he was one of Jack's painting students. He's going to be helping us out. Liam, Noah's a decorator.'

Noah held out his hand and Liam hesitated before he shook it. There was an awkwardness I couldn't quite decipher. It was up to me to put them at ease but I couldn't tear my eyes away from that T-shirt. It had rendered me mute.

We stood in an uncomfortable triangle.

'You've got this, Libs,' Jack's voice whispered, his breath against my cheek. With one last lingering look at the top, which hung looser on Liam's boyish frame than it had on Jack's, I wrenched my eyes back to Noah's face and forced a smile.

'Shall we spend the morning working out what materials we need? And then check out the garden? Liam, outside is where you'll be most use. There's a lot of prep to be done. Sid drew some plans yesterday: I'll show you. There's a shed Sid says is full of tools but I can imagine they're rusty.'

The next few hours were spent jotting down everything we needed to make a start. The list was long. Already I was worried about the budget. That wasn't the only thing troubling me. Noah and Liam were so distant.

'That's pretty much everything,' Noah said when we were back in the kitchen.

I dropped the pad and pen onto the windowsill and linked my arms together, stretching out my tense shoulders.

'That's been productive,' I said. 'Noah has some great ideas, doesn't he, Liam?'

'Suppose.' Liam was picking at his thumbnail.

'And, Liam, you'll be such a great help. Won't he, Noah?' I raised my eyebrows at Noah.

'Um, Yes. Think you'll enjoy it, Liam?'

Again, that shrug.

I was despairing. I knew it was early days but I'd pictured us as the Three Musketeers. In this together. They had barely spoken.

Liam's stomach rumbled. I checked my watch.

'How about I make us some lunch and you two can talk about football or something?'

'Don't like sport,' Liam said.

'What about gaming?'

'I'm not into consoles,' said Noah.

'Right.' It was such a strain. 'What do you fancy to eat? I've some sausages? Bacon? Eggs?'

'All of the above?' Noah smiled.

'In one sandwich,' added Liam. 'With ketchup and—'

'Mayo?' Noah held up his hand and Liam high-fived it. 'Why don't you let us boys rustle up lunch?'

Before I could answer, Liam was already retrieving the frying pan from the cupboard, Noah lifting eggs from the fridge. Finally they had bonded and all it had taken was a shared appreciation for fried food. I was infinitely happier as I turned away. 'I'll be back soon.'

'Libby?' Liam called me as I was leaving the room. 'Do you mind if I change the radio station?'

'You said in the car you didn't mind Nineties music?' I raised my eyebrows.

'It's a bit shit.'

In the snug I picked up the picture of Jack and traced his smile with a light fingertip.

'You'd have loved this,' I whispered. Laughter floated from the kitchen. It was the first time the house had resembled anything like a home. The Beatles began to play 'In My Life', Liam must have retuned the radio, and I sat down heavily on the sofa, the photo frame cold in my hand. Socks leaped onto my lap and butted his head against my arm until I began to stroke him soothingly, rhythmically, until the song had finished. I wiped my damp cheeks with my sleeve and made my way back into the kitchen. The radio was now playing rap. I glanced at it, questioning what I'd just heard.

In my life.

Our song.

I love you more.

'Sit yourself down, Libby, and prepare for a taste sensation!' Liam placed a plate in front of me with a magician's flourish while Noah draped a piece of kitchen towel over my lap.

'Madam …' He began to pour from a teapot. 'This is our vintage PG Tips.'

I took a sip. 'Exquisite.'

The hob was swimming with grease, oil splattered the tiles, cracked eggshells were strewn over the worktops but I didn't care, thankful that Noah and Liam were chatting easily.

'I wish I could paint,' Noah said. 'Pictures I mean.'

'Have you ever tried to work on a canvas?' Liam asked.

'No.'

'There you go. I'd never have thought I was creative until Jack gave me a chance.'

'He was a good man,' Noah said. 'From what I've heard.'

'The best.' Liam was wistful. He squeezed the bread tighter in his hand, mayo-streaked ketchup spilling down his white T-shirt. Jack's T-shirt. Garbled apologies rushed towards me.

'Sorry. Shit. Sorry, Libby, I'll—'

'I don't mind. Honestly.' I placed my hand on his arm. We were both shaking.

'But—'

My mobile began to ring, cutting off Liam's distress.

Sid.

'Hello!' His face filled my screen. He'd become so adept at FaceTiming. 'I was thinking about yesterday, duck. I didn't want you to feel pressured into tackling the garden and the—'

'We've already started,' I said. 'Sid, this is Noah.' I angled the camera around so Sid could see him. 'He's a decorator I met when … well, he's going to help me project-manage—'

'Project-manage! Get you!' Sid laughed which triggered a coughing fit. I waited for him to grab a Polo and compose himself.

'And of course you know Liam.' Liam stood behind me and waved.

'Hello, lad. It's good to see you.'

'You too. I'm …' I could hear the catch in Liam's voice.

'You're being more Jack,' Sid said. 'I know you are, lad, I know.'

'Libby said you've offered to pay me a part-time wage out of the trust. I won't let you down.'

'Too bloody right you won't. I'll be over soon to see what you've done.'

'It'll be a while until it's finished, Sid!' I said.

'Don't underestimate yourself, girl. All it needs is a lick of paint.'

After we'd eaten we were more relaxed.

'There's not a lot we can do until we've got the materials,' Noah said. 'How about I head off and pick up what we need and we can regroup tomorrow. Want to come with me, Liam? Give me a hand? And then I could drop you home? Where do you live?'

'The flats on Bain Rise.'

'In town then. I can pick you up in the morning if you want?'

'Yeah. Cheers.'

'If you want to change your top before you leave I'll try get that stain out?' I said to Liam and after he'd left I held Jack's T-shirt against my heart and hurried towards the sink.

*

Later, the Levi's T-shirt hung on the washing line. I'd scrubbed it until my knuckles were raw and red and finally the ketchup had shifted.

I pottered around the garden before dusk whisked away the remaining light. At the bottom of the plot, right where Sid said it would be, I uncovered a rusty bench. From the shed I fetched the shears and secateurs which were stiff through lack of use, and using force I carefully cut away the bush that had engulfed the seat before I scrubbed it with hot water and soap. It was still ginger with rust but at least it was clean. That night I carried out a cushion and a glass of wine and I sat in the same place Sid had told me he had sat with Norma at the end of a summer's day. Landscapes had changed enormously in the majority of towns through the passage of time but here the sheep remained the constant. The sky turned from pink to lavender to grey as my thoughts floated towards Jack. About the future we thought we might have and the future I could have. The possibilities that this project might bring.

Deep in thought I barely noticed the sense of someone sitting beside me until I drained my glass.

'Jack?'

I looked intently into the space beside me where he should be. Held my breath.

The wind in my hair, the soft bleat of sheep.

He was all around me and yet he was nowhere.

The next few weeks rolled by. My emotions were fierce and frenzied; despair I was doing this without Jack, bursts of joy as his plans took shape. Fatigue gripped me – a tiredness that seemed to bury itself deep into my bones but a desire to keep going, to keep building on the progress we'd made.

Pride.

I felt closer to Jack than ever, his sweet words of encouragement streaming into my ears while I slept. When I woke I'd catch glimpses of light in darkened corners.

Each night I pulled on one of his T-shirts and sprayed his aftershave onto his pillow.

Come to me in my dreams, I urged, desperate for another of the extraordinary experiences I had become an expert on. I was certain that if he was filling my mind when I went to sleep then he would surely fill my dreams.

But you know what they say.

Be careful what you wish for.

Chapter Twenty-Six

The August heat was sweltering.

It was nine weeks since we'd started and I was already in the garden when Liam arrived, carefully carrying a plant in his hands.

'This is for you, Libby.'

'We're supposed to be giving you presents today. Happy birthday, Liam.' I smiled. 'Seventeen!'

He blushed as he thrust the pot towards me.

'It's beautiful.' I crouched to sniff the red roses with the white centre.

'It's from me and Noah,' Liam said, self-consciously. 'It's called "Little Artist".'

I swept him into a hug. 'It's perfect, thank you.'

He wriggled from my grasp. 'It isn't just from me.'

'I shall make sure I thank Noah. It's great how close you've become.' Since that awful, awkward first day they'd formed a strong bond, almost brotherly.

'Yeah well.' In a rare open moment he said, 'You know, I thought after me dad running off and meeting Mum's boyfriends that most men were, you know, wankers but Noah, he's all right. Not as nice as Jack of course. Nor Sid, but you know?'

'He's not a wanker.'

'No.' Liam grinned. 'I can plant the rose under the kitchen window then you'll see it every day.'

'Great, thanks. Where is Noah? Do you want your presents first?'

'He's inside. I'll have them later, I want to crack on.' He was uncomfortable being the centre of attention.

He stripped off his T-shirt and, as always, I automatically handed him a bottle of sun cream.

'Yes, Mum,' he said with a theatrical sigh, but he slathered himself in the lotion without complaint. I think he liked being looked after, and that's what we were doing, looking after each other. A family of sorts. Over the past few weeks various tradesmen had come and gone but Liam and Noah had been my constant. Noah picked up Liam every day when he wasn't at college and drove him over. The roof was repaired. The rooms on the first floor had been plastered. The sash windows on the second floor with the rotting frames, replaced. The woodwork elsewhere rubbed down. At every stage I had taken photos, a reminder – on the days when everything seemed too hard, for I still got days where, without Jack, everything seemed too mountainous – not to give up.

Initially I'd planned to be inside, sanding, painting, but the garden is where I'd found my peace. Working alongside Liam, sometimes talking, sometimes not, but our silence was easy, both of us working through our issues. Often, in my head I spoke to Jack as I hoed and raked the garden, carefully pulled back weeds to discover tender shoots of plants Sid or Norma might have planted, vowing to nurture them. We all needed nurturing sometimes. The pain of losing Jack would come in waves and it was during the periods of intense emotion I would drive my fork into the ground harder and harder. Several times I'd been overcome with dizziness, losing my balance. I was overdoing it, but it was cathartic. At the end of every day I texted a photo to Sid or FaceTimed him. Today he'd be seeing the house for the first time since I'd begun the renovations.

Upstairs, the radio was playing Chuck Berry's 'You Never Can Tell'. Noah was strutting across the room, paint tins swinging from his hands, head bopping to the beat. I could feel the smile form on my face. He must have sensed my presence because he spun round, cheeks colouring.

'I was just tidying up before I fetch Sid.'

'You've got some pretty fancy moves there, Noah.'

He put down the paint and beckoned me to him.

'Oh no.' I started to back away but he raced forward, taking my hand, spinning me round. 'Noah.' But my protest was weak, my feet already moving in time. Our steps in sync, mimicking each other's moves, falling into the scene from *Pulp Fiction*, Noah working his Travolta hips and me momentarily feeling as sassy as Uma Thurman as our eyes remained fixed on each other. The track finished and Noah caught me around the waist and swung me around. I wriggled from his grasp, spell broken, no longer Uma but Libby, grief overshadowing those pure, unadulterated three minutes of fun. Noah's face fell.

'Go and fetch Sid,' I said softly and he opened his mouth but then he turned away without speaking, his footsteps echoing on the wooden stairs.

I clicked the radio off.

*

While I waited for Noah to return with Sid I paced, a writhing mass of nerves in my stomach. I so wanted Sid to love what we'd done so far. Had we done enough? Too much? Retained the heart or stripped it away? By the time Noah pulled up outside, my hands were clammy, my knees weak.

The warmth was stifling as I hovered in the open doorway, watching Sid drink in every detail as he walked slowly towards the front door.

'I'm glad you're here and I can show you everything before we leave for the restaurant. I say everything but we haven't started on the front garden yet. Or the downstairs. Perhaps I should—'

'Perhaps you should relax, duck. I ain't here to judge you. It's … being back here, it feels …'

'Strange?'

'Like home. It feels like home, young Elizabeth. This is where my last memories of Norma are. Your last memories of Jack.' He took my hand. I could feel the tremble in his that had nothing to do with age. 'I ain't one for spirits and all that but …' He cast his gaze slowly around. 'I can feel them here, Jack and Norma. Just like I feel them here too.' He placed one palm over his chest and as I nodded, I placed my free hand over my own chest.

'Let's get inside. See what you've done to the place.'

It took an age for Sid to climb the stairs; when he reached the top, sweat had plastered his hair to his scalp. He hunched over the bannister, gathering his breath.

I crooked my arm and he took it and we slowly shuffled into the first room. Norma's craft room.

Sid sank gratefully into the rocking chair by the open window, his watery eyes scanning the room, the floral pink wallpaper that was a nod to Sid and Norma's bedroom.

'She'd sit here, gazing out at the fields, her fingers busy, knitting, sewing, never having to look what she was doing. She'd just *know*. It was the same with me; if something was wrong I wouldn't have to say anything. She'd just *know*. She was intuitive like that. Like your Jack. She'd have loved him.'

'He'd have loved her, the way he loved you. I'm sorry you lost her, that you've had to live without her.'

'But, Libby, if I weren't living without her then she'd be living without me and I wouldn't wish the pain of that on anyone. It's hard, being the one left, but Norma was always at peace in this room. Fixing things. Making things. She'll be at peace now.'

We fall into perfect quiet, broken only by the occasional squawk of a bird, a buzz of a bumble bee.

'Are you going to use this room as accommodation for the retreat?' he asked eventually.

'No. I'm not sure what I'm going to do with all the rooms yet, particularly that small one off the kitchen. Remember you told me on moving-in day how you and Norma would sit in there eating her scones. But I know what this one is for. It's for Alice when she wants to stay, Alice and her daughter.' She'd found out the sex at the last scan.

'A new life.' Sid smiled. 'Norma would like that. I like what you've done, Elizabeth, what you're doing. Keep going and you'll get there.'

'Square by square.' Standing behind him I squeezed his shoulder and he linked his fingers through mine.

'Square by square.'

The restaurant was blissfully cool, the air conditioning wafting the aroma of curry, sweet and savoury spices hanging heavy in the air. Noah was pouring the wine; there was so much to toast, to be grateful for.

I raised my glass to the reason we were here. 'Happy birthday, Liam.'

We chinked our glasses together. Liam pulled a face as he took tentative sips of the chilled Chablis, screwing his face up as he swallowed.

'Would you rather have something else?' I asked.

He watched as Noah drank from his glass and then he took another gulp. 'Nah. It ain't bad when you get used to it,' he conceded.

'Seventeen. The things you can do at seventeen, lad,' Sid said.

'Like what?'

'My dad were in the Army at seventeen,' Sid replied.

'I can't imagine being in a war,' Liam said. 'It's so brave.'

'It is but we don't always choose the situations we're in and yet we find the courage to face them. Bravery comes in many different forms, Liam lad. Libby here, doing up the house. Noah, carrying on after the loss of his sister, Bethany. Sorry, Noah. Hope you don't mind that Libby told me?'

Noah went as white as the tablecloth. 'Don't,' he said quietly. 'Don't call me brave. I'm not.'

'But—'

'I reckon we should give Liam here his presents.' Sid cut me off, changing the subject, handing a gift over to Liam. Liam unwrapped a battered leather box. Inside were two shiny medals.

'These were me dad's. I had them cleaned for you.'

'For me?' Liam shook his head in disbelief. 'Why? I ain't your family or nothing.'

'Family comes in all different shapes and sizes, Liam lad.

Bravery too. These medals will remind you of both of these things.' Sid's eyes met mine. *I was going to give them to Jack*, they told me. *I know*, mine replied.

'Now mine.' I gently set a mahogany box in front of him. I hadn't sent everything of Jack's to Rhonda and Bryan.

'What's this?' Liam opened it. 'Are these …' He looked up at me questioningly.

'I bought them for Jack, for our anniversary. He … he never got a chance to use them.'

'I can't take them.' Liam ran his fingers over the maple handles of the paint brushes.

'You can and you must. What you're doing at the house is great. You've got a real eye for space and the garden wouldn't look half as good without your input but you have a talent, Liam. Jack knew that and he'd want you to have these. I know the college course isn't what you'd hoped for but don't give up on art. Jack would want you to paint. Okay?'

Liam nodded – he'd give it his best shot – and I squeezed his shoulder. 'I know that you will.'

Noah and I exchanged an I'm-so-proud look.

'I'm giving you the gift of memories,' Noah told Liam. 'We're booked in the bowling alley in forty-five minutes. As it's your birthday, I might let you win.' He grinned. 'But don't count on it.'

While we ate I took some candid shots, using my camera because I wanted to, rather than because I felt I should. Realising this made me think fleetingly again of The Hawley Foundation Prize. Could I still enter my work?

The doors to the kitchen swung open and Liam was visibly overcome as the waiter carried out a huge chocolate cake dotted with seventeen silver candles. His eyes glazed, bottom lip trembling. Having a birthday cake was something I'd always taken for granted; from Liam's expression I wasn't sure he could claim the same.

At the bowling alley Sid opted to go last. Noah and I both knocked down five pins each, Liam two.

'I've never played before,' he said. 'Me mum always said it's too expensive.'

'I'll show you how to throw next time,' Noah said.

'I'll teach you how it's done.' Sid rose unsteadily to his feet.

'Have you bowled before?'

'No. But how hard can it be?'

'Do you want the ramp, Sid?' Noah asked.

'I ain't a baby.' Sid tested the weight of the balls, opting for the lightest orange one, and then shuffled to the line at the end of the lane. He swung his arm back and forth, somehow losing his grip on the ball which flew down the adjourning lane much to the bemusement of the couple using it. Somehow, it gave Sid a strike. I grabbed my camera and took a photo of his triumphant fist pump in the air.

'Did I win?' he asked when he turned around.

We were laughing too much to reply.

Later, I sat alone in the garden on Sid's bench, replaying the day in my mind. Smiling as I remembered Sid's unorthodox method of bowling. Jack would have loved it. Once more, as I thought about him I had a sense of him beside me but of course he wasn't.

If he had been there he'd have spoken. Not of bowling but he'd have told me that tomorrow I'd say something that was inconceivable. Unforgivable. Something I would always regret. He'd have asked me to think before I spoke. But even if there was such a thing as spirits, even though I thought I'd heard him before, he didn't speak.

He didn't warn me.

And so I said it. Oh God, I said *that* thing I could never take back.

Today, still, I hate myself for it.

Chapter Twenty-Seven

My stomach was still swollen with curry and birthday cake the next morning. The lingering taste of cumin and chocolate on my tongue. I worked in the garden alone. I'd told Noah and Liam not to rush in today and it was almost eleven by the time they arrived.

'Morning.'

They sat at the table while I filled the kettle. My head was pounding and I'd only had one glass of wine with the meal and a beer at the bowling alley. Thank goodness it was Friday.

'Phase one is complete then,' Noah said.

'It is.' Steam swirled around my face as I tipped water into mugs.

'What's next?' Noah looked at me expectantly as I distributed the drinks.

'I don't know.' I was bone-weary. I blew against my coffee wishing I'd made a cold drink; everything was too hot, humid, it made my thoughts impossible to decipher.

'We've all earned some time off. Shall we take a break next week? It'll give me some time to plan the next stage.'

'I could help you make a plan?' Dejected, Liam clattered his half-eaten digestive back onto his plate.

'Go and have some fun, Liam. There's no college for a few weeks.'

'But—'

'I'll still pay you. You are entitled to holiday pay,' I added quickly before he could tell me he didn't want charity.

'It's not the money, it's …' He stared miserably at the table, jabbing biscuit crumbs with his finger.

'It's just a few days,' I said gently. 'This isn't the end. Take some time for yourself, do some drawing or painting.'

'Whatever.' He shrugged.

My eyes met Noah's in a question and as I rose from the table and headed upstairs he followed me.

'Will Liam be okay next week?' I asked when we were alone.

'He'll be fine. I'll take him to the cinema. We both want to see the new Marvel film. We can go for a pizza after.'

'That's so kind of you.'

'Not really. He's like a little brother to me. An *annoying* little brother at times but he's a good kid.'

'I guess it must feel odd? No, that's the wrong word. But growing up with a sibling and then becoming an only child.'

'Liam isn't a replacement for Bethany.'

'No. Of course not. Just it's nice for Liam to have a role model and…' I didn't quite know how to finish. Had I said the wrong thing?

For a moment we were quiet. Noah took a step towards me but still we didn't speak.

'I suppose I'm coming to think of us as a family,' I said eventually.

'A dysfunctional one,' Noah said, but his tone was light. 'I really enjoyed yesterday.'

'Me too. Even if I did need to duck every time Sid took his turn, just in case.'

We both laughed but then he was suddenly serious.

'Libby.' His eyes met mine but I didn't understand what they were expressing that he couldn't say.

But the way he looked at me …

In my head I could hear the music from yesterday, the intensity of our dance.

It didn't mean anything.

A shiver snaked down my spine. 'Libby,' he said again, softly. He moved closer, gently smoothed my hair away from my face. I could feel his warm breath against my skin, my lips. My heart galloped with a fear he was about to ruin everything by trying to kiss me.

He wouldn't try to kiss me, would he?

I couldn't move. I didn't want him but his palm felt soft against my cheek. I placed my hand upon it. I'd missed being touched.

Touching someone.

'Libby?' We sprang apart at Alice's voice, my heart pounding, cheeks burning as if we'd done something wrong. 'Liam said you were up here. Oh, hello, Noah.'

'Alice. You haven't seen this room finished, have you? Do you like it?'

'It's amazing!'

'I've got to go. I'll see you in a week.' Noah slipped away before I could speak. Flustered I turned my attention to my sister who was rocking in the chair I'd bought, gazing out over the fields.

'It's so peaceful here,' she said.

'Well this room is yours. Yours and the baby's whenever you want to stay.'

'You'll love her, won't you? Whatever?'

'Alice, of course I'll love her. I can't wait to be an auntie and what's all this "*whatever*"? Your midwife isn't concerned about anything is she?' Up until now all the appointments had gone well.

'No, it's just … promise me you'll never judge her.'

'Alice, you're worrying me.'

She lifted her hair from her neck before letting it drop. 'Ignore me, I'm sweltering. Being pregnant in August isn't fun. How can it be this hot before midday?'

'There's a fan in the snug. Want to sit in front of it?'

She nodded.

'I'm just going to grab a shower and get changed. I'm covered in soil. I'll be down as soon as I can and we can have an early lunch.' I wanted to wash away Noah's gaze. His touch. The words he did not say. Did he see me as more than a friend? If Alice hadn't interrupted would he have tried to kiss me?

Would I have let him? I dismissed that thought immediately. I never wanted to kiss anyone but Jack.

But still, I covered my cheek with my own hand, feeling the warmth of his palm upon my skin.

I was notably cooler, dressed in clean shorts and T-shirt, when I went downstairs but I was still feeling rough. The relentless heat and too many thoughts making my head pound. I could hear the loud whirr of the fan. Inside the snug Alice was oblivious to my approach. She had a photo of Jack in her hands and she was crying.

'I don't know how to tell her, Jack.'

I was hit by a bolt of fear. 'Alice?' My voice was so low and gravely it was unfamiliar. 'Tell me what?'

'Nothing,' she said defensively.

'It must be something. What?'

She shook her head. 'I can't.'

'It can't be that bad?'

'It is.' She couldn't look at me.

What? What did she mean? I ran through things in my mind; what was the worst thing I could possibly think of?

It hurt as it barged into my mind. I didn't really believe it for a second but she wouldn't talk and I couldn't stop putting two and two together, coming up with entirely the wrong answer. And her silence made my treacherous mind fork over the possibility even more.

Jack and Alice.

Again I shoved the notion away; it was ridiculous, impossible and yet Alice sat before me, covering her face with her hands.

I had to be wrong though, Jack wouldn't do that. Alice wouldn't do that, would she?

Do we ever properly know anyone?

My mind cast back, Alice at the twelve-week scan. 'Artistic! He'll take after Jack.'

Faith's text. 'Have you spoken to Libby yet?' She'd explained this away with the Norfolk painting but what if she were covering up for Alice? Preserving Jack's memory.

I jumped forward again; today Alice had been strange, making me promise I'd love my niece, that I wouldn't judge her.

Wouldn't judge her for what? Her mother's mistakes?

I didn't feel the words rise from my gut, words I would never be able to take back. They formed their toxic shape on my tongue. I didn't even know if I believed it when I asked, 'Alice, is Jack the father of your baby?'

The very second I accused Alice of sleeping with Jack I knew I was wrong. I wanted to grab the hateful words with my fists and stuff them back into my mouth and that was before I saw her face crumple.

I'd hurt the person I loved most in the world, immeasurably, and all I could do was apologise.

Where had that come from? Why did I say it? It was like I wasn't in charge of my own thoughts, my own words.

'I didn't mean that. I've been … It's grief. I get these odd moods, irrational thoughts, I'm sorry.'

'So am I, Libby. I'm sorry that you … you think that … that *Jack* is … that me and *Jack* …' She swiped away angry tears.

'But …' My thoughts were muddled, I couldn't think clearly. Why wasn't she denying it? 'He's not …' I waited for her to say no. 'Is he?' I couldn't stop the question bursting from my mouth again.

'No. No he isn't but … fuck you, Libby. Fuck you for thinking you're the only person going through something. Fuck you for using grief as a get-out-of-jail-free card every time you're a cow. Jack would be ashamed.'

'I know and I'm—'

'Fuck you,' she said quietly as she walked away.

The first thing I did when I woke on Saturday was to text Alice again. **I'm sorry.**

Again, she didn't reply. I called for the umpteenth time but she didn't pick up.

I needed to see her in person. I wasn't sure if she was working so I drove to her house but her car wasn't outside. I'd come back later, in the meantime I wasn't far from the care home.

Sid was in front of his mirror, running a comb through his hair.

'Even lifting me comb to me head hurts. Bloody bowling, I've rediscovered muscles I'd thought were lost. Is everything all right? I've a cab coming at ten-thirty,' his reflection told me. 'A few of us are heading out for brunch.'

'Brunch?'

'It ain't a prison here, duck.'

'I know. I just had you down more as a full English man.' I settled myself onto the edge of his bed.

'Yeah well, Ethel lost at bridge for the third time running and she's paying. I was worried she'd think it was a date when I heard her ask Helen, the care assistant, something about a padded bra, so I'm taking Bert. Safety in numbers. We'll probably go to The Happy Bean. At least you can get a decent sausage there. I can't be doing with them places that serve smashed avocado on a roof tile. What's so fancy about mashing up a bit of fruit with a fork and not even serving it on a proper plate? Is Alice working today, Libby?'

At the mention of my sister I dropped my head into my hands.

'Uh oh. I know that look. What's happened?'

'Nothing.' My voice was muffled, the word a lie.

'Elizabeth,' Sid said sternly but not unkindly. He peeled my fingers away from my face. I couldn't look him in the eye. He thought the world of us, of Jack. I was ashamed to repeat my terrible accusations and yet if I didn't Alice might tell him later.

'I accused Alice and Jack of having an affair.' I stared miserably at my shoes which were caked in mud from my gardening endeavours. 'I asked Alice if Jack was the father of her baby.'

'Jack loved the bones of you.' Sid didn't show the disappointment he must have felt. 'He'd never have been unfaithful, particularly not with your sister.'

'I know,' I said quietly.

'Well then why?' The mattress sank a little as he sat beside me.

'Remember I told you about Owen, my first boyfriend?'

'I do.'

'I caught him with Alice a while ago, they were holding hands. She said there was nothing going on but …'

'You put two and two together and made a baby?'

I nodded. 'And when she explained … it was all innocent anyway but I demanded to know who the father was if it wasn't Owen but she wouldn't give me a name. I can't understand why she won't tell me … and yesterday I found her crying and talking to a photo of Jack telling him she didn't want to lie to me or to break me and … I …' I couldn't say it again.

'Put two and two together and made a catastrophe?'

'Pretty much. I can't believe I said it. I can't believe it even crossed my mind.'

'So why did you?' Sid never told me when he thought I was wrong, instead he gently guided me towards finding the answers on my own; he would have made a wonderful father.

'I think … I think that losing Jack in such a violent, unexpected way has shaken my faith in … in everything. I've thrown myself into the renovations and … and it helps while I'm busy. When I'm doing something it feels like I've turned a corner but when I'm not I've got this constant edgy feeling. It's like I can't trust the world any more. Nothing feels safe.' I could hear the quiver in my voice and Sid must have heard it too because he took my hand, his thin fingers encircling mine, and waited until I could carry on.

'At home, with Liam in the garden and Noah in the house, I feel safe. Protected. We're in our own little bubble almost but when I'm somewhere else, like shopping, I look at people differently, thinking you could have a knife. A gun. You just don't know who to trust.'

'You can't let one rotten apple sour the cider. Most people are good.'

'I know. If I stop and consider it properly I do know that but these random thoughts come out of nowhere and … Last week we'd had such a good morning. Noah was about to begin painting the last room and Liam was digging the vegetable patch. I was feeling so positive and happy and I went out to get some cakes for them. I was perusing the shelves trying to choose when someone touched my shoulder and I screamed. I made a fist and swung around and it was …' The thought of it caused my face to burn with shame. 'It was this little old lady and she looked *terrified*. "I just wanted you to reach a box of French Fancies," she said. I almost lashed out at her and all she wanted was some Mr Kipling.'

'Perhaps it's time you talked to somebody. That Victim Support lady you didn't want to speak to?'

'I don't know what to do.' I leaned against him, the scratchy wall of his tank top rough against my cheek. He smelled of tobacco and mints.

Of comfort.

'I wish Alice would tell me who the father of her baby is.'

'Perhaps she wishes you'd stop asking.' Sid offered me a Polo and I took one. 'Perhaps she believes having a father isn't the be-all and end-all.'

'But it was horrible for us.'

'Was it? Or is that only how you felt? Did Alice feel the same?'

I contemplated this as I sucked my sweet, feeling it shrink on my tongue. I was incredulous to think that Alice might not feel the same as me.

Driving home, my temples throbbed with the effort of trying to focus on the road when my head was full of Alice.

Without her, without my family, who did I really have except Liam and Noah? And I was paying them to help me.

I had never felt so alone.

So utterly, unbearably lonely.

Broken.

Afraid of the present, afraid of the future. Desperately needing comfort but unsure where to turn.

Jack.

The only person I wanted was Jack.

I tried to summon him in my mind's eye.

I need you.

I parked outside the house – our house – remembering moving-in day, his hand in mine, my laughter as he swept me into his arms and carried me inside. Now, instead of being held in arms that loved me, I took a lonely walk into my empty hallway.

There was no one to greet me, no Socks purring, curving around my ankles.

I was alone, except, when I stepped into the snug, I saw that I wasn't.

Jack.

He was there, just like before.

Jack sitting in his armchair, the cat on his lap, smiling that smile at me.

It was impossible.

I began to slide to the floor. I couldn't cope with this again. Not tonight.

Was I going mad?

I screwed my eyes shut for several seconds and when I opened them again, Jack was still there.

Still smiling.

Chapter Twenty-Eight

The world let go of me and I crumpled to the floor. Jack stretched out his hand towards me and I felt … nothing. No warmth of blood. No solidity of bone. Nothing.

'You're not here,' I whispered. I closed my eyes. 'You're not here.' I peeped out from beneath my lashes.

'I'm here,' he said softly. 'I've been trying to be here for a very long time.'

I scrambled to sitting and shuffled quickly backwards until the wall was hard against my spine, as if I was afraid of him and – in a way – I was.

'This isn't real. You're not real.'

He looked real though. He looked like … Jack.

'I don't understand what's happening.' My heart broke open as we faced each other. 'Is this one of those extraordinary experiences?'

'I don't know what it is, Libs. All I know is that I've missed you. Really missed you. I've been back before and there are times I was sure you'd heard me, seen me but …'

'You can't be here.' Logically. Scientifically. Everything about this was wrong.

'Don't be shellfish, Libby. This is my house too.'

He tried to lighten the mood and the intervening time melted away, my final memory of him no longer sick in bed but here, now, in front of me.

But …

Tentatively, I reached out my fingers, touched his face, my skin connecting with nothing but air.

'I can't touch anything, I've tried,' he said. 'It makes sense you can't touch me either.'

I recoiled, serpent fast, curling my fingers back into my palms.

Once, when we'd both been ill, Jack and I had curled under blankets on the sofa for days, watching reruns of *Red Dwarf*. We'd laughed so hard, holding our sides which already ached from coughing. In the first episode the technician, Rimmer, died. He was brought back as a hologram, an H stamped onto his forehead. He still had the same thoughts and feelings that he'd had when he was alive but he was unable to touch anything. During later episodes he was upgraded, able to touch solid objects, people, and, later still, he was brought back as flesh and blood.

'Imagine that,' Jack had said. 'Living forever as a hologram.'

'At least you'd still be around the people that you love.'

'But … food!' Jack said, a pained expression on his face. 'I'd really miss food.'

'You're thinking of your stomach rather than … other bits?' I said.

'Other bits?'

'You know.'

'I don't.' He had tried to keep a straight face.

'You just want me to say it.'

'You know I love it when you talk dirty, Libby. What would I miss?'

'Sex. Me. Sex with me.'

He had rolled on top of me and held my wrists above my head. 'I can't imagine being with you and not being able to touch you, it would be torturous.'

I had agreed but now, now the fact I couldn't touch him, that he couldn't touch me didn't seem so important.

He was here.

With me.

But for how long? I wanted time to slow down and speed up all at once. I longed for him to stay but I needed to know what came next.

'Libby?' His voice lifted me from my thoughts. 'Say something, please.'

'Do you remember *Red Dwarf*?'

'Ha! Rimmer.' Jack pointed at his forehead. 'I don't have an H there, do I?'

I laughed but then my sobs choked me once more. Everything was closing in on me, the walls, the ceiling. I grappled for air.

'You're okay, Libby. Just breathe.'

'I … can't.' I dropped my head between my knees, trying to calm down. After a few moments I could talk but my words were not slow and measured, they were fast and hysterical.

'This doesn't make sense. You can't be here, not really. And yet …' My confused heart was breaking.

'Somehow I am,' he said quietly.

'This is crazy.'

'It is.'

'Are you a ghost? A figment of my imagination?' My head just couldn't make sense of the impossible.

'I'm … Jack,' he said simply.

'But you're ...' I was overcome with the enormity that he might not remember what had happened to him. 'You do know that ...'

'That I'm dead?' His face creased with pain and I felt my own expression mirror his.

'Did it hurt? Do you hurt?' My eyes scanned his body. He was wearing his white T-shirt and navy joggers. There was no telltale sign of blood around his middle where his wound was. Could he even bleed any more?

'I don't feel ... I don't want to say anything because here' – he covered his chest with his hand – 'I feel everything. My love for you is still there. But physically, I can't feel the stab wound any more. But my body is ... I can't walk through walls, before you ask.'

It was all too much. I was shaking with shock. My teeth clattering together. It was summer but I was washed with cold.

'Light a fire,' Jack said.

My hands were trembling as I struck a match, once, twice, three times before it lit and I dropped it into the grate. Poking at the logs until flames flickered. All the while I couldn't tear my eyes away from Jack, not wanting him to vanish.

He sat on the sofa and patted the cushion beside him. I curled up on the opposite end.

This cannot be real.

But Socks leaped into the space between us. Gazed up at Jack, purring adoringly.

'Did you ... make him?' I asked, remembering how he came to me. When he came to me.

'I haven't suddenly gained superpowers. I can't make cats.'

'What can you do? I mean, where do you go when you're not here?' I raised my eyes to the ceiling, half expecting to see a fluffy white cloud waiting for Jack to climb back on.

'I don't know, Libby,' he said. 'Truthfully, it's all been a bit hazy. There have been snatches when I'm here and then nothing but blackness in between. If there's a God, I certainly haven't met them yet.'

I wrapped my arms around myself, not for warmth – the fire was throwing out heat – but because I was breaking apart.

This cannot be real.

My fingers found the skin of my forearm and I pinched it as hard as I could.

'Libby?' Jack looked at me with concern.

'I was checking if I was asleep. Dreaming.'

'And if this was a dream you'd want to wake up?' He looked utterly bereft.

'I want … you.' It was the truth. 'I've always wanted you. Can you stay here? With me?'

'I don't know how long I've got, Libby. We need to make the most of this, whatever *this* is.'

'I wish … I wish that you could touch me, just once more.'

'I wish that too, Libby. Lie with me.' He shuffled down on the sofa until he was horizontal and I did the same.

We were curled onto our sides, our faces close. There was no telltale warm breath spilling out of Jack's mouth and yet there was a movement of his ribcage reminiscent of his lungs drawing in and then expelling air. I raised my hand and there was a whisper of a breeze as he placed his palm flat against mine but I couldn't feel him, not really. We were together but divided.

I closed my eyes. Sensibly, I knew that he couldn't be here, this couldn't be real, and yet when I opened my eyes again he was still there, a sad expression on his face. 'I don't understand this either, Libby.'

'But it is you,' I whispered wanting proof, not trusting what I was seeing. 'Tell me …' I needed something that no one else would know. 'Tell me the story of our first kiss.' As the memory came to me I touched my lips; they felt cold without the cover of his. Would they ever feel warm again?

'The first time I kissed you was at the end of our first date, in my flat, as you left—'

'It was not.'

'Back five minutes and I've pissed you off.' He laughed.

'You haven't. It's just you should remember the details like I remember how to make you the perfect cup of tea. Let it steep for four and a half minutes and then a splash of milk and two sugars.'

'Three. I take three—'

'Gotcha.' For a scant second it felt so normal, I couldn't help grinning at him. 'Hurts doesn't it? Forgetting the small things.'

'Like when you forgot who I actually was—'

'You *know* that isn't what happened.' I knew what he was remembering.

'Are you sure, Libby? Because I could have sworn the first time I came to one of your exhibitions you stood behind a complete stranger and slid your arms around his waist because you thought he was me.'

'He didn't seem to mind.' I had been so embarrassed when Jack had tapped me on the shoulder with a confused 'Excuse me.'

'I could never forget you,' I said, serious once more.

'And I'd never forget our first proper kiss. Not the kiss on the cheek at the end of our first date. I so badly wanted to kiss you properly then but thought that after my disastrous peanut butter and banana on crackers dinner I'd be pushing my luck. Honestly, I didn't think I'd see you again.'

I knew how that felt.

'I couldn't believe it when you texted and said you'd arrange our second date. That was the first time we kissed *properly*.'

I nodded.

'You had driven us out to the middle of nowhere and when you opened the boot I'd thought you were going to get out a picnic hamper and a blanket, but instead you handed me a camera.'

'Not just any camera, my Canon A1.' It was my favourite camera. 'You'd told me why you paint, how music inspired you and I wanted to share something with you.' I had felt self-conscious, shrugging my rucksack on my back, fiddling with the settings on the camera looped around my neck. Wondering if this was too much. Too soon. I had led Jack through the trees, away from the well-trodden path of the weekend ramblers and daily dog walkers. We'd stumbled over rough terrain, clambering up steep hills, climbing over fallen trees, thorns snagging at Jack's black jeans – 'Sorry, I should have told you to wear something old' – until Jack was breathless.

'I'm embarrassed at how unfit I am. I'm usually standing behind an easel'. And then suddenly it was the sight in front of him snatching his breath. Water cascading over rocks into a lake which on that day looked brilliant blue but I knew sometimes could be green, grey, colourless.

'I never realised this was here.' The wondrous look on Jack's face had made me pleased I had brought him.

'Not many people do.'

It was later, he kissed me. He'd been swimming in the lake, urging me to join him.

'We'll freeze!' I'd laughed.

'Trust me,' he had said and I did then. I do now as he asks me,

'Close your eyes, Libby. I can't touch you but I can tell you. I can tell you what I'd like to do to you, if only I could.' I'm filled with both fear and anticipation as I allow my eyelids to shut, worried he won't be there again when I open them, everything inside me igniting as I wait for him to speak, and when he does it is soft and loaded with longing.

'Firstly, I'd gently kiss your neck in the way you like, my mouth moving down to your shoulders, feathering across your collarbone.'

I tipped my head back, exposing the hollows of my throat desperately longing for the feel of his lips against my skin.

'And all the while I'd be unbuttoning your blouse, slowly, slowly. My fingers would trail across your stomach, over your hips, dipping below the waistband of your jeans before they lightly stroked their way towards your bra. I wouldn't take it off though, not yet.'

I groaned, arching my back, wanting him to take my bra off, my nipples aching to be touched. 'Jack, please,' I begged. He was driving me crazy.

'Shh. Not yet. We've all the time in the world, Libby,' he said. He carried on telling me what he wanted to do to me and I felt it.

I felt it all.

Chapter Twenty-Nine

When I woke, it was 9 a.m. I had been determined not to sleep while Jack was with me but I must have drifted off in the early hours. I was still in the snug. Still wearing yesterday's clothes. My neck, at an unaccustomed angle, protested as I sat up too quickly.

'Jack?'

His aftershave was a strong presence in the room.

'Jack?'

Where had he gone? I was frantic as I unpeeled myself from the sofa, every part of my body aching and not just because of the sagging cushions and wiry springs that had dug into my back. I ached with sadness.

I ached with missing him.

Where was he?

My heart pounded, breath catching. Last night had felt like the beginning of something but what if it had been the end? A goodbye?

What if it had never happened at all.

'Please. I need you. Please—'

'Libby.' His voice a whisper.

The door pushed open. Alice stepped inside.

'What are you doing here?' I was so confused. I hadn't heard her arrive.

'We need to talk. I looked through the window and you were sleeping on the sofa so I let myself in.' She sniffed the air. 'It … it smells nice in here. It smells of Jack. Were you … were you talking to him?'

'You heard him?'

'*Heard* him?' Alice looked at me with such pity. 'I only heard you.'

'But you can smell him?'

'His aftershave, Libby.' Alice spoke slowly, studying my face while she did so. Her expression was inscrutable.

'Can we talk later? It's not a great time for me. I've got things to do.'

'What are these *things*?' she asked.

Waiting for Jack.

Seeing Jack.

Talking to Jack.

'I just …' I swallowed down my hysteria. Jack would come back when she left, he *had* to. 'What did you want?'

She answered me with silence. A prickly, deliberate silence and then I remembered the last time I saw her, those shameful things I had said.

'Look. I know Jack isn't the baby's father.' My eyes flitted around the room, scared he might be listening, angry, disappointed. 'And I'm sorry I suggested he might be but—'

'There isn't a but,' Alice said. 'You … you accused me, me and Jack. I would never have done that to you, *never*. Jack was devoted to you.'

Her pain cut me deep. With one last glance around the room I forced myself to focus on Alice. My eyes met hers, saw the unutterable anguish in them and I was drenched in spoonfuls of shame.

'I know. God, I'm so, so sorry. I don't know why I said that, it just sprang out of my mouth. Alice I know accusing you was unforgivable but … not having him here … Sometimes I feel I'm holding it together and other times it feels like I'm going mad with grief. He was … irreplaceable.'

'I know that.' Her expression had softened but she didn't make a move to hug me. The distance between us was immense. 'But he's left a huge gap in my life too. He was like a big brother to me. Of course I never looked at him like—'

'I know. I'm so sorry. I don't know why I said it.'

'But you must have thought it to have said it, Libby.'

'I just … I know you loved him too.'

'I did. Completely and it … it fucking hurts that you could take my love and twist it into something ugly.'

'Alice.' We faced each other, a wall of suffering between us. I had to find the right words to knock it down. 'I was wrong.' It was the simple truth.

She dropped her shoulder, calming down. 'That day, when I came to tell you I was pregnant, I wasn't afraid to say it in front of him. I knew he'd support me. I miss him, Libby.' A solitary tear trickled down her cheek. 'And sometimes I feel I've no right to feel so sad because your grief eclipses everyone's. And that's how it should be, of course, but me and Mum … we're hurting too, not just for Jack but for you. You're so up and down we're constantly treading on eggshells around you. One minute you're happy and full of the plans for the house, the future. The next minute you're down again, crying, talking to Jack. We're not judging you but we're not sure how to reach you, Libs. Tell me what to do.' She looked at me beseechingly.

The older kids are being mean at school, Libby. What should I do?

I can't learn my times tables no matter how hard I try. What should I do?

I fancy Sean Richards but he fancies Jenny East. What should I do?

I didn't have all of the answers any more. I wasn't sure I had them then but as a child Alice had had utmost faith that I could do anything. Now she saw me as vulnerable, fallible. Helpless and hopeless. All of the things I didn't want to be.

I could feel myself sagging but I held myself upright, a marionette suspended from strings. I would not fall. I would not fall in front of my younger sister.

'I want you to be happy, Libby,' she said.

I wanted that too and if she left and Jack came back, I just might be.

'I know and I'm sorry and I'm glad we talked and I appreciate you coming, I do, but right now, I want to be alone.'

A look of resignation crossed her face as she nodded.

I stood on the front step and watched her leave before closing the door and rushing back into the snug, convinced Jack would be there.

He wasn't.

In the time Alice had been with me the smell of Jack's aftershave had gone. The lingering sense of his presence, gone.

Alice was right about my moods being so up and down because, unfairly perhaps, I blamed Alice for his absence now too.

I waited for hours and hours for him to come back.

He didn't.

Intermittently I googled extraordinary experiences, trying to find someone who had shared an encounter as detailed and as intricate as mine.

Had it been real? I just didn't know.

234

'Jack?' There was a crack in my voice as I uttered his name.

But he didn't come back.

I couldn't see him.

Smell him.

Hear him.

Nothing. There was nothing.

It was late afternoon. I couldn't bear the sound of my lonely foot-steps against the floorboards any longer. I had raked everything over in my mind and theorised that Jack had only ever appeared after I'd returned home after an outing.

I had to get out for a walk.

On autopilot, my anxious feet carried me to the churchyard.

Noah was sitting on the bench. I hesitated, not feeling like company, but before I could retreat he spotted me, raised his hand in a wave.

'Hello.' I sat down next to him, leaving a gap between us, unsure what that moment we had shared at the house meant. If there *had* even been a moment or if that too was only in my head.

Had he wanted to kiss me?

'How's Liam?' I asked.

'He's fine. I took him for a pizza yesterday. He's not painting. He doesn't have the space at home. He's sharing a room now with his mum's partner's two kids.'

'Did he tell you that?'

'Yeah, not in a deep conversation kind of way but he lets things slip now and again.'

'Because he trusts you.'

'He trusts us.'

As he said '*us*' a creep of heat warmed my face. My eyes met

235

his but thankfully there was nothing in them to say he saw me as anything other than a friend. I allowed myself to relax a little. I'd become dependent on our friendship. I didn't want it to change.

'Three kids in a bedroom must be difficult in a flat so small.'

'It sounds like he's used to people coming and going from his life. He'll be glad to get back to the house, some stability and structure. What have you been up to this week?'

I didn't know where to start. 'Falling out with my sister mainly.'

'How come?'

'I've accused her of something that wasn't true and I wish I could unsay it but I can't. She's keeping the identity of the baby's father secret and it's hurtful. We used to share everything. I hate the thought of being deceived. My ex used to lie to me all the time and it makes me feel so worthless. Does that sound over-dramatic?'

'No.' Noah was choosing his words with care. 'But with everything you've been through – we've been through – we know life is too short to hold a grudge. Alice wouldn't have intentionally hurt you. I … I would never want to hurt you.'

There was something in his expression, something different. Perhaps not attraction as I'd thought before when we'd spun around to Chuck Berry but something else.

Regret?

Longing?

Whatever it was it made me uncomfortable. I shifted away from him slightly.

'You do know that there's no chance that … this … us … will ever turn into a relationship, don't you?' I should have said this before when he'd tucked my hair behind my ear, touched my face. 'I appreciate you helping with the house—'

'Libby!' He looked horrified. 'If I've ever given you that impression—'

'Sorry. It's been a tough few days. Can we just forget I said that?' I regretted pushing Alice away earlier, I didn't want to alienate Noah too. 'I feel that right now, you're the only person on my side. You're the only person I can talk to.'

I spoke truthfully because I had thought then that he was my friend. I had thought he was on my side.

I didn't know that he had a hidden agenda. Soon I would find out, but that day, as we sat in companionable silence, it seemed he was my little bit of sanctuary. My little bit of peace in an otherwise frantic world.

Again, I was a fool.

Chapter Thirty

Three days.

It had been three days since I had convinced myself that leaving the house had been the key to Jack appearing but after I'd returned home after visiting the churchyard the house was still.

Silent.

Cold.

It had been three days since I had seen Noah.

Alice.

Three days in which I'd barely slept, not wanting to miss Jack.

Three days since I had answered my phone.

The doorbell rang.

Mum stood on the doorstep, wind blustering her hair around her face. Her mouth fixed in an expression of determination or perhaps resignation; whatever it was, it wasn't a smile. She couldn't quite meet my eye as she stepped inside.

'I've been trying to ring you.' She bustled into the kitchen.

Normal. Act normal.

'Sorry. My mobile battery's flat. Do you want something to drink?' I could have been reading from a script.

'You look awful, Libby.'

My hand instantly smoothed my hair. It felt limp under my touch, a greasy sheen to it. Had I washed it today? Yesterday?

'… Jack.' The sound of his name jolted me back to Mum.

'What about Jack?' I asked.

Mum tutted. 'Have you listened to a word I've said?'

She pushed my steaming mug towards me. I didn't remember making coffee or sitting down. Panic rose and I quashed it.

I was exhausted, that was all. As soon as Mum left I would take a shower, a nap. Fix myself something nutritious to eat.

'Jack's aftershave,' Mum said. 'Alice said you've been wearing Jack's aftershave, and talking to him.'

'It's comforting.'

'I know but it's been six months and—'

'So I should have forgotten him by now? How can I when he was …' I bit my lip to stop myself saying the word 'here'. I knew she'd never believe me. I stared down at the table, not sure what to say. I had been feeling that I was beginning to move forward. Making a new friend in Noah and starting the renovations had been a turning point for me but after seeing – *thinking* I saw Jack the other day – I had fallen apart again.

'I'm not saying you should even try to forget him.' Mum's voice was gentle. 'But I'm worried that you've taken on too much with this house. The stress is … Libby, I know you accused Jack of being the father of Alice's baby.'

I take a sharp intake of breath.

'We both think … there's no set time to grieve of course and nobody's even suggesting that you move on but … we both think that perhaps you should speak to Victim Support or someone.'

'I am *not* a victim.'

'Don't push me away, Libby.'

I didn't answer. There was only one person I wanted and it wasn't her.

The fridge thrummed. The clock ticked. Outside the sheep bleated. The smell of coffee filled my nostrils each time I drew a ragged breath.

'I'm sorry, Mum, but can you please just go? I'm not feeling great. My head hurts.'

There was a beat or two before the legs of her chair scraped along the kitchen floor as she stood. I watched from the window as she climbed into her car. I could see her head resting against the steering wheel, her shoulders shaking.

I pulled the curtains. Took two paracetamol and climbed into bed.

It was pitch-black when I woke. I had slept the day away. The darkness here was absolute. No lamp-posts shining orange through the window. No headlights from passing cars. Just a luminous glow from a fat round moon suspended high in the velvet sky. The percussive sound of rain splattering against the window.

I hadn't eaten all day. I shoved a minuscule meal for one into the microwave and while the cannelloni turned lonely circles I headed towards the snug to put the TV on so I wouldn't feel quite so alone.

A flicker of something as I passed the dining room stopped me in my tracks. I felt a magnet clamp of longing deep in my chest.

Jack?

I hardly dared take a second look but when I did …

'Jack.'

I wouldn't cry.

He was leaning against the window, his backdrop a smattering of twinkly stars in between the clouds.

I wouldn't cry.

From the kitchen the microwave pinged but instead of moving towards the sound I moved away from it. Towards Jack. Feeling his eyes on me. Wanting his hands on me.

I wouldn't cry.

Rubber Soul was still on the record deck. After our anniversary I hadn't slipped it back into its sleeve. I rubbed the dust off with the hem of my shirt before lowering the needle gently into its groove. 'In My Life' began to play and it was a song for all the feelings words couldn't cover.

There was a hesitancy in me as I stepped towards Jack. Not a shyness, but a wariness. He was holding out his hand but I knew that if I took it, no matter how solid it looked, I wouldn't be able to feel it.

'Trust me,' he whispered.

A shiver swept its way down my spine. I recalled us lying on the sofa, in the snug the other night.

'I can tell you what I'd like to do to you, Libby, if only I could. Close your eyes.'

I had felt it all.

'Trust me.'

My breath was rapid, my pulse light and fast.

I closed my eyes, inhaled and there it was.

Sandalwood.

Jack.

I raised my arms, spread my hands. Felt warm breath upon my cheek.

It was impossible.

It was *all* impossible but it was all I ever wanted.

Jack's hands clasped mine, his fingers … God those fingers.

A tear leaked down my cheek.

John Lennon sang and just like we had on our anniversary, we spun slowly around the room.

This time, if anyone had peered through the window what would they have seen? A crying girl twirling around, arms empty, her hands being held by no one?

'Jack. Jack. Jack.' His name escaped my lips with every breath. 'I'm here.'

But I knew he wasn't, not really.

The song ended. A chill spread from my scalp to my toes. I opened my eyes and he was gone.

I waited until almost midnight before I trudged back upstairs where nothing waited for me apart from a freezing empty bed.

Still I cradled the sensation of us spinning, as though we were still dancing, keeping that feeling close to my chest.

Despite my earlier awkward conversation with Mum, Jack had made this one of the best days since I had lost him.

Tomorrow would be one of the worst.

Chapter Thirty-One

The following day brought a raging storm, rain hurling itself at the windows, wind shaking the frames.

But Jack.

It also brought Jack.

I had been lost in time, lost in the memory of last night's dance when I walked into the snug. Jack was there and suddenly I was lost for words.

Would it always be like this? Appearing and disappearing. Never knowing when or if I would see him again. Instead of confusion, delight, all the things I had felt before, I was overcome with a helplessness so deep it threatened to sink me. I tried to smile at him because I knew that's what he'd be expecting but emotion dragged the corners of my mouth down. I knelt to light a fire, striking a match against the kindling, finding the routine in the midst of such extraordinary circumstances comforting.

The flames danced, orange and bright, and I settled myself on the sofa next to Jack. In the pit of my stomach a tight ball of worry began to uncurl, tendrils of uncertainty pushing impossible questions into my throat. I tried to contain them but they spilled out nevertheless.

'How long are you here for this time?' I fiddled with my cuff. Unable to look at him. Knowing he had no more idea than I did. 'Why *do* you think you're here, Jack?'

'Why are any of us here?'

'Do you think …' I'd given this a lot of thought. 'Do you think you're stuck here until you've completed something?'

'If it's until we've finished this house I'll be here forever.'

'Hey! Have you seen the first floor?' We fell back into banter as though everything was normal but it wasn't. 'What if it's something else?' I had been endlessly speculating. 'Perhaps I'm in danger and you're here to—'

'You're right!' Jack said. 'It's exactly that.'

'It is?' I was nervous.

'But before I can dramatically save you we have to seductively fashion something out of clay so nip out and buy a potter's wheel.'

This time my smile was genuine. 'I absolutely wasn't thinking of Patrick Swayze in *Ghost*.'

'You absolutely were.'

I laughed. 'Remember how hard Sam tried to let Molly know he was still around.'

'How could I forget the utter concentration on his face?' Jack tilted his chin and wore an odd expression.

'Patrick looked sexy, you just look like you're trying not to fart.'

'Yeah. And you look *so* desirable in your panda slippers.'

I stretched out my legs and wiggled my feet so the bears' ears flapped.

From the hallway outside came a fake cough. The sound of shuffling feet.

Shit.

I'd been so caught up in Jack I hadn't heard the front door

open. I threw a worried glance towards the door and then back at Jack.

He'd already gone.

I was torn between fury and embarrassment. How dare someone let themselves in and just stand there listening. It must be Mum or Alice. I dashed out into the hallway. Alice was making a show of unlacing her dripping trainers. Easing them off one by one. Faking a reason to have been loitering. She usually left her shoes on, wet or not.

'I didn't know you'd let yourself in. Again.' My tone was accusatory, my raised voice blanketing my shame – not at talking to Jack, but at being caught talking to Jack. My family were already desperately worried about me. I knew Alice wouldn't get it and she didn't.

'Libby?' She was cautious. 'Were you speaking to Jack again?'

'You must stop using the key. It was for emergencies.'

Alice offered me a smile; it was too bright, almost a grimace. 'Who were you speaking to, Libs?'

She made no move to peer around the door to see if there was anyone there. She knew that there wasn't.

'Jack.' There was a defiant tilt to my chin.

'But …' Alice breathed out heavily. Pasted on another smile. 'We talked about this. Mum talked to you about this. She's upset so I've come to reason with you but now … That was more than saying Jack's name. It sounded like quite a lively conversation?'

'I'm not mad.'

'I know but—'

'You talk to your baby. I've heard you. Rubbing your belly. Telling her all the things she will see when she's born.'

'It's not the same.'

'Why not? You love her and there's stuff you want to tell her.'

'But I don't … You were pausing, Libby. There were gaps in between your sentences. You … you imagine him answering you back?'

'So? If you do your research you'll see it's actually recommended that the bereaved—'

'You were *laughing*, Libby. People speak to those they've lost to tell them how they feel, that they miss them, perhaps to share their news but you … you were laughing. Having a good time.' Alice sniffed. 'I can smell his aftershave again.'

'You smell it too?'

'Of course I bloody can.' She stepped forward and pressed her nose into my neck. 'You're drenched in it.'

Was I? I couldn't remember putting any on.

'We're so worried about you. We thought you'd turned a real corner with the renovation but now … You're not yourself again, Libby.' She placed both her arms on my shoulders and studied me before pulling me close into a hug.

It was the physical contact that undid me. I began to cry. I knew I wasn't myself but how could I be the me before all of this happened? I was a different person then. The world was a different place. 'I'm trying with the house but I don't know who I am without him, Alice.' My voice was muffled by her neck. I pulled away from her and studied my panda slippers which had seemed so funny moments ago but now just looked incredibly sad.

Alice handed me a tissue. 'You have to accept he's not here any more. I'll help you. Mum will help you. This project has been too much. You look so frail. So worn out. We're here for you.'

'I just get the urge to talk to him sometimes.' I wiped my eyes. 'The way you do with your baby.'

'But my baby is real, Libby.' Alice's voice was gentle. 'We just want you to face reality. Start living again. After all, you're not the one who died.'

I don't know where it came from, my reaction.

She didn't mean to be cruel. I knew that as I raised my arm.

She didn't mean to hurt me. I knew that as I drew my shoulder back.

She loved me. I knew that as my palm cracked against her cheek and yet still I did it.

I hit another woman and not just any woman. My sister. My *pregnant* sister.

That was the definitive point when I knew.

I needed help.

Chapter Thirty-Two

I had never hit my sister before, not once, not even as kids when she'd broken my toys or ruined my clothes.

'Alice … I …' I covered my mouth in horror as her cheek instantly reddened, her eyes filled with tears. I stepped forward but she stepped backwards and her palpable fear that I might strike her again was a slap to my own face. 'I'm so sorry. I didn't mean …' I couldn't stop shaking.

She gently touched the mark my palm had left with light fingertips.

'Please … Alice … Please …'

I wasn't sure what I was asking of her.

The thought of her telling Mum and seeing the confusion and disappointment on her face mirroring the hurt and bewilderment that was currently written all over my sister's was unbearable. I had no right to ask her to keep it a secret and yet, still I did.

'Please don't tell Mum.'

'Libby. I love you dearly but that … that … What if I'd fallen?' She cradled her bump protectively. 'What if you'd hurt my baby?'

'I am so, *so* sorry.' Regret slowed my blood. My heart. I could feel every single painful beat. 'I can promise you that nothing like that will ever happen again.'

'You can't promise me that, Libby, because … I know me and Mum keep saying it but you're not yourself. You're not coping. You've taken on too much, too soon.' Instead of brushing aside her concerns the way I usually did, I quietly agreed. 'I know. I don't know what to do.'

'You *have* to see someone. The GP—'

'Okay.' I'd been kidding myself that there was no harm in me seeing Jack, real or imagined, talking to Jack, but the way I turned on my sister the second she called me out, I knew that something had to change. I had to change.

It was only an hour after Alice left that Mum had texted me the time of my doctor's appointment for later that day, telling me she'd meet me there. I didn't know how she'd got one so quickly. I hoped she hadn't told the receptionist I'd had an outburst of violence. My palm stung with shame with every single recollection.

It was a different GP to the one I had seen before. There was a photo of three children on her desk displayed in a 'World's Best Mummy' frame.

'So, Libby. What can I do for you today?' She smiled in the sympathetic way that told me she'd read my notes before I entered the room. She knew about Jack.

'I don't know what to say really.' I didn't know where to start. Not at the beginning, that was too painful.

'What's brought you here?'

I glanced at Mum. She was unusually quiet.

'I don't feel right.' I tugged the sleeves of my thin sweatshirt over my hands. 'I mean, I don't expect to feel happy or anything, not after Jack, but …'

'How do you feel?' she gently prompted.

'I can't sleep but I don't want any more tablets. I didn't get on with the Zopiclone. I feel sick, it's like being permanently worried. Dizzy sometimes. I had an inner ear infection when I had the flu a few months ago and my balance has felt a little off since then. I …' Again I glanced at Mum as I urged myself to spit it out. I was a woman for God's sake. 'I haven't had a period since Jack … I thought I might be pregnant.' This time Mum glanced at me. 'But I did a test and it was negative. I'm just tired. Really tired. I'm renovating my house, it was a shell so I don't expect to be full of energy but …' I shrugged.

'Let's have a little look at you.' The doctor took my blood pressure, peered into my mouth, my eyes, checked my ears. She lifted her stethoscope and listened to my heart. I wondered whether she could hear it was broken, the shattered pieces rattling around my chest. Eventually, she sat down again.

'Everything seems okay. I'd like to run a blood test to check your thyroid. Are you okay with needles?'

I nodded.

'If it isn't Libby's thyroid,' Mum said, 'what could it be?' Instead of the usual bravado in her words, the 'my neighbour's best friend's daughter has experienced the same thing so I'm an expert', there was a vulnerability I hadn't heard before. I realised how much she'd been worried about me. The doctor saw it too.

'I can understand how concerned you are, Mrs Emerson, but I'm not seeing anything alarming here. Grief can often cause physical symptoms. The stress can cause a chemical reaction in the body with glands releasing more hormones than they should. This wouldn't be a problem in the short term but when the stress of grief continues for weeks or months and we have abnormally high levels of hormones circulating in the blood it affects our immune system. It isn't surprising, Libby, to hear that you're feeling so off, particularly with project-managing a house renovation. They can be very fraught.'

'I'm enjoying it. I've made really good progress. I'm not used to manual work though—'

'It isn't just the physical,' Mum interrupted. I threw her a look but she still carried on. 'She's been talking to Jack.'

'It's quite common – and quite comforting to talk to those who are no longer with us. It's not—'

'She hears his replies. She has conversations with him.'

My face flamed. 'I am here, Mum.'

Undeterred she carried on. 'She's just not … herself. And she thinks he's sent her a cat.'

'I … I don't.' How could she have said that out loud?

'Libby?' The doctor leaned forward. There was no judgement on her face. 'Do you hear Jack?'

I shrugged. Fidgeted on my chair. I'd agreed to come here to appease Mum, so the doctor could tell her it was normal to feel low. Tired. All of the things I had been feeling. 'I … I like to talk to him. It …' My voice cracked. 'It makes me feel that he's still with me.'

'Have you ever experienced any hallucinations? Auditory or visual?'

'No.' My treacherous knee began to jiggle up and down, I fisted my hand and pressed against it so it would stop.

'I'm … sad. It's okay to feel sad, isn't it?' My attention flickered between the doctor and my mum. I wanted to tell them I felt scared too. Scared I was losing my mind. But what if I was? What if it wasn't real? What if Jack was gone forever? I just couldn't bear it. My lips quivered.

'Libby, I don't want to upset you. Of course it's natural. But sometimes the normal grief reaction can morph into something deeper and I just want to make sure you are okay.'

'Sorry.' I pressed my fingers to my eyes to keep my tears back. 'I am okay. I just miss him.'

'Her mood swings are terrible.' Mum patted my arm. 'She lost her temper with her sister.'

'Unpredictable moods will likely carry on for quite some time I'm afraid. Libby, have you talked to anyone about how you feel?'

'My friend Noah. He's a decorator and he's been helping me with the house. He lost his sister, Bethany, a few years ago so he understands.'

'That's great you've got some support. Look, my receptionist will text you an appointment with the nurse for your blood test. It'll be in the next few days. I'm also going to give you the number of a grief counsellor. You can say I sent you.' She scribbled on a piece of paper and handed it to me. I took it between my thumb and index finger but she didn't let go. Reluctantly I met her eyes.

'Before you go, I need to ask you whether you've thought about hurting yourself, Libby?'

I pictured those tablets snug in the bathroom cabinet. The bottle of vodka in the cupboard under the sink. But that was ages ago. Things were different now.

'No.' And I meant it. I felt more stable now than I had all those weeks ago.

But that was before I made a shocking discovery and everything changed once more.

Chapter Thirty-Three

The questions the doctor had asked me bounced around my mind.

'Have you ever experienced any hallucinations? Auditory or visual?'

Is that what Jack was? A hallucination? Before Jack passed I had never thought about the afterlife, I hadn't experienced the painful loss that forced me to confront my own mortality and everything that came after. Would a grief counsellor help me unpick my feelings? Sift through what was real and what wasn't?

Instead of going home, suddenly I was desperate to talk about it all, but not with a stranger. Someone who was my age, who knew what it was like to lose somebody young.

Noah.

'Hello, it's Libby isn't it?' Noah's mum asked when she answered the door.

'Yes.' I smiled.

'Noah isn't here. He's taken young Liam for a burger. Do you want to come in and wait? He shouldn't be long now.'

I hesitated, remembering Noah telling me his mum wasn't good with people, preferred to be alone and yet she was opening the door a little wider. I stepped inside.

It was hot inside the house, the type of stifling day you get after a period of heavy rain. I shrugged off my denim jacket as I followed her down the hall, past those photos on the wall in dust-free frames and polished glass. Bethany as a baby, a toddler, a grinning schoolgirl, hair in bunches. Bethany leaning on the bonnet of a small white car, joyfully dangling keys in front of the camera. Bethany and Noah licking dripping ice cream cones on the beach, cross-legged under a blazing sun. She would always remain suspended in time.

'Tea?'

'Yes thank you, Mrs—'

'Call me Sandra.'

'Sandra.' I loitered in the doorway as she moved around the tiny room, measuring out tea leaves into a floral pot, fishing a strainer out of the drawer.

'So …' She handed me a cup and saucer. I balanced it precariously in one hand as I spooned sugar from the small silver dish she held. 'How are you?'

'You know …' I shrugged. 'Up and down.'

'I can't imagine.'

But she could and I needed to know. 'Do you … I don't want to upset you but can I please ask a question? I know you'll understand. It's about Bethany.'

'What do you want to know?' she asked.

'Does it get any easier? Losing someone young … How can you stop picturing them moving through their life? Thinking about all the things they are missing?'

She didn't speak at first. My questions were intrusive, should probably have remained unasked. 'She doesn't like to talk about Bethany,' Noah had said. Understandably so.

'Bethany … it's difficult to talk about.'

'I appreciate that but …' I was holding back my tears. 'It's just that sometimes …' My voice dropped to a whisper. 'I feel I'm going mad with it all.' My cup chinked against my saucer. My trembling hand placed it on the worktop.

'After we … lost Bethany it was like the heart had been ripped out of our home but you have to carry on as best you can. That doesn't mean you forget that person. When you lose a child, you grieve not just the person they are but the person you thought they would be,' she said, sadly.

'After, did you talk to her?'

She looks confused.

'I mean,' I expanded, 'after you buried her. Did you talk to her, here or at her grave or anywhere?' My voice was tiny. The room unbearably warm. I rubbed my hand across the back of my neck and felt the sweat that slicked my skin. Sandra's eyes were brimming with tears and I wished I had never come. Wished I had never started this conversation.

'Libby,' she said finally. 'Bethany … Bethany isn't dead.'

Seconds ago I was boiling hot. Now I was freezing cold. My blood, my bones, nothing but ice. My tumbling questions were pushed back by one thudding thought.

Bethany. Wasn't. Dead.

It didn't make sense and yet as I looked at Sandra I saw it. The shame in her eyes, the slump of her shoulders, the pinch of her mouth. She recognised my despair and I recognised her guilt. I knew. I had felt it. The weight of responsibility we carried. The ceaseless 'if-only's that spun around my head.

Noah had lied.

'You grieve for the things that you had hoped your child would be,' she had said moments ago.

Honest. Open. Kind.

Noah wasn't any of those things. Perhaps it wasn't Bethany she had been talking about at all. Perhaps she was grieving for the man she wished Noah had become instead of the liar he was.

But … why?

Had I misunderstood?

'Bethany isn't dead?' I repeated. 'Are you sure?'

'I think I'd know if my own daughter wasn't alive.' Her tone had changed, anger poking her words.

'Of course. Sorry. It's just that … Where is she?'

She pushed her chair back, knocking the table as she stood, the china rattling together. 'You should leave.'

'I'm sorry. I only—'

'I'll tell Noah you called.' She crossed her arms tightly across her chest defending herself against any more questions.

I couldn't help glancing at the photos on the wall as I hurried down the hall. The photos of Bethany which stopped abruptly at her teenage years.

Was Sandra confused? So overcome by grief she pretended Bethany was alive? I had to find out.

The churchyard was empty. I was frantic as I raced around, examining the names on each and every headstone, even the ones that were obviously too old, squinting as I deciphered the faded lettering.

I read them all.

'Bethany isn't dead.'

'Bethany has gone … I lost Bethany …'

Gone.

Lost.

She was no longer here.

All the terms Noah had used circled back to me. I had thought it was so he didn't have to use the death word, but it wasn't that.

There was no Bethany.

I paced, around the churchyard, looking back over the times Noah and I had been together in my head. The things we had talked about.

Grief.

That was always, understandably, our main topic of conversation.

I recalled the first day I had met him. His shadow falling over me as I had fallen to pieces at Jack's graveside, my heart breaking over the headstone. He'd come from nowhere and left when I did.

'Bethany isn't dead.'

'Libby?' I tensed at the sound of Noah's voice. Not wanting to turn around and face this man I believed was my friend. He had deceived me in the cruellest way possible. 'Mum said—'

'You lied.' My hands bunched into fists.

'Please.' He looked distraught. 'Let me explain.'

'You. Lied. To. Me.' I began to walk away before marching back towards him. 'Why? Why? I don't understand why you … why anybody … would pretend …' I trailed off because suddenly I knew why. 'You … knew. That day I first took you to the house. You said how awful it must have been Jack being mugged after going out for Lemsip. I never told you he went out for Lemsip. How did you know that?'

Noah could have answered my question a myriad of different ways: 'because I'd read it in the paper,' 'because Alice mentioned it', 'because I'd heard it on the news,' but instead he said none of those things. The colour drained from his face.

How did Noah know? And not just about the Lemsip but … I thought back again to our first meeting at the churchyard. He knew Jack's name before I had told him. He knew the date of his death. He'd said he read it from the headstone but I had been leaning against the writing, masking it.

But that wasn't our first meeting, was it? He had come to the house, the day of Jack's funeral. 'I'm sorry,' he'd said over and over while I had told him that we didn't want quotes at that moment, assuming he was a builder. What if he had come for something else? Was apologising for something else?

'Are you even a decorator? Noah? What's going on?' I asked but I already knew.

I shook my head wanting to toss up other thoughts, different thoughts, a snow globe craving a change of scene. But there was only one thing in my mind. The knowing that I had never shared with anyone what Jack had bought at the shop. It hadn't seemed important.

Until now.

There was only one way Noah could know.

If he had seen it.

'Jack wasn't on his own that day was he?' I backed away from him. 'You were there.'

Chapter Thirty-Four

'You were there that day, Noah,' I repeated.

Noah folded in on himself, his legs no longer supporting him. He crouched on the ground, covered his face with his hands and wept. My knees buckled and I sank onto the grass next to him. An odd numbness spread through me as I watched him sob. I couldn't offer him sympathy – I didn't feel any. I didn't have to ask him again if he was there. As he sat up his bloodshot eyes and tear-stained face told me that I was right.

I had so many questions I didn't know where to start. I couldn't begin to articulate all of the things I wanted … I *needed* to know. Instead I violently tugged up handfuls of grass, tossing the blades aside before reaching for more.

Noah was still crying loud against the birdsong, the leaves rustling in the breeze. I could have placed my hand on his shoulder to comfort him.

I didn't.

'I …' He gulped a breath. Tried again. 'I'm sorry.'

It wasn't enough.

It would *never* be enough.

'It should have been me.' He could barely scratch out those

words. Still I couldn't speak but I nodded. Yes. Yes it should have been anyone except Jack.

'It all happened so quickly,' he began in a low voice. 'I was cutting through the alley when I heard footsteps behind me. I was shoved into the wall. My head hit the brick and … and I remember blood trickling down my face. He … Kenny, I found out his name from the newspaper later, he stood blocking the sun, his shadow … I felt … cold. I remember that more than anything else. Feeling cold.'

I wrapped my arms around myself as I listened. I couldn't envisage ever feeling warm again.

'Suddenly Jack was there. He asked me if I was okay. He had a bottle of something tucked under his arm and was holding a box of Lemsip. He offered me his other hand to help me up and he pulled me to my feet. It …' Noah huffed out a stream of air. 'The knife … I hadn't seen it before but it glinted in the sun. Kenny asked for our wallets and phones in this really calm, really cruel voice. Jack handed his over and I was just getting my phone out of my pocket when there was a bang, a car backfiring. Kenny turned around and Jack said to run, so we did. I … Jack's footsteps were right behind me – *right behind me* – I wouldn't have left him, I swear, but then I heard a shout. I stopped and turned and Kenny, he … he had Jack and I could see … the blade. I screamed at him and ran back towards them to help Jack but before I could reach them … Jack went down. The bottle smashed as it hit the floor. Kenny looked … he looked scared. I chased him. He ran towards the other end of the alley and before I could grab him he … he ran right into he road. I … I chased him right into the road.'

Noah took a second. 'There was a screech of brakes. A thud. People came streaming from the shops to help. Somebody heard

Jack call for help and I thought … I thought if he was conscious, talking, he'd be okay. I … didn't know he'd been stabbed. I … wasn't thinking straight. All I could see was Kenny running in front of the car. I could hear the sickening noise of the car hitting Kenny. I … I turned back and someone was with Jack and I just … left.' This time he met my eye. 'I will be ashamed of that until the day I die.'

'He never told me … about you,' I said, but Jack had been in shock too. Scarcely speaking.

'I waited for the police to knock on the door. For them to appeal for witnesses. I felt like a murderer but Kenny was dead, an accident the paper called it, and that seemed to be the end of it.'

The end of Jack.

I saw it all unfold in front of my eyes. My beautiful selfless Jack stepping in to help out while all the time I was at home with Alice.

Laughing.

Texting him that he was taking too long.

'You're needed here. I'm dying!'

No wonder he didn't tell me. He hadn't wanted to talk about it and he hadn't needed to. Kenny was dead, Jack's things had been recovered and the nurse had assured us he would be fine.

'When I heard about Jack's death on the news, I was heart-broken. I came to your house to tell you my part in it but I didn't know it was the day of the funeral and I couldn't. I just couldn't …'

'You're a coward.' I would not feel sorry for him. He wasn't the victim here. Jack was.

'I am sorry, Libby.'

'It's not enough. If it wasn't for you …' I left the rest of my sentence unspoken but he knew. 'So you sought me out to appease your guilt.'

'No. I didn't.'

'How could you have pretended to be my friend? I told you things I haven't told anyone else.'

'I am your friend.'

'You're not! It was a lie. All of it. How could you do that to me? Pretending to want to help. Taking Liam under your wing. Acting like you're a good person. You are NOT a good person.'

'I am. I wanted to help and I—'

'Thought you'd lie your way into my life.'

'I never planned to. I swear. I came here to pay my respects to Jack and you were already here and … You wanted to talk and I wanted to offer you some comfort.'

'And you thought making up a dead sister—'

'It wasn't cold or calculated, it was … Bethany was my hero. I idolised her. Growing up we were inseparable. Our parents were religious. Strict. But Bethany always found a way to have fun. She loved life. She … she had an affair with one of the church congregation. He was thirty years older than her and married with kids. My parents disowned her immediately but she didn't care. Her lover left his wife and they moved up north. I never saw her again. Mum never recovered from Bethany leaving and then, ironically, Dad ran off with a woman twenty years younger. I don't know where my sister is. It felt … it feels like such a loss.'

'It *isn't* the same thing.' I was furious he thought the two things were comparable.

'I know.'

'You don't or you wouldn't say something so bloody insensitive. *You* get a choice. *You* can track her down. Make up. Ignore her for the rest of your life. Choices I don't get to make any more because … because …' Noah reached out and touched my arm. Angrily, I shook him off.

'You know what, Noah? I don't really care.'

'Please, Libby. I've been a mess. I've been signed off work with depression since the mugging.'

'It was more than a mugging.'

'I know that. And I know I deserve to feel this way but you … you and the house have given me a focus and—'

'You're no longer welcome at the house so go back to your real job, Noah.' I glared at him. 'What is it that you actually do?'

'I'm a journalist.'

'That figures. You lie for a living.'

I walked away, barely holding my head up, barely holding myself up. I don't know how I managed to drive home but somehow I did.

Jack wasn't there.

I floated around the house studying every photo. Tracing his face. That smile. The curl of his hair where it touched his shoulders. He could have been here if he hadn't helped Noah. He *should* have been here.

Minutes dissolved into hours.

Jack didn't come.

I wasn't sure how much time had passed, whether it was even the same day, before the front door opened and shut. Alice and Mum.

'Libby?' Alice asked cautiously. 'Noah called me and said you were upset. He's worried about you—'

'Give. Me. Back. My. Key.'

I held out my hand. The noise was too much. I wanted to be alone.

Mum began to speak. I wished everyone would stop talking. Their voices were expanding. Filling the room. Filling my head.

Shut up.

I paced over to the window but the sunshine was too bright. My vision flickered.

Shut up.

Mum and Alice swam in and out of focus. I couldn't see properly but I could still hear their voices. Worried. Angry. Loud.

Shut up.

Emotions built. Noise built.

Shut up.

My knees weakened. My hands gripped the radiator in a futile attempt to keep myself upright. The sky outside strobed light, dark, light, dark.

I could feel myself slipping, sliding, aware but not. I was still conscious but I couldn't move. Couldn't speak.

I could feel Alice shaking my shoulders, hear Mum calling my name but all I could see was Jack.

Chapter Thirty-Five

By the time the paramedics came, it – whatever 'it' was – had passed.

The paramedic, Christine, crouched down before me.

'Libby, I'm going to take your blood pressure.'

While Christine tightened the band around my arm I told her that no, I wasn't diabetic, I hadn't had episodes of fainting, I didn't have a history of cardiac problems. I was adamant I didn't want to go to hospital. I was exhausted. Stressed. Not eating properly. That was all.

Mum had told Christine that I'd completely zoned out. That it had been terrifying to watch. She'd told Christine I hadn't been 'right' for ages. Was there really something wrong with me?

In the corner, Mum sniffed into a tissue while Alice wrapped a comforting arm around her. I had caused them so much stress these past few months.

'It's best we get you checked out properly, Libby,' Christine said.

'Do you think it's something serious?' Mum was alarmed.

'I'm not saying that,' Christine said carefully. 'It could be a multitude of things or it could be absolutely nothing. But if we take Libby to A & E her symptoms will be investigated straight away.'

'The doctor said Libby needed a blood test. She's waiting for an appointment with the nurse.'

'I'm okay now. There's other people who need you more than me.' I didn't feel okay at all but all I wanted to do was to flop into bed. Sleep it off.

'Better to be safe than sorry?' Christine formed it as a question. She squeezed my hand. 'Will you come with me?'

I nodded, feeling very small and very scared.

Christine's promise that with an A & E admittance I'd be investigated straight away was horribly inaccurate. Initially I was left in the corridor on a trolley, Mum and Alice acting like bookends, standing stiffly at my head and feet, protecting me from the sheer volume of traffic passing through; porters briskly pushing wheelchairs, nurses walking with purpose, patients shuffling past in slippers and dressing gowns, cigarettes and lighters clutched in hands, visitors with furrowed brows and downturned mouths. I felt self-conscious lying down. I wasn't really sick. I had asked if I could sit up but had been told no wheelchairs were available and there still wasn't a cubicle free which would have had a proper seat.

Alice let out a soft groan. Rubbed the small of her back with both hands.

'Alice, please go home. You shouldn't be standing.'

'I'm not leaving you.' She shifted her weight uncomfortably from foot to foot.

'Mum. Tell her to go home.'

'I can't make either of you do anything,' she muttered.

'You made me see the GP, twice,' I said.

'Fat lot of good they both were. *Stress*. The man who works at the newsagents had a—'

'Libby?' A kind voice. A hand on my arm.

'Angela.'

'I was just on my way back to the ward and I thought it was you. What have you been doing to yourself, lovey?' Her voice was just as reassuring as it had been when Jack had been admitted to her ward.

'Nothing. I had a … thing. I was brought in as a precaution.'

'How long have you been here?' she asked.

'A couple of hours,' Alice said flatly, rubbing her bump.

'I'll be back in a sec.'

When Angela came back she wheeled me out of the corridor into a cubicle. 'I'm going to give you my mobile number in case you need anything else.' Alice had already sunk down onto the chair squeezed into the corner. Mum sat on the edge of the trolley her legs tucked under her to avoid Alice's in the small space.

'Alice, you should go home. Get some rest.' My sister's eyes were closed.

'No. I'll stay.'

'She's right,' Mum said. 'We could be here for ages, Alice. You should—'

'You should go too, Mum. Mabel won't have eaten and—'

'I'm not leaving until you've had those tests.'

'About that …' The curtain swished back. A nurse with an apologetic look on her face. 'It's getting so late. We've a radiographer off and you might not get one today now.'

'Please. Go,' I said to Mum. 'There's no point us all being here.'

'I can't leave until I know the results of your tests.'

'Even if Libby does have a scan, which is unlikely now, she won't find out the results. We're going to try and find you a bed for the night. I'm sorry I can't be more helpful, we're run off our feet.'

'You're only ten minutes away,' I said to Mum. 'I can ring you if I need anything. Please. You both look shattered.'

'I do have a piece of haddock in the fridge for Mabel. Alice?'

'Yeah, okay. But text the second there's news. Text even if there isn't. You've got your phone and charger. Use them.' She hugged me close. 'Love you, Libs.'

'Love you too.'

'Yes.' Mum patted my hand as though that said it all and funnily enough, it did.

Typically, twenty minutes after Mum and Alice had left I was told I was being taken for a scan after all.

I was met by a nurse with a swinging golden ponytail, the lightness of her hair a contrast to the dark shadows under her eyes.

'Elizabeth Emerson?'

'Libby.'

'I'm Rowan. I just need to ask you a few questions.'

I fought to keep my voice steady as I told her there was no chance I could be pregnant.

Inside the scanning room my nerves increased as I looked at the machine.

'They're really loud aren't they?' I remembered what I'd heard. 'People have panic attacks in them.'

'You're thinking of an MRI scanner. This is a CT scanner. It won't surround your whole body so you shouldn't feel claustrophobic. It's quieter too. It works on X-rays not radio waves. You just need to lie still. The radiographer will be able to talk to you through a microphone. He might ask you to breathe in, breathe out or hold your breath at certain points. It will be over quickly and completely painless.' She smiled.

I lay down. Closed my eyes. There was a faint whirring.

A buzzing. A few minutes later I was told it was over. I hadn't felt a thing.

There was no one else in the waiting room. Impatiently I drummed my fingers against the arm of the wheelchair I had again been told to sit in. Footsteps clacked against the floor behind me but it wasn't Rowan telling me I could leave now. Where was she?

I picked at a stray thread hanging from the hospital gown as I waited. And waited. What was taking so long? My scan finished ages ago. My eyelids drooped with tiredness. I wanted my clothes back. My phone. I'd call Mum and ask her to come and pick me up and with a bit of luck I'd be back at home in half an hour.

The double doors to the scanning room swung shut with a bang. I looked around. Rowan headed towards me.

'Sorry about the delay. We've found a bed for you and a porter will be along to take you to the ward in just a—'

'I've still got to sleep here? Why? I've had the scan.' Despite the warmth a chill slid through me. 'Was there … something wrong with my results?'

She yawned. 'Sorry. Double shift today because we're so short-staffed. The results aren't immediate. The radiologist needs to analyse the images and write a report. In the meantime we're keeping you in for observation.'

'Is there something I should know?' Dread churned my stomach. I knew how precious hospital beds were. They wouldn't keep me here unless they thought something was wrong.

A cloud passed across Rowan's face. 'It's late and—'

'Please. If there's anything you can tell me.'

'Try not to worry. The radiologist has to write his report.'

'Can I see him please? The radiologist.'

'He won't be able to tell you anything. Look, here's the porter.' She faked a smile. 'Cedar Ward please, Trev.' She hurried away from me. Away from our conversation and my questions, leaving me alone with my fear and this strange man who began to push my wheelchair without warning. Without speaking. Our journey through the almost empty corridor swift and silent. He put the brakes on the wheelchair and with a 'I'll tell someone you're here,' I was left.

Again, I was alone.

Cedar Ward elicits an image of trees, sunshine, nature – a happy place to be.

It wasn't.

My neighbours were elderly. One had skin so pale she blended into the pillowcase. The other rattled out a chesty cough every other minute. Neither had baskets of fruit or get well cards on their bedside table.

I shuffled under the covers, the blankets and worry weighing heavily on me.

'Try not to worry,' Rowan had said.

Was I reading too much into that sentence, interpreting it to mean I did have something to worry about? Was I making something out of nothing?

Perhaps being kept in for observation was standard. I wasn't sure how CT scans worked. Whether the radiographer could see live on a screen during the scan or whether a computer needed to transcribe images. I texted Angela.

Can a radiographer tell at a scan if anything is wrong?

A radiographer will send the results to a radiologist who will write a report for the doctor.

Yes. But if something was wrong could they see it?

Radiographers aren't trained to interpret what they see.

But could they see something wrong?

I waited for the buzz of Angela's reply. I waited for the screen to light up.

But …

But …

But …

At last my phone vibrated. Her answer just one word.

Yes.

Chapter Thirty-Six

It wasn't long after breakfast that Mum's heels click-click-clicked down the stuffy ward until she reached me.

'Libby.' She leaned in to kiss me and the lightness of her perfume reminded me I hadn't washed, cleaned my teeth. I must stink. 'I came early so I can be here when they do your scan.'

I hitched myself up in bed, adjusting the pillow behind me so it supported my back. 'I had it yesterday.'

She drew in a sharp breath. 'Yesterday?' Her hands fluttered to her neck. 'Why didn't you tell me?'

'I didn't want you to worry and I knew I wouldn't get the results straight away.'

'So if you've had the scan, why are you still here?'

'They kept me in for observation in case I banged my head or something when I fell.' As I said the words I so wanted them to be true. They sounded plausible. Perhaps that's all it was. Routine. Procedure.

Better to be safe than sorry.

'So what's happening now?'

I shrugged. Twisting the corner of the sheet round and round my fingers, tighter and tighter.

'Libby?' Mum laid her hand on mine to stop me fiddling. 'Is there something you're not telling me?'

'No. I haven't been told much. The nurse said the doctor will speak to me later and then I suppose I can go home.'

Home. I wondered if Jack was there, why I couldn't see him here, if I'd ever see him again.

The day stretched. Each time Mum asked the nurse what was going on we were told they were busy, someone would be with me when they could. The menus came round for the following day. 'Best pick something,' the nurse said. 'If you're not here, whoever gets your bed will need to eat.'

For lunch I had the choice of the lady who'd been here the day before. Fish with new potatoes and overly orange tinned carrots.

'Mabel would be glad of that,' Mum said as I pushed it away.

It was late afternoon when a porter came with a wheelchair.

'I've been told to take you to the doctor,' he said. Mum trot-trot-trotted to keep up with his gait.

The shiny brass plaque on the door said Mr Baxter. Inside a desk and three chairs. Official. Terrifying. Nothing good could come of being taken to a private space in a hospital.

Mum was unusually quiet as we waited. A few minutes later the door opened and, for some reason, we automatically stood. There was a solemnness to the occasion somehow.

'I'm Mr Baxter.'

Unlike the medical staff I'd encountered so far in their uniforms and scrubs, he wore a shirt and trousers and a brief look of sympathy before his face fell into a neutral mask. I tried to make sense of the hierarchy. Was a 'Mr' more qualified than a doctor? I'd never dealt with illness before. I just didn't know.

He shook hands with me and Mum and gestured for us to sit back down. I held my gown together while I sat on the chair; the plastic squealed as I slid my spine hard against the backrest, trying to put as much space as I could in between me and this man who I already knew would change my life.

Mum reached across for my hand, squeezing it hard.

'Libby, you were brought in after a seizure—'

'Oh no!' Mum released her grip on my fingers. 'Libby didn't have a seizure.' She glanced at me and smiled an 'it's okay, they've mixed you up with someone else' smile. 'Libby did have some sort of episode but you've made a mistake. Donald, a customer in my shop, is epileptic. I've seen him having a seizure twice over the years. They are nothing like what Libby had.'

Mr Baxter rested his elbows on the table and steepled his fingers together. 'Mrs Emerson, seizures aren't always convulsive with loss of consciousness and twitching limbs. There are many different types of seizures. These range from feeling a bit spaced out to—'

'Don't you lose your driving licence if you've had a seizure?'

'Yes. It will be suspended though you can reapply after you've been seizure-free for a year, but—'

'Epilepsy.' Mum was clutching my hand again. 'It's not so bad, Libby. There's medication and—'

'I'm afraid,' Mr Baxter cut in, 'it isn't quite as simple as that. Libby's scan showed a mass on the brain.'

'A … a mass?' Mum's words were light, floating away. The room was floating away.

'I don't …' I tugged at the neck of my flimsy hospital gown, the tie choking me.

Mr Baxter pushed forward the cup of water on the desk. I picked it up but I was shaking so much that every time I tried to raise it to my mouth water splashed onto my lap. Mum plucked a tissue from the strategically placed box in front of us. I wondered how many other families Mr Baxter had given bad news to. How many tears had been shed in this bleak room in this bleak building.

'You must have lots of questions,' Mr Baxter said.

Mum and I glanced at each other.

We should have lots of questions, we probably did, but there was only one pressing thing Mum needed to know.

'Are you sure? I've heard of test results being mixed up.'

'I'm sorry, but yes, I'm absolutely sure.'

'But Libby's recently lost her boyfriend, Jack,' Mum said in a strangled voice like that might make a difference. I'd already had bad luck. I couldn't possibly have any more.

I sucked in air.

Breathe.

There were things I needed to know.

Breathe.

'This ... this mass ...' I paused to formulate my question. Associating the things I knew with the word.

Nothing came to me.

'It ...' I licked my dry lips. 'It isn't cancer or anything?'

Fleetingly a pained expression crossed his face until he rearranged his features into calm once more.

'Libby, we don't know what it is right now.'

'Cancer. You're telling us Libby could have cancer?' Mum broke down in tears. I sat mute with shock.

Cancer.

'A mass is an abnormal growth of cells dividing in an

uncontrolled way. It could be benign or malignant, we can't tell that yet.'

'How could I have something in my brain and not know about it?' My fingertips drifted to my forehead as though I might feel it pulsing beneath the surface. Already I thought of it as a writhing black swarm of cells. My throat stung with rising bile, as my eyes stung with the tears I struggled to hold back. I had the bizarre notion in my head that if I cried it would mean I was accepting this, somehow cementing it in truth. I wasn't. I wouldn't.

'There are a multitude of symptoms you might have been experiencing. Headaches, nausea, vomiting, tiredness.'

I processed this before I replied. 'I've had all of those,' I said quietly. 'I thought I was pregnant a few months ago.'

'Hormones can be affected. Your menstruation cycle disrupted.'

'But …' I cast my mind back. 'I've felt unwell for ages. Months. I had the flu and my ears were blocked and my balance felt unsteady but … Could those things have been caused by the … it?'

'Indeed.'

'But other than that I've felt …' What had I felt? 'Not fine, obviously, because of Jack but not … ill. Sad. Angry. But nothing I shouldn't have been feeling.'

'You've been through a tough time, Libby, I appreciate that but mood swings can also be attributed to your condition.'

You're not yourself, Libby.

'No, wait.' Mum stood up, circled the room like a frightened animal. 'I've taken my daughter to see a GP *twice*. Libby is stressed because of Jack. Because she's grieving. Two different doctors agree. They can't both be wrong. They're *doctors*.' She turned to face Mr Baxter, hands on her hips.

'Unfortunately there are more than a hundred different types of tumour and no two people's experiences are the same. There isn't always a conclusive list of symptoms a GP could be presented with and automatically link them to a tumour. The brain affects everything from irrational thoughts to evoking a sense of déjà-vu.'

Irrational thoughts. I had accused Alice of sleeping with Jack. Owen.

'But they're doctors,' Mum said again. 'They *should* have known. That's misdiagnosis. That's … wrong.'

'Diagnosis isn't always easy,' Mr Baxter said. 'The tumours are more common than we'd like but still relatively rare.'

'How rare?' I don't know why it seemed important to know just how unlucky I was, but it did.

'In the UK there are roughly 11,000 people diagnosed a year and more than 100,000 living with a tumour.'

'And what's caused this … thing?' Mum was almost hysterical. 'Is it because Libby's been so upset over Jack?'

'I had symptoms before I lost Jack.' I remembered the day we moved into the house. My thumping headache. Dizziness. The exhaustion I experienced almost on a daily basis, even then.

'We don't yet know the cause although research is being carried out all the time.'

There was a tap at the door. A woman entered. Blonde hair in a chignon.

'Libby …' She stretched out her hand as she strode towards me. 'I'm Charlotte, one of the neurosurgeons here. Mr Baxter asked me to pop in and see you.' After she'd introduced herself to Mum she sat lightly on the edge of the desk.

'I appreciate this is a shock for you both and a frightening time. We've seen your scans and we can't be absolutely sure what it is at this stage but we are going to do the best we can to remove it.'

'But that sounds so dangerous. Libby's *brain*,' Mum was wringing her hands in her lap. 'You don't even know what it is and Mr Baxter said it could be benign. What if you left alone?'

'Now Libby has experienced a seizure we want to remove what we can before she has further complications. There isn't much room in the skull for anything other than the brain. Our priority at this stage is to remove it and then histology will help us understand what it is and what further treatment Libby might need.'

Surgery. Further treatment. It was all too much.

'What's the waiting list like?' Mum was asking.

'Things don't always move this quickly but we've a space unexpectedly become free tomorrow.'

'Become free …' Mum covered her mouth with her hand.

'Nobody died, sorry – badly worded.' Charlotte leaned forward and briefly touched Mum's arm. 'The gentleman due for surgery has a really high temperature. We've postponed his op. Rest assured Libby is in safe hands. We'll do absolutely everything we can to safely remove as much of the mass as we can and then we'll take it from there.'

'And afterwards? Libby will be herself again? She's been acting so … odd lately. Looking back I knew it was more than grief. She …' Mum patted my knee to take the sting out of her words. 'She hit her sister.'

My face was hot with embarrassment. At least Mum hadn't shared that Alice was pregnant.

'And Alice is expecting.'

'Acting out of character is definitely something a lot of patients experience. Were you aware it was your sister, Libby?' She went on to explain, 'With the location of Libby's tumour she may have been having visual hallucinations.'

'Hallucinations?' My stomach lurched.

'Seeing things that aren't there. Of course not everybody will experience this but—'

'Hallucinations can be caused by this …' I press my hand hard against my skull. 'This thing in my head?'

'Yes. Some patients see or hear things that aren't there. Tumours can also sometimes cause psychosis. Patients might experience things that are very real to them but—'

'They aren't really there,' I said flatly.

'Is there anything you want to talk about, Libby?'

Jack.

I began to cry.

Mum's eyes locked on to mine. I could almost hear her mind whirring. The times I had talked to Jack. I gave an imperceptible shake of my head. I didn't want to share. I didn't want her to share. There was nothing to tell.

It wasn't all in my mind.

Jack had come to me.

Delusions.

Jack *had* come to me.

Seeing or hearing things that aren't there.

Jack had come to me.

It had been real. It had *felt* so real.

Jack.

I tried to pull myself together. I tried to listen as Charlotte ran through what would happen during the surgery, Mum rubbing my back rhythmically as I leaned forward, elbows on knees, head in my hands, but I couldn't focus. All I could think of was Jack.

The ward was quiet. Lights dimmed.

Jack.

I whispered his name but he didn't come. Surely if he was a figment of my imagination I could summon him at will. I stared into the not-quite-dark until the shapes around the ward sharpened and shifted, bedside cabinets swaying from side to side, an IV drip sliding across the floor.

Jack.

If my seeing him, hearing him, being with him was caused by the tumour then removing it would almost certainly remove Jack from my life and I couldn't bear that, not again. A life without him wasn't the life I wanted or needed.

If I didn't have the surgery he would still be with me. Always be with me, until …

We'd be together.

It was the early hours when I slipped out of bed.

Noiselessly I padded down the ward.

I turned the corner, the gloom swallowing me.

One step.

Two steps.

Three.

I carried on walking towards the glowing green of the fire escape exit sign.

As quietly as I could I pressed down on the bar and opened the door. Stepped out into the night.

Carried on walking.

Chapter Thirty-Seven

The sun was rising by the time I'd arrived home, shivering in my hospital gown, my feet bloodied and sore.

Irrational behaviour.

I had jogged much of the way, ducking behind parked cars, taking cover in ditches whenever traffic crawled by, sure that someone must have realised I was missing, be looking for me.

But they didn't seem to be.

Several times I had stopped to vomit in a hedge. This time I couldn't put my sickness down to a suspected pregnancy. Whether it was the exercise, the mass in my brain or just the knowing it was there that was making me sick I didn't know. I didn't know anything any more.

Still, my heart hammered as I stumbled up the lane, convinced there'd be a nurse, a police car, Mum or Alice at the very least waiting for me at the top, but there was no one.

The sight of the house caused a painful tightening in my chest. I remembered the day we had moved in. How I had drunk it all in. The pops of yellow as daffodils had poked their cheerful heads through the tangle of stinging nettles. The front garden was just as unkempt as it had been then, although the back was much improved. The paint still peeled on the front door I had vowed to restore to a glossy British racing green. The brass lion's head door knocker remained ginger with rust.

It had all gone so horribly wrong.

The smokeless chimney towered into the pale sky. There had been no making love in front of dancing fire. No toasting of marshmallows. That day my dreams had burned strong and bright and now they were nothing but ash. I lightly touched my temples with my fingertips. It was in there, even then, this mass that had brought me pain and suffering. Confusion and … Jack? Had it brought me Jack?

He was there at the window.

Watching.

Waiting.

I no longer felt the sweat dampening on my skin as I stepped towards him. No longer felt the gravel cut into my soles.

Jack.

My lips formed his name as I touched my head again, no longer trusting what was in front of my eyes.

But my heart. I trusted my heart that was still full of love for the man I could see. My heart that would always be full of love for the man before me. I hurried forward, reaching for the handle, knowing that Mum or Alice had likely locked the door when I was taken to hospital and I'd have to find another way inside but it slipped open. I bolted it behind me.

Jack.

He stood before me, his brown hair curling over his collar, his grey eyes holding mine until I broke away. Slowly I scanned the room. The mustard sofa, the open fireplace. My brain processed every object. I knew that if I wanted to, I could touch them. Feel the smoothness of the polka-dot vase. The chill of the silver picture frame. I could lay my hands on everything in this room and feel the weight of them beneath my skin.

Everything except Jack.

Still I tried, reaching for him as he stepped away. My hand connecting to air that felt thicker somehow.

Something *was* there.

Someone.

Jack.

I screwed up my eyes. Opened them again. Saw the concern on his face and I wanted to cry.

'I'm sick.'

'I know.' I didn't ask him how. It wasn't important. There was only one thing I needed him to confirm.

'Are you real?'

'I'm here.' Two words that didn't bring me comfort. I no longer trusted him. I no longer trusted myself.

Hallucination. Auditory and visual.

Lightheaded, I sank onto the sofa, not sure if it was the trek to get here, the tumour or the heavy swell of needing his comforting arms around me so badly that knocked me off my feet.

'You should be in hospital, Libs,' Jack said quietly.

'What, and let them operate? Let them remove possibly the only thing that allows me to see you? Hear you?' I spoke quickly, knowing that tears were only moments away. 'I can't do it, Jack. I won't.'

I waited for him to tell me that he'd always be with me, whether I had the operation or not.

But he didn't. A sick feeling sloshed in my stomach.

Hallucinations.

Psychosis.

Had any of this been real?

I raised my face to Jack's. I had to choose. My life or the one I'd created here with him? Greedily I wanted both.

'It's time for you to move on, Libby. Time for me to move on but I can't do that until I know you're safe and well. Perhaps that's why I'm here, to make sure you—'

'Then you'll be sticking around as long as I do because I'm not signing the consent form for surgery—'

'You have to.'

'Make me,' I challenged. I could feel the anger pulling in my veins. I wanted an argument. I would welcome one but my rage was misdirected. I wasn't even sure who I was furious with. The world? My circumstances? Everyone? Everything? But not Jack. 'Sorry.'

Jack gave me a sad smile. 'You know how you've felt since I … left. Do you want your Mum to feel like that? Alice?'

'I don't care …' I trailed off. I did care. But was it wrong if I cared about myself more? About what I wanted?

'Libby.' Jack crouched down before me. So close, but not close enough. He would never again be close enough. 'You could have a good life. A life without me.'

'I've had months without you and it hasn't been good, it's been horrible. Awful.'

'It doesn't mean the future will be. You have such a lot to look forward to. Finishing this house. Becoming an auntie …'

'But none of those things means anything without you to share them with.' He just didn't get it.

'You get to make a choice. You can choose to be happy.'

'I don't want to chose a life without you. I won't.'

'But it could be—'

'I know exactly how it will be.' It would be just like every day has been since he died.

Long.

Empty.

Hollow.

'You don't know how it could be, Libs. It would be a different life but not necessarily bad. Don't knock it until you've tried it.'

'I have—'

'Properly tried it. And if you don't have the op you're being a crab.'

I didn't answer. I couldn't. Despite Jack trying to lighten the mood I began to cry.

'I meant shellfish—'

'I know what you bloody well meant, Jack.' I struggled to speak through my tears. 'It's my life. Mine. I get to choose, not you. You … You left me. You made your choice. Helping Noah or coming home to me and guess what? You made the *wrong* choice. Oh I know things too,' I added as I registered his confusion. 'I know all about Noah.'

It was unfair. I could tell my words had wounded him and I was glad. The anger rising up once more.

'Mood swings,' Mr Baxter had said, but my resentment didn't necessarily have anything to do with my illness. I was justified in feeling pissed off, wasn't I?

'I want to be with you, Jack. Properly with you. Whatever that takes,' I said, firmly.

'Think of your family,' Jack implored. 'Think of Alice's baby.'

'It isn't my baby. Our baby. ' We would never sit around the dining table coaxing them to eat vegetables so they could have chocolate ice cream.

'You could still have all of that, Libby. A husband. Kids. A new life. A second life and I …' His voice quivered. 'I would know that I had always been your first love.'

'My last—'

'Libby. Stop. It.'

'I won't have the surgery and you can't make me.'

The silence was heavy and uncomfortable until Jack broke it. 'Maybe I can't make you sign the consent form but I won't stay here and watch you die. I'm leaving, Libby, and this time I won't be back.' He strode out of the door and after a fraction of a second's pause I hurtled after him.

'Jack!' But the hallway was empty. He was gone.

I raged and I screamed and I cried. I begged Jack to come back. He didn't.

His resolve and morality, the strengths I once admired, were keeping him away. I knew that. But I also knew he'd come back to save me if he had to. He wouldn't stay away if he thought I was in danger.

Would he?

I climbed the stairs, two a time. Swiped the box of sleeping tablets from the bathroom cabinet and headed back downstairs into the kitchen.

'Jack.' I filled a glass with water and then shook the pills. 'Jack. You'd better come back.'

Still, nothing.

He was staying away to save me, but I didn't want to be saved. I settled myself on the sofa in the snug. I'd been goading Jack, forcing his hand, but the more I mulled it over, the more it made sense. Could I be made to have the surgery against my will? My irrational behaviour and erratic train of thought was already being blamed on my tumour. If it was deemed I wasn't capable of making a decision, could the surgery consent form be signed on my behalf? I didn't want to take the risk. I wasn't sure and I didn't want to take the chance.

'Jack?' I gave him one last chance before saying loudly, 'Fine. If you won't come to me, I'll come to you.'

Thoughts were rocketing around my mind so hard they stung. Was I doing the right thing? I just didn't know but what I did know was that I didn't have much time. The nurse must have noticed I was missing by now. Mum was listed as my next of kin. If I was going to act I needed to do it quickly.

A miaow cut through the silence. Socks jumped onto my lap. I buried my face in his neck, my tears dampening his fur. 'Sorry,' I muttered. I wavered. My heart felt as though it was breaking as I pushed him off my lap.

'See you soon, Jack,' I whispered into the empty space that surrounded me as I emptied the pills onto the table before me.

It was then the landline began to ring.

The fourth phone call.

'Libby, it's Mr Baxter, from the hospital.'

I had known that it would be the hospital, so why did I answer? On some level did I want to be talked out of what I was about to do? Tension pulsed behind my eyes. My forehead tight. I felt like the mass might explode, splattering the walls with my redundant hopes and dreams, my flesh and bone, my sadness and regret.

'I know you're scared, Libby.' And until Mr Baxter said that I hadn't even realised I was. But under the numbness, the shock, the disbelief, my body trembled and dread spidered its way up and down my spine. 'But now that you've had one seizure you're at risk of having another and that's why we want to move with urgency. If you come back in—'

'I'm not coming back in.'

'You're lucky a space has opened on the list today—'

'*Lucky?*'

A sigh. 'Libby—'

'I don't want the operation.' But I could hear the doubt in my voice.

'I understand—'

'You don't.' That much I knew was true.

'So explain it to me.'

The line crackled while I fumbled around for the right words, any words. 'Have you … have you ever lost anyone you loved?'

'My mum died last year.' His voice gentle.

'And what if you had the chance to see her again?'

'I don't believe in the afterlife.'

'I'm not talking about the afterlife. I'm talking about here. Now.'

'I don't quite—'

'I can see Jack. Hear him. Not fleeting glimpses, although it started that way, but proper conversations.'

'Libby. Perhaps it wasn't made clear enough. It's very rare but the side effects of the mass could include psychosis—'

'But don't you see, I don't care. Maybe I can only see Jack because I'm sick but if that's the reason, and you make me better then … then …' My voice broke.

'Then you won't see him again.'

I wiped my eyes with the edge of the hospital gown I was still wearing.

'But, Libby, you might have limited time to have this operation and if you don't—'

'I could die, but …' I trailed off. Not wanting to tell him that was what I was trying to do when he called.

'Not necessarily. There can be many complications. Too many to predict and don't forget until we've performed the histology we don't know exactly what we're dealing with. But you could have more seizures, a stroke, paralysis, loss of speech. Loss of memory.'

It was this last one that floored me. 'So I might be alive but not remember Jack? At all?' My voice was tiny. Lost in a wave of utter sorrow.

'Potentially. Yes.'

'But you don't know for certain?'

'We don't know for certain.'

Without saying anything else I replaced the handset in its cradle. From the corner of my eye, a movement. I swung my head around, the sudden shift causing pain to radiate through my skull.

It wasn't Jack, it was Socks running out of the room.

I was alone.

Alone and terrified.

And that was when there was a hammering on the front door.

PART TWO

Chapter Thirty-Eight

It crosses my mind not to let Mum and Alice in as they pound frantically on the door but I know they won't just give up on me and leave. I wouldn't if I was in their position because that's what families do, they stay.

They endure.

I withdraw the bolt and they almost fall into the hallway, Mum clasping me in a hug that squeezes the breath from me. For once, she doesn't speak. I wriggle out of her arms and head back into the snug, not caring that my hospital gown is flapping open at the back, that my knickers are on display. It is the least of my worries.

'I know you're both here to persuade me to go back to the hospital but—'

'Oh my God.' Mum covers her mouth with her hands in horror. I follow her eye line to the sleeping pills scattered over the table.

'It's not what you think,' I say weakly although it is *exactly* what they are thinking. 'I can't deal with this right now. I need some time to process everything. Some space.'

'We're not leaving you.'

'Please. I'm not going to do anything stupid. ' I stuff the pills back into the box. My hand is trembling and several tablets fall onto the floor. I scoop them up so Socks doesn't find them.

'You've already done something stupid.' Alice's tone is hard now, she and Mum playing good cop, bad cop. It won't work. 'How could you have just … run away?'

'Like you have run away from your problems? You haven't even told the father …'

'At least if I don't tell him, I won't *die*.'

'Alice!' Mum is distraught but I don't blame my sister for her bluntness. She is speaking out of a place of fear. Of love. Sometimes there is only a fine line dividing the two.

'Sorry.' Alice is shamefaced. 'But we don't understand why you left the hospital. It's crazy—'

'But I might be crazy.' I tap my head. 'This thing might be making me crazy.'

'All the more reason to have it removed then, surely?' Alice asks. I don't answer. My head full of nothing. The swirling mass of cells crawling around, devouring my rational thoughts. Causing irrational thoughts.

'Please talk to me, Libby,' Alice begs but I don't have any words. How has it come to this? Jack gone. Mum crying into a tissue in the corner. My sister crouching broken before me, her baby bump hard against my shins. There's a tightening of her abdomen, the baby is moving. Did it all circle back to this life inside her? Jack going out for prosecco. Did it start the day we moved in here when she called and asked if she could pop round? If I'd said no, she couldn't visit, would things be different? Would Jack still be here? If only I hadn't answered the phone.

Four phone calls.

It has taken four phone calls to spin my world off its axis

and I remember them all with sharp clarity; the things I wanted to know – I was going to be an auntie – the things I wished I'd never been told.

Paralysis.

Memory loss.

The shock, the fear, the hope. The impossible, impossible decision I am faced with. To let go of Jack and have the operation, not knowing what the doctors will uncover, not knowing if it will be a success, the future uncertain and terrifying. Or to remain as I am, here with Jack, not knowing what the tumour might do to me, that future also uncertain and terrifying.

A stroke.

Loss of speech.

But … Jack.

You might have limited time to have this operation.

How limited? Is it safe to take a day to let things sink in? Two days? A week? I want everything to slow down.

Stop.

'I can't …' What I can't do is look my sister, Alice, in the eye. It's too much. All of it.

Death.

'Mr Baxter has told us the risks if you don't go back in.'

'I know. He told me too.'

Alice thinks I don't understand, but I do. Or perhaps she thinks it doesn't scare me or that I'm too scared.

I don't know which I am.

Both, perhaps.

'Say yes.' She is crouching before me, reaching for my hand but I snatch mine away. 'Say yes to the surgery and I'll take you back to the hospital now. You deserve to live. A fresh start.

You'll feel better with that … that thing out of your head. You can begin to move on. You will …' She swallows hard. 'You will find happiness again.'

I remain silent and still but my mind is noisy. Deafening thoughts scream for attention but the loudest one of all is yelling that if I have the surgery I might not see Jack again.

Ever.

But if I choose Jack, am I effectively saying goodbye to my family? My friends? My resolve not to have the surgery earlier is weakening now that I am faced with the distraught, tear-stained faces of Mum and Alice.

A quieter voice now whispers that I haven't seen Jack at all. It was psychosis, a hallucination, a side effect of the tumour that has lodged inside my brain, and it is this thought that makes me hesitant to agree or decline. That makes me question the times I have spent with Jack since he's been gone, seen him, heard him. Were they real? Any of them? I understand that there may be a medical explanation, of course I do, but it *felt* so real. Solid. Nothing like a dream. We talked. We laughed.

'I saw him. I heard him.' It's all I say but Alice knows, she heard me talking to him after all.

'I know you thought you did.' Alice squeezes my hand. 'And I know it must have felt very real to you. But it was your mind manifesting things, Libby.'

I'm only half-listening as Alice also says shock has the power to whisk memories behind a hazy curtain, sometimes replacing them with a better, shinier version – the way we wished things were, Jack still being here.

'But I'm here and I need you,' she says. 'Your niece needs you. We'll get through this together.'

She is offering out hope when I have none, a gift for me to unwrap and hold close. She places my hand on her bump and I feel a fierce kick. Strong. Undeniable. Absolute. A surge of love floors me. I draw back from my sister who winces and shifts her position, but as uncomfortable as she appears, she still doesn't leave my side. Can I consciously choose to leave hers?

Another pulse of pain. Another wave of nausea. I'm dizzy. Sick. Afraid.

Alice is talking me round. She's always been able to wrap me around her little finger. Sometimes I hate her. Not often, since we were kids, but on days like today when she just won't leave me alone. She won't let me go without a fight. I wouldn't if it was the other way round but it's my choice to make and mine alone.

'I think …' I tail off, unsure what I think. What I know. She's been telling me a new life, a better life is what I need. What I deserve.

That word plucks a hollow laugh deep from my belly. *Deserve*.

Do I deserve … *this*? To have lost the only man I've ever truly loved. To have lost the life I should have had. To have this … this thing inside my brain?

'You *know* what you have to do, Libby. You *must* have the surgery.' Her voice is thick with tears. 'For your sake. For Jack's,' she adds softly. 'For mine.'

Should I do what she is asking? If I agree, it's an admission that my life has been built on a lie, it's accepting that these past few months have been nothing more than a figment of my imagination. Dancing with Jack, lying on the sofa together, I'd be admitting it was all fake. And it isn't only that, if I'm honest; the childish part of me taunts. Why should Alice get what she wants when I can't have what I want?

Jack.

But I know that's a ridiculous way to think. If nothing else, I do at least accept that the mass on my brain is causing my erratic moods. But I'm not convinced I have conjured Jack up. He was as real to me as Alice is right now.

'Please, Libby, please,' she pleads. 'I know it's a big ask. I know you weren't expecting this – none of us saw it coming. We never thought for a second you were seriously ill. We thought it was grief. We put everything down to grief, all of your symptoms, and God I wish we hadn't, but now we know.' One whispered word, 'Please.'

Neither of us speak. The clock ticks. In the distance, the sound of a tractor. Alice's perfume fills my throat, something light and floral. She whimpers as if I am causing her physical pain and I probably am.

'Jack—'

'Don't speak his name—' I bite before she can tell me what he'd want because I know she would be right. He would want me to live.

'I won't stay here and watch you die.'

He *wants* me to live.

Alice flinches as I snap at her, perhaps wondering if I might slap her again, but still she doesn't leave. She's waiting for an answer as she tucks her long blonde hair behind her ears. Mum is waiting for an answer. She doesn't add anything, she knows Alice has said everything she can and I'm more likely to listen to my sister than anyone else. I lean back in my chair, eyes flickering over the nicotine-yellow ceiling we never did get round to painting bright white, as though I might find the right response written there.

Yes or no. Yes or no. Yes or no.

The words are loud. I raise my hands to my head, fingertips digging hard into my scalp.

Mum and Alice or Jack?

I can't decide.

Mum and Alice or Jack?

I won't.

Limited time.

I have to.

Think.

'You know if I could change things, I would,' Alice says softly. Evenly. 'If I could travel back in time I wouldn't have come round that day. Jack wouldn't have gone out for booze and—'

'I'd still have a brain tumour,' I finish.

'But Jack would be here and you'd feel you had something to live for.' She places her palm against my cheek; it's cool and I lean against it, allowing her to take the weight of my head which is heavy with thought. With doubt. For the first time I look at her properly, her eyes, the same green as mine, are rimmed red. The whites streaked with tiny blood vessels from where she's been crying and I realise despite her steady voice she is no more together than I am. 'If I could go back ...' She falls silent before she can blame herself, again. I can't bear her guilt. Her shame. I have enough of my own.

Slowly I look around the room for all the places Jack should be, but isn't: leaning against the radiator, gazing out of the window, eyes lighting up at the sight of his art students traipsing down the path. Sprawled on the sofa, patting the space beside him, my head fitting into the hollow between his shoulder and neck. Crouching down, building a fire, his skin glowing orange from the flames.

Pointing the remote control at the TV, popcorn balanced on his stomach, as we watched yet another home improvement show, picking out all the things that we would do to our house.

I carry them in my heart, the plans we made, the dreams we nurtured.

I will always carry them in my heart.

'Alice. Mum. I love you both dearly but I need you both to leave. I promise' – I raise my hands as Mum opens her mouth to protest – 'that I won't do anything rash.' I hold out the box of pills to Mum. 'But I just need a little time to think everything through. Please.'

'Fuck!' Alice says sharply.

'Alice, please don't …'

But I don't finish because Alice has doubled over in pain. It isn't my words that have hurt her.

It's the baby.

Chapter Thirty-Nine

Alice lets out another cry and all thoughts of Jack, of my diagnosis, of the decision I have to make fade away to nothing as I drop to the floor next to my sister and reach for her hand.

'The baby ...' she mumbles. 'Hurts ...'

Both Mum and I lightly touch Alice's stomach. Feel the tightening and release. I don't know what to do. I wish I'd paid more attention when she'd told me about practice contractions. Brackon Hicks or something. Why had I been so wrapped up in myself?

'This could be Braxton Hicks.' Mum has read my mind.

'Hurts. Too. Much.' Alice whimpers again.

Helplessly I turn to Mum. 'We have to get her to the hospital.'

'I'll call for an ambulance.' Mum grapples around in her bag for her phone.

'We can take my car.' I try to stand but Alice squeezes my fingers tighter.

'You can't drive, you've had a seizure,' Mum says. 'I can't drive in this state. Ambulance please,' she says firmly into her handset, giving them her name and my address, relaying that Alice is only thirty-four weeks pregnant. 'I think she's in labour,' she adds. 'They're on their way.' She tosses her phone back into her bag and kneels the other side of Alice. 'Go and get changed, Libby,' she says, not looking at me as she speaks.

'What? I don't need—'

'You're still wearing a hospital gown for God's sake.'

At the hospital Alice is unloaded from the ambulance on a trolley. Me and Mum trot alongside as we wend through the corridors, battering our way through double doors. We reach the maternity unit. Mum gives Alice's details.

'Is dad on the way?' we are asked.

'No. It's just us. The three of us.' Mum's eyes meet mine and I nod. We had always been a three. We had always coped.

We would now.

'Only one of you can come in the room.'

'Libby,' Mum says before I have had time to speak. 'You two have always—'

'Needed you.' I am out of my depth.

'You can do this. Be there, for your sister.'

Alice grips my hand tightly.

'Okay.' I can do this. Even if this is the last thing I can do.

From Alice's screams, her pants of pain, I had expected the baby to come quickly but there is still no sign of her. The midwife, Samantha, stays in the room with us. She had explained they'd keep a very close eye on Alice because she is only thirty-four weeks pregnant but they'd let the birth progress naturally as long as the baby isn't showing signs of distress.

'I need to tell you something,' Alice says in between contractions. She is nine centimetres dilated and apparently that means she could be giving birth very soon. 'The father, it's …

it's …' She takes another suck of gas and air before she carries on. 'Michael.'

'Michael?' For a second I am confused, searching my mind for all the Michaels we know, but there is only one. 'Faith's husband?' I don't let go of Alice's hand. I don't judge her.

'I'm so sorry.' Again a draw of gas and air for pain relief. 'He called into the coffee shop on Valentine's day after work for a cup of tea. He asked me what my plans were that night and when I told him I didn't have a date he—' Another contraction hit. 'He said that Faith was away in Norfolk and then asked if I wanted to get something to eat. As friends.'

I gritted my teeth. Fucking liar. Faith *had* been in Norfolk but was back for Valentine's. That was the night she showed up at our flat. Eager to show the photo of the beach with the bunker to Jack.

'He'd always seemed okay on the couple of occasions I'd met him with you. I thought …' A beat. 'I thought he was harmless and I was upset about being on my own. I'd recently broken up with Kris. It was stupid but we went back to mine with a takeaway and a bottle of wine and … he kept topping up my glass and …' She is crying now.

'Alice, he's fifteen years older than you. He should have known better. I don't blame you.'

'Don't you?' Alice lets out a roar. 'Libby …'

Samantha springs forward.

'It's time.'

I am nervous and excited. Distressed to see my sister in so much pain and elated I am about to become an auntie.

Alice screws up her face and clenches my fingers so hard I fear they will snap.

It seems to take an age.

303

Alice is told to push. To stop pushing. We pant together. I cheer her on, my vision clouded with tears.

'Come on, Alice,' I urge. In my mind I am standing by the red ribbon that stretches across the finishing line while eight-year-old Alice jumps towards me in a sack.

'You can do this, Alice,' I encourage, the way I did when my seventeen-year-old sister had hesitantly climbed into the car to take her driving test.

'I believe in you, Alice.' I reassure her as I had so many times over the years when she'd been lost. Alone. Afraid.

With one last push, one almighty scream, it is over. There's a brief, terrifying moment of silence before there's a cry.

The baby is crying.

Alice is crying.

I'm crying.

'It's a girl.' It is confirmed and they show her to us and she looks so small and helpless I am scared.

While she is checked over I soothe the damp hair back from Alice's brow.

'You did it. You did it,' I whisper over and over.

The rosette for coming first at sports day.

The driving licence.

A daughter.

She did it all.

My niece – Chloe Norma Emerson as she's named – is a fighter. She's tiny but breathing unaided which I am told is encouraging. I gaze at her in wonder through the glass window leading to the neonatal unit.

The rows of cots all cradle new life.

I recall the lyrics of The Beatles song Jack loved so much about those who have come before. The circle of life. People have to leave the earth to give way to someone new. New babies. New families. New hope.

I love you more.

Reluctantly I turn from the window and take the lonely walk down the corridor.

I know where I'm heading.

I have made my decision.

Chapter Forty

It is early when I wake, the sounds of the ward rousing me. I slept here last night after I'd spoken to Mr Baxter and told him that I wanted the operation. I hadn't expected them to fit me into surgery so quickly, sure I'd be added to an infinitely long waiting list but, possibly because they were worried I'd run away again, they told me they would operate today.

But I won't run away.

Seeing Chloe make her noisy and dramatic entrance into the world had changed mine. The love that filled my heart was different to the love I felt for Jack. It is solid. Tangible. Something I know to be true.

I'm scared though.

It has been twenty-four hours since I saw Jack and a larger part of me than I'd like wonders if I had ever really seen him at all. It's discomfiting to pick apart our sense of normal to realise it's not normal at all. The nausea I had grown accustomed to, the headache that always thuds away in the background, this is how I thought it felt to be me, but it isn't, not really. I can't fully remember what healthy feels like. Happy.

But loved?

I can remember the feeling of being loved. Safe. Adored. Mine and Jack's limbs entwined as we lay in bed, my head resting on his chest, his fingers twirling strands of hair around his finger.

The whisper of forever.

And we had lasted forever, Jack's forever anyway, and even now I am not letting him go. I'm not moving on, not forgetting him. But I am choosing to live, partly for Mum, Alice and Chloe but, undeniably, also for me.

It is Angela who approaches me with a smile.

'You don't work on this ward!' I am delighted to see her.

'I heard you were here, hospital jungle drums. How are you feeling?'

I battle to keep my shoulders down, surpassing the shrug that fights to rise. I lick my lips. My mouth is dry and it isn't only because I am not allowed to eat or drink.

'Terrified.' One word but it pretty much sums everything up.

'Don't be. I've checked the list, they'll be taking you down before lunch.'

'Have I got time to see Chloe?'

'Absolutely, Auntie Libby.'

Auntie Libby! I can't help but smile all the way to the neonatal unit.

He's there, he has his back to me as he gazes through the glass. I don't need to say anything. He senses me watching, turns and greets me with a huge grin.

'Sid. Should you be here?' I ask.

'At eighty-two probably not, but—'

'You know what I mean.'

'Your mum brought me in. She's just helping Alice have a shower and whatnot. They'll be along in a bit.'

'She's gorgeous isn't she?' I turn my attention back to my niece.

'Norma used to feed me tinned prunes and custard for pudding every Thursday. She looks a little like that. All wrinkly and—'

'Sid!' I object to my niece being compared to a dried fruit.

'And I loved those prunes, Libby. Really loved them.' His pale blue eyes water. 'You've all become like family to me. I'm lucky to have met you all. You've brought me much happiness.'

'And grief, and worry, and—'

'But that's what families are for, Libby. Not just the good but to support each other through the bad. Life isn't all beer and skittles, you know that.'

'I know,' I say quietly.

In her cot, Chloe stretches her mouth into a yawn and waves her tiny fists. I worry she'll dislodge the tubes and wires but a nurse had run through everything with me and I knew an alarm would sound if she did. Besides, it isn't like Chloe is alone. There is someone with her at all times. She begins to open her eyes but then, as if it's too much effort, she closes them again. It doesn't matter. She's got plenty of time to see the world, the beauty of it all. I only hope that one day she gets to see my face. We watch her wriggle. The tiny rabbits on her sleep suit look like they are hopping.

'I'm having an operation today,' I tell Sid.

'I didn't think you are dressed like that for fun,' he says, nodding at my dressing gown, my panda slippers. 'I know, duck. I know. Your mum told me.'

'What if … What if something goes wrong and I don't make it and I don't live to see Chloe grow up and—'

'But what if you do? What a privilege and a joy that would be. Me and Norma were never blessed but now … now through you lot it's like I've got a family of my own again. A daughter. Granddaughters. A great-granddaughter. People who will give me a good send-off when it's my turn to go, rather than the empty church I'd resigned myself to. Chloe will have plenty of people to love her with or without you but, Libby, I reckons you'll be fine. I really do. I know the thought of the tumour' – he doesn't flinch from the word and I love him for it – 'being in your brain is enough to give you the heebie-jeebies but there's no reason to think the worst of the surgery.'

'Except the consent form I signed. All the things I've been told might possibly go wrong.'

'You must stay positive, duck. You're doing the right thing having the op.'

'Am I?' Now it is almost time I am petrified I'll go to sleep and never wake up again. Never see Chloe grow, fall in love, have children of her own. I pinch the bridge of my nose to stop myself from crying. It doesn't work.

'Yes it's absolutely the right thing. If you hadn't agreed, your mum would have been devastated. You're a good girl. Not shellfish at all.'

I laugh through my tears. 'That's what Jack would say if he was here.'

'You know what else he would say? Live your life to the fullest. Laugh. Love. I never thought Norma would go before me. I wanted us to slip peacefully away together in the house. Now I've a very different life to the one we'd planned but' – he glances back at Chloe again – 'it's a good life and yours will be that too. Different to when you had Jack. The before and after life. But it will be what you make it. Life's an adventure. Don't knock it til you've tried it.'

I nod, too overcome to speak. He hugs me tightly. As ever, he smells of tobacco and Polos and safety. I never want to let go but he releases me.

'Squeeze me any tighter and I'll be piddling all over your slippers, duck. I'd better find the loo. My bladder ain't what it was.' He hobbled down the corridor, his walking stick tap-tap-tapping out his goodbye.

For the longest time I watch Chloe. Every minute movement, a kick of her leg, a shift of her head, is miraculous. It is while she is screwing her face up to demand her breakfast that I sense him, next to me, shoulder to shoulder.

'You're back.'

'I've come to say hello to Chloe.' Jack nods at the glass before turning to me with sad eyes.

'And goodbye to me.' It isn't a question. There's a deep knowing inside me that this is it. The end of us.

It is too much.

'I don't want you to go.' I am properly crying now, not caring if anyone sees me.

'Do you remember when I asked you to move in with me?' Jack asks gently.

I do. It is as clear in my mind as it was that day. I had been bushed. The hours spent running between my flat, Jack's flat on the other side of town and trying to build up the business with Greta had taken its toll.

Early on a Saturday morning Jack had woken me. 'Let's go out and get some fresh air.'

'I really don't want to.' I pulled the pillow over my head. 'I want to sleep.'

Jack whipped the pillow away. I groaned.

'You can sleep on the way.'

'On the way where? I can't go far, Jack. I need to go home, do my laundry, put my rubbish out. I've been here for days. My bin must stink.'

'Who said romance is dead?' Jack had tugged the covers. 'Your stinky bin will have to wait. Get up and wear something warm. The forecast isn't great today.'

'All my warm stuff is at my flat. We'll have to stop off on the way.'

'No. If we do you'll find a million things to do. You can wear one of my jumpers and I'll dig out a spare coat.'

I had pulled on my jeans, splattered with a red stain where I'd spilled pasta sauce down them the day before, a spare pair of knickers I now carried in my handbag since I'd been caught out before.

'I look a state,' I had said.

'You look beautiful, Elizabeth Emerson.'

'I'll have to go home later, I've no clean underwear left.'

'Me neither. But you can make the same pair last for days. Inside out, back to front …'

'Jack! You do *not* do that. And how would I wear a thong backwards?'

'It would look better. You should definitely try it.'

'You first.'

'It would take more than a strip of silk to contain—'

'Enough!' I laughed.

Cocooned in the warmth of the car, The Eagles taking it easy from the stereo, I had drifted off.

Sometime later, I realised we had stopped moving, the engine was quiet. I stretched, yawned as I blinked the sleep from my eyes and took in our surroundings.

'Norfolk!'

Jack grinned. We'd stepped out of the car, sea air zinging into my mouth. Hair whipping around my face. Already I was refreshed. Jack hoisted a large rucksack onto his back and then offered me his hand. I slipped mine inside his. We headed over the sand dunes until we were there.

The bunker.

Jack unzipped his rucksack, and took out a crowbar.

'What are you doing?'

'It's the key to the bunker,' he said as he levered off the man-hole cover. It wasn't as easy as he had perhaps thought. His arm pumped up and down, sweat forming on his brow, until at last there was a give. He toppled backwards.

'Idiot.' I'd peered into the blackness. As kids, Alice and I had thought nothing of jumping into the unknown, not fazed by the dark. Now, I shivered.

'Let there be light.' Jack produced a torch.

'You've thought of everything. Have you got the kitchen sink in there?'

'I do have something else.' He reached into the side pocket. 'Libby, this is the place I first told you I loved you. Here, I gave you the key to my heart. Today the key to the bunker.' He toed the crowbar on the floor. 'And now I want to give you the key to my home.' He opened a small jewellery box. On scarlet velvet nestled a shiny silver Yale key.

'But …' I was confused. 'I've already got a key to your flat. You've got one to mine.'

'Umm yes. I was *trying* to create a moment. It's a gesture.'

I looked at him helplessly.

'I want you to move in with me, Libby. I want you to bring

your jumpers and clean knickers and never have to worry about running out of stuff again.'

'I … Move in together?' I was stunned.

'Yes. It'll be an adventure. Just like when we go down there.' He glanced at the bunker. 'You said it yourself. There's an entire world waiting to be discovered.'

Our eyes met; I hope mine reflected the love that I saw in his own.

'What do you say?' he asked, shyer than I had ever seen him before.

'But … I'm grumpy in the mornings and I always forget to take the rubbish out and—'

'I know.' Jack traced my lips with his fingertips. 'I know all of those things, the good and the bad. I'll be the one to deal with the bins, I won't talk to you before you've drunk your morning coffee. There's an art to loving you, Libby, and I think I'm rather good at it. Don't overthink it.'

We both watched a butterfly flit, a carefree dance before alighting on a nearby shrub.

'What if—'

'That's a sign,' Jack cut in.

'The butterfly?'

'He has a heart-achingly short lifespan but he doesn't live his life in fear, worrying about the what-ifs and the buts. Instead he sees a landscape brimming with possibilities as he flies across the limitless sky. Don't live in fear, Libby, it's only a half life.'

The butterfly dipped and hovered in front of us before soaring off to pastures new, making a leap into the unknown.

'Yes,' I said, a smile spreading over my face. 'Yes!' Jack lifted me into his arms and I wrapped my legs tightly around his waist.

Unlike in the movies where the boy twirls the girl around giving the impression she weighs virtually nothing, his knees buckled and we tumbled onto the sand. 'Yes.' I pressed my lips against his over and over again.

'Elizabeth Emerson, I promise you this,' he said once we had finally stopped kissing. He looked at me with such intensity as he ran his fingertips tenderly down my cheek. 'I will love you for the rest of my life.'

The memory was bittersweet.

'And I did,' Jack says now. 'I made you that promise, Libs, and I kept it. I loved you for every single second of my life, still love you now. Will always …' He is crying too. I want to wipe away his tears but know that I can't. It's agony. More than anything I long to feel his skin one last time. 'I'm going to make you another promise now. You *will* be fine.'

'You can't know—'

'I can't be here and yet somehow I am. Libby, all you have to do is believe it. Want it. You can be happy and that is my wish for you. I want you to remember that.'

'I'll try.'

'I'll leave you a reminder,' he says but before I can ask him what he means a nurse waves at me from the end of the corridor.

'Libby. We're ready for you now.'

I turn to my left. Jack has gone. But hurtling up the corridor in his place is Mum pushing Alice in a wheelchair.

'We've come to say good—'

'Don't.' I can't bear another black-and-white movie farewell.

'Good luck,' Alice says simply, instinctively knowing I don't want a fuss.

'We'll be here when you come round,' Mum says and

like a child I want her to promise me that I will come round, but even if she says the words it won't make them true. One thing I've learned over the past few months is you can't take anything for granted. Our little family of four is still a family of four but instead of Jack, there's Chloe. We don't know how long we have left with the people we love. Whether each time we see them will be the last.

See you soon, Jack had said that fateful day when he went out to the shops. Norma had told Sid goodnight and never woken up again. It's impossible to predict when people will leave our life, enter our life. All we can do is make the most of the here and now. The people we have.

I hug Mum tightly. 'I love you so much. Sorry about everything I've put you through.' She strokes my hair as she had when I was small when I'd woken from a nightmare.

'None of that self-pity, young lady,' she gently chides.

'It's shellfish.' Alice stands and wraps herself around us both and when the nurse calls me again and they let me go, for the longest time I can still feel their arms around me. Jack's too.

I am staring at the ceiling. The nurse telling me in a second she'll count me down from ten and then the anaesthetic will take hold and I'll step over the line that separates the conscious from the unconscious.

'You'll be okay, you know.' She smiles down at my worried face. 'That young man of yours will look after you. From the way he was gazing at those babies you could tell he is kind.'

I wrestle to sit up as she eases me back down. She had *seen* him. *She had seen Jack.*

I attempt to speak but my tongue is too big for my mouth.

Jack, I try to say, but his name is only in my head.

Suddenly he is next to me, taking my hand, only this time I feel it, warm and soft around mine.

'I love you, Elizabeth Emerson.' His whispered words cross worlds, coming from his heart to mine.

It's the last thing I hear.

I don't know how much time has passed when my awareness begins to kick in. Everything is hazy. Someone is calling my name.

Jack?

He's come back to me.

Or have I gone to him?

Perhaps we've met in the nothingness in between.

I struggle to open my eyes, but I can't. My lids are too heavy.

Jack?

'Libby?' he says softly. 'It's time to wake up.'

Chapter Forty-One

It has been a month since my operation. A month in which my house has been filled with visitors bearing cards and flowers, well-wishers carrying casseroles. Everyone and everything.

Except Jack.

He's gone and as hard as it is, I have to accept that he was never really here. That he was a symptom of my tumour.

But sometimes I still wonder …

I've become close to Angela, Jack's nurse, and I was going to ask her to trace the nurse who was with me when I had my anaesthetic and ask her to describe who she'd seen when she'd said 'That young man of yours will look after you.' She couldn't have meant Sid.

That young man.

But in the end I'd decided I didn't want to know. Perhaps I'd imagined she'd said that, the tumour, the anaesthetic, the stress of surgery playing tricks on me. I'd rather not know. Anyway, there was something else that made me think … perhaps?

'I'm going to make you another promise now. You *will* be fine,' Jack had said minutes before my surgery. And I was. Charlotte, my surgeon, had removed all of the mass and thankfully, as it stands today, no further treatment is needed although I'll be having regular check-ups. As for the future, I don't know what that might hold, but none of us can predict it, can we?

Chloe wriggles in my aching arms. Since she was discharged from the hospital she has gained weight at a healthy rate. I shift her onto my shoulder.

'Shall I take her from you?' Alice offers but as tired as I am, I shake my head reluctant to relinquish my hold on this little girl that I adore. I'm weaker than I'd like but Mr Baxter assures me that will pass. I'll get back to normal. My new normal anyway.

The downstairs rooms of the house are still as they were except they appear brighter now; there's a warmth the snug didn't have before. Chloe's yellow and orange chequered baby quilt stretched out on the carpet under the patch of sunlight that beams through the window. Socks somehow knows to stay off of it. He's sleeping on the windowsill, above the radiator. A wooden crate stands in the corner full of brightly coloured plastic toys waiting for Chloe to grow into them – they all seem to take batteries – and next to it, now there is a hand-carved wooden farmyard. Sid had lugged it inside this morning.

There is a creak to his knees, a pain on his face as he kneels to set it up, but he waves away offers of help. You can tell that it means a lot to him to do this. That the farmyard means a lot to him.

'I've had the paint checked in case Chloe chews the animals,' he says as he slots the roof onto one of the barns. 'You know, in case it was toxic because of its age. There's no lead in it.'

Mum raises her eyebrows to me in a 'where did it come from?' gesture and I give the tiniest of 'how would I know?' shrugs.

Sid picks up on our curiosity as he struggles back to standing, this time accepting Mum's hands to steady himself. 'There was a time,' he says as he sinks down on the sofa – his old sofa where he'd once sat with Norma – 'just once. When I could have been a dad. Me and Norma, we didn't dare get too excited. The farm was the first, the only thing we bought. I couldn't resist it. But … it wasn't meant to be.'

My heart swells. 'You would have been a great dad.'

'You are a great dad.' Mum crosses the room and gives him a hug. 'Perhaps not in the way you'd thought but … to me … you know. Thanks for everything, Sid.'

She's crying. I'm crying. 'You're a wonderful grandfather,' I add.

'And a fabulous great-grandfather.' Alice is tearing up too. 'We all love you.'

'You know …' Sid takes his handkerchief out of his pocket and dabs his eyes before blowing his nose. 'Sometimes life *is* all beer and skittles.'

Chloe begins to whimper, the whimper that I've come to recognise precedes a cry so deafening I can't fathom how it bellows from her tiny lungs. Quickly the focus switches back to her and I think Sid is glad.

'I'd better get her home,' Alice says. 'She's overtired and with a bit of luck she'll nod off in the car.'

Before I hand my niece over to her doting mum I lower my lips to her forehead and kiss her goodbye, breathing in her newness. Johnson's baby lotion and innocence. Her tiny fingers swipe at air before landing on Jack's beanie. Before she can inadvertently tug it from my head, I gently unknot her fist.

The first time I looked in the mirror after the surgery I had been distressed. I told myself a shaved head and a scar were unimportant in the great scheme of things but still I couldn't bear to look at myself.

Sid had sensed how uncomfortable I was when he first visited me when I'd been transferred to the ward. As his stick tapped towards me I wished I'd thought to ask Mum or Alice to bring me a headscarf in. It hadn't seemed important after I'd come round; being alive seemed the most, the only, important thing.

Self-consciously, I'd touched my scalp as Sid lowered himself onto the hard blue chair by my bed.

'Hair don't make a person, duck,' Sid said. 'It's the heart that counts and you've got the biggest one. Still, you might want to wear this until it grows back.' He handed me a cream scarf patterned with pink roses. I was too overcome to say thank you but from the way I gripped his hand, he must have felt my gratitude.

At home now, I generally wear Jack's hat, still splattered with paint. My hair is beginning to grow, my head now itchy, but sometimes I run my fingers over the bump of my scar and I'm glad of it. It represents life.

Alice gathers Chloe's things together. It never fails to surprise me the paraphernalia she now carries with her: wipes, changes of clothes, muslin cloths, toys. Mum helps Sid to his feet.

As they leave I hug them all in turn and tell them that I love them as I do every time we say goodbye, aware that sometimes people leave and don't come back.

Can't come back.

I'm still sad but the violent mood swings I suffered seem to have dissipated, my anger with everyone, everything abated. Even though I am reassured it was not my fault, that I know it was not my fault, I am still ashamed of the way I acted out of character and the worry I put Mum and Alice through. It's something I talk through with Angela now that we've become friends. She insists that my erratic behaviour wasn't the cause of Alice going into labour, but how could she know? Sometimes I still feel the sting of that slap, hear Alice's cries of pain when her contractions started and I think what if …

What if Chloe hadn't survived?

What if it was all my fault?

Again.

Outside the sun is shining. It will be good to feel it on my skin. Because of the seizure I am still not allowed to drive but a walk will do me good. 'Blow away the cobwebs,' Sid would say.

Momentarily I consider bringing my camera but I dismiss the thought. I don't want to feel my emotions through a lens, particularly when I'm still figuring out what they are.

Grief is ever-present, in my stance, my gait. I walk down the lane, slower than I did before, all too often staring at the potholed track in front of me, every now and then forcing myself to look up. To see the sky, a fresh ice blue. Watch the flap of wings as a flock of birds takes flight to pastures new.

What would it be like to feel that freedom?

The fields are still clinging on to their summer green despite the leaves of the trees crisping to autumn orange. It's so beautiful here. Me and Jack had such hopes, such plans. Despite his life insurance pay-out taking away the urgency to decide what I want to do with the rest of my life, I know that eventually I'll have to. I glance back at the house – our house. It would break my heart to sell it but perhaps a fresh start is what I need. I'll talk to Mum about it. We've become so close, the once fragile relationship with her now strong as steel. I appreciate the lengths she has gone to, still goes to, to help me navigate my way on this dark and lonely path I've found myself thrust onto. I've realised it isn't always about what you say or don't say, what you do or don't do. Sometimes as a parent it's enough to just be there. Show up.

She always shows up.

My energy is low and it is too far for me to walk but still my feet make their own way to the churchyard. I have such a lot to tell Jack. Ask him. It isn't quite the same talking to him at home now he no longer replies. Here, at least, I feel close to him still.

The hedgerow rustles its hello as I push my way through the wrought-iron gate.

I see his profile, sitting cross-legged on the place where Jack sleeps his last sleep.

Liam.

His mouth is moving but I can't make out what he's saying.

But he's crying.

My heart aches for him.

Its unsettling to hear a teenage boy so distressed and I don't know whether to let him know I am there or not.

'So …' He gulps back his tears. 'It's all gone to shite. Libby ain't working on the house no more 'cos she's sick. Not that I want anything to do with Noah now. It's all his fault you're … you're … I hate him and I miss him and then I hate myself for being a twat because he was only being nice to me and Libby because he felt guilty. And I thought … I thought he liked me.' There's a gut-wrenching sob before his broken voice continues. 'Me dad's back inside and me mum's new fella is a complete wanker. He makes out he's me mate, shakes my hand and stuff when he comes round but really he's squeezing it too hard. He ruffles my hair but he pulls it. I told him he's a dick and Mum said if I can't be civil I can't stay under her roof but where can I go?

I've got no one else. My college course is rubbish, we hardly ever paint. Not that a talent for painting will get me far but you were the only one who believed in me, Jack, and … and you fucking well went and left me—'

It's raw and personal and I desperately want to comfort him.

'Liam,' I call as I walk slowly towards him, giving him time to wipe his face, his nose with his sleeve. I kneel beside him and wrap my arms around him. His body is shaking with grief.

'It's going to be okay,' I soothe, stroking his hair.

'How?' His voice is muffled against my shoulder.

'I don't know yet. But it just is.'

While he cries I think of the way he'd been written off by the teachers, the authorities, even his own mum but with me he is kind, hardworking, gentle. I'd noticed while he worked on the house that he carried a bag of cat treats in his pocket, saw the way he tenderly stroked Socks. I think about the other kids Jack had wanted to help. I think about all of it. All of them. Can I help them?

Can I help Liam?

He deserves it.

The boy who graffities walls, the boy who had stolen my laptop and purse is worlds away from the optimistic helpful boy who had painstakingly, gently, moved the snails from the back garden so they wouldn't eat the plants.

There are different sides to us all, aren't there?

Eventually Liam stops crying. We sit, backs against Jack's gravestone, legs stretched out before us.

'It wasn't Noah's fault.' I've come to accept this. 'Jack was … he chose to help because that's the sort of person he was.'

'But if he hadn't—'

'You can't dwell on the what-ifs. It will drive you mad. Jack would want you to forgive Noah. You need good people in your life, Liam.'

'Why?' He looks sideways at me. 'Are you … are you going to die?'

'Not yet, I hope.' I smile. 'I've got a lot of living to do first. So have you.'

'Yeah.' He sniffs, stands. 'I've gotta go. I'm meeting me mates.'

'Don't vandalise anything.'

'I won't.'

'Or punch anyone,' I call after him.

He raises his hand in a wave, and then he's gone.

I want to help Liam. I want that so much but …

A red admiral butterfly hovers over Jack's gravestone, fluttering its delicate wings and I recall watching a similar butterfly in Norfolk on the day Jack asked me to move in with him. How Jack used the tiny creature to brush away my doubts.

'He has a heart-achingly short lifespan but he doesn't live his life in fear, worrying about the what-ifs and the buts. Instead he sees a landscape brimming with possibilities as he flies across the limitless sky. Don't live in fear, Libby, it's only a half life.'

Jack had a heart-achingly short lifespan but his life was full to the brim with plans for the future.

The butterfly spins corkscrew spirals before he heads off to his next adventure.

It is time for me to go.

The instant I step inside the hallway I smell it.

Jack's aftershave.

I freeze. Not sure what to do.

Think.

Say.

Panic builds. Is my tumour back? Am I going crazy?

'Jack?' I tentatively call, desperately hoping he answers me, desperately hoping he doesn't.

Silence.

Closing the door, I try to calm myself, pressing my hand against my scar. The surgery was a success but what if the mass is coming back? My heart is pounding as I step into the snug, breathe in deeply. I can't smell anything here. Back in the hallway it's still there, the smell of him. I try the dining room, remembering when we danced. Our cheeks pressed together, The Beatles spinning on the record player.

In here the scent is of lavender polish; Mum is always whizzing round with a duster.

At the bottom of the stairs the aftershave is stronger. I follow it, feet creaking on the steps. Scared of what I'll find. Scared of what I won't.

The smell leads me to the room on the second floor where I'd stacked Jack's art supplies. He's not here. Of course he wouldn't be. Tears prick at my eyes. What was I expecting, that he'd be waiting to welcome me with that huge grin of his and his comforting arms, and what if he had been? It would have meant I am sick again.

The painting of Norfolk is still covered. The one Faith had brought round telling me it was to be his proposal. The 'Please will you …' never finished, his question left unasked. I remove the sheet.

Gasp.

It's finished.

My knees buckle.

It's finished.

I screw my eyes up tight; I'm seeing things again. But when I open them I know that I am not.

It's finished.

'You can be happy and that is my wish for you. I want you to remember that,' Jack had said in the hospital immediately before my surgery.

'I'll try,' I had replied.

'I'll leave you a reminder,' he had said, and here it was. My reminder.

The painting of the beach, the glistening sea, the white light-house and the barely visible entrance to the bunker, a hidden world.

Finished.

'Will you please be happy?' painted in Jack's cursive script. It isn't a question, it is a statement. A command. No, gentler than that, it is forgiveness. Permission to move on. Let go of the guilt.

Proof.

It is proof that Jack didn't blame me for any of it. Not him going out for Lemsip, for me not checking his dressing, for not realising just how sick he was.

Will you please be happy?

It doesn't cross my mind to call Faith to double-check that the painting hadn't been finished. To confirm that the wording was incomplete when she brought it here. To check that perhaps it isn't a blip in my memory. After all, I had been ill then, the mass in my brain growing.

But I don't need confirmation, explanation.

I know with certainty.

Jack *had* been here all along, and if it wasn't real, any of it, then I don't want to know.

Will you please be happy?

I nod. Smile through my tears.

Happy.

I know, for Jack, I will try. I will try and be that butterfly and see the world as brimming with possibilities, the sky limitless.

I know what I'm going to do. I reach for my phone, scroll until I find exactly the right app to download.

Chapter Forty-Two

On my phone I download a journal app and write my first entry, marking the date, and then Liam's name and one word. Home. My digital version of Norma's kindness book. And then, as intimidating as I'd found Liam's mum, I call a cab. Knock on her front door, hoping Liam is home and not still out with his mates.

'You again?' she sneers. 'What do you want?'

'To talk about Liam.'

'Dunno why you're so obsessed with my boy. Like some kind of weirdo.'

'If by obsessed you mean taking an interest in and caring about him, then yes, I suppose I am obsessed.'

'Caring about? You gave him a job, some hope, and then you dumped him.'

'I didn't …' I lower my voice. 'I didn't *dump* him. I've been in hospital.'

She shrugs, uninterested. 'Whatever.'

'Look.' I take a moment to swallow the irritation that's on the tip of my tongue. 'Do you think he's happy?'

I expect her to shout, to scream, to tell me to get lost but instead she says quietly, 'It ain't easy bringing up a teenager.'

'I know you've done your best.' When that sentence formed I didn't believe she had but once the words are out, hanging between us, I see something else on her face. Guilt? Sorrow? And I think that perhaps she has done her best and really, that's all any of us can do, isn't it? But before she can respond her new man appears behind her, reeking of alcohol. 'What the fuck do you want?'

His spittle hits my face, the scar on my head throbs but I do not walk away.

'Liam?' I call and I wait while he tentatively walks towards me.

'You shouldn't have come.' He scowls, probably worried about what might happen when I leave, but I am not leaving.

Not without him.

I take my question and hold it out to him. 'I'd like you to move into the house.'

'What are you, some fucking paedo?' The man steps forward but I stand my ground, my eyes on Liam's.

'You're seventeen, you can leave home if you want to. Look, I can't drive yet,' I say. 'I'll pay for you to take an intensive course to get your licence, you can use my car, it'll be handy to get out and choose things.'

'What things?' he asks.

'To finish the new art centre. To furnish the rooms. For Jack.' I give that a moment to settle, my pulse skipping lightly in my veins. 'You hate your college course and I can set up an apprenticeship for you until you're eighteen.' He doesn't speak. The wait is agonising. 'What do you think?'

Ten minutes later we are both in the cab, his meagre possessions in a bin bag.

'Thanks,' he says.

'Please don't thank me. You've worked so hard over these past few months and I shouldn't even have considered—'

'There's one more thing you can do to make it up to me,' Liam says. 'I'll make us dinner when we get home but promise me I can choose the music while I cook. Honestly. Nineties pop. You old people.'

'Old? I'm only twenty-seven!'

I laugh and it feels good.

There is somewhere else I have to go. Someone else I have to see. And when he isn't at home I know where to find him.

Noah is on the bench when I arrive and for a few moments I watch him, waiting for the hate I had felt for him to fill my veins, heat my body, but it doesn't. More than anyone, I know that life's too short to hold a grudge, and not just Jack's life. My life. My fingers find my scar before I drop my hand back to my side.

'Hello.' I offer him a bottle of Lucozade. Hesitantly, he takes it.

'It's okay. I haven't poisoned it or anything,' I say.

'I wouldn't blame you.'

'Blame' – I gaze into the distance, into the sky, where an aeroplane cuts across a white puffy cloud – 'is toxic and I don't blame you. Jack would say forgiveness is a gift you give to yourself.'

'I don't …' Noah rubs his hand over his chin; he hasn't shaved. 'I don't want you to say you forgive me just because Jack would.'

'I'm saying it because' – I take his hand – 'it wasn't your fault.'

His fingers curl around mine and for a long time we don't speak.

It is me who breaks the silence.

'Are you back at work?' I ask.

'No. I've been having counselling though. Trying to reduce

my anti-depressants. I've … I've been coming here every day. Hoping you'd be here but—'

'I've been sick.' I touch my head.

Noah's eyes flicker towards my hat before landing on my eyes. 'Libby.' My name barely audible.

'I'm going to be okay. I have to be. I'm going to finish the centre. For the kids. For Liam. For Jack. But … mainly for me.'

'How is Liam? I've texted him but he doesn't answer.'

'He was angry but he'll be okay. I've offered him a full-time job. Asked him to move in.'

'That's brilliant. Can I come back? Help out?'

'No. You were never much of a decorator.' I smile. 'Go back to work, Noah. Don't let guilt ruin your life.'

He nods. 'I could help in other ways. Writing features, publicity, I know my way around the system when you need to apply for funding. Grants.'

'That would be wonderful.'

It's another small step.

Another square.

Today, we are waiting for Faith. I had called her to ask whether I could talk through Jack's plans with her.

'The notes you emailed were great and we've made a really good start with both the house and the garden but the practicalities of running the courses and workshops are something I can't quite figure out. Can I pick your brains?'

At first we had spoken about the business side but then she had asked, 'And you, Libby? How are things with you? You haven't messaged me for ages.'

'I've had a brain tumour.'

I heard her gasp. 'Oh my God.'

'It's okay. I'm okay. I'm one of the lucky ones but … I thought I didn't want to be saved. I thought I wanted to be with Jack. You know when you have a love that precious and you can't let it go? You have that with Michael, moving around the country, giving up so much for him. You—'

'Don't,' she said. 'Don't compare Jack to Michael. Jack was a good man. The best. Michael is … Well it doesn't matter. Are you really going to be okay, Libby?'

'Promise. I had a great surgeon. What's …' I hesitated. We hadn't been that close. 'Is there a problem with Michael?'

'I'm leaving him.' She explained that Michael had always had a problem remaining faithful. She had tried to keep him happy, had treated him with love and kindness and affection that perhaps he didn't deserve. She was fed up of moving from town to town after he'd broken yet another heart, not just that of his wife. I was amazed, they'd always seemed happy but then I guess you never really know, do you?

She asked if she could visit. I didn't tell her about Alice and Michael. Chloe. It wasn't my place to, but when my sister heard Faith was coming she made sure that she was here too.

'I've something to tell you, and I am so, so sorry.' Alice's voice shook as she relayed the details. It was just one night. Valentine's. She had been drunk. Upset. She hadn't meant to destroy a marriage.

'You didn't,' Faith said. 'It was broken long before you. Please don't give it another thought. It doesn't matter.'

'But it does. There's something else.' Alice told Faith about Chloe. How she had tried to tell Michael she was pregnant but he didn't want to hear it. He hadn't been in touch since they'd moved away.

Faith had cried. Alice had cried. Eventually they had hugged, not quite friends but both recognising the hurt in the other, the way the same man had betrayed them, lied to them.

Mum and I had been waiting in the kitchen with Chloe and when Alice called us through we carried the sleeping baby gently to Faith.

'Oh!' Faith covered her mouth with her hands. Tears pooling in her eyes again. 'She looks … she looks like Michael.' Her voice wavered. 'She looks like the child I imagined we'd have one day if I managed to fall pregnant. Can … can I hold her?' Faith cradled Chloe in her arms, scanning her face. 'Actually, she has your mouth, Alice. She's beautiful. Don't ever apologise for her.'

Chloe opened her sleepy eyes and studied this new person holding her.

'What will you do with your life?' Faith murmured before raising her face to mine and asking beseechingly, 'What will I do with mine?'

'Move in.' I didn't hesitate. 'I've plenty of room and we can fulfil the plans that you and Jack made. Open the centre in his name, in his honour.'

She nodded, tears spilling down her cheeks. No matter what is taken from us there is always hope, and that was the exact moment I decided to go ahead and enter The Hawley Foundation Prize.

Days later there is a knock on the door. I open it to a delivery man. 'Sign here,' he says before leaving me with a long cardboard box.

It's heavy. I carry it through to the kitchen. Through the window, beyond the garden, I see Liam and his friends clustered around one of the outbuildings, deep in conversation. They've all offered to help out in return for beer and snacks.

'It would probably be cheaper to pay them, duck,' Sid said doubtfully and I will – but in the meantime they are learning about paying it forward.

Kindness.

The ripple effect, that smooth pebble dropped into a pond.

I open the box; inside is a guitar, the Gibson, Jack's guitar, and with it, a note.

In retrospect, we took too much from you. Rhonda and Bryan.

I curl my fingers around the neck, hearing Jack strum 'Lay, Lady, Lay' the night we first made love, feeling his lips on mine, his hands.

Too much *had* been snatched from me but in return, thanks to the doctors, I've been offered a future. Thanks to the support of everyone surrounding me, a chance to make Jack's dreams come true. A chance to give back to the community he loved.

We're all doing it, together.

We're all being more Jack.

Epilogue

It is spring again. The time for new beginnings, fresh starts. A year since Jack and I had stood looking up at this house, marvelling how lucky we were that it had become ours. The front garden is no longer overgrown; Liam has cut everything back and now the daffodils have once more pushed their hopeful heads through the nettle-free borders. I was worried he'd dislodged the bulbs when he'd dug the earth over, that they'd never bloom again, and yet here they are. We could learn a lesson or two about determination from these sunshine-yellow flowers. No matter how hard it is to break from the clutches of darkness with a cheerful smile they do exactly that, time after time. Today, once more, I can smell honeysuckle and happiness.

The front door, now restored to a shiny British racing green, is open.

Round the side, Faith is hanging bunting from the barn, Alice holding the ladder steady. Chloe sleeping in her pushchair, her skin slick with sun cream although she's shaded by an umbrella. My once impetuous little sister is an incredibly responsible mum.

Sid is here early. I have a surprise for him.

'Follow me.' I lead him through the kitchen, to the small room where he and Norma used to sit and watch the sunset, munching on cheese and crackers with homemade chutney, scones and jam with fruit from the garden.

I'm anxious as I wait for his reaction, remembering how sad he was over FaceTime on moving-in day when Jack had brought the phone in here and he'd seen how the room looked. 'A shell' he had called it.

It isn't a shell now.

Sid doesn't speak. He can't. He's too overcome. I can feel my own hot tears building behind my eyes.

He lightly touches the newly papered walls. I had the wallpaper custom-printed with pages from Norma's kindness journal; rows of her neat writing covers the space between ceiling and floor. He turns to me and opens his arms and I step into them, feel his fragile spine beneath his shirt, the fluttering of his heart.

'Let's sit,' I say softly.

He takes one of the leather burgundy armchairs I'd sourced, I take the other. On the small table between us is a plate laden with scones, with pots of clotted cream and jam. They won't taste as good as Norma's but I've tried.

We gaze out over the fields but I know Sid isn't seeing the grass, the sheep; he's seeing his bride, his life. A tear spills down his cheek and for a second I worry I've done the wrong thing, but he turns to me and says quietly, 'It's a beer and skittles day, Libby. I'm so proud of you.'

'I couldn't have done it without—'

'Shh. You may not have my blood in your veins but ...'

'I know.' I reach out my hand and he takes it and we sit, quietly, for the longest time.

*

Later, I search out Liam. He's in one of the barns. The outside walls are covered with graffiti. I'd given him free rein to express himself creatively and the images are bright and joyful. In the centre is Jack. He has his arms splayed and is surrounded by words: love; live; laugh; art; hope. It's stunning. Jack was right, Liam is immensely talented. Faith has already asked him to assist her in teaching but I'm not sure he'll be here for long; he's destined for great things, I truly believe that. The first showcase we host will be of his work.

On the door of the barn is a brass sign; each of the outbuildings has a name. This is the Sid Butler Teaching Room. My photography studio, which Greta will share, is named after my adorable niece, Chloe. Inside, a skylight beams sunshine onto a semicircle of easels. My mouth lifts into a smile as I recall sitting in the centre of a similar set-up, naked, vulnerable, Jack's eyes on mine.

'This looks great, Liam. Thanks.'

'Why don't you go and get ready?' Liam says. 'I'm going to go and blow up some balloons for the exhibition space and then we're done.'

'We really should have hung more pictures in there, it's so bare. What if—'

'What if you go and get changed? Honestly, everything is under control. Your mum is in there sorting out the refreshments. Everything is fine.'

'But—'

'Get ready,' Liam says, no longer the child.

I check my watch and hurry back to the house. It's a big day. I want to look my best.

I stand in front of the mirror, nervously smoothing down my orange dress – it isn't the day for black – and the pixie cut that feathers my skull. There's the sound of car doors. Chatter below my window. People are beginning to arrive.

Downstairs, the house is full of colour and life. It is packed with lots of people I don't know – Noah has done a fabulous job with publicity – and some that I do. Alice and Mum are waiting at the bottom of the stairs. The hallway has been decorated; I chose a burgundy similar to the original.

My mind travels back to moving-in day, gazing at the faded patches on the dark walls where family photos had once hung. Jack's arms around my waist, his lips on my neck.

'We'll fill the house with new memories,' Jack had whispered.

Now myriad frames display before and after photos of the house, the project that once felt insurmountable tackled with love, bit by bit.

Square by square.

Mum squeezes my arm. 'You look beautiful.'

'You smell good too.' Alice smiles.

I take a deep breath, Jack's aftershave filling my nostrils. I've taken to wearing it on special occasions and it doesn't get more special than this. I begin to wobble and take a breath.

Happy thoughts only tonight.

I scan the kitchen. Sitting on one of the chairs is Mum's neighbour, Mabel. Leaning on his walking stick, engaging her in deep conversation, is Sid. Mabel's fingers play with her necklace as she laughs.

Mabel Mackay, you flirt.

I smile.

It's never too late for love.

Mum nudges me. 'I brought Sid round for tea once and he

338

came with me to give Mabel her dinner. We ended up eating together and they really got on well. I saw him get out of a taxi last week and assumed he'd come to visit me but instead it was her door he knocked on,' she tells me. 'They've really hit it off, more than I'd realised. They've been texting non-stop. Mabel made a joke yesterday about having a toy boy.'

I'm glad.

'Libby.' A voice to my left says my name. It's Noah.

'I want to introduce you to someone.' He ushers the woman standing behind him, forwards. I spot the resemblance immediately.

'This is Bethany, my sister. I kept thinking about our conversation, choices, and I found her online and reached out.'

'I'm so pleased for you both. Hello Bethany.'

'Hi,' she says shyly.

'Thanks, Libby,' Noah says.

'What are friends for?' I swiftly hug him before I move away to gather my thoughts. If it hadn't been for Jack dying they wouldn't have found each other again. Mum and Alice would likely never have got to know Sid properly. Liam would never have been given so much responsibility and the opportunity to shine. Mabel might never have met Sid, had a second chance at love.

The butterfly effect. The delicate flutter of wings. The tiniest change doesn't always lead to chaos, catastrophe, an ordered life falling apart as I'd thought.

Sometimes it leads to new beginnings. Friendship.

Love.

There's the sound of a metal fork against a glass, a hush falls.

'If you could follow me, everyone,' Faith calls.

I follow the throng, those butterflies now dancing in my

stomach as we wander outside, passing Socks under the shade of a tree, licking his paws.

Outside the larger barn – the grandly named Norma Butler Exhibition Hall – Liam stands in front of a red ribbon, scissors in hand. His friends begin to clap as I approach. I'm touched they've all made an effort tonight, wearing shirts and trousers, part of their old school uniform, some trousers too short, ankles on show, dirty trainers on feet, but none of that matters. They are here to support me. We've become a mismatched family. At the centre of their cluster is Faith. Michael, now her ex-husband, might have become a father but in an odd kind of way she has become a mother. Nurturing. Protective. Encouraging. A Wendy to the Lost Boys in *Peter Pan*.

Everyone has joined in with the applause and I hold up my hands, laughing, giving a wave as I see Angela standing at the back.

'Faith.' I call her over. It's as much her night as it is mine.

'Thanks for coming.' I address the crowd before I scan my notes. I've practised my speech over and over.

'Many things have brought us here today. The kindness of Sid who allowed us to buy this house and generously set up a trust. The vision of Jack who strived to make the world a better place. He made my world a better place.' I falter. Screw up the paper in my fist. It doesn't feel right to recite prepared words. I want to speak from the heart.

'A wise man' – my eyes find Sid's – 'once told me that "everything will be all right, it usually is" and although there've been times I've doubted that, I think that this' – I make a sweeping movement with my arms – 'is all right.'

'More than all right,' someone shouts.

'When Jack first came up with the plans for the centre I thought it was too ambitious, but to Jack everything was limitless. He loved a challenge. He taught himself to play guitar in days because I ... well, because ...'

'You thought it was hot,' calls out Alice to laughter; heat rushes to my cheeks, perhaps I should have stuck to my notes.

'Jack liked nothing more than an adventure. On one of our first dates, I wanted to share why I loved photography and so I took him to my favourite place, a waterfall. I rummaged around in my bag for the right lens and by the time I'd found it Jack had stripped to his underwear and was swimming in the lake. "I haven't brought any towels," I called to him. "How are you going to dry yourself?" He smoothed back his hair and laughed. "Live in the moment, Libby," he said. "Don't always worry about the what next," and after a moment's hesitation, I joined him. I've never forgotten how cold I was that day, but I've also never forgotten how it felt to be present. Alive. Grateful. Jack taught me those things and I miss him immeasurably.' I pause. Take a moment to let the lump that has risen in my throat settle. 'Jack isn't here and yet he's everywhere. This is his dream and I feel so privileged to finally say Alethic, the Jack Gilbert Centre for Art, is finally open.' With a snip, I cut the ribbon while Liam uncovers the shiny plaque.

'Now we can all—'

'Just a moment.' Greta steps forward, cutting me off. 'I'd just like to say something. Twelve months ago Libby was invited to submit an entry for The Hawley Foundation Prize and although, due to the circumstances, she didn't want to enter, I accepted the invitation on her behalf. The theme was "hope" and last month, after persuasion, she chose her final pieces and they were taken away to be judged. Tonight, I am delighted to tell you that she has, very deservedly, won first prize.'

I cover my mouth with my hands. I've won. It's overwhelming. My dreams, Jack's dreams, all coming true.

'He'd be so proud of you.' Greta pulls me into a hug before there's a pop and a glass of fizzing champagne is thrust into my hands.

I take a sip and tell myself it's the bubbles that are making my eyes water, but it isn't. It's everything.

I look around.

This is everything.

'Please feel free to wander around.' Faith takes control while I compose myself.

'I've a surprise for you.' Greta leads me into the barn that Liam had been trying to keep me from going into earlier.

I step inside.

Four photos.

It took four photos to cement my world back onto its axis.

Every entrant to The Hawley Foundation Prize was invited to submit a selection. One they'd be judged on and three supporting pictures that fitted the theme. Mine had been sent away but Greta must have collected them because now they are hanging on the newly plastered, freshly painted walls of the barn, alongside a silver sign which says 'Elizabeth Emerson – First Prize.'

Hope.

My first photo, and my showpiece, is of Chloe of course. Alice stands in front of it now with her daughter; she looks a world away from the tiny baby pictured in an incubator, vulnerable, tubes and wires. A too-large hat falling down over one eye.

'That's you,' Alice says.

'Mumumu,' babbles Chloe.

The second photo is of the house. It was after my surgery when I was moving forward with the centre. Faith and I had decided to remove some of the internal walls and rejig the upstairs. We'd been so excited when the builder had knocked the first wall down. He'd asked me if I wanted to dump the rubble into the skip. I'd wobbled the wheelbarrow up the wooden plank. Faith had raised her hand, fingers splayed.

Five.

Four.

Three.

Two.

One.

I'd tipped up the wheelbarrow, a cloud of dust rising as the contents clattered into the bright yellow skip. Faith, Alice, Mum, Liam and all the other teens who'd come to help punched the air simultaneously and cheered while Socks looked on, each person's face shining with excitement. We didn't fully realise then there would be so many challenges – the top floor wasn't in anywhere near as good shape as the first floor. But that day nothing was insurmountable.

The third photo is black and white. I didn't take it but the rules stated you could submit one photograph that wasn't your own if you'd enhanced it, and I had painstakingly restored this image which was faded and worn. It fitted the theme perfectly and I had to include it. It's Sid and Norma in front of their house – this house – mine and Jack's house. It was their wedding day and the first time they would be spending the night together. He is wearing a suit and tie. She is radiant in a floor-length lace gown, sparkling with pearls. Pride is written all over Sid's face as he smiles directly into the lens, holding the hand of his new bride. Norma is gazing up at Sid adoringly.

'Feels like yesterday,' Sid says.

'Thanks for letting me share it.' I turn to him but he can't take his eyes off his wife and I can see why.

'You both look so in love. So excited for the future.'

'That we were and we had a good life – not all beer and skittles mind – but then life ain't like that, is it?'

I squeeze his arm and move on to the next photo. The last photo. It's one of me and Jack on moving-in day. Our faces pressed close together, matching goofy grins. Paint-plastered beanie on Jack's head. His brown hair curling around his neck; it always needed cutting. Jack dangling the key in front of the camera, the sun glinting from the metal. The single bird in the background soaring through the clear blue sky. I remember it all. The soft bleat of the sheep in the fields, the lazy buzz of the bumblebees. The smell of the wildflowers.

And hope.

I remember the hope.

Jack.

Oblivious to the crowd in the barn I trace his face with my fingertips. His smile. The pure joy of knowing that he was following his dream, that now I am following both his and mine.

One of the girls from the village who I'd hired to hand our refreshments breaks my thoughts.

'Canapé?' She offers a tray laden with the snacks I had ordered. Crackers heaped with peanut butter and banana. I notice the slight frown that creases her forehead as I take one and raise it to my mouth.

'Don't knock it til you've tried it,' I tell her, turning my attention back to Jack and beaming. He'd have loved this. He'd have been so proud of me.

Will you please be happy?

I am, Jack. For the first time in a year. *I really am.*

A movement in my peripheral vision catches my eye. I think I see Jack, his posture relaxed, but when I turn round there's nobody there.

I am nowhere near the door but a breeze comes in from somewhere and I shiver as it brushes the back of my neck.

It feels like a kiss.

Author's note

CONTAINS SPOILERS

Hello!

Thanks so much for reading my second love story, *The Art of Loving You*. I do hope you've enjoyed it.

At primary school I read a book called *The Ghost and Mrs Muir* and I became a little obsessed with spirits. It was so different to the stories I had read before and I thought it was so clever that one of the main characters was a ghost. It was around this time I almost lost my mum. She had been discharged from hospital, after a routine operation, when a couple of days later she was suddenly, terrifyingly, struck with sepsis. If it wasn't for quick action, a middle-of-the-night ambulance ride to hospital, she wouldn't be here today.

I began to question what happens after we pass. Is there another place? A happier place? After watching, and loving, the film *Ghost* as a teenager, this brought about a whole new set of questions. What if somebody we loved was trying to communicate with us? How would we know? What if they couldn't quite find a way to connect or what if they did and we assumed it was a figment of our imagination, a trick of the mind? This is something I thought about a LOT, visiting spiritualist churches and events and trying to work out what I believed. I still remained unconvinced either way until I lost one of the people I had loved most and my entire world folded in on itself. It was then I experienced something extraordinary. Something impossible. Something for which there was, there is, no rational explanation. Love crossing worlds became something I very much wanted to explore through fiction.

Of course, in this story there is a medical explanation (and I chose this condition due to personal reasons) why Libby was able to communicate with Jack, but was that the only reason, or could he have reached out to her from the other side? I'll leave it up to you to decide. I'd love to know your thoughts. You can find me at www.ameliahenley.co.uk or come and chat to me on social media at https://twitter.com/MsAmeliaHenley https://www.facebook.com/msameliahenley https://www.instagram.com/msameliahenley/

Amelia x

Acknowledgements

It's such a joy to write the acknowledgements to my second love story. Firstly a BIG thanks to everyone who read, recommended, reviewed my debut, *The Life We Almost Had*. In addition to readers, the support of book bloggers has been overwhelming and SO very appreciated, with special thanks going to Anne Cater of Random Things Blog Tours who turned my new release into a real celebration, and Linda Hill who tirelessly championed my story. Despite the challenges of releasing a debut during a pandemic, it felt like such a special event.

It takes a village to publish a book and I'm very grateful to my editor, Manpreet Grewal, who took Libby and Jack's story and, with a gentle hand, helped me make it better. Lisa Milton and the entire HQ family who have worked so hard through such extraordinary circumstances to get books onto shelves with a special mention to Melanie Hayes, Melissa Kelly and the production team. Cari Rosen for the copyedit. My agent, Rory Scarfe, and all at The Blair Partnership for standing behind my new direction.

I couldn't have written this book without the help of Piers Townley at The Brain Tumour Charity who has been so generous with his time, answering endless questions. For the sake of fiction, I have taken artistic licence with some of the information I learned, particularly regarding the rare side effect of psychosis. Please do visit The Brain Tumour Charity website here (https://www.thebraintumourcharity.org/) to read about the invaluable real-world work they devote themselves to and if you have any concerns about your own health do speak to your GP.

Louise Molina, thanks for your nursing expertise. Any mistakes are purely my own.

Gratitude to readers and writers on social media who chat to me; writing is such a solitary business so the interaction really means a lot. My friends, especially Sarah Wade, and Natalie Brewin, who came up with Sid's wonderful catchphrase – we will have more beer and skittles days!

My family, the ones who are here and the ones who are sadly no longer with us – Glyn we miss you very much – in particular Mum, Karen, Pete and Rebecca. My husband, Tim, who has been thrilled to gain a second wife in 'Amelia'.

My children, Callum, Kai and Finley who are, and always will be, my ENTIRE world.

And Ian, who is present in both this book and my heart.

Book Club Questions

1) Libby and her mum have had a strained relationship, partly due to lack of communication. Is it ever too late to repair past hurt?

2) Alice has kept a secret from Libby. Do you think she should have been honest from the start?

3) Libby's ex-boyfriend, Owen, was a terrible person when they were together, and yet has since settled down and turned over a new leaf. Do you believe that people can change?

4) Noah put his life on hold following a family tragedy. Should he have repaired the damage earlier? Why do you think he didn't try?

5) Jack always helped strangers, sometimes putting their needs before his own. Is this selfish or selfless?

6) Liam's teachers had written him off as a troublemaker, and yet when he's given a chance to prove himself, he shines. Are we too quick to judge kids today?

7) *'Life isn't all beer and skittles'* Sid is fond of saying. His generation are often incredibly optimistic. Why do you think this is?

8) The theme for The Hawley Foundation Prize is 'hope'. If you had to submit one photo to fit this theme, what would it be?

9) When Libby is being prepped for surgery, the nurse mentions seeing Jack outside the baby unit. What explanation could you offer for this?

10) Do you believe any of Libby's experiences could have been real?

11) What would you like for the characters after the story has ended?

Turn the page for an exclusive extract of Anna and Adam's beautiful and heart-breaking love story in Amelia Henley's debut novel

Available to buy now

PROLOGUE

Seven years. It's been seven years since that night on the beach. I had laid on the damp sand with Adam, his thumb stroking mine. Dawn smudged the sky with its pink fingers while the rising sun flung glitter across the sea. We'd faced each other curled onto our sides, our bodies speech marks, unspoken words passing hesitantly between us; an illusory dream. *Don't ever leave me*, I had silently asked him. *I won't*, his eyes had silently replied.

But he did.

He has.

My memories are both painful and pleasurable to recall. We were blissfully happy until gradually we weren't. Every cross word, every hard stare, each time we turned our backs on each other in bed gathered like storm clouds hanging over us, ready to burst, drenching us with doubt and uncertainty until we questioned what we once thought was unquestionable.

Can love really be eternal?

I can answer that now because the inequitable truth is that I am hopelessly, irrevocably, lost without him.

But does he feel the same?

I turn over the possibility of life without Adam, but each time I think of myself without him, no longer an *us*, my heart breaks all over again.

If only we hadn't…

My chest tightens.

Breathe.

Breathe, Anna. You're okay.

It's a lie I tell myself, but gradually the horror of that day begins to dissipate with every slow inhale, with every measured exhale. It takes several minutes to calm myself. My fingers furling and unfurling, my nails biting into the tender skin of my palms until my burning sorrow subsides.

Focus.

I am running out of time. I've been trying to write a letter but the words won't come. My notepaper is still stark white. My pen once again poised, ink waiting to stain the blank page with my tenuous excuses.

My secrets.

But not my lies. There's been enough of those. Too many.

I am desperate to see him once more and make it right.

All of it.

I wish I knew what he wanted. My eyes flutter closed. I try to conjure his voice, imagining he might tell me what to do. Past conversations echo in my mind as I search for a clue.

If you love someone, set them free, he had once told me, but I brush the thought of this away. I don't think it can apply to this awful situation we have found ourselves in. Instead I recall the feel of his body spooned around mine, warm breath on the back of my neck, promises drifting into my ear.

Forever.

I cling on to that one word as tightly as I'd once clung on to his hand.

I loved him completely. I still do. Whatever happens now, after, my heart will still belong to him.

Will always belong to him.

I must hurry if I'm going to reach him before it's too late. There's a tremble in my fingers as I begin the letter, which will be both an apology and an explanation, but it seems impossible to put it all into words – the story of us. I really don't have time to think of the life we had – the life we almost had – but I allow myself the indulgence. Memories gather: we're on the beach, watching the sunrise; I'm introducing him to my mum – his voice shaking with nerves as he said hello; we're meeting for the first time in that shabby bar. Out of order and back to front and more than anything I wish I could live it all again. Except that day. *Never* that day.

Again, the vice around my lungs tightens. In my mind I see it all unfold and I feel it. I feel it all: fear, panic, despair.

Breathe, Anna.

In and out. In and out. Until I am here again, pen gripped too tightly in my hand.

Focus.

I made a mistake.

I stare so intently at the words I have written that they jump around on the page. I'm at a loss to know how to carry on, when I remember one of the first things Adam had said to me: 'Start at the beginning, Anna.'

And so I do.

Speedily, the nib of my pen scratches over the paper. I let it all pour out.

This is not a typical love story, but it's our love story.

Mine and Adam's.

And despite that day, despite everything, I'm not yet ready for it to end.

Is he?

ONE PLACE. MANY STORIES

Bold, Innovative and
empowering publishing.

FOLLOW US ON:

@HQStories